FreeForm Combo: Beginnings & Reborn

FreeForm

Orrin Jason Bradford

Published by Porpoise Publishing, 2019.

FreeForm

Beginnings

Orrin Jason Bradford

An unseen invasion: the ultimate threat...

When a mysterious spacecraft is uncovered in the North Carolina mountains, agent Pat Vogt's life begins to look increasingly alien. Betrayed by her own government, she's forced to unravel a conspiracy that holds implications for existence on Earth...and beyond.

Years later, Vogt returns to find the mountain town of Waynesboro fostering secrets much darker than she'd ever imagined. Even her closest ally, Dr. Allen Pritchard, withholds crucial information, and his desire to mend a painful past may jeopardize the human race.

Who is genetic engineer Fredic Homlin, and what connection does the Biogentrix Corporation's chilling technology touted as the 'play dough of life' represent? Can one headstrong woman reveal the truth in time, or will something else be sown?

Beginnings is the shifting shape of much that lies ahead...

Orrin Jason Bradford's style has been compared to the "early works of Dean Koontz and the late great Michael Crichton." ***Freeform: Beginnings*** is the first novel in the action-packed, sci-fi Freeform series.

mybook.to/freeformseries

Pick Up the Rest of the FreeForm Series Today

Available at
amazon

The Adventure has Just Begun[1]

1. http://mybook.to/freeformseries

Part One
Something Wicked This Way Comes

Mountain Mystery
Saturday, March 5, 1993

THE HELICOPTER SWOOPED low over the crest of the mountain, and Pat Vogt held her breath and her stomach.

"Ease up, James," she said as soon as she could take another breath. "If we catch a downdraft off one of these mountains, we're likely to be wearing those trees."

James, an ex-Gulf War copter pilot, often flew as though he was being pursued by some unidentified enemy aircraft. Pat suspected he occasionally experienced flashbacks of those grueling war years.

"In fact, climb a couple hundred feet, and let's take another pass from a different perspective."

James nodded affirmatively and gave her a sly wink, which Pat ignored. She drew a lot of winks from her male co-workers and once in a while a pinch on the ass from some brave fool...but only one.

Her five-foot, two-inch frame of muscular curves had stopped plenty of men in their tracks, but they didn't around Pat long without discovering she was a woman with whom you did not fool around. Oh sure, a little kidding around was okay; it was to be expected, and Pat was far from being a prude. She knew she was attractive, even sexy. Pat had spent many long hours in the gym and karate dojo in the pursuit of a healthy frame, but it wasn't for her shape she worked so hard. It was the desire for excellence in everything she took on in her life, especially her career.

"We're getting low on fuel, sweet thing!" James shouted to her over the whirl of the blades. "We'll have to take it in for refueling."

"One more pass," Pat replied. "I thought I saw a glint over the ridge. It could be a metallic surface reflecting the sun."

"These babies don't stay afloat long when the blades stop rotating," James answered.

Pat turned and stared at him for a long few seconds. "One more pass," she mouthed slowly.

"Whatever you say. You're the boss."

The helicopter eased over the ridge. Pat placed the set of binoculars to her eyes. She studied the rough terrain below, looking for the scar in the thick growth of trees she'd noticed on the previous pass. It looked like someone had selectively cut a thin line through the dense growth. A fast-moving object striking the surface at an acute angle as the report had suggested could have caused such damage. Yet with heavy snowfall, it could go unnoticed.

She lowered the glasses for a moment. There, to the left—a long thin line angled obliquely across the crest. She raised the glasses back to her eyes and traced the scar, shouting to James as she did.

"Turn east about fifteen degrees and come in a little slower! I think I see something." She felt James make the adjustment quickly.

As she studied the defect in the landscape, her gaze stopped at the end furthest from the crest. As they passed over the area, a flash like a flashbulb, momentarily blinded them; or was it the reflection of the noonday sun? But from what?

"See that thin break in the trees we passed over? I want you to put down there."

"No way, babes," James replied. "Not with this wind and us sucking on fumes. One little hesitation and we'll be eating those trees."

"I thought you were the great Gulf War copter pilot with ice water flowing through his veins."

"I'm not interested in picnicking in these woods for several days while a search party tries to find us. Not even with a gorgeous dame like yourself."

"Okay, fine. Set me down with the crane. Note the spot on the map and return for fuel. Bring the others back in the other copter while this one is being refueled."

"Are you crazy? I can't lower you—" James stopped short as he noticed Pat already strapping the rigging around her slender frame.

"Lower me as close to the ground as you can, and I'll cut myself free. Don't worry, I'll take full responsibility."

"Our orders were to return to base and report anything we found to the rest of the search team. Not to investigate on our own!" James shouted.

"I'm in charge here, James!" Pat shouted back. "Your orders were to follow my directions. We haven't found anything to report. I'm simply going down to take a closer look. If there is anything there, you'll be back with the team. I'll be hanging around waiting. Don't worry, I'll be fine." Pat patted his arm. "Lower me down."

"What in the world could be down there worth risking your neck?"

"Oh, nothing except the most likely candidate for a bona fide UFO in the last several years. I intend to be the first person to set eyes on it." She placed the glasses under her seat and picked up her camera, slinging it around her neck by its strap.

She left the passenger seat and scurried to the rear of the chopper. She clipped the crane rope to her rigging and waited for James to give her the go-ahead.

As James made a final pass over the site (a second pass beyond what the fuel gauge indicated was possible), James signaled for her to ease out of the door. As they approached the narrow gully in the trees, Pat wondered if she'd made a wise judgment call. Who was this James character, anyway? She'd only met him a few hours ago. How good of a pilot was he? Hell, she couldn't even remember his last name; she'd known him for such a short time. How did she know if he had really flown in the Gulf War? For all she knew, he could be as new at flying copters as she was at investigating UFO reports. She wasn't comforted by the thought as she glanced down at the Longleaf Pines reaching their long fingers to tickle the bottoms of her feet.

Pat hung from the undercarriage of the copter as James continued to lower her with the crane while dropping the helicopter closer to the trees.

A gust of wind started Pat turning slowly on the end of the thin fiberglass cord.

He better know what he's doing, Pat told herself as she tried to slow the spin, growing more uncomfortable with her situation by the moment.

Just as she was sure James was about to plop her into the thick growth of trees, dashing her body against the pines, the thin break appeared, and she was deftly lowered into it. Heavy tree limbs whizzed by on both sides. She felt like she could reach out with either hand and grasp a handful of needles. Despite a reduction in the wind gusts, she continued to spin out of control. She thought on one pass that she could see the gleaming metallic object at the end of the thin canyon formed by the trees, but she couldn't be sure.

She estimated that she was a good thirty feet in the air when she felt the shudder of the helicopter through the line. *Oh, shit, James is running out of fuel,* Pat thought as she glared up at the copter's underbelly. *Lower me quicker, you fool.* She continued to hang as though suspended in the web of a monstrous spider, waiting for the spider to return home for his evening meal.

She had to do something and quick. She couldn't count on James. She realized you couldn't rely on anyone when the chips were down—only yourself. She continued to hang for several seconds trying to decide what to do.

She stared below her at the rough terrain of the mountainside; she estimated there was a good twenty-five feet to the ground. The copter shuddered a second time. Enough was enough. She'd take control of the situation herself. She punched the safety release on her chest and felt the familiar rush of free fall.

She'd spent a summer between her sophomore and junior years of college skydiving her heart out. In a three-month time span, she'd made over fifty jumps, most of them free falls. The training paid off as she fell toward the irregular surface of the mountainside. As the ground came up fast, she held her feet and knees firmly together. She did not stay on her feet but rolled to one side, her hands and arms clasped tightly across her chest.

She rolled down the mountainside, picking up speed as she fell until her left shoulder struck a large rock embedded in the ground. She came to an abrupt and painful stop. She lay there for several seconds, wincing in pain, then staggered to her feet to give James the okay sign, but the helicopter had already sputtered over the crest, dragging the line behind it.

Pat dusted herself off with her right hand and felt a sharp pain shoot through her left shoulder. She gently moved her left arm to be sure it wasn't dislocated and was rewarded with another shock of pain which threatened to black her out. *Not dislocated*, she thought, *but sure as hell not one hundred percent, either*.

Pat stared in the direction where the helicopter had disappeared. *I sure hope he makes it back to camp*, she thought. *He's my ticket out of here*. Having had the thought, she placed it out of her mind. There was nothing else she could do about it right now, so why worry? It was time to go looking for a UFO.

Before setting off in the direction where she anticipated finding the UFO, she made a thorough inspection of her camera. *A bit scuffed and dirty. Still serviceable.* She snapped a picture, relieved to hear the familiar click-click of the shutter.

She picked her way across the terrain, occasionally stopping to enjoy the rugged scenic beauty of the mountain. She took a deep breath of fresh air and let it out slowly. What a great job. No sitting behind a desk all day for her. Being a part of the new team assigned to explore the highly secretive "Waynesboro NC UFO Case" was a little hard for her to believe. She had finally found a position that fit all of the passions she'd inherited from her parents. Her interest in investigative work was passed down from her father's thirty-year career as a police detective in Atlanta. She had undoubtedly inherited her love of science and speculation from her mom's career as a science fiction novelist. It was quite an accomplishment to be the newest member of B.I.U.F.O. (the Bureau of Investigation of Unidentified Flying Objects) and to be assigned to a field case, particularly one as juicy as the Waynesboro case.

She'd been with B.I.U.F.O. only three months, and she knew her being on the case had irritated some senior investigators back in Washington. Well, as her dad had said, "Fuck 'em if they can't take a joke."

She'd earned the opportunity, and it wasn't by sleeping with some high-level politician as she knew several of the other investigators suspected. She had worked her butt off for this chance, and if people would stay out of her way, she'd make sure the hard work paid off.

The early spring thaw and rain had been a good omen, although the wet ground made walking a slippery mess. Since the initial reports from the Strategic Air Command over three months ago of a high-speed UFO originating from outside the earth's atmosphere, no one had had any luck locating where it might have gone. North Carolina had suffered one of its worst winters ever, with a heavy burden of snowfall that surpassed all previous records. It had been two days after the radar sighting before anyone could investigate the report. By that time, a good eight inches of snow had fallen in the region. If the UFO had struck the earth, it had been buried under a heavy blanket of white.

B.I.U.F.O. had spent several days of reconnaissance and several thousand dollars of taxpayer money with no results, so they had called off the search until the spring thaw. The thaw had come early, and in the interim Pat had joined the investigative team. She was about to make all that hard work worthwhile.

As Pat neared the end of the thin clearing, it became more apparent how the UFO had avoided detection. Evidently, the object had come in low and hard, burrowing its way into the side of the mountain, leaving behind a thin gully covered by the snow. The sides of the ravine had partially collapsed, leaving only the upper few feet of the dull gray dome exposed.

Pat ignored the patches of the last remnants of snow, strolling straight through the slush to reach the alien object. *I may be the first human to ever see an alien spaceship,* she thought. She didn't believe it. More likely she had joined the club of a select group of other humans who had witnessed similar objects, although she suspected few people had been as close to one as she was at this moment. Most UFO sightings were of strange objects streaking across the sky. There were much fewer reports of people visiting crafts that had landed.

As she reached the metal dome poking out of the side of the mountain like a giant cold sore, she strolled around it, looking for a way in.

There's no question; it's man-made—oops, alien-made. She stopped. Could it be man-made? What if this wasn't an alien vessel but one from some foreign country or even a top-secret American project? Standing next to the craft, her bold move to explore the ship on her own didn't look like such a wise decision.

I could have asked James to loan me his revolver. The Colt .45 he wore strapped to his waist wasn't Pat's favorite weapon, but it sure would be comforting to have in case the inhabitants of the ship proved less than cordial. She stopped long enough to be sure the knife, a present from her dad, was securely strapped to her left leg. Small comfort if she met a foreigner with an automatic rifle or an alien with a death ray, but better than nothing.

She turned her eyes casually to the trees around her but could see or hear nothing except the usual sounds of the forest, the chirping of the first spring birds mingled with the rustling of the trees. She started walking around the metallic dome again, searching for a way into its interior. She strolled around the complete circumference, finally arriving on the other side of the deep channel. She peered over the edge of the channel. She thought she could make out a slight irregularity at the base where the ship's exterior disappeared into the side of the mountain.

Pat scooted down the steep side of the gully, struggling to maintain her balance on the slippery mud, but within a few yards she found herself sliding on her backside out of control. Within moments, the wet mud had soaked through her jeans. As she reached the bottom of the chasm, she threw her right arm out against the ship and caught herself, sending another lightning bolt of pain coursing down her left side. She found the ship's surface surprisingly warm. Could it be from the sun's radiation or did the heat come from within?

She regained her footing and squinted her eyes, trying to pierce the dark shadows created by the sides of the channel. What was that in the dark hole next to the ship's surface? An irregularity or dried mud packed against the smooth side?

She stumbled over to the short tunnel, finding it difficult to balance on the rocky, muddy surface. It was mud caked on the side—and an irregularity. As her eyes adjusted to the dark, she could make out a raised circular pattern. She dug into the pocket of her jeans and pulled out the small flashlight, another present from her father. She twisted the head to turn it on and shone the light beam into the dark recess.

"Yes!" The word slipped from her lips with a hiss that sounded eerie as it bounced off the metallic surface. An entrance, it had to be.

Did she dare enter the ship before help arrived? It was an insane thought. Her orders from Oliver had been specific. *Do not investigate any findings on your own. Wait for backup from the rest of the team.* She should climb out of this dark muddy ditch, back to the sunny surface where she belonged, and wait for James to bring Oliver and the rest of the search team. She had had enough heroics for one day. Already, she would receive top recognition for finding the alien vessel, if that's what it turned out to be. Please, dear God, let it be alien. She would get credit for the discovery, whatever it was. Yes, it would be best to wait.

She shrugged her shoulders in one of her favorite gestures and winced at the pain on the left side. "Daddy said I didn't know what was best for me." She slid into the dark tunnel.

Confrontation

The bear groaned softly as it stretched its long body, touching the two sides of its lair. It rolled onto its back and wiggled, trying to reach the itchy spot in the middle. As it turned, it bumped against the frozen carcass, mostly bones, lying next to it. *Is it time,* he wondered? *Is the metamorphosis complete?*

The grizzly lumbered onto its feet, kicking the carcass to the side. It stood frozen to the spot for several minutes, its nose in the air, its eyes closed. Something was amiss. He'd been awakened by something—something besides hunger. The metamorphosis was not quite finished. Almost, it would do, but something was wrong.

After a couple more minutes, the bear lowered itself onto all fours and strolled outside. Once again, it stood on all fours and waited. The ship. Something was wrong with the ship. He must get back. His link with the ship, although weakened in this form, clearly indicated an intruder. Perhaps only a curious animal sniffing around the perimeter. Or not.

His adaptation to the new planet was all but complete. The little that remained would have to wait. He was safe. His body had made the necessary re-calibrations. The foreign environment was his; he owned this planet as his own.

He stood there for a moment longer, debating whether to transform back into the hunter-survivor form of his people. No, the bear would be better. It was less likely to draw attention from other inhabitants of the planet. At least until he found other forms to add to his repertoire.

He returned to his lair. Stepping over the carcass of its former occupant, he crouched down so he could reach the back of the cave. In the dim light that filtered from the mouth of the cave, he could make out the two objects upon which his entire mission rested—the cocoon and the crystal.

Amazing, we are indeed an amazing race, he thought. For as long as he had been settling planets, he never lost his appreciation for these two pieces of technology. Hard to imagine that in the small sphere of the cocoon, far smaller than the size of the bear's head, could be housed ten thousand souls of his people. Equally amazing was the crystal, so small that it could easily be worn around his neck as an adornment, yet it held the entire technology of his people. His people were the most advanced civilizations of the galaxy, at least as far as they'd been able to determine in the five hundred plus years they'd been exploring it.

The question is, do I leave these two precious objects behind or take them with me back to the ship? There was something wrong with the ship. Every fiber of his body blared the warning. He could not afford to let either of these objects become lost. No, better to leave them here where they'd be safe and return to them when he was satisfied the ship was okay.

Having planned his course of action, he backed out of the narrow part of the lair to where he could once again stand up. He started to take a final meal from the frozen carcass but decided against it. He wanted fresh food. Perhaps on his trip back to the ship, he would be lucky and find some.

THE SOUND OF A SPUTTERING helicopter pulled Oliver's attention away from the stack of reports lying in front of him.

It's coming in low, he told himself, glancing in the direction of the sound. *Too low and on fumes.* He jerked his large frame out of the director's chair and lumbered out of the tent in time to see the whirlybird's landing sled scrape the top off of several trees. It wobbled in midair like a huge eagle that had been shot, then amazingly stayed in the air long enough to make a bumpy landing at the edge of the clearing. As he ran towards the copter, Oliver noticed only the pilot was inside. Where the hell was Pat? A familiar burning sensation in the pit of his stomach had already begun. He was certain he wasn't going to like what he heard from James.

A few minutes later, the burning from the "dormant" ulcer flared into a full force bonfire, and he reached for the economy size bottle of antacids in an attempt to extinguish the familiar blaze.

"YOU DID WHAT?" HE SHOUTED. "Why in the world would you do such a foolish thing?"

"Damn it, Oliver, she insisted. I don't need to remind you how persuasive Pat can be. Besides, she was calling the shots. That's what you told us when we started the search."

Oliver groaned. "Well, as soon as the second helicopter is back and yours is refueled, we'll go see if we can find our roving dare-devil. You made sure she was all right before you left, didn't you?"

James nodded. "She's fine. I have to say, she's got guts. I'm not sure how smart she is, but she sure has guts."

Oliver started walking back to his tent then stopped and turned back to James. "What did it look like? Could you make anything out?"

"DAMNATION!" PAT YELLED for the third time in the last thirty minutes as her fingers slid off the lip of the door. She winced at the familiar pain in her shoulder. In the forty-five minutes she had been wedged against the ship, she had broken three fingernails and scraped her knuckles—and moved the door half an inch. The most frustrating thing, the door had moved. Within the first couple of minutes, it had moved. She was certain.

Which means it wasn't locked, only stuck. If it's not locked, then I'm going to get inside, one way or another. If only I had the full use of both of my arms, she thought. *And if—*"...the queen had balls she would be king," she heard her father's familiar voice ringing in her ears.

I'm getting in, she told herself again. *There is no way in hell I'm getting this close without finding some way into the damn thing.* What if she ran the blade of her knife along the crack again? Maybe that would dislodge something. *I'll try it again.* "Third time's the charm," her father added. *Buzz off,* Pat retorted.

THE ALIEN SPOTTED A stag in the woods above him. *Does it smell me?* The alien wondered. *No, I'm upwind. A gorgeous beast. Much more attractive than this clumsy body. And fresh meat*, he thought. *What about the ship? I should get back to the ship. The intruder is still there, although outside.* He hesitated. *I'll be fast. Fresh meat and a new form to add to my collection.* It made sense to take a few minutes. But not in his present form. The bear was too slow, too cumbersome. The hunter-survivor was not. Without moving, he called his natural body forth. He felt the familiar surge of energy and the welcome sensation of coming home to the body he was most comfortable in.

Welcome home, Sluneg. Nice to be in my own body again, he thought. Such a fine form. There was nothing in the galaxy that could compare. No other structure was as efficient—the perfect killing machine.

As he completed the transformation, he glanced down at himself. The customary black coloration would not do in this situation. Too visible. He gazed around at the browns and greens of the forest and called them forth out of himself. Not as attractive, but more functional. *Let's go have some fun.*

He crept forward on padded feet, being sure to keep the three-inch stiletto-like nails retracted. *Just a little closer*, he thought, *before I let it know I'm here; a little closer.*

Now! the alien thought as he reached out and purposefully stepped on a thin branch on the path. Crack!

The stag had returned to grazing on the lush new grass of the meadow. At the sound of the breaking branch, it raised its head again, a clump of grass hanging out of its mouth. It looked around, the skin on its neck twitching nervously. It sniffed the air. Nothing.

It was alert. A worthy trophy to add to his collection. He thought of his ship again. *Okay, mustn't dawdle. Get on with it.* He stepped out into the clearing as the stag lowered its head for another nibble of grass. The two animals stared at each other, both frozen in an instant in time. The stag was the first to break. It reared on its hindquarters, turning to its left.

Even as the alien leaped after the stag, it marveled at the beauty of the beast. The deer fled across the pasture, picking up speed with each stride. The hunter-survivor matched it step by step for the first fifty yards, still studying its beauty. As the two of them neared the edge of the forest, the alien picked up its pace, closing the gap between the two of them.

Ten yards from the forest, the alien left the ground in a leap that covered the final five yards. As he sailed through the air, his front legs fully extended, he protracted the twelve razor-sharp claws, each of them already spinning on their axis at full speed. He hit the right flank of the stag like a freight train, knocking the rear legs of the animal out from under itself. Each claw spun their way deep into the stag's flank, easily piercing skin, fat, and muscle.

As the two animals fell into the woods, the alien withdrew the claws of one paw, holding on with the other, leaving behind six holes, each an inch across and three inches deep, blood gushing from each one. He jabbed the nails in again, farther up the flank, and again, reaching for the stag's backbone. The panicked stag flung its head back in an attempt to free itself. The alien ducked under the rack of antlers. As the stag turned its head to take another swing, its antlers caught in the low-lying branches of a nearby tree.

You're all mine, the alien thought as he walked his way up the stag's back, leaving behind a set of deadly fingerprints.

PAT WEDGED THE KNIFE in the narrow crack again and twisted, holding her breath as she did so. Each time, she risked breaking the thin blade, leaving it stuck in the crack as an additional obstacle. The tempered steel had stood up to the punishment. The method worked. Slowly, painfully slow, Pat pried the door open.

A little more, she told herself. *Hold on a couple more times*, she instructed the knife, *and I'll be able to get enough of a hold on the door to wrench it open with my one working arm.*

She paused for a moment to wipe the stream of sweat from around her eyes. By this time, her entire body was drenched in her perspiration. Her short dark hair lay matted against her scalp. *I'm beginning to smell like a men's locker room*, she observed. *Come, take me now, James.* She kidded with herself. *What, you aren't interested? Why, you fickle bastard. How like a man.*

She wedged the edge of the knife in again and twisted, holding her breath once more. *Holding my breath, that's the key. If I don't hold my breath, I'll get cocky, and the knife will sense it. It'll think I'm taking it for granted and 'snap!' it will be all over.*

As she continued to work, she speculated about what she would find on the other side. Poisonous gas? A ten-foot cockroach waiting hungrily for its next meal? Maybe a ship filled with gold and diamonds. *If I were an alien, I'd be sure to bring along plenty of booty for the natives.* If aliens had been studying them for the past fifty or more years, as many experts claimed, wouldn't they know how much earthlings valued gold and diamonds?

One particular question kept haunting her though. Was the ship occupied? Was there something waiting inside for her, ten-foot cockroach or other? Who was to say this was a manned or alien-occupied vessel? All indications pointed to the contrary. The landing had been a far cry from smooth. If there were aliens on board, would they still be alive, and what had they been doing for the last three months? Certainly not waiting for Pat Vogt to arrive to rescue them.

"All in good time," she mumbled out loud then smiled. Another one of her father's favorite lines, used whenever an overly inquisitive little girl would ask too many questions. "All in good time, Patti. All your questions will be answered—all in good time." Pat hoped he had been right.

Pat adjusted the beam of the flashlight to take in the next section of the door. The flashlight was stuck in the mud wall a few feet from the door, and it was a simple matter to move the beam where she needed it.

She shoved the knife into the crack again and levered it back. She felt the usual resistance; then the knife slipped. She scraped another knuckle, and the knife fell onto the ground. She picked the knife up from the mud and wiped it on her pants. She started to insert the knife back in the crack when she noticed the blunt end.

Damn! She placed the knife more directly in the beam of light. About a quarter inch of the tip had broken off. *I wasn't holding my breath,* she chided herself. She inspected the knife closer and decided she had been fortunate. It was still serviceable, and when she got back to town, she could get someone at the hardware store to grind the end to another point without damaging the rest of the knife. *Hold your breath*, she reminded herself as she went back to work.

The next time she wedged the knife in the crack, she felt the door move a little more than before. The next time she was sure. *It's coming. The damn thing is finally giving me a break.* She continued to hold her breath. No point in getting cocky.

Ten minutes later, she carefully placed the knife back in its case strapped to her leg and wiped her face again with the soaked sleeve of her right arm. Okay. Time to pop this son-of-a-bitch open.

Wedging herself firmly between the ship and the back of the mud cave, she took a firm grasp of the ledge at the top of the door. One, two, three—heave! At first, nothing happened, except for her face turning red and the pain in her left shoulder reminding her to take it a little easier. She didn't relax, only strained even harder. Still nothing.

"Come on, you bastard. Give me a fucking break!" she shouted at the top of her lungs.

The door moved. A half inch, then another half inch.

"All right. There you go!" Pat shouted again. "Now we're cooking." She readjusted her hand-hold down a quarter turn and pulled again. The door moved easier this time.

She reached a hundred eighty degrees across to the other side. It was more challenging to get a firm grip, but she found the door had loosened sufficiently to be able to pull it another three-quarters of an inch out. She bent to the top and repeated the process again. Although she could not see them because of the mud, she'd calculated the door was hinged at the bottom.

"Any moment!" she said out loud to give herself encouragement.

The dark tunnel was far too quiet. The other side? What would be on the other side?

She stopped. *Let's not be foolish,* she told herself. The thought of poisonous gas returned. How would she be able to tell? Not all toxic gases had an odor. Take natural gas. Odorless. The smell came from an additive. She pondered the question, finally deciding there was no way she could be sure. The best she could do would be to sample it, slowly, carefully. If she felt the least bit light-headed, she'd get the hell out of the tunnel and wait for the team.

Sometimes, life is risky. Her father used to remind her often. This was one of those times. She grasped the top of the door again and pulled. This time it came easily, and Pat stepped to her right to give the door room to open and held her breath.

No sound, she noticed; no hiss. Nothing to indicate a change in pressure. Didn't mean the gases were the same, but it did make her feel a little better. She sniffed the air. Was that a sweet smell? Had it been there before? It was hard to tell. Mostly, all she could smell was herself. Oh well, here goes.

She took another whiff, a little stronger this time, and waited. Smelled the same as it did. Right? Feel fine so far. Right? Yes, she concluded as she pulled the flashlight from its spot in the mud wall and shined the light into the ship. Slow and easy. Take it slow and easy. She took a short breath, then holding it again, she stuck her head through the crack and looked around.

"Holy, mother-of-pearl!" she said in a hushed voice as though she was entering an ancient cathedral. It felt that way. She half expected to find herself looking into a small air-lock with the inside of the ship on the other side of yet another door. She wasn't prepared for what she saw.

It looked like the central section of the ship. The room stretched at least fifteen feet into the center and was nearly that wide. Pat estimated the distance between the ceiling and the floor to be eight or nine feet. So much for a ten-foot-tall cockroach, she thought as she stepped over the rim of the door and entered the ship. Roachy was no more than seven feet. She smiled at her own joke.

As she did so, she felt the first wave of dizziness. Toxic gas! Her mind screamed at her. Get out—get out! Fighting the panic, she stopped in midstride and realized she'd been holding her breath for at least a minute and a half. She slowly let it out and inhaled slowly, quickly feeling better. The air was stale but harmless.

As her foot hit the decking of the ship, Pat heard a low-grade hum followed seconds later by a blast of light from overhead. She ducked for a moment as though she'd been attacked by a flurry of bats, but there was nothing there. She stepped back, and as she did so, the lights flickered off.

Not bad. She wondered how you turned them off when you're ready to let the cat out and go to bed. She re-entered the ship, and the light cut on again, so she switched her flashlight off.

The room was austere with only a few unfamiliar objects along the far wall. A storage room? It was possible that this was not the main entrance. Likely, in fact. If the ship had come in right side up, the main hatch was buried fifteen or twenty feet. More than likely, this was an auxiliary way in and out of the ship, close to the top of the ship in case of unexpected crash landings.

Besides the door to the outside, there were two other doors which led to other parts of the ship, one directly across from the exit door and a second one on the wall to the left.

"Which shall it be?" Pat asked herself out loud and was startled by the sound of her own voice. It was too damn quiet. She whistled a tuneless melody.

She walked over to the door directly across from the exit. What if the doors were locked, waiting for the unique thumbprint of the ship's owner?

Please, Lord, let it be open, she prayed as she approached the door. Much to her amazement and joy, when she was a couple of feet from the door, it noiselessly slid open.

"All right!" she exclaimed. *Now we're cooking.*

Pat strolled through the ship. Each room seemed more amazing than the one before. As she left one room, the light automatically cut off in it and on in the next one. *Like having an individual ray of sunlight following you around*, she thought, her mood lifting with every minute.

She didn't understand anything she saw, but it was definitely high tech. Much more advanced than anything she'd ever seen, even in the hundreds of sci-fi movies her mom had taken her to.

And definitely alien. No way could any of it have been made by or for humans. The equipment lacked the usual symmetry she'd come to expect of human design. There were no right angles or rectangular objects. Everything was free-flowing, amorphous. The shape appeared to depend on the need or function, without any preconceived expectation that it had to look a particular way. Pat found her mouth gaping open for the third time and clamped it shut. She snapped a couple of pictures in each room, being careful to ration her only roll of film.

It was in the fourth room where she found the two empty cylinders. They spanned from the floor to the ceiling and Pat estimated they were about three feet in diameter. As she studied them, cold, creepy fingers danced along her spine. Empty, but she felt sure there had been something inside. She didn't know why she felt so strongly about it, but there was no question in her mind. What had been inside? More importantly, where were they?

She jerked her head around, looking in every corner. In a millisecond, her mind flashed through a half dozen of the most gruesome aliens of her movie-going days. Despite squinting her eyes and looking into every deep recess, none of the aliens materialized.

Pat sighed with relief, but the breath caught in her throat as she heard a faint metallic clink behind her. A second later, the lights overhead blinked out. The sound had been so soft. Had she imagined it? Her heart rate doubled for the second time in the last few minutes. Her palms dampened with sweat, and she feared she'd drop the flashlight she still held in her hand. It was slick. She switched it on.

Time to leave. *Calm down, it's nothing.* The ship was empty. No, not empty. The only thing empty was the two cylinders in front of her. *Leave. Leave quickly.* Her mind raced. Meanwhile, her body knotted from the rush of adrenalin. She took a deep breath and let it out slowly. Be calm. No matter what, getting all worked up would only make things worse. If there was something in the ship with her, she didn't know if it was dangerous. It was possible, despite all the stories to the contrary, that aliens could be friendly.

The second sound, louder and much closer behind her dashed the notion of friendly aliens from her mind. Friendly or not, she was not equipped to meet them on their ground. To them, she was an intruder. How would she react coming home and finding someone in her home?

She was alone without any idea how far away help was. She was unarmed and vulnerable—as vulnerable as she could ever remember feeling. It was time to visit the cold reality of the light of day. Now!

Hunter-survivor

The alien stood in the entrance, looking at the small object that had fallen from the console. He didn't like what he had found on his return to the ship. He had, in fact, left a well-deserved meal when his sensors notified him that the outer security of his ship had been breached. Whatever had been on his ship had not been a harmless creature of the woods. Somehow, it had found its way into the ship and was here this minute.

Had his presence been discovered by the primary species of the planet? Shortly after his arrival, he had on a couple of occasions observed from afar a small village of bipeds. These strange, bipedal creatures appeared to own this world and were probably the cause of the poor condition it was in. Could one of the bipeds have stumbled upon his ship? Could his luck be so rotten? Having been on several other settlement missions, he knew the answer to the question was a resounding yes. The unexpected twists and turns were what he lived for, and at the same time, he had noticed of late, he sometimes found himself wishing for one smooth, trouble-free mission. Clearly, this was not to be the one.

He considered his options. If his ship had been discovered by a biped, his entire mission must be considered in jeopardy. If the biped had in some way communicated with others of its kind, they could be on their way at this moment. Which meant he didn't have much time to rectify the problem. This called for bold, immediate action.

The ship would have to be destroyed. He could not afford to have his enemy study it. There was nothing in the ship that could not be replicated, given enough time and resources. All the plans for the necessary equipment to recover his people from the cocoon were housed in the memory crystal, both of which were hidden back in the cave. Destroying the ship would be a definite setback but not one from which he could not recover. His was a patient race.

He stared at the small object that had fallen from the console. He picked up the detonation unit where it had fallen. Clumsy of him, but it could still serve his purpose. The noise would certainly bring the intruder running to the entrance and give him the opportunity to revenge the invasion of his privacy. He'd then leave the ship in the ready mode. He'd wait for others of the intruder's race. If they came, he'd destroy the ship by remote. If not, he'd return and defuse the system. Either way, the intruder would pay for stumbling on the ship. Most important of all, his secret would be intact.

A sound from deeper inside the ship drew his attention away from the warning lights of the detonation unit. His first direct contact with his enemy was about to occur. He shivered with anticipation. Perhaps he'd be surprised. Maybe the intruder would put up a better fight than his previous encounters. He enjoyed a good match. Should he cut off the lights? No, not yet. What did he have to worry about? Let the biped get a good look at him. It would be fun to see its reaction.

He was disappointed when the intruder entered the room. As he had suspected, it was one of the bipeds, which meant his mission was definitely in jeopardy. It was also a female of the species, which meant he wouldn't even have the pleasure of a good fight. Seeing one up close like this, it became evident to him that this species was much more fragile than he had first imagined. *Hardly worth playing with,* he thought as he strolled forward, still holding the detonation unit. Best to end it quickly in case others were on their way.

As he narrowed the distance between them, the biped backed out of the room and deeper into the ship.

It's apparently terrified of me, Sluneg thought. *No wonder. No doubt it's never seen the likes of me. At least it appears smart enough to realize it's about to die. Well, I'll have a little fun with it before I snuff out its life.*

PAT RETRACED HER STEPS as quietly as possible, forcing herself not to run. Three doorways still separated her from the outside when she came face to face with the alien. For a heartbeat or two, she stood frozen in the bright light of the room, staring in disbelief.

Before her eyes had fully adjusted to the light, Pat backed out of the room, adding a new image to her impressive collection of alien memories. This one was far more horrible than all the made up ones if for no other reason than this one was real and standing before her blocking her exit from the ship. As the door closed behind her, Pat switched the flashlight to her left hand and pulled the hunting knife from its sheath with her right hand. She kept the flashlight on but pressed it against her leg to hide the light. If she was to get out of this mess alive, a surprise was her only hope.

The biped had retreated to one of the storage units of the ship. The clutter of supplies and equipment would make the hunt a little more challenging. He would play with it a little while. Let it think it had a chance to escape before killing it. *Not long*, he promised himself. There was too much work ahead to indulge too long. Before opening the door, he signaled to the ship to keep the lights off. As he entered the storage room, he paused for a moment to let his eyes adjust to the darker room. He scanned the room with his multiple senses and found the creature hiding behind one of the backup computers.

He wondered how such a helpless species had become so dominant on the planet. Many of the other animals he had come in contact with seemed more likely candidates. He ran his razor sharp claws along one wall, adding a deep-throated growl for effect. He had seen larger animals break their cover, fleeing in fear from the combination of sounds. This one did not. *Interesting*, he thought. *Could it be paralyzed to the spot? Whimpering in the corner in terror?*

Probably so, he thought as he stepped around the console to take a look. As he did, he was blinded by a brilliant flash of light, and in the next instance he felt the searing pain of cold metal penetrate between the protective plates of his chest.

He screamed in pain and anger, stumbling back in confusion. It took him an instant to realize he'd been wounded. Not a severe injury, only irritating and disturbing. The biped had drawn first blood.

What was this? The human must be insane with terror. It was coming after him again. Through the glare of the unexpected light, he saw the gleam of metal as it slashed through the air. He raised his left arm to fend the human off and felt a second explosion of pain as the weapon sliced through the sinewy muscles of his forearm. Again, not serious but aggravating to think the sick little beast was actually trying to kill him. He roared with rage and was surprised to hear an edge of fear in his voice.

He leaped away from the attack onto a storage container several feet above the biped. The sudden quick movement and distance of the leap seemed to catch it by surprise. The beam of light shining from the end of one of its appendages did not follow the path of the jump. Instead, it scanned the room in front.

He took the opportunity to examine his wounds. Already, the clotting mechanism of his blood had started to seal off the wounds. Neither injury was substantial. More blows to his pride than anything. It was time to stop playing with the human. He had serious work to accomplish. Time to kill this aggravating animal and be done with it. His next approach would be more careful, more deadly.

He slipped behind the storage container before the search beam found his hiding place. He would slide up behind it and finish it off. When he came around the container, the animal was nowhere to be seen. The beam which he had counted on to locate the intruder had been snuffed out. He stopped his own breathing for a moment and listened carefully for its breathing. Nothing.

Had it died from fright? Not likely. Given what he had recently learned of his enemy, he had a new respect for it. Fear did not seem to control this species as it did most of the others on the planet, which would, in part, explain its dominance.

Then he heard the biped. It could not hold its breath as long. The sound had come from the other side of a stack of food cylinders. The long cylinders were seldom needed on an expedition but were included on the ship in case of emergency landings on inhospitable planets. They were tied together by a thick elastic band.

He crept to the other side of the stack and listened again. A second breath confirmed the beast was still hiding on the other side. Protracting one long nail from its sheath, he slid it under the strap, sawing easily through the plastic. As the final strands were cut, he pushed the cylinders towards his enemy and then leaped away to safety. The biped, caught by surprise, was buried under the cylinders.

He waited for the last cylinder to come to rest and then strolled over to the still form. As he did so, it moved, groaning softly. The light source it had used earlier to blind him lay, still on, a few feet away. Not a bad little fighter, he thought as he stopped several yards away from it and studied its small frame. Smarter than he had expected. As he watched, it turned over on its back and stared at him. It shook its head as though trying to clear its vision. The eyes opened wider as it realized its fate.

Time to end it, he thought as he took a step closer. A distant sound from outside the ship stopped him. He cocked his head, listening carefully. He could not identify the sound, but it grew louder as he listened. Something was approaching at a fast rate of speed. Others of its kind? Had the small, resourceful animal lying before him somehow called for help? His eyes darted around the room, looking for any way it could have accomplished this.

His eyes came to rest on the slender figure lying on the floor. As he stared into the biped's eyes, he was shocked by what he saw. No fear—only hate. Then it also turned towards the distant sound. A thin smile formed on its lips, and a torrent of short staccato sounds shot from its mouth. He regretted he had not taken the time to simulate his enemy's language. If the biped recognized the sound, it could be persuaded to tell him what it was. It would be best simply to kill and be done. Get away from the ship and watch for signs of new visitors.

Having decided his course of action, he started towards the biped again, determined to make the killing swift yet as painful as possible. After all, it had ruined his plans for an easy takeover. It deserved to suffer a little. He was only a few yards from it when he noticed the quick flick of the human's right arm. He watched in sudden surprise as a gleaming metallic object flew through the air, implanting itself deeply in his neck.

A new and much more intense shock of pain soared through his entire body. His defense mechanism instantly alerted him to the serious nature of the injury he had received. The scream of anguish that escaped from his lips was strangely guttural. His windpipe had been severed, and part of the cry had escaped from the wound.

He fell backward in pain. As he hit the floor, the sound from outside grew in his ears. Must escape. Must get away from the ship. Must survive—survive—survive. The instincts of the hunter-survivor took over his bodily functions. He reached up to claw the sharp piece of metal from his neck but then stopped. If he removed the object, it would leave a larger hole for his defenses to close. Better to leave it in place for now and let his body seal around it.

As he struggled to stand, he felt a sudden jolt of energy as the hormonal mechanism of survival strengthened his body with new reserves. He found himself standing, his legs were shaky but able to direct him towards the door. He stumbled against the entrance, his head slapping painfully against the metallic corner. His mental processes threatened to shut down from the blow, but a new jolt of hormone released from a gland beneath his brain cleared his head sufficiently to allow him to stumble towards the exit.

As the hormones coursed through his system, he was able to think beyond the instinctual drive to survive. Should he go back and kill the intruder? No, it was incapacitated enough. It would not be able to escape before he destroyed the ship. The loud whirring sound from outside demanded his attention. He should transform out of his hunter-survivor form and protect his identity. Certainly the noise was from others of the dominant race. It was important he not be seen like this. Could he transform or had the wounds weakened him too much? He had to try, but to what form? The bear was too slow. The form of the biped would draw too much attention from other of that kind. The deer form was the answer. Quick and strong, but more importantly, it would be natural for a deer to run away from the noise outside. It would draw little attention.

As he exited the ship, his body began the alteration, slowly at first and then with more speed. He was operating entirely on hormonal energy at this point, and he'd pay dearly for it in the long run. It would take weeks for him to recoup, but that was not important right now. All that was important was to survive—at any cost.

Deer Run

As the blades of the helicopter slowed, Oliver opened his eyes and took a breath. He hated flying, but most of all he hated flying in helicopters. As far as he could tell, they weren't made to fly. They defied all the natural laws. But this had been the worst flight ever. As they had approached the thin separation in the thick foliage of the mountain forest, he couldn't believe there was any way for the two copters to slip safely between the two lines of trees. Space was simply too tight. As he had closed his eyes and gripped his knees with white-knuckled hands, he imagined one of the helicopter's rotors clipping a tree branch, forcing the copter into the path of the other one. The two copters falling to earth in a massive fireball seemed to be more of a premonition of what was about to happen than his vivid imagination.

Although not a religious man by nature, Oliver gave a prayer of thanks as he opened the door and climbed out. By some miracle, they were still alive. He tried not to think about the return flight out of the wooded canyon. Maybe he'd stay until a road was built. It wouldn't take more than six months.

Leaning over to avoid the slowly turning rotors, Oliver glanced around at the surroundings. About fifty to seventy-five yards ahead the metallic hump they'd seen from the air lay mostly submerged in the side of the mountain.

"Damn! Can you believe it?" he said. He straightened up to get a better look then realized he was still under the rotors. He scurried away from the copter, cursing at it quietly under his breath.

Oliver jogged a safe distance from the helicopter, then stopped to study the mysterious object again. He stood there for a moment, appreciating his first sighting of a legitimate UFO when he noticed a large stag appear from nowhere. Had it come from the ship? No, that didn't make sense. It probably had been there all along, Oliver thought, *I didn't notice it until it starting running.*

Such a majestic form of nature was in sharp contrast to the alien form behind it. The deer continued to gallop down the deep chasm favoring one leg, apparently frightened by the noisy intrusion of his sanctuary. As it neared the two helicopters, it made a sudden and ungraceful detour up the left side of the chasm. As it turned, Oliver noticed the bright red blood stain on its neck and caught the glint of sunlight on metal. Had something been sticking from its neck? He couldn't be sure.

Oliver squinted his eyes closed for a second then reopened them to be sure of what he saw, but by the time he looked again the deer was at the crest of the channel and had turned away from him.

"Did you see that?" he asked as James came up from behind him.

"Yeah, a deer—a beauty. They're common in these mountains," James answered.

"Did you notice anything unusual about it?" Oliver asked as they jogged towards the other men exiting from the second copter.

"No, can't say I did, but I didn't get a good look. Mostly only saw its backside."

They joined the other two men from the second copter. As the four of them strolled towards the UFO, Oliver determined he had been the only one to get a good look at the deer. No one else had noticed anything unusual about it. Oliver wondered what he'd seen himself.

They were still fifty yards from the ship when they saw Pat sprinting through the gully following the exact path of the deer. *She's limping some too,* Oliver thought, *and favoring her left side. What's going on here?* he wondered. As she drew nearer, she shouted at the top of her lungs between gasps for air.

"Get outta here. It's going to blow! Get out!"

All four men stopped short in their tracks as Pat's warning reached them.

"What did she say?" James asked, the color draining from his face, suggesting he had understood.

Oliver made a quick decision. "No time—do what she says. Back to the copters—now!"

Without hesitation, the other three men followed their boss's order and hightailed it back to their respective copters. Oliver hung back a little and waited for Pat to catch up. As the two of them ran towards the copters, he asked, "What's going on here? Did you get pictures?" Oliver noticed the bruises and scrapes on her face and neck. A fresh trickle of blood stained her right temple, and deep creases of pain lined her face.

"No time!" Pat gasped, then came to an abrupt stop. Her right hand flew to her neck, a look of anguish deepening the lines of her face.

"Oh, God, my camera. It's still in the ship." She turned back towards the ship, but Oliver grabbed her arm.

"No time," he repeated her own words as he dragged her towards the helicopters. They reached the copter and climbed in, gazing out the window to study the alien object. It had taken on a strange glow, resembling hot flowing lava.

"We've got to get away from it." Pat voice was little more than a whimper.

She needn't have worried. James had already started the rotors.

As the two copters lifted from the ground simultaneously, the second copter drifted towards them then, with a sudden jerk, veered in the opposite direction towards the brightly glowing sphere. The pilot fought for control while at the same time climbing for altitude. Meanwhile, James struggled to keep his own copter from crashing into the trees on either side. The crosswinds of the mountain made it difficult for both pilots to judge which direction to turn their sticks.

James finally got enough altitude to fly above the searing wind. The second helicopter was not so fortunate. The wind caught the copter under its belly, pushing it down the chasm towards the alien vessel.

"Pull back—pull back, Jerry!" James yelled. Oliver reached over and grabbed James' shoulder.

"Steady there, James. Jerry knows what he's doing." It dawned on him why James was so concerned. The two pilots had come to work at B.I.U.F.O. at the same time, having flown together in Iraq. James was watching one of his best friends fight for his life.

After a struggle which seemed to take hours but actually lasted only a few seconds, Jerry finally mastered the controls, and the helicopter stabilized about twenty yards above the glowing sphere. He had begun his upward descent when the alien ship reached critical mass. The resulting fireball enveloped the helicopter like the flames of a campfire consumes the unsuspecting moth.

Oliver watched his pilot closely as James pressed his face hard against the window, staring for several moments at the spectacle below. Finally, James leaned back in his seat and through tear stained eyes turned and looked at Oliver and Pat.

"He was a better pilot than me," he said simply. "He didn't deserve to die."

THE ALIEN FINALLY STOPPED his flight up the mountain, leaning heavily against a tree to rest and watch the scene below. As he relaxed his body, it returned to the hunter-survivor form so it could continue to heal itself. He turned in time to see the ship that had carried him across light-years of space explode in a glorious fireball. He was surprised and delighted when the explosion engulfed one of the biped's machines, but he knew it was only the first of several encounters that would no doubt result in bipeds dying. At the same time, he had a new respect for this species. They only looked fragile. They could actually prove to be a worthy adversary, he thought as he resumed his trek up the mountain and back to the cave that would have to serve as his primary home, at least for a while longer.

Cover Up
Friday, April 1

Pat gazed out the office window to the postcard view of the Washington Monument. The cherry blossoms were at their peak, and hundreds of tourists were busily strolling the gardens around the monument, taking thousands of pictures.

The blossoms are early, Pat thought. Like the winter thaw down in North Carolina. A month ago, the thaw had looked to be a blessing from heaven, but with what had happened since then, it appeared more of a curse from hell.

Three men sat across the table behind Pat, listening to the tape of her story that had been made less than 24 hours after the disaster on the mountain. Oliver sat at one end of the table, separate from the council.

Separate from me as well, Pat noted. Despite telling herself differently, she was nervous about the meeting. 'Government bureaucracy can be a strange and dangerous animal,' her father had told her. In the past couple of weeks, she'd witnessed it for herself.

She had begun to suspect something was up the day after the explosion of the UFO. She and Oliver had been flown to Washington D.C. for their debriefing where they'd been held in tight security; "protected" from the press, they'd been told. It had been entirely by accident when she stumbled upon a copy of the morning paper. It had been left by someone in the room where she and Oliver were waiting before the debriefing. On the front page was the headline:

MILITARY AIRCRAFT CRASHES IN NORTH CAROLINA MOUNTAINS

As she read on, she realized the story was a cover-up for what had happened near Waynesboro. Her fears mounted when she showed the paper to the official conducting the debriefing. He was obviously embarrassed and upset that the article had so carelessly been left in the room.

In the last month, she'd been interviewed only by government officials, given no access to legal counsel, although until recently she hadn't thought she'd need it, and kept completely isolated from the outside world. She'd only been allowed to send her parents a brief, censored telegram informing them she was fine and that she had been assigned to a vital mission which would have her out of touch for a while. Sending the telegram was preferred over email or phone because they could control what the final outcome of the telegram would be. Looking back, it had been the telegram that had warned her she was in a lot of trouble.

As the tape came to an end, one of the men across the table shut off the recorder. Pat took another moment to look out the window and wished she could be an innocent tourist enjoying the nation's capital and the cherry blossoms, and then she returned to her seat. The three men stared at her for several seconds as though each of them was waiting for the other to begin. Finally, the man who had turned off the tape, cleared his throat, smiled blandly and said, "Ms. Vogt, I'm William Hartford and this"—he nodded to his left—"is Mr. Stephen McAllister, and this"—he nodded to his right—"is Dr. Henry O'Donnell. Of course, you know Mr. Sykes," he said as he nodded toward Oliver.

The formality of the names made Pat more nervous. *What is this, a trial, or what?* She decided to find out. Resting her arms on the table, she leaned across it and smiled demurely at the three men.

"Well, Bill, Steve and Henry, is this a trial or what?"

The three men looked at each other as though uncertain how to answer the question. Finally, Bill said, "No, Ms. Vogt, this is not a trial. We simply want to ask you a few more questions."

"That's good, Bill," Pat replied, continuing to ignore his attempts at formality. "Because if it were a trial, I would have to insist on having my attorney here." She turned and winked at Oliver and was surprised when he didn't so much as return a smile. The two of them had been on good terms. What was going on here?

"Ms. Vogt, as Mr. Hartford said, we only want to ask you a few questions." Dr. O'Donnell took the lead. "You must understand. What happened on that mountain is of major importance to national security. We want to be clear about exactly what did happen."

"I've told you what happened. It's all on the tape we listened to. What more do you want to know? By the way, who are you guys? Really. I don't mean your names. I want to know what agency you belong. And what is this meeting? If it's not a trial, what exactly is it?"

Hartford looked first to O'Donnell, then to McAllister before answering. "I'm with the Defense Department, Ms. Vogt. Dr. O'Donnell is with NASA, and Mr. McAllister is with the CIA. This meeting is, well, a meeting to determine your future with B.I.U.F.O. and to determine what, if any, actions are to be taken following the incident on the mountain."

"What? The three of you are supposed to determine 'my future with B.I.U.F.O.,' but you aren't even with B.I.U.F.O. Doesn't that seem a little strange?" Pat turned towards Oliver. "Oliver, what exactly is going on here? I feel like I'm under attack. I didn't do anything wrong up there. Oliver, tell them I didn't do anything wrong." Pat pleaded with her former boss. Oliver did not answer but simply looked down at the notepad in front of him.

Finally, without looking up, he said, "Tell them what they want to know, Pat. They're conducting this investigation at the request of the White House. If you don't cooperate, it'll only make things worse for you."

Pat groaned softly under her breath. *The White House. Oh shit, I've had it. They think I blew the damn UFO up. They don't believe a word I said.* She felt herself tearing up from frustration. The stress of the last month that had been all bottled inside her threatened to escape all at once. No! She'd not cry in front of these bastards. She wouldn't give them the satisfaction. She straightened her back and glared at the three men across the table.

"I refuse to say anything else until I have legal counsel. Now, if you gentlemen will excuse me—"

McAllister spoke up for the first time. "Ms. Vogt, that won't be necessary. You have made your position perfectly clear." He glanced at O'Donnell and Hartford. "Now, we'll make ours clear as well.

"You acted out of poor judgment on your last mission. What's more, you disobeyed a direct command from your superior, Mr. Sykes. You were a young rookie at B.I.U.F.O., on your first assignment. You acted rashly and without forethought. In so doing, you greatly jeopardized the mission and placed the rest of your team in grave danger. Two men lost their lives on your account."

"We will never know exactly what happened inside the structure that was dug into the mountain nor will we ever know what the structure was. You saw to that. You claim there was an alien inside and that it destroyed its own ship. No one else saw anything remotely like what you described. The only thing reported leaving the ship was you and a deer." McAllister paused for a moment and leafed through a folder of papers in front of him. When he looked up, his jaw was firmly set, and his eyes stared intensely into Pat's eyes.

"We're sweeping this one under the rug, Ms. Vogt, and you will cooperate. If you don't, you will be arrested as a spy and charged with espionage. We can make a case, a solid case, that you were operating for a foreign interest and your purpose was to find and destroy a top-secret military craft which had gone down on U.S. soil.

"The story we expect you would prefer to support is this. You have been under a lot of pressure lately. It took everything you had to get accepted into B.I.U.F.O. You then lost two team members on your first mission through a bad call on your part. It was more than you could handle. You've accepted B.I.U.F.O.'s offer to undergo extensive psychotherapy as well as accepting their suspension. Six months from now you will voluntarily resign from the bureau. You will never mention anything about the Waynesboro assignment. If anyone asks, you will simply say it was a difficult time of your life and you'd rather not discuss it. Is that understood?"

Pat sat in her seat, her back still straight, icy fingers running down her spine. They'd set her up to take the fall. Whatever it was that had been on the mountain, B.I.U.F.O. was not prepared to share it with the rest of the world. What about the alien? Had it died in the explosion? What if it hadn't? It could still be out there somewhere.

"Ms. Vogt." Hartford's voice interrupted her thoughts. "Do you understand what Mr. McAllister said?"

Pat nodded slowly. "I understand."

She glanced over to Oliver, but he would not meet her gaze.

He knows something that he isn't saying. He saw something, and he's afraid to say what. Somehow, she had to find out. What happened on the mountain might be swept under the rug for the rest of the world, but she would not forget it. She had walked through an alien spaceship, had almost been killed by its occupant. More importantly, what if it were still alive? She'd cooperate, but for only one reason. If the alien were still alive, it would be up to her to find it. She would not be able to do anything if she were behind bars.

A vivid picture of the alien standing over her flashed in her mind. It had meant to kill her but had misjudged her. She'd gotten a good look at it and, despite being dazed by the blows from those cylinders, she would be able to recognize it again. How could such an ugly beast hope to hide? Even if it was mistaken for a panther, which it only vaguely resembled, how many reports of panther attacks did you hear about in this part of the world? It would turn up, and when it did, she would be around to be sure it received the proper welcome it deserved.

She tossed her head back in a carefree manner. "I understand perfectly, gentlemen, and you can count on me to cooperate fully. You've made it clear. Is there anything else you need of me?"

"No, I think that will be all, Ms. Vogt," Hartford said as he glanced at his two companions for the last time. "We appreciate your cooperation."

Pat stood up to leave. As she turned towards the door, her eyes fell once more on Oliver, who continued to study the pad of paper in front of him. *You know something, Oliver dear, and I'm going to find out what role you played in this. You owe me that much.*

"Are you coming, Oliver?" she asked innocently.

Oliver shook his head and, without looking up, said, "No, I have a couple of things to go over with Bill, uh, Mr. Hartford. I'll see you in the next day or so." *You bet your sweet ass you will,* Pat thought as she left the room. *You bet your sweet ass.*

THE COFFEE HOUSE WAS in the basement level of a run-down apartment house. Although Pat had walked by it dozens of times before, it had not been the kind of place she'd consider frequenting—until now. It was the perfect place, reasonably close to her home, but more importantly, it was dark and secluded. Oliver had made a good choice.

She hesitated at the top of the stairs. She wanted to look around her to be sure no one had followed her, but it would only make her seem that much more suspicious. With all her willpower, she resisted the temptation. She'd been careful, and her father had taught her well how to keep from being followed. She was sure the van that had been parked outside her apartment was still there. She'd left her television running and a tape recording of extraneous sounds she had made a couple days ago. She had at least an hour before anyone listening in on the bug would suspect the apartment was empty.

As nonchalantly as possible she strolled down the short flight of stairs as though she was going to her favorite neighborhood coffee house. Inside, she paused in the foyer, waiting for her eyes to adjust to the sudden darkness. The only word she could think of to describe Benny's Coffee House was dingy. No, two words —dark and gloomy. Perfect for the meeting with Oliver. She walked through the beaded curtain and into the main room. A middle-aged lady looked up from her *Reader's Digest* and smiled through heavily made-up lips.

Before Pat had a chance to describe Oliver to the lady, she pointed over to the far corner booth. Oliver sat there with a cup of coffee in front of him and a thick cloud of smoke partially obscuring his face. He's taken up smoking again, Pat observed as she walked over to the table. After six months of proudly accusing others of not having the willpower to stop, he'd picked it up again.

I'm not the only one under a lot of pressure these days.

"Thanks for agreeing to meet with me," Pat said as she slipped into the booth across from Oliver.

"No problem," Oliver replied simply. "I can't stay long. My secretary is covering for me, but..." He didn't bother to finish the sentence.

"I understand. Let me get right to the questions then. What did you see on that mountain?"

Oliver looked down at his coffee and back to Pat. "Nothing, really. It was all in the report. We didn't have much time. I saw a large metallic object dug into the mountainside. It was difficult to determine its shape, but I'd guess it was spherical or oblong. When we first approached the site, it was resting quietly, but by the time we landed, it had begun to glow." The words sounded well rehearsed as though memorized straight from the report.

The hostess came over to the table to take Pat's order. Pat looked at the thick brew in Oliver's cup and decided to pass on Benny's special coffee. The hostess nodded and left without saying a word.

"What else? Was there anything else? Think hard. I know you saw something you're afraid to say. Damn it! Oliver, I'm taking the rap on this one. Okay, I'm willing, but you've got to help me. I've got to know what you saw."

Oliver hesitated. He studied his cup, twirling the dark liquid as though he would find the answer in the bottom of the cup. After a minute, he shook his head and without looking up, said, "It's all in the report. I don't know what you're looking for from me, but I can't help you." He picked up his coffee cup and took a sip, then sat back in the booth as though he was finished with the interview. Then he sat forward again.

"I like you, Pat. I really do. I liked you the moment you walked into my office for our first interview. I'm going to tell you something. It won't make any difference, but you need to hear it.

"You're not a team player. Oh, you're a great individual player. You've got a lot going for you, but you're not a team player. In this world, if you're not willing to go with what's good for the team, well...you get cut."

Pat nodded. "And you're a team player, right?"

"Yeah, that's right." Oliver took another long sip of coffee and winced at the bitter taste. He lit another cigarette and then grinned sheepishly. His face turned red. "I'm not going to smoke much longer. Only until this stuff blows over."

Pat nodded. "One more question. Are you sure what you saw was a deer?"

"Yeah, I'm sure. I'm not as much a city boy as most people think. I was raised on a farm. We had deer all over the place. It was definitely a deer. A stag to be accurate; quite handsome."

Pat picked up Oliver's cup of coffee and drained it. She put the cup back down and patted his hand lying on the table. "Thanks. You've been a lot of help," she said with an edge of sarcasm she couldn't quite keep out of her voice.

She was sliding out of the booth when Oliver grabbed her arm. "Let it go, Pat. You'll have a much happier life."

Pat extricated his fingers from her wrist. "I'd like to. I can't." She turned and walked out of the coffee house.

OLIVER SAT PUFFING on his cigarette long after Pat had left. *I should have told her*, he thought as he studied the thick cloud of smoke which hung like a veil in front of him. She could have explained why the deer had been bleeding and what had been sticking out of its neck. Perhaps she could have told him why those two details had been left out of the report, although every other minuscule point had been included.

He crushed the cigarette out in the ashtray and left its corpse with its companions. No, he had done the smart thing. What was important to remember was that the report had been censored. Someone had decided not to include the details about the deer. Someone on the team more important than himself.

"I better take my own advice," he muttered as he slid out of the booth and dropped a couple bucks on the table. "Shut-up and go with the team.

Part Two
The Miracle of Birth

C-Section

Monday, June 7, 2003

The giant dog waddled into the exam room. For a moment, Dr. Allan Pritchard thought the dog would get stuck in the doorway because her mid-section was distended and as wide as the door. She passed with a couple of inches to spare.

"Looks like a cross between a St. Bernard and a double-wide mobile home," he said with a smile to the petite lady being dragged along by the hemp rope tied to the dog's neck.

"Oh, but such a sweetheart she is," Alice Parker replied. "She wound up on our doorstep a couple of weeks ago, in a motherly way. She was wet, cold, and hungry. One look with those soft brown eyes, and I was hooked. She's come close to eating us out of house and home since then, but I can think of worse ways to end up in the poorhouse."

Alice and her family had been clients of Dr. Pritchard ever since he'd opened his practice in Waynesboro six years ago. Like most of his clients, the Parkers were good ole southern folk, not high on the cuff of life financially but with a wide-open heart. Somehow they always paid their bills, although not as quickly as he'd like all the time. At last count, Alice had three other dogs and no telling how many barn cats, and her two-footed family was almost as large. If the truth was known, a hundred-pound pregnant bitch was the last visitor they needed on their doorstep, but for some reason, Providence seldom stopped to consider such details.

Allan noticed two of Alice's strapping teenage sons standing awkwardly outside the door. *Thank goodness for strong help*. He'd already called Dawn, his receptionist and right-hand assistant, but it would be another twenty minutes before she would be dressed and at the clinic. Hopefully, by then he'd know whether a C-section was in the making for the early morning hours or not. Gazing down at the rotund mid-section of the dog, he suspected that would be the case.

"Boys, how 'bout coming in here and giving me a hand? Given the size of mamma dog here, I don't think we'll lift her on the table. But I'd like to check to see if she has a puppy in the birth canal. She's less likely to drag us into the next county if you two help hold while I do it."

Dr. Pritchard turned to Alice and smiled at her. "No offense, ma'am, but I'd like you to take the bow. Get in front and talk to her. All this is really frightening to her, and she could use your comforting."

"No offense taken, Doctor Pritchard. Lord knows, I ain't got much control over her. I'm no more than a fly pestering at her neck with this here rope."

Alice relinquished the rope to her two sons and knelt down in front of the dog and spoke softly in her ear. "It'll be alright, Molly. Doc here is going to take good care of you."

She looked up at Allan with a sheepish grin. "Don't rightly know what her name is, but she reminded me of Molly O'Brien when she was carrying her triplets. Since she don't come to any other name, we figured Molly was as good as any."

"And better than some," Allan replied as he slipped the long fingers of his right hand into the latex glove. "I'm going check to see how far along she is and if I can tell if we've got a pup lodged in the canal."

"If she's breech, does that mean you'll have to cut the puppy up to get it out of her?" Buster, Alice's younger son, asked.

"Where'd you get such an idea?" Alice asked, her eyes growing large at the thought.

"That's what Doc Williams had to do with Jimmy's milking cow a few months ago. She couldn't have the calf, so he went in and sliced it up and yanked it out piece by piece."

Alice turned to him, her face white with fright. "I don't care so much if we save the pups, that's not what's most important here, but you won't have to put Molly through such an ordeal, will ya, Doc?"

Allan smiled reassuringly. "Don't worry, Alice. Small animal practice is a bit different from a farm practice. I'm going to see what's what in here first. If we have a breach, we'll simply do a C-section. Molly will be asleep, and she won't feel anything. Let's not jump to conclusions." He smeared the glove with lubricant.

"Hold her still, fellas. This may be a bit uncomfortable for her."

A soft groan of anguish worried Allan at first as he inserted the gloved finger into the dog's vagina, but he relaxed a little when he realized the sound came from Molly's concerned owner. Molly continued to stand patiently, apparently unconcerned by the invasion of her privacy.

"It's times like this that I'm glad I have such large hands," Allan said. He felt around for a few seconds and didn't like what he found. "There's a pup in the canal, no doubt about it, and it feels huge. How long did you say she'd been in labor before you called me?"

"I'd say a good two, three hours," Alice replied. "At least half that time she's really been straining, but she wasn't having any luck."

Allan pulled his finger out, slipped the glove off his hand, and tossed it in the trash can. "Well, we could take an x-ray to confirm what I suspect, but all indications point to a C-section."

"To tell the truth, Doc, if it's all the same to you, I'd just as soon avoid the extra expense of the x-ray. As it is, I'll have to pay for the surgery over time, but you know I'm good for it."

"I'm not worried about that, Alice. You sit here with Molly and make her as comfortable as you can. I'm going to get the surgery suite set up so we can begin as soon as Dawn gets here. We'll take good care of mamma and the pups."

Alice patted the dog's broad head, and Allan noticed her eyes glistened more than usual. "Take good care of her, Doc. I've gotten attached to her. Like I said, I'm not so concerned with the pups. If it's a question of her or the pups, save old Molly here."

Allan understood what Alice was saying. There were to be no heroics saving the puppies if they were in trouble.

"KEEP THE GENERAL ANESTHETIC as light as you can and still keep her down, Dawn. I'm also using a local so she won't feel the incision," Allan said as he draped Molly's newly shaved and washed belly. "We want to get in and out as quickly as possible and get her awake."

Dawn nodded and smiled. Allan knew what she was thinking. In the six years she'd worked with him, she'd heard the same speech many times before. More than once he'd used her as his sounding board extolling the virtues of quick surgery. Not so fast that you were sloppy, but not so darn fired slowly that you lost the patient from too much anesthetic. She squeezed the bag of the anesthetic machine, then refilled it with fresh oxygen.

The two worked like a well-oiled team. They both knew what to expect from each other. That's why even though Allan had two other fully trained and qualified technicians, he called Dawn for the emergency surgeries. Besides, she lived the closest to the clinic, and she was divorced with only a teenage daughter. She didn't mind the late-night calls. At least that's what she told him whenever he asked.

Allan finished clamping the last drape in place and reached for the scalpel. He made a bold incision along the midline between the two rows of engorged mammary glands and watched as the blood mixed with the milk of one of the glands where it had been nicked. It fascinated him that tissue could bleed milk as well as blood. He sponged the incision for a moment before making a second incision through the connective tissue of the midline of the abdominal muscles.

"It feels more like I'm operating on a horse than a dog," Allan said to Dawn as he finished the incision and laid the scalpel down on the instrument tray. "Do you have a box and towels ready? In a minute, we'll be up to our knees in squirming yelping pups."

"All ready, Dr. Pritchard. You start tossing them out, and I'll start catching them. Don't worry about the umbilical cords. I've got the suture material ready to tie them off."

Allan smiled behind his mask at Dawn's formal use of his title. It didn't make any difference how often he told Dawn it wasn't necessary to call him doctor after hours. Old habits die hard, and since she'd been in human medicine for five years before starting with him, she was trained to use the formal title long before she came to his clinic. Besides, as she often said, "Once you're a doctor, you're always a doctor."

He reached into the incision and pulled the right horn of the uterus out. As he did so, Molly's side collapsed to normal size. "Whoo-wee, we've got some large puppies here. I wonder if she mated with one of old man Jacob's Shetland ponies."

He rested the thick tubular uterus onto the surgery drape and worked to free the left horn from Molly's abdomen, looking for an area without major veins coursing through it to make the next incision. Blotting the glistening surface with several gauze sponges, he reached for the scalpel.

"How's she doing, Dawn?" Allan asked as he prepared to cut through the muscular organ.

"She's stable, and her gums are nice and pink."

"How 'bout increasing her I.V. drip a little? This is about the time her blood pressure is likely to drop."

"It's done," she replied in a few seconds.

"Good. Well, get ready for some pups that might resemble Shetland ponies." He slid the scalpel smoothly across the body of the uterus so he could pull all the puppies from both horns through the one incision.

Allan was always thankful when he cut into a uterus for his years of training at the emergency clinic where C-sections had become a routine piece of surgery. A cut too deep could leave one or more puppies missing a toe or worse. He made the incision lightly through the uterus, deftly stopping short of the fetus that lay beneath.

Placing the scalpel back on the tray, Allan reached into the incision to pull out the first puppy. His hands made contact with the creamy white surface at the same time his eyes told him he was touching a huge pulsating maggot. Without thinking, he yanked his hands away and stepped away from the table, feeling an involuntary shudder course along his back.

"What is it, Doctor? What's wrong?" Dawn asked at the sudden movement. "Did you hit a bleeder?"

Allan stood frozen to the spot, a good two feet from the table, his hands clutching the surgery gown at his chest. A wave of nausea passed through his body and up his throat. He swallowed once, twice, tasting the foul stomach acid.

"No, no bleeder. Everything is fine—I think," he finally said.

He felt a droplet of sweat trickle down his temple and had the absurd urge to ask Dawn to wipe his brow but refrained. Taking a final gulp, he stepped back to the spot he had so recently vacated. He stared into the incision at the pulsating mass partially hidden by the pooling blood that seeped from the incised uterus but didn't take his hands from where they were glued to his gown.

"Are you okay, Dr. Pritchard?" Dawn asked as she rose from the stool she sat on next to the anesthetic machine.

"I'm fine; stay where you are," he said too brusquely. "I'll let you know when I need your help," he added in a softer tone.

Taking the longest forceps from the surgery tray, Allan gently prodded the blunt end of the mass. It retracted itself away from the probe. As it did so, he could see what appeared to be a similar mass lying beneath the first one. *How many of these horrible things could there be*? he wondered. As the shock of the discovery subsided, the inquisitive mind of the scientist emerged. *How could these things have gotten inside her? Were they parasitic? Had they eaten the puppies that should have been in there?*

Allan noticed the pool of blood slowly expanding, seeping from a medium-sized vessel. He clamped it off with forceps then cleared the pool with a wad of sponges. Molly still needed help in delivering whatever it was inside her. With another shudder, he reached into the incision and gently cupped his hands around the swollen lump. It had a firmer feel than he had expected and was warm to the touch. Still feeling the pulsating motion through his gloves, he fought a strong urge to withdraw his hands.

Allan pulled the mass out of the uterus. It slipped out with a sucking sound like pulling a shoe out of the mud. At about eight inches, it was much longer than he had imagined. Pulling the wormlike mass out of Molly's abdomen, Allan looked for some sign of an umbilical cord but couldn't find one. As the other end reached the surface where he could see it, he noticed it was lightly attached to the inner lining of the uterus and was a little more sharply tapered. *Could this be its head*? he wondered. He wiped the glistening surface with the partially blood-soaked sponges and as he did, he heard a gasp of astonishment escape from Dawn's lips.

"Oh my God!" she whispered when she finally found her voice. "What in God's name...?"

Allan gently laid the larvae-like mass in the towel-lined box that Dawn had prepared—the box that had been intended for cute, cuddly puppies. The lump wiggled much like a newborn pup, but there was no chance of confusing the two.

"I don't know what in God's creation it is, or if it even is of God's doing, but there are plenty more where that one came from," Allan replied as he pulled the second squirming mass from the incision. By this time the beads of sweat dripped from both sides of his face, but he ignored the tickling sensation. He was repulsed by the eight-inch maggot-like masses and at the same time drawn by curiosity.

Surely they can't live, he thought. *What if they did? What would they grow into, and from where did they come? How could nature be so arbitrary with such a miracle as birth?* He continued to pull them out of each horn of the uterus until six white sausages lay in a row in the box.

Finally convinced he had the final one, he looked up for the first time at Dawn's pale face. He tried to smile and was glad the mask hid the feeble attempt. "Well, Dawn, aren't you going to goo-goo over the little bundles of joy like you always do?"

"No way!" she screamed at him, an edge of hysteria in her voice. "I'm not touching those horrid things, whatever they are." She stared down at the box despite herself. "What are they, anyway?"

"Well, they might be the ugliest litter of pups ever recorded, but I kinda doubt it," Allan joked in an attempt to lighten up the atmosphere of the room. "All I can guess is they are some bizarre parasite that somehow made its way into Molly's reproductive tract. Not that I've ever seen or heard of such a thing."

"What are you going to do?" Dawn asked.

"I'm going to finish this piece of surgery first. Alice wanted me to go ahead and spay Molly if possible. Given what we delivered, I think it's an excellent idea."

"What are you going to do with those?" Dawn pointed to the box, a look of disgust still glued to her face.

"I don't know. I suppose we could save them for a barbecue this weekend." He knew as soon as he said it that it was a mistake. He'd been accused more than once of having a sick twist to his sense of humor.

"Dr. Pritchard! Sometimes you say the most horrid things—really."

"Well, don't worry about them. I'll dispose of them. I'm sure whatever they are, they don't have a chance of living."

Several minutes went by without either one talking as Allan concentrated on the surgery. As he finished removing Molly's enlarged uterus, he paused and looked at Dawn. "Alice wasn't concerned with saving the puppies as much as she was with Molly. I think it would be best to tell her the puppies were born dead. No reason to have her all worried about something we can't explain."

"You don't have to worry about me, Doc," Dawn replied, glancing down at the box one last time. "As far as I'm concerned, the less said about this night, the better."

Mother Molly

Despite the unexpected development of the surgery, Molly came through with no complications. Dawn's masterful handling of the anesthesia had her chewing at the endotracheal tube as Allan tied the last skin suture.

"She'll be up and around in no time," Dr. Pritchard said as he snapped his gloves into the trash can. "You are one fine anesthetist, Dawn. Despite our surprise, you maintained her at the right level. I might have to start paying you for these late nights." He smiled at her and laid his arm around her shoulders.

"Damn right you're going to pay me," she chided back. "Any more like this, and you won't be able to pay me enough to come in."

Walking into the prep room, Allan slipped out of his gown and, folding it into a ball, tossed it in the general direction of the clothes hamper.

"If you don't mind, how about going up front and let Alice know Molly is doing fine. I'll be up in a few minutes after I clean her up a bit. Tell Alice we'll be keeping Molly overnight but to call us in the morning around nine. No, better make that ten. Considering the hour, I expect I'll be in a little later than usual."

"Do you think we can keep you out of here until at least after eight?" Dawn asked. The entire staff gave their boss a hard time about the long hours he kept.

"Well, we'll see," he answered as he turned to walk back into surgery then stuck his head back out the door. "Remember, the pups were born dead, but Molly is doing great. Tell her she can say goodnight to her in about ten minutes. Then come back and help me get her off the table."

Allan returned to the surgery room, untying his mask as he went. He tossed the disposable cap and mask toward the trash can and watched as they fluttered in the air like two wounded ducks then fell short of the can by about a foot. As he stood looking at them lying on the floor, he could hear Laura's voice reverberating in his mind. Although his wife had been dead for four years, she was seldom far from his thoughts.

"Allan Pritchard, if you aren't the messiest man I have ever seen. Why in the world would God be so cruel as to have me fall in love with such a messy man?"

"Probably has to do with keeping balance in the world, sweetie," he'd answer back. "If we were all as neat and perfect as you, He'd not have any fun watching us."

Allan caught himself staring at the cap and mask lying next to the trash can. Four years since the fire that took Laura and Todd, and their presence was still so strong. *When will it end?* he wondered. Would the pain of his loss ever leave him alone? When would he stop hearing their voices and seeing their faces each time he missed a trash can, or cleaned the dishes, or did any of a hundred other mundane, day-to-day activities? How long would he have to detour around Waynesboro Elementary School whenever he traveled north out of town?

He strolled over to the debris lying on the floor, picked it up, and placed it in the can. *That's for you, Laura, to let you know I still love you.* As he straightened up, his eyes fell on the delivery box. He wasn't surprised to find three of the white sausages had already turned a pale gray and were no longer moving.

It's just as well, he thought. *It saves me the trouble of figuring out how to put them to sleep*. As he continued to stare at the box, he noticed something about the three that were still alive that had escaped his first inspection. Towards the tapered end, what he imagined was the head end, were two dark splotches, less than a centimeter across. Allan bent lower to get a better look. Sure enough, each of the living larvae had the marks, but they were missing from the dead ones. What could it mean?

The scientist in him began speculating. *It could mean that is the hind end, and those are developing gonads indicating that those three are males*, he thought. *It would make sense the males would live longer than the females*; he kidded with himself. No, he was pretty sure that was the front end, assuming the front end would be the one attached to the uterine lining for nourishment.

Ok, if he assumed the dots were at the front end, what did they represent? *Of course,* he thought, *those must be primitive eyespots. If that was the case, why didn't the other three larvae have them?*

He took one of the towels from the pile and used it to pick up one of the dead larvae. For some reason, he was not anxious to handle them without something between him and their white skin. He turned it over in his hands, confirming there were no marks. Inspecting the other two revealed the same information.

"Interesting, Doctor," he said softly to himself. "What does it mean?"

As though to answer, a low moan startled him so much he almost dropped the larva before realizing the sound came from Molly. He took the three dead larvae and placed them in a plastic trash bag. He started to tie it shut but stopped. He still needed to decide what to do with the other three. Molly moaned again to remind him that she needed his attention first.

Allan placed the trash bag next to the box and untied Molly from the surgery table. Laying her on her side, he placed a few clean sponges against her incision to absorb the seeping blood. He stood there for a couple of minutes, stroking the soft fur behind her ear.

"Poor Molly, you're going to wake up expecting to be a mother, and you're going to be awfully disappointed. You'll have to give all that love to those kids out there. They can be your pups instead."

He heard Dawn come back into the treatment room adjacent to the surgery suite. "Here comes the cavalry to help this old doctor get your large carcass off the table and into a cage. Lord help me not to throw my back out again."

Dawn pushed the surgery door open and propped it with the rubber wedge. "Are you sure you don't want me to get those boys back here to help us with this?" she asked. Dawn knew the long history of her doctor's back ailments.

"No. I don't want to take any chance of them seeing those things." He pointed to the box and bag. "They'd have fun scaring the dickens out of their mom. I promise to be careful and to bend at the knees. Let's put her in the recovery cage in the treatment room. We can move her to a run in the morning when she's awake enough to walk out there on her own."

After moving the half-awake dog to her cage, Allan straightened up slowly and was relieved to feel only a mild twinge in his back. It'd be a little sore in the morning but nothing he couldn't handle.

"I see half of them are already dead," Dawn remarked as she walked into the surgery room to clean up.

"Yeah. I doubt the other three will be far behind."

"You are going to put them to sleep, aren't you?" Dawn said with a note of surprise in her voice.

Allan hesitated before answering. He hated to lie to Dawn, but putting animals to sleep was one thing he hadn't been able to do since Laura and Todd's accident.

Dawn walked over to him and touched his arm. "You want me to do it?" she asked in a soft voice. He felt her shudder as she said it.

"No. It's alright. You go home and get whatever rest you can with what's left of the night. Marva can clean up in the morning. I'll leave her a note."

Dawn stood there for a couple of seconds, her hand still resting on his arm as though thinking of what else she could say. She sighed softly and dropped her arm.

"You're the boss, Doc. Don't stay here the rest of the night cleaning up though. I know your tricks. I'll be mad as a wet hornet if I find out that's what you did."

He smiled at her. "I promise to be a good little boy and go home and get some sleep. You run on home."

Allan was returning to surgery when h remembered the Parkers.

"Did they want to see Molly?" he asked.

"No. They said if she were still sleeping they'd wait until morning. They were tired too."

"Good night, Dawn, and thanks."

"Anytime, Doc. Not for a couple more days, okay?"

He laughed. "I promise."

After Dawn left, Allan walked back into surgery and gazed down at the three living lumps. They continued to pulsate and squirm next to each other like three newborn pups.

But they're not pups, he thought. *They're probably not even mammals. God only knows what they are. Probably would grow up to be giant flies.*

They'd be frustrated all their lives because they'd be unable to find a large enough heap of cow dung to fly around. He smiled at his ridiculous thought.

He knelt down in front of the box and felt another warning twinge from his back. He continued to stare at them for a couple of minutes. Finally, he reached out with his hand. What would they feel like? They'd been warm when he'd removed them from the womb, but that would have been expected. The uterus was a nicely regulated incubator. His hand continued to close the gap. Two inches from the closest one, he stopped as a shudder formed between his shoulder blades.

Oh, go ahead. Don't be silly. He touched it and was surprised to find it felt like a hairless puppy. It was warm and soft. *Well, it sure the hell isn't cuddly,* he thought. *But two out of three isn't bad.*

Allan watched in amazement as the lump turned its "head" in the direction of his hand. It knew he was there. It was responding to his touch. He realized what it was looking for. The tapered end sucked in and out, looking like a fish lying on the deck of a boat. It brushed against his hand then reached for his small finger.

It was suckling his finger! He jerked his hand back and cracked it against the surgery table above his head.

"Sorry, guy. I'm not your mamma. I don't know who is, but I know it isn't me."

Allan watched the three small lumps of life as they continued to wiggle next to each other. Could they be puppies that hadn't fully developed? The thought was ridiculous. As much as he had hated embryology class in vet school and despite the number of hours he'd spent asleep in it, he'd learned enough to know there was no larval stage in the dog's fetal development.

Well, the choice is simple, he thought. *I can either put the tiny creatures to sleep and stay up the rest of the night with a guilty conscience, or I can let them live and spend the evening trying to figure out how to keep them alive.* Either way, it didn't look like sleep was on the agenda, but as he considered the alternative he knew which one he'd choose.

Whatever they were, they had made it this far, and they had the right to live. If they died, it wouldn't be at his hands. Until he knew more about them, he'd treat them like three orphan puppies. He couldn't see putting them back with Molly. His entire staff would quit on him if they walked into the clinic in the morning to three eight-inch maggots suckling on a hundred-pound hound.

He could give them some of Molly's milk though. She had plenty, and if they had been pups, that first milk would be important. Dr. Pritchard walked back into the treatment room where Molly lay on her side in her cage, snoring softly. He took a small bowl from the cabinet and milked the thick colostrum from Molly's glands. She opened one big brown eye and stared without much enthusiasm at him then closed her eye and went back to sleep. He collected enough to give each of the pups at least a couple of feedings. He noticed as he gathered the milk, he had shifted how he thought about them. They were no longer unknown lumps but had become puppies.

"Strange puppies, but puppies," he muttered to himself as he poured the warm milk into a baby bottle. *If Dawn finds me feeding these little things, she'll have me committed, and I wouldn't argue with her.*

He walked back into surgery with the bottle. Would he have to hold them in his hands to get them to nurse? The thought made him feel a little queasy. Although he'd decided they should have a chance at life, they were still repulsive. He picked up the towel lying next to the box and picked the largest one up with the towel, placing the nurser in front of its "head." The suckling motions resumed as the white lump of life drained the bottle.

Amazed at the appetite and the volume of milk it could hold, he realized he'd have to milk Molly again if he was going to give them two feedings of the colostrum as he'd planned. When the bottle was about a third empty, he placed the pup back into the box and picked up the next one. It also tried to suck the bottle dry, but when he picked up the third one, the smallest of the litter, it refused to take the nipple.

"Not a good sign, little one," he said as he stuck the nipple in its small orifice. "Let's see; I do have the right end, don't I?"

He checked and found the eyespots. That wasn't the problem. He continued for another ten minutes with little results. Finally, frustrated with the battle, he took an infant feeding tube from the next room and fed the remaining milk through the tube.

"If you think I'm going to feed you in that manner every time, you better rethink it," he told the tiny pup as he placed it back with the other two. "You're too ugly for such special treatment."

He walked back into the treatment room and glanced at the wall clock. 2:30. He rubbed his tired eyes. With a little luck, he could still get a couple of hours of sleep. He milked another bottle of colostrum from Molly then grabbed a couple more towels and a heating pad, placing them in the box with the pups. As he started to leave, he noticed the garbage bag with the three dead pups. He picked it up and dropped it into the special can reserved for deceased pets for animal control to pick up.

It didn't occur to him until late the next morning that it would have been a good idea to save the bodies for autopsy, but by then, animal control had already made their rounds.

Biogentrix
Tuesday, June 8

Allan slept a dreamless five hours and awoke groggy and grumpy. He stumbled into the bathroom and was in midstream of emptying his bladder when his eyes fell on the three white sausages lying in the box next to the tub.

He staggered back in shock, the stream of warm urine spraying the carpet next to the john. Allan grabbed one of the spare towels he had brought home from the clinic and cleaned up the mess. As he did so, he remembered the previous evening's occurrences. Filling the sink with cold water, he soaked his head until he was able to open his eyes without them crossing. He hated mornings. A large part of staying up at all hours was because he knew when he finally gave in to sleep, it would mean going through the hell of waking up.

It hadn't been that bad when Laura and Todd were around. Todd was usually the first one to wake up. Allan remembered many mornings when his young son would sneak into his parents' bedroom and slide beneath the covers between the two of them. He missed those mornings. He missed a lot of things about those days.

When he could hold his breath no longer, Allan lifted his head out of the water and felt a familiar twinge of pain course down his lower back and into his right thigh. *Damn, not yet forty and already falling apart. Life isn't fair,* he thought, chuckling. *Typical early morning thoughts. If any of my clients saw me in the morning before I'm fully awake, they'd think I was Dr. Jekyll and Mr. Hyde. Could this be the kindly Doc Pritchard, who coos over the puppies and kittens and extends credit to everyone who needs it?*

Allan shook his head, sending tiny water droplets spraying around the room. He reached for a fresh towel, careful to pick up one of his own and not one from the clinic to save him from the displeasure of picking animal hair out of his mouth the rest of the morning.

He bent over slowly, partially supporting himself with his hands on his knees, and gazed into the box. He realized the smallest pup had died during the night.

"I wouldn't be surprised if they all croaked," he muttered. *Well, good morning, Mr. Sunshine. Aren't we in a great mood this morning?*

He decided to take a shower before feeding the remaining two pups. In his present attitude, he'd choke them to death. A shower and a cup of coffee had wondrous effects on his morning temperament.

Twenty minutes later as Allan returned to the box, he noticed the remaining two pups didn't look the same.

"Why, I'll be..." he said as he set his coffee cup on the back of the john and bent over to pick up the larger pup. It took him a couple of seconds before he realized he had picked it up without a towel, but it didn't seem to matter as much now since the small lump had transformed itself during the night. It no longer looked like a giant maggot. It had features that suggested it really was a puppy. Not a normal pup by any means since none of the features were fully formed, but where the dark eyespots had been were tiny slits. He could make out two tiny holes where the nose should be, and the mouth had shifted to one side.

Allan picked up the second pup and studied it. It too had altered its structure during the night, although not as completely as the larger one. Were those tiny nubs at the tip of the head going to be ears? The body itself hadn't changed as much as the head, but even there it looked like it had been molded. No legs, but on the larger one there were tiny bumps where it looked like legs could be forming.

He placed them back in their box and walked to the kitchen for their milk. *Fascinating,* he thought, shaking his head. *Whatever the tiny creatures were, they were altering their shape at a miraculous rate.*

As he returned from the kitchen, Allan stopped for a moment in the den. It was one of his favorite rooms in the sprawling log cabin, probably because of the rows of pictures that lined the walls. Each one showed Todd and Laura at some special moment: Todd's first birthday; Todd swinging on the swing set that Santa had given him when he was four and that had put his young parents in hock for months; Todd going off on his first day of school. Only one room had more pictures in it—Todd's room. It was Todd's room even though neither Todd nor anyone else had slept in it since the accident. The den would be a better place than the bathroom to keep the pups. It was warmer and less drafty. Allan pushed a recliner a foot or two farther away from the wood stove to make room for the box and tossed a couple of new logs onto the coals. The nights and mornings had been nippy even for early April. For some reason, it seemed important that the remaining two pups stay alive. The morning didn't look quite so grim.

After feeding the pups, Allan placed their box in its new location next to the stove and realized his stomach was urging him to the kitchen for breakfast. He glanced at his watch. Almost eight o'clock. Usually, he'd be at the clinic, reviewing the appointment and surgery books. Breakfast was not a normal part of his routine, but today was different in many ways. He grabbed the portable phone on his way to the front door. He punched in the speed-dial number to the clinic. Dawn answered the phone as he was bending down to pick up the paper, grunting as another shockwave reverberated down his back and right thigh.

"Hello, Waynesboro Animal Hospital, this is Dawn."

Allan straightened up and cradled the phone against his neck. "Hey, Dawn, this is Doc."

"I thought that was a familiar groan," she replied. "Your back bothering you this morning?"

"A little," he lied. In truth, it was hurting like hell. He closed the front door and headed toward the bathroom for his bottle of aspirin and muscle relaxants. "I'm calling to let you know that I'll be in a little late. How about checking the appointment book—"

"Don't worry, Doc. It's already taken care of. You're clear until 9:30 when Ms. Talmon is bringing in her poodle for shots and to check her ears. We can take her in as a drop-off if you like."

"You're a gem, Dawn. Now I know why I keep you around. Keep Ms. Talmon down for her appointment. I'll be in before they arrive." Allan contemplated tell Dawn about the two live pups but decided to wait until he saw whether they were going to make it or not. Somehow, he didn't think Dawn would be too keen on him keeping them alive.

"How's Molly?" he asked instead.

"She's doing wonderfully. She's up and around, and she ate of her breakfast. Alice has already called to check on her. I told her she'd be going home later today."

"Great. I'll check her when I get in." He shook a couple of aspirin and a muscle relaxant into his hand and took them with the lukewarm coffee.

"Are you sure you should be coming in this morning?" Dawn asked. "You know how your back can flare up."

"Don't worry. I'm taking good care of it. I promise to hang in my torture chamber for at least fifteen minutes before I come in." Allan's "torture chamber" was a gravity boot system he used to help stretch his back. Hanging upside down like a bat did wonders for straightening his spine and relieving the pressure on the pinched nerves.

Allan walked into the kitchen, the phone cradled against his head. He finished the call and set the phone and paper down on the table; his mind focused on a big batch of French toast. As the paper hit the table, it fell open to the front page. He glanced down at it, and the headlines caught his attention.

Biogentrix Denies Charges

Says Genetic Engineering Projects Meet Federal Guidelines

They're at it again, he thought. Biogentrix was not the largest employer of Waynesboro, but they were the one most often in the headlines. The feud had raged ever since the company had moved into the area three years ago. They virtually brought their entire staff of 850 people from the outside, rather than hiring locals as the Waynesboro founding fathers had suggested.

On top of that, Biogentrix was hush-hush about projects they were working on, something else that made the rest of the community uncomfortable. A small town like Waynesboro loved to gossip but preferred to have a few facts to seed the stories. In recent years there had been a lot of talk about the genetic engineering projects, rumored to be a large part of Biogentrix's research. Most of the locals, both merchants, and farmers, saw such experimentation as dabbling in work rightfully belonging to God.

Finally, the townspeople made such a fuss, the federal agency responsible for monitoring such experiments inspected Biogentrix's facilities. According to the paper, the final verdict was out, but Biogentrix was pleading not guilty to all charges.

Allan's thoughts flashed to the young forms resting quietly in his den. His mind toyed with the idea that there may be a connection. *No, surely not. How on earth could there be?* The nagging thought persisted like a kernel of popcorn lodged in the back of his throat.

Alice had said Molly had been a stray. Could she have escaped from Biogentrix's facilities? It didn't seem likely. Most labs used much smaller dogs, like beagles, to cut down on the care and feeding costs. Of course, that could vary, depending on the project. What kind of project could they be up to that would result in eight-inch-long maggots?

Okay, smarty, if not from Biogentrix, from where did Molly's surprise package come? He spent the rest of breakfast munching on French toast and pondering the question.

Marva the Mouth
Tuesday, June 15

A week later, Allan found the smaller of the two puppies curled up next to its littermate, cold and stiff, having died during the night. Again, he wasn't surprised. It hadn't done well for the past two days, and although it had continued to look more like a puppy, its transformation remained far behind the larger one, which was indistinguishable from the real thing.

The remaining pup's eyes opened on day ten, right on schedule, and was taking solid food by the end of the third week, which was a little ahead of schedule. Allan was thankful since he had been skipping out three or four times during the day, driving the seven minutes to his house, feeding the pup, and running back for the next appointment. Such action didn't go unnoticed by the staff, particularly his full-time technician, Marva Chamblis. He overheard a typical conversation she had with Dawn one afternoon as he slipped quietly into the clinic through the back door.

"Come on, Dawn, play the game with me. What do you think Dr. Pritchard is doing when he runs home every day? Do you think he's got a mistress stashed away? Maybe he met her down at Quincy's."

"Marva, I don't want to play your silly game. It's none of my business what Dr. Pritchard is doing, and neither is it yours," Dawn answered with an icy tone that sent goosebumps down most people's backs and usually shut up further gossip from them—but when it came to gossiping, Marva wasn't most people. She was an award winner, and she saw Dawn's cold response as a challenge to her title, so she continued the game.

"It isn't any of our business, but aren't you the least bit curious? I mean, in the last couple of weeks, every time we turn around we see his backside going out the door. You have to admit that's pretty strange for a guy we normally can't drag out of the clinic during regular hours."

"Marva, you ask more questions than any black person I've ever known," Dawn replied. Allan knew when she referred to Marva's skin color the shit was about to hit the fan. Dawn's Southern Baptist upbringing in the mountains of North Carolina had left her with a thin yet deep streak of racial prejudice, one that usually remained well hidden but was about to surface.

"I'm going to say this one more time, and that's it. Dr. Pritchard is your boss. He was nice enough to take a chance with you when no other veterinarian in this area would. I need not remind you that you'd been fired from three other places for gossiping when Dr. Pritchard took a chance. If you don't want to find yourself back out on the street living on food stamps, I suggest you find a way to curb your tongue even if it means *cutting it out*." She added that last bit with a biting emphasis. "Do I make myself clear?"

Allan smiled despite himself. Dawn rarely got angry, but when she did, Lord protect anyone in her path. He found himself feeling a little sorry for Marva.

"Yes, ma'am, I understand." Marva's meek reply was almost too soft to hear. "You know how much I need this job, Dawn. You wouldn't tell Dr. Pritchard on me, would you?"

"Marva, sweetie, I love you to death, I really do. But unrestrained curiosity will be your downfall." Dawn's mothering instinct had already replaced her anger. "I suggest you keep your nose squarely in the center of that pretty face of yours and out of other people's business. You'll make people a lot happier."

Allan reopened the back door and closed it again, harder this time. He coughed a couple of times to be sure they heard him as he walked into the clinic. The conversation came to a sudden stop, and by the time he walked into the reception area, Marva was busily dusting the dog food display, and Dawn was filing records. He thought he smelled the stale odor of tobacco smoke and wondered where Marva had stashed the forbidden cigarette but did not press the issue.

Allan stopped next to the counter, intending to tell both of them about his houseguest. At as he gazed at Marva dusting the same row of cans for the third time, he knew that telling her would be like placing a full-page ad in the Waynesboro Chronicle. No matter what he said about keeping it a secret or what he threatened, Marva would not be able to be quiet about it. It wouldn't be that she wouldn't try to keep quiet. He knew Marva liked working for him and wouldn't do anything to hurt him or intentionally breach his trust. Asking a chronic gossiper to keep a secret was like expecting a dog to share his food with a strange dog freely. It was simply against the laws of nature. Allan decided he'd tell Dawn about it later when she was alone and elicit her assistance in coming up with a harmless white lie to appease Marva.

MONDAY, JULY 12

The puppy was five weeks old when Allan noticed further alterations in its appearance. The changes, subtle at first, became more noticeable as the weeks passed. The nose, which had grown into a short muzzle, began to shorten again; the earflaps became smaller and slid down the sides of the head. The tiny toes on the front feet elongated and looked more like fingers. It was the hands that gave it away. The small vestigial dewclaw which generally remains the smallest digit grew like the rest of them and by week eight had taken its place next to the other four fingers. The pup was growing an opposable thumb.

During this time Allan kept the puppy a secret. Each day he'd go into the clinic fully expecting to tell Dawn about the miracle of life that was evolving at his home, but each evening he'd leave the clinic, making a new agreement with himself to tell her the next day. By the tenth week, Allan gave up the game. It was at the same time he bought a used bassinet from the Goodwill Store and moved his 'baby' from the den into Todd's room.

As he placed the small bundle onto the soft cushion of the bassinet, Allan felt a familiar warm glow in the pit of his stomach. It had been years since he'd felt it, not since the last time he had tucked Todd into bed and read him a chapter of *Aesop's Fables*. He continued to stare into the rich brown eyes that had locked onto his own. It was as though they were playing a game to see who could stare at the other the longest. Allan lost.

He strolled into the den and took Todd's baby picture off the wall where it had been hanging over the cardboard box next to the wood stove.

He carried it and another picture of Todd at two years of age from the coffee table to the bedroom. He removed the hand-stitched embroidery pictures, one of a puppy and the other of a kitten that his mother had stitched for her only grandson from the wall over the bassinet and replaced them with the pictures of Todd.

Nanny Kendra
Monday, August 2

Over the next few weeks, Allan started showing videos he'd taken of the real Todd whenever he was home, several of which also had Todd talking and singing. It seemed to work as the likeness to his son grew noticeably. At the same time, Allan realized he needed help. Todd had kept him up several nights with his crying. Added to that, Allan had two late emergencies that pulled him back to the clinic after eleven. He felt more and more uncomfortable about leaving Todd at home alone. What if he climbed out of the bassinet? He could break his neck. Allan solved part of the problem with another trip to Goodwill, returning with a baby crib and playpen. Allan shopped at Goodwill for these articles, not to save money but because it was on the far side of town in an area seldom visited by his clients. His purchases remained a secret; not an easy feat for a town the size of Waynesboro.

He knew he had to tell someone. He needed help and didn't know where to get it. Dawn seemed a natural choice. He even toyed with telling her the truth. Surely if anyone would understand, she would. Even so, when he considered it, he couldn't imagine anyone understanding what he was doing. He didn't understand himself. He was raising a little boy who looked like his son but had come from a stray dog's belly. When he stopped and thought about it, he doubted his own sanity. He couldn't expect anyone else to believe the story.

Allan's only choice was to lie to Dawn for the first time since he'd known her, seven years. He called her into his office to avoid Marva's elephant ears for gossip. Dawn closed the door on his instructions and sat on the edge of the chair across from his desk. He noticed she wrung her hands as she sat there trying to look calm and wondered what she must think, being called so unexpectedly into his office.

"Relax, Dawn. This isn't about you or your work, which by the way is outstanding. It's personal, very personal, and I'm asking you to treat it with the utmost confidence. Do you understand?"

"Oh sure, Dr. Pritchard," she answered as she visibly relaxed. "I was certain that I had done something wrong."

"You haven't done anything wrong except to continue to call me 'Dr. Pritchard' when we're in private. Do you think you'll ever be able to call me Allan?"

Dawn smiled. "I've tried, Doc. I've tried, but it always comes out the same. I'm afraid I'm a creature of habit."

"Okay, I can accept it." Allan hesitated, unsure how to begin the well-rehearsed lie. "This is a matter which is rather difficult to discuss, Dawn. I'm sure you've been wondering why I've been running home so much the last several weeks."

"Well, the thought did cross my mind, as well as some other minds." She nodded in the direction of the outer office where Marva sat manning the phones.

"Yes, I'm sure it's driving Marva crazy, poor girl. Unfortunately, it'll have to be that way for now. I'm going to tell you what's going on, but under no circumstances is Marva or anyone else to know."

"I understand."

Allan took a deep breath. "I am temporarily keeping my three-month-old nephew while my brother and his wife work out some marital problems."

"Your brother from Maine?" Dawn asked, a look of surprise on her face.

"Yes, he drove down a few weeks ago on his way to Florida." He plodded along with the made-up story, feeling as though the words were stuck together with peanut butter. Dawn knew little about his brother, only that the two of them didn't see each other often. The fact was they seldom saw each other. They hardly acknowledged the other one's existence. For that reason, Allan thought the story would hold. It was unlikely his brother would actually visit him.

"I didn't think you ever saw your brother?" Dawn asked with a confused look on her face.

"Well, we don't, or didn't," Allan stammered. "The truth is"—his eyes flitted to the blotter on the desk and back to Dawn—"we've been getting along a little better lately since his problems at home started. Warren doesn't have many friends, and when your marriage is breaking up, you need to talk to someone. I'm the someone for Warren. It certainly shocked me."

"Why didn't you mention this sooner?" Dawn continued to ask questions that forced Allan to dig himself deeper into the lie.

"Warren asked me not to say anything to anyone," he replied. He was alarmed to find the lying was becoming easier. "He thought it would only be for a week or two at first, but now it may be for months." He bit his tongue to keep from saying that Kitty, Warren's wife, had been caught fooling around with another man. Once the lying started, it was difficult to cut it off.

Dawn smiled. "You're a father again. Well, I'll be. I shoulda guessed, the way you've been dancing around here. Why, that's wonderful." She was beaming. "But you don't mean to tell me you've been keeping that little boy; you did say it was a boy—"

He nodded.

"You've been keeping that little boy alone at your house without anyone to look after him during the day?"

Without hesitation, Allan answered with another lie. "Warren was here for most of that time, but he had to head out to Florida the other day. I don't know when he'll be back. He asked me to look after..." He realized he hadn't thought of another name for Todd. He sat there with his mouth open, panic gripping him by the throat. *This isn't going to work*, he thought. *She sees right through this sham. She's playing along to see how much rope I'll take before I hang myself.*

Allan's eyes finally focused back on Dawn, and he saw the poster behind her with the words Upjohn Pharmaceuticals boldly printed across the front.

"...John." He finally finished the sentence. "We call him TJ. It's a little difficult looking at the little bundle and thinking of him as John." *Nice re-*

covery, he thought, but he was aware how close a call it had been. What other questions did Dawn have to trip him up?

Before she had the chance to think up a new one, he grabbed the initiative. "Warren left abruptly, as is his nature, and I realize that I need someone to help out while I'm here at the office. I thought you would know of someone who could handle this discreetly. I don't want my name or Warren's becoming the popular gossip."

Dawn pondered the question for a moment, her brow knitted in thought. Then her face brightened with a smile.

"How about Kendra? She's out of school for the summer. She's planning to sit out a semester while she decides whether to go to college or not. To tell you the truth, I'd love to get her out of the house for a while. She's beginning to drive me crazy."

Allan had watched Dawn's seventeen-year-old daughter grow from a scrawny adolescent into a young woman. There was no doubt in Allan's mind she was capable of looking after his new son. But could she keep a secret even from her mom? It was risky, but it seemed to be his best bet.

"Do you think she'd do it?" Allan asked tentatively.

"Are you kidding? She'd fly to the moon for you. Besides, she loves to babysit, if the kid is fairly well behaved. How is TJ?"

"Oh, he's easy to care for," Allan answered. *If you don't mind him changing shapes in front of your eyes,* he thought. It raised an important question. If Todd, alias TJ, continued to grow as quickly as he had been, how would he explain it to Kendra? His plan was developing holes in it—large ones.

He'd have to figure it out as he went, Allan concluded. Kendra was the best choice he had. She adored her "Unc-Doc." Even at home Dawn had perpetuated the formal title. He hated to do it, but if necessary he felt he could bring Kendra into the conspiracy without her spilling the beans. At least until he thought of something else.

"Well, does she have the job?" Dawn asked, shaking Allan out of his thoughts.

"Yeah, great. It would help me out. Speak to her tonight and let me know."

"Oh, don't worry. I know she'll jump at the chance. I don't want you paying her more than the going rate for babysitters. I know how you like to spoil her." Dawn stood up to leave. At the door, she stopped and looked back at her boss. "When do I get to visit your little nephew?"

The question sent a cold chill down Allan's back. "Uhh, not for a little while, if you don't mind. He's getting over a bad cold, and I want to keep his exposure to other people to a minimum. I'll let you know when."

"Okay, but don't think you can hide him from his Aunt Dawn forever." She started to leave again but paused once more. "What's it like after all this time to have a baby in the house?"

Allan smiled at her as he leaned back in his chair. "It feels a bit like the old days." As Dawn left the office his mind was racing. It was nothing like the old days. Things were moving too fast. Todd was growing too fast, and it seemed only a matter of time before someone would find out the truth.

The thought struck him funny. *The truth? What was the truth?*

TJ's Disorder
Wednesday, October 13

Allan turned into the driveway of his log cabin and cut the engine of his Chevy Blazer. Through the twilight of the early summer evening, the light from the kitchen window caught his attention. Kendra's figure was highlighted on the other side. For a brief moment, Allan experienced a painful stab of déjà vu as he was reminded of the many similar nights he had come home late to his home but with a different figure waiting in the kitchen for him.

He shook his head to bring himself back to the present. No, it was not the same. Kendra was not Laura, and Todd was not his son. The first was easy to remember. Kendra was only seventeen, not thirty-five, and although she had begun to spoil Allan as much as his wife had, he did not confuse the two. Though tall for her age at five feet, six inches, she wore her brunette hair pulled back in a perky ponytail, while Laura kept her blonde hair too short to pull back.

Todd, on the other hand, was an entirely different matter. As the weeks flew by, it seemed more and more natural to have his son back—too natural. When it came time to introduce Kendra to the baby she'd be helping to take care of, he called him TJ—part Todd and part...what? He'd not come up with an adequate answer to that question.

He pulled the bag of groceries out of the back seat and walked towards the back door that led into the kitchen. Was he going crazy? The thought had popped unexpectedly into his mind a number of times lately. Or was he already a bona fide nutcase? Raising a creature that had come from the uterus of a mutt dog, obviously not a puppy but that was taking on the unmistakable identity of his deceased son. *Sounds pretty certifiable to me*, he thought as he reached the door.

As he strolled into the kitchen, Kendra stopped rinsing the dishes and placed the last one in the dishwasher. She held the portable phone cradled against one cheek.

"Dr. Pritchard just came in. I'll need to call you back later tonight, Mimi."

As she hung up the phone, she turned, a troubled look on her face, obvious to Allan even through the smile she used to try to mask it.

"Who was that on the phone?" Allan asked as he set the groceries on the kitchen table and walked over to the refrigerator to get himself a beer.

"Mimi Rawlins. You know, she's Bo Rawlins' niece. She lives over in Foster Flats, but well, she's having some family problems, so she's been spending a lot of time at her uncle's. We've become good friends. I think she needs a friend."

"Well, that's nice of you," Allan replied.

"She's easy to be friends with," Kendra continued. "Even though she's a year younger than me, she's more interesting than most of my other friends. She wants to be a reporter when she grows up. Most of my classmates don't seem to know what they want past next week."

"How's TJ been today?" Allan asked, changing the subject. "He hasn't been giving you any trouble, has he?"

Kendra wiped her hands with a towel and tossed it on the counter. She walked over to the kitchen table and reached into the bag of groceries. She stopped in mid-motion. Taking her hands back out of the bag without removing anything, she turned to Allan.

"No, TJ has been a little angel, as usual, Doc." Since turning sixteen, she'd dropped the "Unc" part of the name. "But something is wrong with him, isn't there?"

"What do you mean, sweetie? Isn't he feeling well?" Allan asked, a growing concern beginning to gnaw at his stomach. *Was TJ sick? Was he going to follow the path of the rest of the litter?*

"I thought it was my imagination at first, but I'm certain it's not," Kendra continued as though she hadn't heard Allan's questions. She sat down in the chair next to the kitchen table. She rested her hands in her lap, but they refused to sit still.

She's nervous or scared about something, Allan thought as he pulled a chair out from the table and sat down facing her. The gnawing sensation in his stomach grew. *The jig is up*. He wondered what had happened today. *Had TJ turned back into a dog or worse? How could he ever have thought he could get away with this crazy game?*

"He's growing too fast," Kendra said simply. "Like I said, at first I thought it was me. Babies usually seem to grow faster than they should. But not like TJ. I weighed him two weeks ago and again today. He's gained four pounds. That's abnormal by anyone's standards."

Allan nodded. He knew she was right. He'd suspected it would be only a matter of time before Kendra suspected anything, so he wasn't completely caught off-guard by the comment. In fact, he felt a little relieved. So many other things far harder to explain could have happened. He took a long draught on his beer before answering. When he did, he spoke with the smooth tone of a professional liar. Why not? That is what he had become.

"I know, dear. You're right. I've been meaning to tell you, but I haven't quite known how. TJ has a rare disorder. Doctors don't quite know what is causing it, but he is growing much faster than normal. There have been a few other cases similar to TJ's reported, but it is quite rare. It's part of what has caused the trouble between my brother and his wife. The two of them are under a lot of stress trying to cope with it. I should have told you sooner. I'm sorry."

The look on Kendra's face broke Allan's heart. Kendra had fallen in love with the infant at once. To hear that TJ had a serious illness was harsh news to deal with for a seventeen-year-old.

What am I doing? Allan wondered. *I'm digging myself deeper. I'm only putting off the inevitable. Sooner or later someone else will have to know the truth. Why not just get it over with and confess to Kendra? Have her call her mom and Marva and the newspapers. Get it out in the open.* Even as he argued with himself, he knew why not.

They'd take TJ away. They'd want to study him—figure out what he was and from where he had come. Allan couldn't let that happen. He couldn't lose his son a second time. Not yet.

He turned his attention back to Kendra's troubled look. "It'll be okay, sweetie. TJ's dad is talking to as many doctors as he can. That's part of the reason he left TJ with me. We may have to take him to some specialists soon, but in the meantime, you continue to do a great job caring for him. Everything will be alright."

Kendra brightened a little bit. "Do you think they can find a cure?"

"I don't know for certain, but modern medicine is making major discoveries every day."

Kendra walked over to the refrigerator and pulled out one of TJ's bottles. She took it over to the stove to warm. "Well, we'll have to be sure he gets everything he needs in the meantime. I'll tell Mom that I'll have to spend more time over here to be sure he's getting the proper care."

"I'd appreciate it if you didn't say anything to your mom about TJ's condition. It would only worry her. TJ's parents don't want other people to know. Tell her he has a condition which makes it not a good idea to have visitors. We can't afford to have him catch anything else."

"Oh sure, she'll understand. You're right. Mom is a natural worrier when it comes to babies. She wouldn't want to do anything to jeopardize TJ's health. I'll tell her without letting her in on our secret."

Allan finished his beer. He walked over to toss the can in the recycling bin. He felt elated. The lie had gone smoothly. *I'm getting good at this.* The thought disturbed him. He was particularly concerned by the sense of pride and satisfaction that came with it. Proud to be a good liar? What was he turning into?

He walked over to Kendra and put his arm around her shoulders and squeezed her.

"I appreciate what a good job you're doing, and I know TJ thanks you as well. After giving him his bottle, you run on home. You must be getting hungry yourself."

Part Three

"People think the FDA is protecting them—it isn't. What the FDA is doing, and what people think it's doing, are as different as night and day." –Herbert Ley, Jr. MD, former Commissioner of the FDA

Vogt's Return
Saturday, October 23

Pat Vogt edged her new Jeep Cherokee onto the shoulder of the state highway. She slipped it out of gear and pulled the emergency brake. With the engine and air conditioning still running, she climbed out of the car to stretch her legs and get her bearings. The ride of the Cherokee wasn't as comfortable as the Mercedes she'd traded in, but it was more her kind of automobile. The Merc had been fine in Charlotte. Her clients expected her to drive such a car. The owner of one of the most successful private investigation agencies in the southeast should drive a Mercedes, or BMW or Porsche. But deep down, Pat was more of a Chevy truck kind of woman, or a Jeep Cherokee.

She stretched her arms and legs and bent down to touch her toes, feeling the familiar pop of her lower back. For the first time in years, she'd missed her workouts this past week. Something she rarely did. Her hours in the gym were a sacred discipline. They were what kept her alive, as crucial as a policeman cleaning his gun or a surgeon sterilizing their instruments. But this week had been an exceptional week. Completing her important cases and turning more routine matters of her agency over to her employees for an indefinite period of time was no small matter.

It seemed to be more difficult than it should be, but delegating anything to anyone was tricky. You couldn't count on most people to do a good job. But the agency took a back seat to the case on which she was working. Sometimes Pat thought the only reason she even bothered with her P.I. firm was to have a way to support the one case that meant everything to her. The case that had become her sole purpose in life—even her obsession.

As difficult as the turnover of the business was, Pat had gotten pretty good at it. In the past eight or ten years, she'd pulled herself out of the rat race of her own business at least four times that she could remember, each time without knowing how long she'd be gone. Some had been as short as a couple of weeks. Once she'd stayed on the road for six months, and the business had almost gone under. Tracking down clues on her own case—the Case of the Missing Alien, she affectionately called it—wasn't easy work. No one else knew where she went or for what. She didn't dare tell anyone.

B.I.U.F.O. had made sure she'd keep her mouth shut. She had been on the edge of being declared certifiably crazy by the time they let her out of the organization. The intensive therapy sessions that had been recorded in her permanent files didn't help her mental state or her reputation. They'd done an excellent job of setting her up so, if by chance she went to the papers with her story, she would have no credibility. Not that papers cared about their sources' credibility these days. Such papers as the *National News, the Sun Times*, and the worst one, the *Global Inquiry* out of Atlanta. Pat suspected few people read those papers' stories as though they were true, but they still had effect. To ensure Pat's cooperation, B.I.U.F.O. had made it perfectly clear to her they would not hesitate to pull her back in for a long-term lease on a padded cell.

Pat didn't dare tell anyone about The Case of the Missing Alien, not even her parents, which was tough. They did not know why she had left B.I.U.F.O. Her dad, who had been so proud of her when she'd gotten the position, was confused when she left. Both parents had been concerned when they found out about the therapy. She had finally told her dad that it wasn't as it seemed and although she couldn't tell him what had happened, she asked him to trust her. Without a moment of hesitation he had. He'd been around long enough to know about the political pitfalls one could fall into, but most of all, he knew and trusted his daughter.

Pat reached into the jeep and pulled the map off the dash. Opening it on the hood, she studied her progress. Only another thirty to forty minutes, she estimated, to the outskirts of Waynesboro. It was the third time she had returned to the quiet township that sat nestled in the foothills not far from the mountain of her nightmares. She'd not been back in over five years. *Third time's the charm*, she recited another of her father's favorite sayings. *Well, it had better be*, she told herself, *because if I don't find anything on this trip, the Case of the Missing Alien will be permanently put to rest.*

Over the past couple of months, she had given it a lot of thought. Ten years was long enough to put her life on hold, waiting for something, anything, to happen that would suggest the alien was alive. Oh, there had been tidbits in the news from time to time. They had turned out to be someone's wild imagination. As far as Pat was concerned, this was her last trip to the mountains. A final goodbye to a stage of her life she was quite ready to move beyond. She promised herself she would move on this time.

It would be interesting to see how much the little town had changed in the five years, if indeed it had. Many of the small towns in the North Carolina mountains seemed stuck in time. It was as though they grew to fit the size of one of the narrow valleys then stopped. With no additional land flat enough for new growth, Waynesboro had grown to its maximum capacity.

Pat folded the map in the open position in case she needed to look at it while driving. She was about to climb back in the Cherokee for the last leg of her journey when she heard a low moan, a whimper. She stopped abruptly, her hand automatically reaching to the small of her back where she kept her revolver. As her hand touched the vacant spot, she remembered she'd placed it in the glove compartment so she wouldn't have to endure the discomfort of sitting on it for the three-hour trip.

Should she go fetch it? The sound repeated itself. It didn't sound very threatening. She reached down and felt for the stiletto knife strapped to her ankle and, as she often did when checking for the knife, she had a momentary flash of another time she'd reached for a similar knife. The comfort of the cold steel reassured her.

She walked around the back of the jeep, pausing every few steps to listen. The sound repeated itself for the third time, a little louder. She continued her search. She pulled the knife from its sheath and used it to push away the dense underbrush along the road. As she thrust deeper into the thick bushes, the whimpering repeated, this time blending into a low threatening growl.

It was an animal. It had to be. The permanently implanted image of the alien as it towered over her in the ship flashed before her eyes. No, it couldn't be. What were the chances of her running into it along the side of the road like this? *Maybe not that one alien*, she thought. But what about one of its offspring? What if in the past ten years, it had done nothing but continue to multiply? There could have been a second alien of the opposite sex. Who's to say the alien needed two different sexes? There were plenty of examples in the animal kingdom of asexual reproduction.

She'd have heard of other people running into strange animals. Pat had been looking for such clues. Who could say what was hiding in the bushes? She regretted leaving the revolver behind in the glove compartment. It should be in her hand. *Wouldn't Dad be pissed to find out his daughter had been killed because she hadn't gone back for her gun.* He'd never speak to her again. The ridiculous thought made her giggle. With a second low growl, the giggle caught in her throat.

"Easy boy, I'm not going to hurt you," Pat said in a soothing voice. She'd grown up with animals and, although the growling made her nervous, it wasn't going to stop her. She pushed a clump of low-lying branches to one side and took another step forward. The deep growl continued as Pat finally found its source. Lying partially hidden by the brush and with leaves and twigs hanging from its thick coat was a Golden Retriever. As it saw Pat for the first time, the growl turned back to a whimper, and it wagged its tail.

A good sign. It must be used to people. She spoke softly to the dog as she bent down to take a closer look. "Good boy. I'm not going to hurt you. Take it easy."

She put the stiletto back in its sheath and held out her hand palm up, making sure it was below the level of the dog's head. After a moment, he took a sniff of her hand, followed by a tentative lick. She let the dog check her out thoroughly before petting its head. When he didn't shy away from her, Pat quietly moved closer to the dog to get a better look at him. As she did so, he moved deeper into the brush, exposing his left rear leg and the deep gash that had caused him to take refuge.

"Oh, you poor boy," Pat said as she stared at the nasty wound. "What happened? How did you get in such a mess?" She slowly moved among the brambles to get a better look at the wound. It was a nasty one, deep and dirty. There was no doubt it would need a vet's attention.

Keeping her eyes on the stray, she carefully removed her belt from her jeans. There was no question she'd take care of the poor fellow. Pat had spent most of her life around animals, and it didn't occur to her to abandon one in such obvious need. At the same time, she knew how dangerous an injured creature could be, and she wasn't interested in being bitten.

She eased up closer to the retriever and was relieved to see him wag its tail at her. The soft whimper did not turn into a growl. It was as though he was telling her he was ready to be helped. Pat gently stroked the dog's head and scratched behind his ears for a few minutes, building his trust. She slipped the belt around his neck, through the buckle, and around his nose.

She'd have to pick him up and carry him to the car. If she moved the leg the wrong way, it could hurt him and his instincts would be to bite first and ask questions later. Still talking soothingly to the dog, she moved deeper under the bush and gently eased one arm under his belly. Holding onto the belt with the other hand, she placed her knees well under her body and lifted up, being thankful for the many hours on the exercise machines that gave her the strength to help an animal in need. He was lighter than he looked.

"You're nothing but a bag of bones, boy," she said to him as she adjusted his weight close to her body. The dog struggled for an instant before relaxing in her arms.

"That's a good boy. We're going to take care of that nasty wound. Don't you worry. We'll get some food in you as well." She carried him back to the Cherokee and placed him in the back compartment.

"I wonder if Waynesboro is large enough to have its own vet?" she asked herself as she shut the rear hatch and smiled as the Retriever spun around a few times then lay down.

WAYNESBORO HAD GROWN, Pat noticed as she drove through the outskirts of the small town, but not enough that anyone living there every day would have noticed. She stopped at the first filling station and asked for the directions to the nearest veterinary hospital and was relieved to learn the town did indeed have its own. Two, in fact. She asked if either one specialized in pets and was again surprised to learn Waynesboro had a small animal vet—Dr. Allan Pritchard.

"He's my vet," the attendant said. "I take my dogs and cats to him. You won't find a finer one around. He's a little on the expensive side but worth it. Lets most people pay as they can, though I don't know about a stranger. You tell him Jake from the station told you about him. It might help."

As Pat pulled into the parking area of Waynesboro Veterinary Hospital, she was surprised for the third time. The building, although smaller than most veterinary hospitals she was accustomed to, was of contemporary design and had a well-manicured lawn. She parked in front of the clinic door. There was only one other car in the area, a gray and black Blazer which she hoped belonged to the vet himself. She glanced at the lettering on the door, which gave the hours the clinic was open, and frowned. The clinic closed at one, and it was already past two.

She glanced back to the Blazer, deciding it was the kind of car a vet would drive in a small town like Waynesboro. Leaving the engine of her car running to keep the cab cool, she walked to the front door and found it unlocked. She strolled into the small but impeccably clean waiting room. Along two walls were benches, the pastel blue of the cushions matching the small squares in the wallpaper. The corner between the seats was taken up by a small table, a set of recent dog and cat magazines neatly fanned out for display.

Set up for the next business day, Pat thought. Someone runs a pretty tight ship here. As the door closed behind her, she heard the muffled sound of a bell somewhere in the back of the hospital. In a moment a tall, lanky man in his late thirties to early forties came down the hall, wiping his hands on a towel. He wore a crisp white lab coat that came down to his knees. By the time he reached Pat, she'd decided she could trust this man with her parents' lives, and certainly any of her pets.

"Yes? May I help you?"

"Yes. I know you're closed, and normally I would wait until your regular hours, but I have a stray dog outside that's been seriously injured." Pat stopped as she noticed the man smiling.

"I'm Dr. Pritchard, Allan Pritchard. Most people around here call me Doc, but you're not from around here, are you? You may call me whatever you're comfortable with."

"No, I've driven up from Charlotte, but I didn't know it was quite so obvious," Pat replied, returning his smile.

"It's not, not really. It's what you said about regular hours. I don't think anyone else around here considers that I have regular or irregular hours. I'm pretty much always available. Anyway, let's take a look at your friend." He reached into the large pocket of his lab coat and pulled out a leather leash. They walked out to Pat's car.

"I do need to let you know one thing," Allan said with some hesitation. "My receptionist, Dawn, will kill me if I don't mention it. It's regarding taking care of a stray. If it's as serious as you've indicated, treatment may be rather extensive." He hesitated again. "In which case, I'll be happy to administer whatever first-aid is necessary, but—"

"Oh, don't worry Dr. Pritchard. I don't expect you to take on the financial obligation of a stray. I'll assume full responsibility for whatever needs to be done. I couldn't think of walking away from a hurt animal."

The doctor noticeably relaxed. Pat smiled. *I bet he has a significant amount of money on the books*, she thought. She'd see to it that her bill didn't become a part of it. Between the two of them, they were able to get the retriever out of the car and into one of the exam rooms without hurting him further.

"I don't suppose you recognize him, do you?" Pat asked.

"No, can't say I do. The shape he's in, it'd be hard for even his owner to recognize him. Still, Golden Retrievers are pretty rare in these parts so it shouldn't be too difficult to find his owner. If not and you decide not to keep him, I'm sure we can find him a good home. He looks like a purebred," he said as he slipped a muzzle over the dog's nose. "I'm going to clip and clean the leg, which may hurt a little. If you wouldn't mind helping? My staff has already left for the day."

Pat moved to the front of the animal and put one arm around the dog's neck.

After a few moments of shaving the leg with a pair of electric razors, Allan looked up at Pat and smiled again. "You hold him like a pro. You're not looking for a new career as a vet technician, are you?"

To Pat's surprise, she found herself blushing at the smile and the remark. "No, I'm quite happy with what I currently do, but I'll certainly keep your offer in mind."

"By the way," Allan continued as he washed the leg wound, "what brings you to our fair town of Waynesboro?"

I'm looking for an alien who tried to kill me not far from here ten years ago. The thought almost leapt out of Pat's mouth. Instead, she said, "I love the mountains and I needed a little time away from Charlotte to recharge my batteries. But I didn't want one of the usual touristy type places."

"Well, Waynesboro definitely isn't one of those." Allan laughed. "If you're looking for peace and quiet, we have it in spades. What do you do in Charlotte?"

"I run a private investigation agency," Pat replied, noting how unusual it felt to be on the other side of the questioning. This Dr. Pritchard would make a pretty good investigator himself. He seemed competent at gleaning the information he needed without appearing to pry.

"I love my job, but it can be pretty stressful at times." Pat moved a little closer to get a better look at the leg. After the clipping and cleaning, the wound didn't look as bad as before.

As though reading her thoughts, Allan said, "Our fella here isn't too bad off. I'll dress the wound and get him started on some antibiotics for the infection. In a couple of days, if the infection responds as it should, I'll be able to stitch most of it closed. The rest will heal with a little time. He should be as good as new within a week to ten days. Were you planning to be around that long?"

Pat nodded. "I don't know how long my stay will be here. It depends on how well things go back at my office. If it stays quiet, I'll stay longer."

In truth, she knew the office could manage itself. She'd trained her people that way. What would determine the length of her stay was what information she came up with from the mountain and surrounding countryside. She was at a blind end everywhere else. If she couldn't pick up the trail here, her ten year long investigation might come to a close.

Allan applied a yellow antibacterial ointment to the wound and wrapped it with stretch gauze. "Do you plan to camp or stay at one of our fine hotels?"

"A little of both. I was up here four or five years ago and found several nice camping areas. I also have found about three days of camping is as long as I can stay away from civilization and a hot shower. Is the Waynesboro Tourist Lodge open?"

"Oh sure and still run by the Adkins family. Elma has turned most of it over to her daughter, Lorna, but it continues to plug along like the rest of us."

Allan finished wrapping the leg and patted the retriever on the head. "Well, I don't like taking in a dog without knowing his name and since we aren't likely to learn yours, we'll have to make one up." He continued to rub the dog's ear, but his eyes were on Pat. "What do you say we call him Lucky for awhile? It seems to fit."

Pat found herself blushing for a second time as she gazed into Allan's steel gray eyes. "Yes. That fits him."

"If you'll help me get him in a cage, I'd say we're about done. It looks like we'll be seeing you a bit over the next few days."

"You can count on it. If you don't mind, I'd like to visit him each day."

Allan nodded and smiled. "Mind? No, I don't mind. That would be fine—just fine."

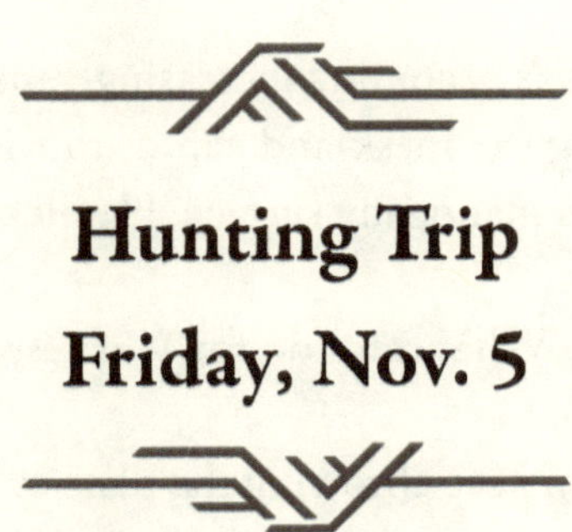

Hunting Trip
Friday, Nov. 5

Dawn stuck her head into the surgery room and interrupted Allan's humming.

"It's Bo Rawlins on the phone. He's calling again about your annual deer hunt. It's the third time in the last two days he's called. What do you want me to tell him?" Dawn asked, the unpleasant look on her face suggesting what she would like to tell him, but Bo was one of their most influential clients, particularly among the hunting crowd, a large number of which supported Allan's practice. Besides, Allan found Bo's down-home humor refreshing despite the fact it occasionally stepped over the boundary of good taste.

"Tell him I'll be with him in a moment," Allan said as he tied the next to the last suture. "I'm almost done in here. Oh, by the way, any word from Kendra?"

"Yes, she called a few minutes ago." Dawn replied, her look instantly transforming to a smile. "She said not to forget TJ's food, especially another box of Cheerios. He's eating you out of house and home." Dawn laughed. "She loves taking care of him. She says she's never seen a child eat so much or grow so fast."

Allan pulled his mask off and scratched the end of his nose where it had been tickling for the last five minutes.

"He is a growing boy," he answered, but the thought made him nervous. Since telling Kendra the fable about the growth problem, she'd kept her word not to say anything to anyone, but how long could she be counted on not to let something slip? He felt as though he was skating across a lake of thin ice, listening to the dull thuds of the ice cracking.

Living a life of lies was becoming increasingly uncomfortable. Allan sat behind his desk, tossing the mask and cap onto the clutter of paper that habitually hid the desk's mahogany surface. He picked up the receiver and leaned back in the chair.

"Bo, good morning. What can I do for Waynesboro's finest hunter and fisherman?"

"For starters, you can keep throwing the blarney my way. Others might begin to believe it if an upright citizen like yourself keeps saying it. Secondly, you can join me and a few of the guys this Saturday. We're going deer hunting, and we'd like to invite you to come along."

"Well Bo, you know I'm not much of a hunter. I doubt I've shot my rifle since vet school."

"You say that every year, Doc. Neither have some of these other fellas, least not close enough to any game to make a difference on the ecology. It's mostly an excuse to get together and freeze our butts for a couple of hours. It's also a good excuse to indulge in a little 'medicinal' to warm the blood. We'll go down to Jake's after we're through hunting. Whatta ya say?"

"You can count on me," Allan relinquished. It was the same every year. Bo would pester him to go hunting with "the boys" as soon as the season opened, and continue to hound him until he said yes. Once Allan went with him, Bo would feel his social obligation was over until next year. Allan had done it for the last three years and so far had never even seen a deer or fired his rifle. He figured it was a good excuse to clean the old firearm if nothing else. It didn't hurt his business any either.

"Great! I'll pick you up at your place around six; how's that?"

Allan groaned. Six on a Saturday morning; there ought to be a law against it.

"I'll meet you at the clinic at 6:00 a.m. I'll need to check a couple of cases." The last person he needed down at his cabin was Bo. If he found out about TJ, it would be all over town before the sun set.

"Okay, it's a date—and Doc, we're going to get us a deer this year; you wait and see."

Allan hung up the phone but remained in his seat, shaking his head. *Get us a deer, would we?* He could hardly wait. He pushed the intercom button and in a few seconds, Dawn's voice came through the phone. "You rang?" she asked, her voice poorly disguised as a butler.

"Yes. I was wondering if we have Lucky cleaned up and ready to go. Pat, uh, Ms. Vogt will be here in a few minutes."

It would be Lucky's first excursion out since coming into the hospital. The leg had responded well to Allan's careful attention. Pat had asked to try him outdoors with her over the weekend while they continued to look for a permanent home.

"Yes, Dr. Pritchard. For the third time, Lucky is ready. I promise Ms. Pat will be pleased. You will definitely be a hero in her eyes."

What was Dawn talking about? Be a hero in her eyes? He wanted to be sure his newest patient and client received the proper care. He smiled to himself at the thought. Well, maybe he was being a little more attentive than usual.

Pat had made it a point to visit Lucky every day since he had been admitted to the hospital, and Allan had made as much a point to be around to talk to her. Evidently, his actions had not been missed by Dawn's trained eyes. Well, so be it.

"Thank you, Dawn. That will be all." He cut the connection in the middle of her giggle.

A few minutes later, Allan's intercom beeped.

"Dr. Pritchard, Ms. Vogt is in Exam Room 3. I thought you'd like to go over Lucky's instructions for the weekend." There was a syrupy quality to Dawn's voice that was unmistakable. Allan ignored the implication.

"Thank you, Dawn. I'll be right there." He returned the receiver to its cradle, grinning in spite of himself. He noticed a light flutter in his stomach similar to the sensation he experienced when he had to speak to one of Waynesboro's civic groups. He knew the reason for the butterflies. The thought had been in the back of his head for the last two days. He'd allowed it to come to the foreground only twice, both times without resolution.

Now, when the moment was upon him, he knew he'd made his decision. He would ask Pat out on a date for Saturday night. At least, he had decided that it was a good idea. Would he follow through? That was another question entirely. He remembered when he'd asked Laura out on a date. They were both in college. It had taken him two weeks to get up the nerve to ask. Surely, in the past several years he'd improved. He was a successful veterinarian and businessman; as Bo said, a well respected 'pillow' of the community.

And yet, when it comes to attractive women, I'm as nervous as a cat about to have kittens, Allan thought as he pushed away from his desk. Already, the palms of his hands were sweaty and his mouth dry. *Hell, by the time I get into the room I'll be lucky if I can even get the words out.*

Despite the discomfort, he had to admit he enjoyed the sensation. It had been a long time since he'd been interested in anyone of the opposite sex. He'd begun to think he never would be. Pat Vogt had changed that. *Let's see if she'll be willing to go out with an over-the-hill widower.*

As he entered the exam room, he smelled the light scent of Pat's perfume. It was a fragrance he'd come to look forward to each day. Pat stood as he entered the room. She wore a pair of faded jeans that fit snugly in all the right places. The cuffs were stuck in the tops of a pair of well-worn hiking boots. Her flannel shirt had a multi-colored checkered pattern which matched the light blue turtleneck underneath. Her medium length black hair was pulled back in a ponytail, revealing small ears. The blues of her shirt and turtleneck highlighted her blue eyes, which met Allan's gray eyes in a steady gaze.

After a couple of seconds, Pat's lips turned upward into a demure smile. "Is anything wrong?" she asked as Allan continued to stand frozen, staring at her.

Realizing how long he'd been studying her, Allan shook his head and returned the smile. "No, nothing. Nothing's wrong. You look"—he struggled to find the word to describe what he was thinking—"lovely."

Pat's smile broadened.

"Why, thank you, kind sir," Pat replied in an exaggerated southern accent. "You say the sweetest things."

Remembering why she was here, Allan reviewed the case with her, telling her how well the wound had healed and what to look for over the next couple of days. Pat listened intently, occasionally asking a question for clarification. When he was finished telling her how to care for Lucky, there was a long pause.

"Well, I'll go tell Dawn to bring Lucky up to you," Allan said awkwardly, but he didn't move to the door. Instead, he stood in place, the fluttering of his stomach intensifying. *I'm going to blow I! Go ahead, ask her. What's the worst she can say? She can say no. She can say how inappropriate and unprofessional it is for a veterinarian to ask a client out. She could say—*

"Is there anything else?" Pat's words interrupted Allan's argument with himself.

"No. Yes. Well, what I mean to say is no. That's all I think you need to know about Lucky. Do you have any other questions?"

Pat smiled. "Well, yes. There is one question. I was wondering what there would be for Lucky and me to do on a Saturday night. I mean, we could stay out at the campsite all night, but I thought if there was some place I could take him, I might find his owner or another person who would like to take care of him."

"Well, most people will be at the high school football game on Saturday. We're playing Morganton. They're one of our biggest rivals. I don't know. You could have some problem getting Lucky through the gate, but if you want to give it a try, I'd be happy to go with you. I'm pretty sure I could convince them to let Lucky in."

"Would you do that?" Pat asked. "That would be great. I haven't been to a high school game in ages."

"Do you enjoy football?" Allan asked, surprised at how easy it was to talk to her.

"No, not really. I mean, I'm not a great fan of the game, but I do love the excitement that's around it—especially with the right company."

Allan found himself blushing. "Well, is it a date?"

"It's a date. Why don't I meet you here at the clinic around 6:30? That'll give us plenty of time to get to the game by 7:00."

"That's fine," Allan replied as he reached for the door to escort Pat into the lobby. He stopped, a confused look on his face. "How did you know the game started at 7:00?"

It was Pat's turn to blush. "I believe it came up when I was talking to Dawn a few minutes ago." She patted his cheek as she walked by. "See you Saturday."

ALLAN HUDDLED IN THE front seat of his Chevy Blazer, his rifle in its case in the seat beside him. He had the engine running and the heat on full blast, but so far the stream of warm air had done little to warm the cab. He shuddered inside the down vest. Six in the morning was his accustomed time to rise during the week, but he usually spent the first hour warming himself next to the wood stove as he made coffee and toast. He hadn't realized how important that time was to his tired body. As he shifted in his seat, he could feel the familiar twinge along his lower back. It felt like a rusty door hinge in need of a good spraying of WD-40.

I'm like an old car, he thought. *Okay once I warm up but not worth a plug nickel until the oil begins to flow.* He thought of waiting in the clinic, but he didn't have any cases to check. There was a thick stack of paperwork waiting on his desk, but it would have to continue waiting.

A beam of light from an approaching car drew Allan back to the real world. He glanced at his watch—5:58. It was one thing you could count on about Bo. When it came to hunting or fishing, he was rarely late. Bringing his dogs in for heartworm testing, that was a different matter.

Allan turned off the engine and grabbed the gun case. Hopefully, Bo's truck would be warmer since he had driven from across town. He locked the Chevy's door and waved to Bo as he pulled up beside him and ran around to the passenger side of the brick red truck. He tried the door before remembering that it couldn't be opened from the outside. He waited while Bo leaned over and opened it.

"Sorry about that, Doc. Been meaning to fix that thing."

Allan smiled to himself. The door hadn't worked for at least three years. Bo's remedy for fixing something was to come up with a pat excuse that could be used whenever needed. He climbed into the seat next to the large man and was surprised to find the cab colder than his own.

"Oh, by the way. The heater went on the fritz a few weeks ago. Gotta get it fixed when I take ol' Nellie in about the door." Bo jammed the truck in reverse and backed out.

"We could take mine," Allan offered hopefully.

"Nah, that's okay. Ol' Nellie's feelings would get hurt, and my reputation would not be the same if I was caught in one of those new fangled yuppy-mobiles. No offense, Doc."

Allan huddled deeper into his vest and stuck his hands into its pockets, seeking even the smallest bit of warm air to thaw his numb fingers. "None taken, Bo," he answered and watched as the fog from his breath collected on the windshield. It was going to be a long morning.

Allan glanced at Bo over the vest's collar. Bo was undoubtedly one of Waynesboro's most unique citizens. Despite outward signs to the contrary, Bo was among the richest and shrewdest businessmen in the county, possibly in the state. He'd made most of his money in real estate, using his down-home good-old-boy technique to keep his competition off stride. About the time they figured they had a sucker, he usually found a way to turn the tables on them. Many a high-roller from the big city had returned home with their tails between their legs and an expensive lesson they'd not soon forget.

At the same time, Bo was one of the most honest men Allan had met. Their friendship went back years, during which Bo had never steered him wrong. He felt fortunate to call Bo a friend.

"Oh, we're going to get us a deer today, today," Bo sang off key. "A deer we're going to get, oh yeah!" Singing was not one of Bo's strong suits.

Allan smiled. Maybe the day wouldn't be such a chore after all.

It was around 7:30 or 8:00 when the buck appeared on the crest of the hill less than fifty yards from where Allan sat huddled next to a tree. He had been instructed by Bo to climb up the tree but had refrained. He wasn't sure his back was ready for such antics. He had dozed off when he heard the slight snap of the twig. He looked up, half expecting to see one of the other hunters approaching.

There it stood, silhouetted against the early morning sky. Allan counted at least ten points on its antlers, a marvelous specimen of deerhood. He raised his rifle and clicked off the safety. The deer remained frozen as though a statue one would place in the front yard. Allan squeezed the trigger, bracing himself for the kick of the gun. His finger froze short of the critical point that would end the deer's life.

What are you doing, Doc? he asked himself. *Going to kill yourself a deer, huh? Mind if I ask you why? You don't particularly care for venison as I recollect. Maybe you're thinking of mounting that gorgeous head. You could place it in the reception area. That would sure impress your clients, wouldn't it? No? Well, how about over the fireplace where little TJ can look up every day and see it. What silent lesson would that be for the boy?*

Allan lowered his rifle but continued to stare at the deer. *Go on, get outta here,* he thought. *The forest isn't safe today.* Allan raised his arm, preparing to scare the buck away. The deer lifted its head at the motion, a split second before the explosion of Bo's rifle stopped Allan's heart for a few seconds and the buck's heart forever.

The buck leaped in the air as though to run down the ridge, but stumbled on the third step then stumbled again, falling forward on the carpus of its right then left front foot, tried to run that way but found it impossible. It collapsed into a clump of bushes and lay motionless.

Allan stood frozen to the spot, wondering from the pain in his chest whether he'd been shot in the same moment. He finally realized he had stopped breathing, took a gasp, then another, like an old car in need of a jump-start. Everything appeared in slow motion for the next few seconds.

He heard Bo yell, "I got me a good on', I sure did!" Bo appeared from the brush about twenty yards to Allan's left, running up the slope towards his kill.

Allan felt nauseous. So this was deer hunting. Now he knew why every year he had been so reluctant to accept Bo's invitation. As he clicked the safety back on, the thought flashed through his mind to keep it off and see how good a shot he was on the moving target in front of him. He leaned the gun against the thick oak he'd been using for support and hiked slowly up the hill.

Why was he walking in that direction? Did he think he could save the fallen deer? Maybe give it mouth-to-mouth until they got it to his clinic. Do emergency thoracic surgery to recover the bullet and sew up the gaping hole it had dug through the heart. No. He knew Bo's shot had been too perfect. The kill had been virtually instantaneous. The deer was dead in its tracks, the last few steps more of a reflex than anything else. He wanted to see—to be sure the deer was dead.

Like he had had to be sure when Laura and Todd were killed. Had insisted on going to the county morgue to view the charred remains. Had insisted on studying the dental charts to verify what was no longer apparent by seeing the bodies. He had to be sure that the blackened twisted logs lying in the morgue were his wife and child—the remains of the two people who, only hours earlier, had been his every reason for living.

Within ten minutes, the other hunters had gathered around the carcass of the dead deer. There was Jake and Jeff Hawkins, father and son. It was Jeff's first hunting trip, and at sixteen years of age, to be this close to a fallen deer was a rare treat. He had a new hero besides his dad: Bo Rawlins, the great white hunter.

The other two men, Lee Reynolds and Larry Withers, were regulars with Bo. They compared the most recent kill with the dozens of other deer Bo or one of them had killed through the years. After ten minutes of jarring, during which it was agreed that this was about the most massive and handsome buck to date, Bo pulled out his hunting knife and wiped the blade on his pant's leg.

"Well, if we want to get any decent meat out of this here carcass, we'd best get with cleaning and gutting it. Lee, how about you and Larry help hold him steady while I slit the belly open. We'll field dress it here and take it into Bryce's Grocers for him to finish the job."

The two men stepped to either side of the deer and rolled it over on its back. Starting at the sternum, Bo expertly stabbed the belly and sawed his way down to the pubic bone. As he did so, the belly glistened open. They rolled the carcass to one side, and the contents of the abdomen slithered out onto the leaf-covered ground.

Allan had seen dozens of autopsies on animals both in vet school and in his practice. Already the procedure seemed to diminish the magnificence of the animal. Less than an hour before, he'd stood watching the deer, awestruck by its regal beauty. It was rapidly turning into a side of meat: a slab of dead, gamey tasting meat.

He turned away from the activity, disinterested in the hunt. A brief glimpse of a familiar white glistening lump pulled his eyes back to the contents of the abdomen.

"What is that?" Jeff Hawkins asked as he leaned closer to the spectacle in front of him, pointing to the white mass that had drawn Allan's attention. The contents continued to roll onto the ground revealing four similar lumps—larvae.

"Must be some sort of worm or parasite," said his father, the least knowledgeable of the group when it came to animal innards.

"No type of worm I've ever seen," replied Bo as he poked gingerly at one of the lumps with his knife.

The larvae were smaller than the first set Allan had seen. He estimated they were not more than four inches across. *Immature, not fully developed,* he thought. *Probably won't live. May not have any signs of life yet.* He continued to study the small lumps as each pair of eyes turned to him for an answer to Jeff's question.

Noticing he had become the center of attention, he stooped down on his haunches and studied the lumps closer, as though seeing them for the first time. He took Bo's knife from him and pushed one of the larvae away from the others, rolling it over as he did.

"Not any type of parasite I've ever seen either, but that doesn't mean a whole lot. Deer autopsies are not my forte. They could be some form of liver fluke or some such that I'm not familiar with. Strange, they're floating free in the belly like this."

"Well, the important question, Doc, do you think the meat will be okay to eat?" Bo asked in a worried voice.

"I can't say for certain, Bo, but I don't see any reason why not," Allan replied. His mind was racing. *What if they find out about the other larvae? They'll find out about Todd—they'll take him away and study him. Don't be a fool. How are they going to find out? Take care of these larvae, and people will forget about them in a few days.*

"Go ahead and finish dressing the animal, Bo. I'll take these back to the office and do some checking into them. I'll let you know if I find out anything."

One of the men handed him a plastic bag left over from a couple of biscuits packed by his wife. Allan placed the four small lumps into it and pressed it shut.

How many more animals are running through the countryside with larvae inside them? Allan wondered. What would happen if they popped up elsewhere? Dawn would undoubtedly hear about it sooner or later and make the connection with Molly's strange C-section.

Could he cover it up? Could he shelter Todd from discovery? What would he do if they found out that his young nephew wasn't what he seemed? As Allan walked back to Bo's truck, he had the strangest thought. What would Pat think of what he had done?

High School Football
Saturday, Nov. 8

As Allan pulled into the parking lot of his clinic, the alarm of his quartz watch beeped six o'clock. Pat's car was already parked near the front entrance, but Pat and Lucky were nowhere to be seen. He eased his car next to hers and cut off the engine but left his lights on.

As he opened his car door, the inside light highlighted the bright bouquet of flowers resting in the passenger's seat. *Dumb. Bringing flowers was dumb*, Allan thought. *She'll think I'm a country hick. Long stem roses would do, but not these flowers.* The local florists had closed early because of the game. Their son was a star defensive back and so despite the loss of business, they closed early for home games.

Allan had had to settle for an assortment of cut flowers from the largest grocery store in town. *She'll hate them. I know she will. Maybe I should take them into the clinic for the staff. Dawn and Marva would like them.*

Allan leaned over the seat to pick up the flowers as Lucky bounded around the side of the clinic with Pat not far behind. *Too late. If I tell her the flowers aren't for her, she'll think I'm a jerk. Relax, man. She'll like them.*

Pat waved to him as she trotted up to the cars. Her cheeks were flushed from running in the cold night air. She was wearing a thick bright turquoise sweater with a full turtleneck and corduroy pants. Allan thought she was the most beautiful woman he'd ever seen. *Why in the world is she going out with me?* he wondered, kicking himself for such a thought. After all, he wasn't such a bad date. He was young, reasonably attractive, and a successful doctor and businessman. There were dozens of eligible young ladies who would be insanely jealous of Pat when they saw the two of them walk into the football stadium. Many of them were his clients. One of Dawn's favorite games was to point out to her boss which of his young and sometimes not-so-young lady clients were flirting with him.

Well, here goes nothing, he thought as he reached into the car and withdrew the flowers.

"Ahh, how sweet," Pat said as she broke out into a gorgeous smile. "It's been quite a while since anyone has given me flowers." She slipped up next to him and gave him a quick peck on the cheek and twirled around him, her arms grasping the flowers to her chest and Lucky prancing beside her, barking.

"It's been such a great day, and I get to cap it off with flowers, a football game, and being escorted by one of Waynesboro's most eligible men."

Allan blushed. "How long did you and Dawn talk on Friday?"

"Oh, long enough. I had to find out if it was safe to accept your invitation," Pat replied with a light giggle. "She assured me that it was, although she cautioned me that I would develop several lifelong enemies of the female persuasion."

The three of them piled in Allan's car and drove to the game. As they approached the high school, the traffic became increasingly thick.

"Wow. I didn't know there were so many people in Waynesboro," Pat remarked as they waited for one of the local police officers to wave their line of traffic forward.

"There isn't, really. A lot of these people have driven in especially for the game. This is the biggest game of the year. Morganton is up the road about thirty miles. Their high school is twice our size but every year our boys give them a run for the championship." Allan gazed in the rear view mirror at the long line of lights behind him. "I imagine half of these cars are from Morganton's fans. They usually have a good showing."

Pat turned in her seat to Lucky, who was sitting quietly in the back seat, and patted his head. "This looks like the perfect place to find your owner or your new best friend."

"How did he do today?" Allan asked.

"He was marvelous. He's obviously been well taken care of. He's obedient and learns fast. In some ways, I'd like to keep him myself, but with my schedule, I don't see how I could."

They arrived at the stadium with ten minutes to spare. "Let's see how much clout as a veterinarian I have in this town. Dogs are normally excluded from being part of the Waynesboro cheering section, but I made a couple of phone calls late Friday and explained to Frank Whiting, the head of security, what we wanted to do." Allan reached into his shirt pocket and pulled out a pair of dark sunglasses.

"Here, put these on. I told Frank that Lucky is your seeing-eye dog."

Pat's hand went out for the glasses and stopped a few inches from them. Her eyes darted from the glasses to Allan and back to the glasses.

"Are you sure we need to do it this way?" she asked, a look of concern and confusion on her face.

Unable to keep a straight face, Allan burst out laughing. "I'm sorry. I couldn't help it. It was too good a story not to try it on you." He put the glasses on the dash.

"Why, you old kidder, you. Dawn didn't warn me about this side of you," Pat said, joining in on the joke with her own smile. "I was beginning to think I was going to have to watch the game through glasses too dark to see anything."

The two of them laughed at the thought. As they did, their eyes met and captured each other for a brief moment.

It's going to be an excellent evening, Allan thought as he studied the fine details of Pat's face. They broke the momentary gaze, and Allan went around the car to open Pat's door.

"Thank you, kind sir," Pat said as she exited the car, turning to help Lucky out over the seat. She clipped the leash to his collar, and he obediently came to her left side.

"Good boy. You look pretty for the people tonight, and see if you can't find your owner. Okay?"

"We need to go to the south gate to get in. Frank said he'd be sure to be stationed there. He has a note for us in case anyone tries to raise a fuss. We should be in time for the pre-game show."

Pat stepped up beside him and took his arm. "Thanks so much for inviting me to the game. I feel like part of the community. It's nice. I've lived in Charlotte for years and haven't felt as much at home as I do here tonight."

"It's the small town atmosphere. It'll get you every time if you give it a chance," Allan replied.

They joined the crowd entering the stadium.

FOR A SMALL TOWN HIGH school, Waynesboro boasted having one of the nicest and largest stadiums to play football, and on this particular evening, the Eagle's Nest, as it was popularly called, was jammed to capacity. The Waynesboro Eagles and the Morganton Bulldogs were in their respective locker rooms. The Morganton band was marching off the field at one end while the Waynesboro band lined up at the other, preparing to make their entrance for the pregame show.

"This is a beautiful facility," Pat remarked as Allan turned over their tickets to a tall lanky fellow wearing a crisply starched security uniform.

"Why, thank you, ma'am," Frank replied as he handed the ticket stubs back to Allan. "You might get a chance to tell our benevolent benefactor what you think. He's here tonight; somewhere."

"Oh? Who's that?" Pat asked.

"Why, Dr. Fredric Homlin, president and owner of Biogentrix, of course."

"Did you say Dr. Homlin is here tonight? That's unusual," Allan remarked.

"Not really," Frank replied. "His 'Honor' usually makes an appearance at the big home games. He thinks it's good P.R. Like he thinks donating the money to build this stadium gives him the right to do whatever he wants in this town and out there in that damn lab of his." The sarcasm in Frank's voice was only slightly masked.

"Dr. Homlin doesn't seem to be the most popular guy in town," Pat said as they wound their way to their seats. "Despite trying to buy some popularity."

"No, I'd have to agree with you there," Allan replied. "I haven't met the man face to face, but despite donating a lot of money to Waynesboro in one way or another and despite the fact Biogentrix is one of our larger employers, most people aren't settled about having them here. Most of the people who work there transferred in. It was great for the economy here, but not everyone saw it that way."

"How long has Biogentrix been here?"

"Only about three years. It's been a hornet's nest from the first. Lately, it's gotten worse. That's why I was surprised to hear that Dr. Homlin has decided to walk among the common folk."

"I'd like to meet the man," Pat said with an edge of intensity that startled Allan.

"You are here for a vacation, aren't you?"

Pat laughed. "That's right. Once a detective, always a detective. He sounds like an interesting fellow, that's all. Don't worry, you're my date for the entire evening."

Allan smiled. "Thanks. It wouldn't do my reputation much good to have you leave me for someone else in front of so many people."

They came to their seats on the thirty yard line. Lucky brought immediate attention to them as the three of them sat down. Allan had purchased three tickets to be sure they'd have plenty of room for Lucky. Several of the kids around them came up to Lucky and patted him. Lucky ate up the attention.

"Neat. We have a new mascot," one of the teenager's said. "But he's not wearing the school colors." Within moments, the problem was remedied. Someone found an old Eagle's sweatshirt for Lucky. Allan helped Pat slip the shirt over Lucky's head and thread his front legs through the arms of the shirt. Everyone howled with laughter and Lucky joined in with a chorus of his own.

"Well, we don't have to worry whether Lucky will fit in or not," Allan said as they finally settled in to watch the game. The two teams streamed onto the field, and the game was underway.

PAT GLANCED UP AT THE scoreboard at the end of the field. "Fourteen, fourteen. Can't ask for a closer game. I can't remember the last time I had so much fun at a football game." She turned to look at Allan. "Can we walk around during the halftime? I think we should find a spot to exercise Lucky."

"Sure. Could I interest you in a cup of coffee or hot chocolate?" As Allan asked the question, his breath formed a momentary cloud between them.

"Oh, I'd love some hot chocolate."

The three of them walked down to the refreshment stand, pausing frequently to give several kids in the crowd time to pat Lucky's head. The refreshment stand was crowded with other people intent on warming themselves up. The mood of the crowd was festive and light. Their team had held their own against the larger high school, and the Eagles were known as a second-half team. The stage seemed set for an upset.

Allan and Pat were two people from the front of the line when they heard a commotion behind them. As they turned to watch, a large man who towered four inches over anyone else pushed his way through the crowd.

"Out of the way, folks. Get out of the way," the man said repeatedly as he pushed people to either side. Several people grunted their complaints as they were shoved out of their spots, but no one attempted to get in the big man's way. As he approached them, Pat stepped purposefully in front of him, planting her left heel into his instep with painful force.

"Excuse me. I'm so sorry. I didn't see you bullying your way through. May I help you?"

The man cursed under his breath but kept his self control. Through tearing eyes, he glared at Pat. "I need to get through here and get Dr. Homlin some coffee," he said as he attempted to wave Pat to the side, but Pat's heel was on his instep. She shifted her weight forward again, and the man winced in pain once more.

"You don't mean 'the' Dr. Homlin? Not Dr. Fredric Homlin? Is ol' Freddy here tonight?"

"That's right. Now if you'll excuse me..."

Pat didn't budge from her spot. She simply applied a little more weight to her left foot. "Why don't you go on back to your boss? I'll be happy to get ol' Freddy a cup of coffee and bring it to him."

The big man hesitated for a moment, unsure whether to proceed with his assignment or not. His attention was finally drawn to the fuming crowd around him as though he noticed for the first time that there were other people around. Pat ground her heel into the tender area of his foot one last time.

"Go on. I'll be over there in a moment with Freddy's coffee."

The thug finally pulled his foot out from under hers and retreated. "Dr. Homlin doesn't like to be called Freddy," he said under his breath. "He's over there next to the restrooms." He pointed to a small group of men dressed in dark cashmere coats.

As the man turned his back on them, Allan slid next to Pat. "You're amazing."

She turned to him, surprised at the comment. "Whatever do you mean?"

"You not only averted a mob scene single-handedly. You completely cowed that giant and got yourself a meeting with the eminent Dr. Homlin."

Pat smiled. "Well, I did say I wanted to meet him. Do you mind?"

"No, not at all, as long as you take me along."

"Of course, silly. You're my date."

As they reached the front of the line, they purchased two hot chocolates, a coffee, and a hot dog for Lucky.

"It's terrible for my reputation for this many people to see me feed such trashy food to a dog, but since the next closest small animal vet is thirty miles away, I don't imagine it'll cost me too much business." Allan bent down and fed the hot dog to Lucky. "Let's go meet this Dr. Homlin."

They jostled their way through the crowd, Allan and Lucky leading the way with Pat following in their wake with the extra cup of coffee. As they approached the group, the men turned to watch their arrival. Pat stepped forward with the cup of steaming coffee.

"Hello, big guy," she said to the man she'd stopped in the crowd. "Here's the coffee I promised."

One of the men stepped forward to take the cup, but Pat ignored him. Instead, she stepped around him and handed the cup to the shorter man standing next to him.

"Dr. Homlin, I presume," Pat said as she handed the cup to him. As she did so, Lucky stepped forward and took a sniff of Homlin's pant leg. The fur on the back of his neck bristled, and a low threatening growl grew in his throat. Allan pulled him back, but Lucky continued his threatening stance.

Dr. Homlin glanced first at Pat, to Lucky, and back again to Pat. "Your dog?" he asked as he nodded in Lucky's direction.

"No, not really. He's a stray I'm taking care of for a few days," Pat replied with a cold smile. She felt her own hackles rise. She'd been a private investigator long enough to learn to trust her instincts. This man was to be watched carefully.

"Fine beast, though a bit silly looking in that garb. Perhaps I'd be interested in him." As he spoke, he took a couple of steps back.

Lucky calmed down a little but continued a low growl in the back of his throat.

"Thanks for considering it. I'll let you know," Pat replied without much interest in the offer. She'd already concluded Dr. Homlin was the last man on earth she'd ever give Lucky to.

She continued to study him as Allan introduced himself. The owner of Biogentrix looked to be in his mid-forties although he had a face that made judging his age difficult. He was an attractive man. What one would call distinguished: dark hair with a dusting of gray at the temples.

Pat was most interested in Homlin's eyes. They were cold yet intense. She had the thought as she studied them that he could literally freeze you with one stare. The slight crow's feet at the edges gave them a sinister quality. Pat felt the goose bumps tingle along her arms and understood why Lucky continued to growl. The dog had good judgment.

"I appreciate the coffee." Dr. Homlin directed his comment to Pat. "You must come out to my place someday soon and let me return the hospitality."

Pat noticed the momentary look of surprise that flashed across the face of the large man, who appeared to be Homlin's bodyguard. It appeared the invitation was an unusual one for Homlin to make.

"Why, I'd love to come out and see what goes on at Biogentrix. Perhaps Allan and I could make it out some afternoon for a tour."

Dr. Homlin laughed, but there was no humor in the sound. "No, no, my dear. I'm afraid you misunderstood. The lab is off base. No one is permitted through there, even one so lovely as yourself. No. I meant my home, Waverly Place. It was once a game preserve. I bought it a few years ago and have been fixing it up. You'd be most welcome there."

Pat smiled at the correction and determined to check out the Biogentrix lab as well as its mysterious owner.

"I am a bit difficult to reach, but you could give Allan a call at his clinic. He's taking care of Lucky, and so I'll get the message through him. Is that okay with you, Allan?"

"Sure, no problem. I have next Wednesday afternoon off. If that would work in your schedule, Dr. Homlin."

Pat appreciated Allan's willingness to come along. The thought of being alone with Homlin had only added to her goosebumps.

"I'll need to check my schedule. I can let you know by the first of the week," Dr. Homlin replied. Pat had the distinct feeling he was not excited about including Allan in the invitation, which was fine with her.

Dr. Homlin tipped his coffee to them as though to make a toast. "Well, here's to an exciting second half. Enjoy the game." With that, he and his entourage turned and walked away.

Only after he was out of sight did Lucky stop growling. "Well, it's for sure, ol' Lucky didn't have much use for the president of Biogentrix," Allan said as the three of them started back to their seats.

"No. I'd say Lucky has good taste in people. I have to admit, Dr. Homlin gave me the creeps as well."

"Then why did you accept his invitation?" Allan asked, a note of surprise in his voice.

"Because he does give me the creeps. I've got a gut feeling something is off about the man, and I intend to find out what it is. I appreciate your offer to come along, but if you would rather not, I'll understand. I'll be fine."

"Are you kidding?" Allan replied. "I'm coming along to protect my own interest. After seeing how you handled yourself tonight, I'm sure you'll be fine. If anything, I'm more worried about Homlin. Remember, you're on vacation."

"Yes, well, I think the vacation has been turned into a working one." Pat took Allan's arm. "But for the rest of tonight it's vacation, and I'll not have another thought about Dr. Homlin. Promise."

Unfortunately, it was a promise she found herself breaking several times throughout the rest of the evening.

Dissecting Larvae

Sunday, Nov. 9

The sharp scalpel blade slid across the glistening white tissue. Being accustomed to seeing a thin line of blood mark where the blade had traveled, Allan was surprised when the red streak did not appear. Of course, the larva had been dead for at least twenty-four hours. You wouldn't expect much bleeding this long after death. Then again, who was to say the damn things even had blood or that the blood would be red?

He wiped a drop of perspiration from his temple with the upper part of his arm. Why was he sweating so much? It couldn't be more than seventy degrees in the treatment room. *You're cutting open one of the things that turned into Todd*, he thought. *It's okay to feel a little strange, even to sweat a little. Your life has taken a bizarre twist lately. This is peculiar behavior even for Halloween.*

He continued to dissect the deeper layers of the larva, surprised to find only a homogeneous mass of off-white tissue—but not entirely homogeneous. Throughout the layers were subtle markings, tissue a bit off-colored, as though it would one day have differentiated into organs.

In his years as a veterinary student and a practicing doctor, Allan had dissected many strange animals from starfishes and mud puppies to horses and cows. He'd never seen anything quite like the larva. There wasn't much to look at. The closest thing it reminded him of was cutting through a brain. You knew it was a complex organ, the most complex of the body, yet when you cut through one about all you saw was white tissue.

Could the larva be just that—an undifferentiated brain waiting for a body to be formed around it? No, the first larvae hadn't formed a body around themselves. They had become the body, first a puppy-like form, then a human baby, and last, a reproduction of his son.

Allan had dissected the remaining larvae. Each one was like the first. What conclusions could he draw from his hour or so of work? Not much. The larvae were definitely not like anything he'd ever run across. He'd known that from the start, and the dissections had only confirmed it. They appeared to be blank slates with little of their inner workings predetermined. It made sense. That's why they were able to adapt to different forms so easily. Their genetic makeup wasn't preset. It seemed like a likely hypothesis.

Allan took the remains of the four larvae and triple bagged them. He placed the bags into a sturdy cardboard box, taped it shut, and placed the box in the freezer reserved for animal pick-up. The city would be around in the morning to remove whatever was in the freezer. They would simply think it was another dead animal waiting for disposal and would burn the whole thing: box, bags, and larvae.

Allan felt like an accomplice to a crime. Destroying evidence to protect a loved one. Well, it was true. He was protecting Todd. He had to. What would they do to Todd if anyone ever found out where he had come from? They'd haul him off to some governmental lab, and a dozen or more scientists would end up doing to him what Allan had done. They'd test him, draw samples, x-ray him, and eventually cut him open to see what made him tick. Allan shuddered at the thought. Not to his son they wouldn't.

He walked into his office and picked his ski jacket off the desk where he'd thrown it when he'd first come in. As he put it on, his thoughts wandered from Todd to Pat. He had invited her to dinner on Wednesday after they were through visiting Homlin's place. He toyed with the idea of introducing Pat to Todd, except it couldn't be Todd; it would have to be TJ. It was a crazy thought. It could only complicate matters, the more people who knew about his secret.

But he didn't want Pat to only know about TJ—not the fabricated story but the truth. All of it. She'd understand what he was going through. She would be able to shed some light on the mystery. After all, she was a private investigator.

The thought sent a cold chill down his back. That's right, she was a P.I. She'd love to know about such a story. What would she do with it? Could he actually trust this woman who he'd only known for a couple of weeks?

Or would she run to the authorities, or worse yet, report him to the mental health people? It was too dangerous. He couldn't take the chance. But the burden of carrying his secret around on his own was becoming overpowering. He had to tell someone soon or he'd burst. If he was going to tell anyone, Pat would be the one to tell. He didn't know exactly why, but he trusted her.

How could he go about it? The question haunted him as he shut out the lights and turned the heat back. He had until Wednesday to figure it out. He had to tell someone soon.

WEDNESDAY, NOV. 12

Allan pulled the latex gloves from his hands and threw them in the trash can.

"Give her two cc's of penicillin, Marva. We'll keep her in recovery until she's fully awake. Please have Dawn call Ms. Curtis and let her know Missy is doing fine and will be able to go home in the morning." He glanced at the work roster and his watch. "It's been a good morning. I love it when the day actually goes as you plan it."

He walked into his office, removing his lab coat as he went. It was one p.m., closing time for the clinic on Wednesday. Pat would be pulling into the driveway in a couple of minutes. They were scheduled to meet Dr. Homlin at two o'clock. That would give them enough time to get a quick bite to eat before driving to the old animal reserve that had become Homlin's private property and another reason for Waynesboro's citizens to complain about the mysterious owner of Biogentrix.

Although Allan was looking forward to seeing Pat again, he wasn't excited about going to Homlin's. The man seemed cold and ruthless, and he didn't trust Homlin's motives. *If he makes a play for Pat, I'll slug him, bodyguards or no bodyguards,* he thought as he glanced at the telephone messages Dawn had neatly laid out on his desk. Only one needed to be called today. He reached for the phone. May as well get it out of the way before he left. He'd call Kendra and let her know he'd be home around four so she could plan the rest of her day.

On his first call, a machine answered, and he left a short message regarding one of his patients. Then he called his home. Kendra picked up the phone on the second ring.

"Dr. Pritchard's residence. Who's calling, please?" Kendra sounded a lot like her mother answering the clinic phone.

"Hey, Kendra. This is Doc. How's TJ doing?"

"Hi, Doc. TJ is doing fine. Had a bowl of Cheerios. I've never seen a kid so crazy for them. He's napping at the moment. I can't believe how well he's walking already, and talking. He's talking up a storm. He even asked for his 'Dada' a few times before nodding off. Cute. Hope your brother doesn't get upset when he learns his son is calling you Dada. What's up?"

"Not much. I wanted to let you know I'll be home around four today, and I'm going to let you have the rest of the day off."

"Great! I've been meaning to ask you for some time off. I have several errands I need to run."

"Well, today is the day for them. Be sure TJ is dressed cute, will you?"

"Of course. I dress him nice for his favorite uncle."

The comment caught Allan off guard. He didn't think of himself as TJ's uncle. He was his dad. After a pause, he said good-bye to Kendra and hung up the phone. As he did so, he glanced out the window. Pat's car was pulling into the parking lot. He glanced at his watch again. 12:58. He loved a woman who was prompt. He took his corduroy blazer from behind the door and stepped into the waiting room.

"You just got a call from a Mr. Homlin," Dawn said from the other side of the counter. "He said he needs to cancel the appointment for today. Said he'd get back in touch with you soon."

Allan nodded. *That's fine with me,* he thought, *but I doubt Pat will be pleased to hear it.*

Meeting TJ
Wednesday, Nov. 19

Allan glanced at the clock on the kitchen wall; five-thirty. Only an hour before Pat was due to arrive. He'd finally made up his mind he would introduce her to TJ and tell her the whole story. He couldn't keep it a secret any longer. His "son" was growing at an incredible rate. It was getting more and more difficult to hide the truth, much less keep him from wandering around. Sooner or later, Kendra would tell Dawn how large TJ had grown, or something else would happen to blow TJ's cover. Then what?

Allan had no way of knowing where that would lead. He also knew Pat wouldn't have any idea either, but the stress of worrying about it alone had become too much for him. At least with Pat knowing everything, he'd have a friend he could talk to about it. Talking things out helped. At least that's what Laura had said. Deep down inside, Allan felt there was some hope that between the two of them, they could figure something out—some way to introduce TJ to the rest of the world without him being looked on as a freak or as dangerous.

He had become even more convinced that today was the day to talk to Pat about TJ when his office received yet another call from Homlin postponing their meeting again. At least this time Homlin offered another date.

When Allan had arrived home around four o'clock, TJ was napping. Allan walked over to the refrigerator to see what he could find to warm up for his son.

He's not your son, a small voice said in the deep recesses of Allan's mind. *Your son is dead, and what you have napping in his room is a mutant larva that you pulled out of a stray dog. He's not your son. He's not even human. You don't know what he is, but he's not your son.*

"So what," Allan said out loud. "He's close enough."

As he said this, he spied the plastic container of food that Kendra had prepared for TJ's meal. God bless her. She sure made his life with TJ easier. Who was to say that this boy wasn't human? He looked human—looked uncannily like Todd when he was three. He ate human food. He talked like a human. He seemed to have a better vocabulary than Allan remembered his son having at three. Other humans, at least one other, related to him as human. For all practical purposes, he was human. Right?

Allan took the plastic container out of the refrigerator and stuck it in the microwave, loosening the lid as he did. He had learned the hard way about firmly applied lids in a microwave. After a minute, the bell to the microwave alerted him that TJ's meal was ready. He took it out and removed the lid to allow it to cool a little. He walked in to waken him. By the time TJ was fully awake, the food would be cool enough for him to eat.

Allan entered TJ's room—the room that had been transformed from a shrine to his deceased son to his replacement son's nursery. Allan stopped in the doorway. *Something is wrong*, the nagging voice said even before he turned on the overhead light. *The crib looks empty...but it can't be; it's empty, I tell you.*

Allan flipped on the light and stared at the crib, the sheets and blanket pulled back as though whoever had been sleeping in the bed had thrown them off. The railing was up. Allan's eyes flitted to the open window at the other end of the room, a light breeze ruffling the curtains. *Someone has taken my son*, was his first thought. *No—that's not possible. No one knows about TJ except Kendra and Dawn.* He was certain of that and equally sure neither one of them would have kidnapped him.

The bitter truth hit Allan in the pit of his stomach like a blow from a boxer pounding on his opponent's body. TJ had escaped on his own. He'd left by the window so as to go unnoticed, knowing Allan would have stopped him. But where had he gone and why?

Allan sat on the chair next to the crib where he read bedtime stories, tears rimming his lower lids and breaking over them. For the second time he'd lost his son, and for the second time he felt the hollow sensation throughout every fiber of his body.

He could simply be outside playing, his mind told him. *You don't know what has happened. He might be back. Go look for him, you idiot. He may have just left*. Even as Allan rose from the chair to go find his flashlight, he feared he'd seen his son for the last time.

He started his search underneath TJ's window and, sure enough, found small footprints that matched TJ's foot size. He followed them across the lawn towards the woods, but before the trail made it to the woods, the pattern changed from child footprints to paw prints.

Allan stared down at the set of prints. *Still believe this is your son?* he asked himself. *Since when did Todd know how to transform himself into a dog?* Allan could feel the energy drain from him. Shoulders slumped, he slowly walked back to the house, obliterating the trail as he went.

"I APPRECIATE YOUR COMING back on your afternoon off," Pat said as she took the leash from Dawn.

"Think nothing of it. Lucky is comfortable in his run, and I was planning on dropping by this afternoon to check on Mrs. Avery's two cats anyway. It was no trouble," Dawn replied with a smile and added, "How's it going with Dr. Pritchard?"

"Well, with your help, it's great. You were right, he is a nice guy. We're having dinner in a few minutes."

Dawn walked around the counter and escorted Pat to the door. "I'm so glad to hear it's going well. I'm not much for meddling in other people's affairs, but you two seemed made for each other."

She paused at the door, her hand on the lock. "I think the world of Dr. Pritchard. He's been good to me and my family. I'd do anything to see him happy." She smiled again. "He's happy when he's around you. I'd say you're good for each other."

Pat returned the smile, a little embarrassed by what Dawn was saying. Good for each other? Yes, she guessed they were.

As she turned out of the clinic's driveway heading towards Allan's house, the conversation with Dawn haunted her. She looked at herself in the rear view mirror. If Allan was happy around her, the feeling was mutual. She'd noticed it herself. Despite everything that was going on with the investigation, she was more relaxed and contented than she could remember being in the last ten years. It even showed on her face. Yes, Allan Pritchard was also good for her. She stopped at a traffic light a few blocks from the clinic and pulled out the directions Allan had given her. When the light changed, she turned right.

Take how Allan had dealt with her plan to visit Homlin's private sanctuary, for instance. The idea of going there alone terrified her, but having Allan accompany her would make a huge difference. That is, if Homlin didn't cancel again. *Funny*, Pat thought. *He doesn't even know what's going on and he's making a difference. What might be possible if I told him what I was up to?*

The thought surprised her. What was she up to? She wasn't even sure herself but deep down inside, the little voice she had learned to listen to, kept whispering to her that somehow Homlin was connected to the Case of the Missing Alien. Maybe he had found the alien, saved its life, and was in cohoots with it. Maybe the alien had died and Homlin was trying to use its genetic material in some way. The voice hadn't come up with many possibilities—at least not any that made sense. Still, it wouldn't let the matter rest.

Oh, so you're going to tell Allan about what you've spent the last ten years of your life on? Tell someone about the Case of the Missing Alien? A man you've only known for a couple of weeks? Are you crazy?

Why not? she argued with herself. *You said Allan made a lot of difference at Homlin's today. What if the two of us were partners in this? Two heads are better than one.*

No way. How do you know he won't go to the authorities? If B.I.U.F.O. ever heard you were in these parts, what do you think they'd do? No, the risk is too high. It could blow the entire investigation. You can't trust people to keep their mouths shut. You can't trust people, period.

She missed her turn. She pulled over to the side of the road to turn around. As she waited for the traffic to clear, the debate continued. For ten years she'd been quiet about what had happened on that mountain, convinced that if she told anyone, it would get back to B.I.U.F.O. and she'd be locked up for life. It wasn't that she did not relish the idea of spending the rest of her life in some room with quilted walls. If they put her away as they had threatened to do, who would be on the watch for the alien? She had to stay free. Sooner or later the alien would surface and when it did, she had to be ready to stop it.

No, as much as she liked Allan and wanted to trust him, it was too dangerous. There was too much at stake.

AT SIX-THIRTY WHEN Pat pulled up in front of his house, Allan was outside looking for TJ. He heard the approaching jeep and walked around the house, flashlight in hand.

"Hello?" Pat said, a troubled frown on her face. "Is anything the matter?"

Her P.I. radar is already on, thought Allan. "No, not really. Just thought I heard something in the backyard. Come on in the house."

In the last half hour, he'd been debating with himself whether to go ahead with his original plan to tell Pat about TJ, but his disappearance changed everything. Was there a need to bring her into this? Given her profession, it was likely she would view his son's disappearance as a possible kidnapping and would want to call in the police and FBI if she even believed his story. Without TJ, there was little reason to expect she would. It was too dangerous.

As they entered through the kitchen door, Pat gazed around as though a potential buyer being shown the house for the first time by the real estate agent.

"Very nice. Cozy. It has that lived-in feel without being messy. I approve."

She strolled into the living room where the wood stove and overstuffed furniture added to the warm, lived-in feeling. She glanced at the wall of pictures and back to Allan, a surprised look on her face. She continued to walk around as Allan stood in the center of the living room, unsure what to do or say. She walked past the partially open door that led into TJ's room, and Allan held his breath. He had failed to come back into the house and prepare it for Pat's visit. His mind raced. *What to do? If she goes into TJ's room, she'll know something is up. I've got to stop her.*

"How about some dinner?" he blurted out too loudly.

Pat stopped a few feet from TJ's room and turned to look at Allan, a confused look on her face. "Aren't you going to show me around first?"

"Well, the rest of the house is a bit messy. I'd rather wait until another time when it's clean, if you don't mind."

Allan walked past her and pulled the door to TJ's room closed. "I've also changed my mind about eating in. There's a new place on the edge of town that opened up a couple of weeks ago I've been meaning to try. I doubt it'll be too busy this evening. Why don't we try it?"

Allan took Pat's arm and gently guided her back to the kitchen. "I'll get my coat and be right with you." He left her in the kitchen and ran to the hall closet to pull out his blazer.

As he walked back into the kitchen, he found Pat standing in front of the microwave, its door open. In her hand was the plastic sectional plate with TJ's dinner. She turned and stared at Allan. The two stood a few feet apart, frozen in place by the mystery between them. Finally, Pat broke the silence.

"What's going on, Allan? You can tell me. I'll understand."

"What do you mean?" Allan replied lamely. He didn't know what else to say.

"You're outdoors with a flashlight. The empty unmade crib in the other room. Everywhere I look, signs that a child lives here—including dinner," she said, holding the dish of baby food out to him.

Their eyes locked onto each other. Would she understand? Allan doubted it, but whether she did or not, he had to tell her. It was too much to keep between them. He laid his jacket on the back of a kitchen chair.

"Sit down, Pat. It's a long story. I don't know if you'll understand. I don't know that I do, but I'll tell you the whole thing." He sat down in the chair where he'd placed his jacket. Already, a heavy burden seemed to be lifting from his heart.

Pat sat down in the chair next to him, placing the plastic plate on the table beside them. She reached out and took his hands in hers and squeezed them gently and waited for him to speak. Allan started with the emergency C-section months ago.

"WHEN I WENT INTO THE room to wake him up, he had gone through the window. God only knows where." Allan finished the story with a heavy sigh and a shrug of his shoulder. He studied his hands that Pat held in her own.

After a few moments, Pat pulled one of her hands away and lifted his chin with it. "Allan, I know this is going to sound strange, but I believe every word of your story. I can't explain what's going on either, not fully, but I suspect what brought me here is somehow connected to what has happened to you."

"What do you mean?" Allan asked, shaking his head. "I thought you were here on vacation."

Pat shook her head. "I'm afraid I haven't been upfront with you either."

She stood up and walked over to the kitchen window. She stared out into the night, struggling with herself. After a minute, she turned and looked at Allan but didn't speak. Another thirty seconds went by.

Finally, she said, "I've never told anyone what I'm about to tell you. To tell you the truth, I had decided earlier tonight that I wouldn't tell you either, but what you shared changes that. If you can keep such a secret. Well, I'm just going to trust you." As she said it, she exhaled a deep sigh.

"It's your turn to sit back and hear my unbelievable but true story. After we're both caught up with what is happening around here, between the two of us, we can figure out what or who is causing it.

"This is not the first time I've been to these parts," Pat said as she walked over to him and sat down. "The first time was ten years ago when I worked for an organization called B.I.U.F.O..."

"I'VE SPENT THE LAST ten years waiting for the alien to turn up. Anything that sounded suspicious, I'd check it out. Every lead has gone nowhere. I finally came back here to the scene of the crime, so to speak, to see if I could pick up anything new. Until a couple of days ago, I'd had no luck."

"What happened a couple of days ago?" Allan asked, a look of wonder mixed with confusion on his face.

"I met Dr. Homlin. I don't know what the connection is, but I know he's involved in some way. Maybe he found the beast. The alien. In my mind I think of it as a beast—a vicious killing machine. Anyway, I don't know how, but I'm sure Homlin is connected in some way. I suspect—no, I know the copy of your son is connected as well."

Allan flinched at the word 'copy'. He realized it was an accurate description, but he wasn't ready to think that way—not yet. Pat patted his knee. She stood up and walked over to the counter where Allan's coffee maker sat. "Do you mind if I make us a pot of coffee? I think this could turn into a late evening."

Allan nodded. "Everything is in the cabinet over the coffee maker."

As Pat filled the coffee maker with water, she glanced over her shoulder to Allan, who continued sitting at the kitchen table, studying his hands clasped together in front of him.

"You know, Allan, this is going to sound awfully harsh of me, but I think it needs to be said." She paused for a moment. "Your son, Todd, died several years ago. Whatever has been living in your house isn't your son. I know you'd like it to be, but it isn't."

Allan nodded but didn't reply. After a minute he walked over to the refrigerator and pulled out a carton of milk for the coffee.

"You know, I seldome used to keep milk in the fridge. I don't drink it often except in coffee. A quart would go sour on me but when Todd—TJ—whoever—I don't even know what to call him—it—when he came, I started keeping half gallons.

"I know what you're saying is true," he continued. "I've been living in a fantasy, knowing all along, sooner or later I'd have to wake up, but the dream was so sweet, I didn't want to face the morning."

His eyes teared, and Pat took a step closer and put her arms around him. He stood rigid for a few seconds then relaxed into her embrace. He laid his head against her neck and shoulder. After a moment, Pat felt his body shudder and his tears moisten her neck. They stood huddled together for several minutes as Allan quietly wept.

Neither one spoke for several minutes. Pat continued to hold Allan in her arms but even as she comforted him, she wondered. *What has been staying with him?*

A LIGHT TAPPING ON the study door brought Homlin's head up from the pile of papers on his desk. "Yes, what is it?" he asked gruffly. Hadn't he told them he was not to be disturbed?

The door opened, and Alex Yadkin, Homlin's right hand man, stuck his head and shoulder in through the crack. "I'm sorry to disturb you, but it's rather important. There's a small boy here to see you. About all we can get out of him is his name. TJ—TJ Pritchard," Alex said with an amused look on his face.

"I don't know anyone by that name. Find out what he wants. Wait a minute. What did you say his name was?"

"TJ Pritchard." Alex repeated.

"Any relation to that ass, Allan Pritchard?"

"He says he's Dr. Pritchard's son."

"Oh, he does, does he?" Homlin shut the file in front of him and rose from behind the desk. "I didn't think Pritchard had any children."

"That's the interesting thing." Alex replied. "He doesn't, although our research on him revealed he did have one who died in a fire a few years ago. His name was Todd."

Homlin glanced at his bodyguard. "What's going on here? What are you smirking at?"

"You'll see in a moment," Alex answered.

"This had better be good, or you'll be answering to me. You know I don't care for practical jokes."

"Oh, you'll enjoy this one. I'll stack my next three days off on it."

The two of them walked down the stairs to the library. Alex opened the door and stepped aside to allow his boss to enter first. As Homlin walked through the doorway he saw the child sitting in the center of the plush sofa, his legs dangling in mid-air, a confused, worried look on his face. When Homlin first entered the room, the boy was looking around as though he'd never been in such a large room, but his eyes drifted over to Homlin and stayed fixed. The boy's furrowed brow relaxed, and his face took on the calm composure of a man nestled in his loved one's arms.

Homlin studied the small child for several seconds before turning his attention to his amused escort. "Why didn't you tell me? He's one of us!"

IT WAS WELL AFTER MIDNIGHT. Allan had lost track of how long they'd been talking. He lay on the sofa in the den enjoying the warm cozy heat of the wood stove. His head rested on Pat's lap, and as they talked, her hand lightly stroked his temple. Despite the intensity of the conversation—how their two stories might fit together—Allan couldn't remember a time when he'd been more at ease. It felt so natural. It was hard to believe he'd known this woman for such a brief time.

As the evening progressed, the talking grew softer and less frequent. Allan found his attention drawn to Pat's light caresses. He studied the fine details of her face—the slightly upturned nose, the full lips, the high cheekbones, the creamy texture of her skin.

Slowly, Allan raised himself up on one elbow and brought his eyes level with Pat's. For the moment, thoughts of mysterious larvae and alien spaceships evaporated. The only thing Allan was aware of was Pat's slightly parted lips. So lovely, so sensual, drawing him in so much. It had been so long since he'd allowed himself to think about being with a woman. He had dating a couple of times in the past two years. Both had ended in disaster. He'd simply not been ready. With Pat it was different. This didn't feel like a date. This felt as natural as if they'd been together for years. She belonged here in his den, and he belonged in her arms. That's the way it was supposed to be.

His lips lightly touched hers once, twice. He turned his head slightly and kissed her again, harder this time, then harder still. The passion mounted like a freight train rumbling down the side of the mountain. Pat's supple body pressed against his, a willing player in the love game. They explored each other—two children discovering that their best friend isn't exactly the same after all.

Finally, when Allan felt like he would burst, Pat gently pushed him away for a moment. "Not on the couch. Let's go to your bed." Her face was flushed, and the look of desire matched his own.

Allan was uncertain. It wasn't that he didn't want to make love to Pat. He did, more than anything he could think of at the moment. The question shot into his head. *Could he?* It had been so long. He'd been a satisfying lover to Laura, but that had been years ago and the two of them had practically grown up together. What would Pat expect? She was probably used to experienced lovers with special talents that came from sleeping with many different women. Meanwhile, he was a small town boy who could count on one hand the number of women with whom he had slept.

Pat seemed to notice his hesitation and patted his cheek. "Don't worry, honey, we're going to bed. Who knows what will happen? We could fall asleep." Her warm smile and light teasing reassured him. True, he didn't know what Pat liked, and finding out would be half the fun.

As they entered Allan's bedroom, he was momentarily embarrassed to find he'd not made up his bed, but Pat didn't seem to even notice. She excused herself and walked into the bathroom. As soon as the door closed, Allan rushed to put the bed linens in some order before stripping his clothes off. Pajamas? Should he put something on? Hell, he didn't even know if he owned a pair or not. Certainly, Pat wouldn't have any gown to put on. Not unless she had a teddy secretly hidden in her handbag.

He decided against looking for pajamas. *What the hell, go for broke*, he thought as he stripped off his underwear. It felt funny to be so self-conscious about what he did or didn't wear. He pulled the sheet and bedspread back and slipped into bed. The cool sheets felt good against his warm body. Despite his sexual arousal, he felt a calming drowsiness start to play at his eyelids. Wouldn't Pat be shocked if she came out of the bathroom to find him snoring away in bed. She'd never forgive him. There was no chance of it happening. His body was too tingly—too aroused.

In a moment, Allan noticed the crack of light under the bathroom door disappear, the door opened and Pat strolled out towards the bed. She wore his bathrobe she'd found behind the bathroom door. She approached the bed, her slender form silhouetted by the light coming through the bedroom door from the other room. She stood next to the bed for a moment, gazing down at him, and pulled the tie loose from her slender waist. She slipped the bathrobe from her shoulders and let it drop to the floor. The light from the other room cast an eerie glow across her slender shape.

Allan slid himself to the other side of the bed, giving Pat room to slide into the warm spot he'd vacated. As she pulled the sheet over her, she turned towards him and pulled his head to her breasts. Allan inhaled the sensual fragrance of her perfume mingled with the aroma of arousal. He closed his eyes and enjoyed the visual fireworks discharging behind his eyelids. His hands and tongue danced across Pat's body as her hands did their own dance across his.

Allan smiled to himself. *Making love is a little like riding a bike*, he thought. *Some things you don't forget.*

Poaching
Sunday, Nov. 23

The buck raised his head, sniffing at the air for possible danger. Noticing no change, he resumed his grazing at the edge of the open field. The muscles of his shoulders twitched slightly. He stepped from patch to patch of the dry grass, seemingly unconscious to his surroundings. His head lifted again, a large tuft of grass in his mouth. Before the buck could take a step, the arrow entered his chest, penetrating deeply through the lung, puncturing the heart.

Despite the fatal wound, the buck flung himself back on his rear legs and leaped into the air, galloping across the clearing. With each beat, the heart pumped the life-giving blood into the chest cavity. In the middle of the field, the deer stumbled, righted itself and stumbled again. Ten yards into the woods it crashed to the ground, its brown eyes already glazing over. By the time the hunter reached it, the heart had stopped pumping its blood through the wrong channel.

"Damn, what a shot! Convoy!" MacMillan shouted. Realizing where he was, he clamped a hand over his mouth. He ran across the edge of the clearing, keeping his eye on the spot where the deer had disappeared into the woods. He wasn't worried. The arrow from his crossbow had traveled straight and true to its mark. He would not have a long search for this one. God only knew how he was going to get it out of here by himself. But he wasn't that far from the opening in the fence and his pickup truck. He'd field-dress it as quickly as possible to reduce the weight and drag the remains out. It would be worth the hard work. He could already imagine the look on Bo's face when he drove up to his place with the buck in the back of his truck. The look alone would be worth the effort.

As Convoy entered the far edge of the woods, he slung the crossbow across his back and pulled the hunting knife from its sheath. It would pay for him to be quick with his work. One could not be too careful when poaching on a game reserve. *Especially this one*, Convoy thought. Ever since the strange doctor had taken it over, it gave him the heebie-jeebies to hunt there. He'd seen the patrols, each man with an automatic rifle that looked like it came from a Rambo movie. He suspected the men were the type who would shoot first and ask questions later. He wasn't interested in finding out if this was true. Best to move fast, take the spoils and vamoose.

As he spied the still carcass a few yards into the woods, Convoy smiled. *What a shot!* he thought again. He loved hunting with a crossbow. It was the weapon of a true sportsman. It took cunning, patience, and a high level of skill. Not like hunting with a rifle where you could take a beast like this one down from a hundred yards. Anyone could do that. Hell, even Bo got lucky on occasions.

Convoy pulled the deer onto its back and jammed the knife into the warm belly. As the knife penetrated the cavity, steam rose from around the opening, and the glistening innards pushed their way through the wound. Convoy continued to saw across the thick muscle of the abdomen, working his way towards the chest. Concentrating on his work, he missed the quivering lump of white tissue until one of them fell out of the wound and landed on his boot.

He glanced down nonchalantly at his foot to see what had hit it. Spying the moving mass, he jumped back from the buck, dropping his knife in the leaves.

"Holy mother-of-pearl. What the hell? Shit! Not these damn things again. What is it with you guys?" He addressed the question to the dead buck. "This is disgusting. How can you look so damn healthy and be eaten up inside with such disgusting worms or whatever the fuck they are?"

He wiped the boot the larva had landed on in the leaves. He stopped for a moment and considered his next move. What had Bo said about these things? He'd seen them too, hadn't he? It had been from a deer outside the reserve. That vet friend of Bo's had been there and had seen them too.

What had Bo said about it? Hell, they'd been drinking a good while by the time the subject had come up. His mind was a bit foggy about the whole conversation. The vet hadn't known what the damn things were either. Wasn't that what Bo had said? They'd taken the carcass and dressed it anyway, but no one had dared eat the meat yet. Fuck! What was he to do?

He stared down at the deer's carcass. He could take it over to the next county and sell it to some of his buddies over there. It was doubtful anyone there had heard about these things. Yeah, that's what he'd do. He'd cut the head off and have it preserved, and he'd sell the meat, or if he couldn't sell it, he'd trade it for some 'shine. He'd get something out of his hard work besides a queasy stomach.

He kicked the quivering lump with the same boot he'd been cleaning and watched the white mass sail into a clump of bushes several feet away. As he watched the mass disappear into the bush, he realized he was not alone. Standing a few yards deeper into the woods behind the bushes where the lump had disappeared was a thickly muscled brute, his automatic rifle resting comfortably in the crook of one arm. The cold smile on the man's face turned Convoy's stomach for another loop.

I'm in deep shit, he thought as he found his lips stretching into a fake smile. Thoughts of the meat and the rack of antlers evaporated into the cold winter air. Survival was the only thing that mattered. Getting the fuck out of the reserve without ending up like the buck. He turned in the opposite direction of the man and started tearing through the bush, zigging from side to side. As he ran, he thought he could hear the man behind him raise the gun and cock it. The cold air burned deep into his emphysemic lungs.

He'd begun to think the man had been all threat and no action. *Hell, he's one of those who can't pull the trigger*, he thought just before the burst of gunfire lifted him off the ground and crashed him into a tree. It was his last thought before the shattering pain enveloped him, followed closely by a wave of darkness.

HOMLIN LEANED BACK in the plush leather chair and pulled deeply on the cigar. *A strange habit*, he thought for the hundredth time as he enjoyed the sensation of smoke entering his chest. Nowhere else had he ever heard of any civilization that inhaled smoke as a pastime. It was even stranger that he had adopted such a habit. He leaned a little further back in his chair and stared at Alex through the thick haze of smoke.

"Well, what do you have to report on our Ms. Vogt?"

Alex didn't respond at once. He'd learned to choose his words carefully when reporting to his superior. Homlin was not above killing the messenger for being the bearer of bad news. It could get dicey sometimes, even when the news wasn't so bad, as in this instance.

"I have two of my best men on her in twelve hour rotations. She has moved into the Waynesboro Inn and is no longer camping out. For the most part she seems to be enjoying her vacation. Nothing suspicious to report at this point."

"Good. But I don't want your men to relax. She's unpredictable," Homlin replied, remembering too well his near fatal first meeting with Pat Vogt. "She's a cunning member of an equally cunning species. Don't relax, do you understand?"

Alex nodded, hesitated for a moment again, and went for it. Homlin appeared in a good mood. It wasn't any harm in giving it a shot. "There's one thing I don't understand," Alex started tentatively, as though testing the water with his toe before jumping in.

"Yes? Go ahead," Homlin urged.

"Well, if this woman is so dangerous to our plan, why not snuff her out? I mean, after all, she is the only human who could be able to figure out who you are. Why not get rid of her? I'd have no problem—"

Homlin righted himself in his chair and leaned forward across his desk. He opened his mouth, a quick retort ready to put Alex in his place, then stopped, the first words hanging in his throat. Instead, he stood up and walked over to where Alex sat. "Even though I know you are here not to think but to act on my thinking, I'm feeling benevolent today, so I'm going to explain the situation to you." He smiled down at Alex, who was visibly relaxed, then strolled towards the window.

"Vogt is dangerous, no question. She's dangerous. As you said, she's the only human who actually saw me when I first landed. But the entire situation is dangerous at this point. We are at a critical time. Until we get the FDA approval for FreeForm, everything is in a sensitive balance. One wrong move could jeopardize the entire project. I need not remind you what that could mean for our race."

"Killing a human right now, any human, could tip the balance. The one thing I do not need is to have attention drawn to this area or to Biogentrix or to myself. Not yet. I'll be flying back to Washington in a few days. I expect by this time next week everything will be in place for the final approval. It'll be downhill from there. For right now, we are at a critical point. Very critical."

Homlin turned from the window and faced Alex. "Therefore, I want you to do only one thing. Follow my orders. Thinking on your own is dangerous." Homlin smiled. "When the time is right for our Ms. Vogt, I'll let you know. I'm quite aware of your interest in her. You be a good soldier, and I'll be sure you get your reward."

Alex started to rise from his chair. Before he could do so, there was the sound of footsteps running down the hallway outside and a moment later a loud rap on the door.

"Come in," Homlin said, turning back to his desk.

Lenny, Alex's second officer in charge of the guards, burst through the door. One look at his face raised the hackles on the back of Homlin's neck. What had happened? He was only seconds from finding out.

"I'm sorry to barge in like this—"

"What is it?" Homlin interrupted him.

"There's been some trouble on the southwest quadrant of the grounds," Lenny replied, staring nervously at his two superiors.

"What kind of trouble?" Homlin asked as he flipped the ashes from his cigar.

"One of our men caught a poacher," Lenny continued.

Homlin relaxed at the news. He continued to his desk and sat down.

"Okay," he said in a more relaxed manner. "That's not so bad. You know what the procedure is for poachers, don't you?"

"Yes," Lenny replied. "I know, but I'm afraid the man panicked. The poacher was killed."

"What!" Homlin and Alex shot out of their chairs as though pulled by the same string. "You've got to be kidding. You can't mean to tell me after the warnings I've given your men that one of them had the nerve to disobey me."

Homlin felt the veins in his neck bulge and his face grow warm. "Of all the stupid, avoidable accidents..." Homlin struggled to find the words to express his anger.

"Who was the poacher, do you know?" Alex asked.

"Yes. His ID was recovered. His name is Daniel MacMillan."

Daniel MacMillan? Homlin searched through his memory. He didn't know a MacMillan. He turned and glared at Alex.

"Well?"

"The name sounds familiar, yet it doesn't quite fit," Alex replied. "MacMillan? I know of a MacMillan but his first name isn't Daniel. Wait a minute." Alex turned to his second in command. "Was he wearing an old blue cap with some trucking emblem on it?" Alex asked as Homlin paced back and forth between the desk and the window.

"Yes, that's right," Lenny replied.

Alex let out a big sigh. "I don't think this is going to be as bad as it looks." He glanced first to Lenny and then to Homlin.

"Why not?" Homlin and Lenny asked at the same time.

"Well, I happen to know about our poacher. He's a no-count drifter. Seldom has a steady job. Drinks like a fish. It's not unusual for him to go on benders all the time. Might disappear for months on end. No one will be surprised if he disappears. Hell, I doubt anyone will even notice."

Homlin considered what Alex had said. He chewed on the half smoked cigar like it was meant for eating rather than smoking. "Are you sure?"

"I'll go down and verify who he is," Alex said. "If he's who it sounds like, yes, I'm sure. No one will miss him."

Homlin continued to gnaw on the cigar. Finally, he replied, "Okay. Go check it out and let me know for sure. I want you to pull everyone together. I'm going to get the point across once and for all. I'm not going to have our entire mission jeopardized by some trigger-happy idiot. I want you to get a message to your two 'experts'. Under no circumstance are they to touch a hair on Vogt's head. They are simply to watch her and report all actions to me. Is that clear?"

Alex nodded. "Very clear." He rose from his chair. "I'll take care of it right away."

After the two men left, Homlin sat behind his desk and considered the situation. Everything would be fine if only he didn't have to depend on such idiots to get the job done.

He smiled as he lit his cigar and blew a new cloud of smoke. *Not much longer*, he thought. Soon, the most critical part of his job would be accomplished and he could relax. He would be able to give Alex the treat he so much longed for. Maybe he would arrange to watch the fun.

Homlin's Home

Saturday, Nov. 27

Pat pulled off the road onto the narrow driveway and found the road blocked by a formidable wrought iron gate. *It's about time I get a look beyond that gate*, she thought. Homlin had put her and Allan off several times, offering various excuses, but once again her persistence—some would call it stubbornness—had paid off. A guard stepped out from the small house next to the gate and walked up to the jeep.

"Hi. I'm Pat Vogt, and this is Dr. Allan Pritchard. We have a two o'clock appointment with Dr. Homlin."

"May I see your driver's license? Both of them," the guard replied coldly.

Allan and Pat glanced at each other as they pulled their licenses out and passed them to the guard, who studied them carefully before passing them back.

"Drive straight to the house. It's .6 miles from here. Do not stop along the way for any reason. Drive fifteen miles per hour. No faster or slower. They will be expecting you. Is that understood?"

"Oh yes, quite well. You have a nice day now," Pat answered sweetly.

As the gate opened, she threw the jeep in gear and slammed her foot down on the gas pedal. The rear wheels kicked stones in all directions as they fought for traction. The jeep leaped ahead, passing fifteen miles per hour in the first few seconds.

Pat turned to Allan. "Did he say fifty miles per hour? That seems a little fast on such a narrow road." But she kept her foot to the floor.

Allan grabbed instinctively for the handhold above his head and smiled nervously.

They arrived at Homlin's home in less than a minute. Pat waited until the last second before slamming on the brakes. The jeep squealed to a stop in a cloud of dust and burning rubber, inches from the front porch. The door burst open, and four large men poured out onto the porch, automatic rifles and revolvers in their hands.

"Well, what a warm reception," Pat said as she undid her seat belt and opened her door. She started walking towards the house, then stopped to look back at Allan, who continued to sit in the jeep, grasping the strap over his head. Pat walked around to his side and opened his door.

"Relax, Allan. I promise not to get us killed. I want to play with them for a little while." She'd already proven her point. Dr. Homlin was hiding something. No one had so much security just for the fun of it. The question was, what was he hiding?

As she walked towards the house, she held her hands high in the air. "Don't shoot, don't shoot. It's just us. The guard said at the gate that we should go exactly fifty miles per hour until we got to the house. I thought it was a bit too fast, but who am I to argue with house rules?"

As she passed one of the guards standing on the first step of the porch, she lowered her hands and patted the automatic rifle he held in his hand. "Nice pea shooter you have there, Charlie. Do you know how to use it?"

Allan slowly exited the jeep, a sheepish grin on his face. "Hello, boys. No hard feelings, huh?"

When there was no response, he stepped up his pace and caught up with Pat.

"Take it easy, will you? You're not making any friends at the moment."

"You wouldn't want these gorillas as friends anyway," Pat answered loud enough for the "gorilla" holding the door to hear.

As they entered the foyer, they were met by the man who Pat had first confronted at the ball game walking down the wide, spiral staircase that led to the second floor. *Quite a place Homlin has here,* Pat thought as she smiled politely.

"Ms. Vogt and Dr. Pritchard. How nice of you to pay us a visit. Dr. Homlin is on a long distance call at the moment. He'll be with you in a few minutes. In the meantime, if you'd like to step into his study..." He pointed to a set of double doors to the right.

Pat and Allan nodded and entered the study. The room was large and spacious. Lining three walls were bookcases from floor to ceiling. Most of the fourth wall was taken up by a large picture window lined with heavy drapes that could be pulled shut to exclude the light. At the moment the drapes were open, letting in the breathtaking view of the game reserve forest. Visible through the trees was a large lake.

"May I fix you a drink while you wait?" The bodyguard asked with more manners than seemed natural for him.

Obviously, Homlin has instructed him to be on his best behavior, Pat thought.

"Do you happen to have lemonade?" Pat asked with a flutter of her eyelashes.

"Why, yes, uh, in the kitchen," the temporary host answered. "I'll go see if I can find it."

Pat nodded and watched as he left the room. As soon as the door closed behind him, she was in motion, prowling around the room like a bloodhound on a hot trail.

"What are you doing?" Allan asked with a note of surprise in his voice.

"I'm checking out Homlin's interest in reading material. The books in a person's library say a lot about them." She continued to study the shelves of books.

After a few moments, she seemed to lose interest in the study and walked over to the window.

"Well, what's the verdict?" Allan asked as he picked up a book at random from one of the shelves.

"If he's read all these books, he's well read," she answered. "There doesn't seem to be a particular pattern, which is unusual. Most people have one or two favorite subjects or types of books they read and collect. Homlin doesn't. There is a high concentration of classics, but they span the entire Dewey Decimal System in subject. The fiction is just as varied."

After a few more minutes of gazing out the window, she turned with a puzzled look on her face. "What do you think is out there?"

"What do you mean?"

"There." She pointed out the window. "In the game reserve. Our instructions were to not stop on the road. I dare say if we had been more than a minute or so late, we'd have been sought out. What is out there that Homlin doesn't want us to see?"

"It's the rules," came a voice from the study doorway. Homlin stepped into the room, a smile on his face that sent a cold shiver down Pat's neck.

"I hired this protection agency after I received some threatening phone calls. My research is controversial as I'm sure you are aware if you read the paper. The agency agreed to protect me only if I followed their rules. Coming straight to the house at *fifteen miles per hour* is one of the rules. That's all."

Homlin gazed first at Pat and then at Allan as though checking to see if they were buying his explanation. As he spoke, he strolled over to the overstuffed leather upholstered chair and motioned them to a matching sofa.

"Your drinks will be here in a moment. I apologize for not being available to welcome you personally, but it was an important call I've been waiting for all morning. To answer the question you were posing, I have maintained and added to the game reserve. What is out there"—he waved one arm in the direction of the picture window—"is game. Quite an assortment of game, both indigenous to the region and some that are not, but they do well in this climate. I have a strong interest in preserving nature, especially the endangered wild animals. How about you, Ms. Vogt? It seems I've met you somewhere before. I was wondering if it could have been at some meeting on wildlife preservation?"

"No, I doubt it," Pat replied. "I've only a passing interest in it. Like many people, I'm an avid animal lover, but I'm not what you'd call an animal activist."

"Strange. I seldom forget a face, particularly such a charming one. Do I not ring a similar bell with you?" Homlin stared intently at Pat as she replied.

"No, I'm quite sure I've never met you," she replied with a casual shrug of her shoulder. "I am also good at remembering faces and names." As she smiled sweetly back at their host, she felt a strange feeling that she was lying even to herself. She had never met this man, and yet there was something strangely familiar about him. But what?

"Have you lived in these parts long?" Homlin continued to question, her but before she could answer, Homlin's bodyguard entered with their drinks. She waited until he was finished serving before answering.

"No, actually I'm visiting for the first time," Pat said and was relieved when Allan gave no indication otherwise. "Unless you spend a lot of time in Charlotte, I'm afraid we've never met."

"Well, it's not important," Homlin answered, but Pat was unconvinced by his statement. Homlin was not the type of man to ask such questions if they were not important. Something about Pat troubled him as much as he troubled her.

Homlin turned his attention to Allan, asking polite questions as though to cover up the fact that it was only Pat in whom he was interested. After a few minutes, he turned the conversation to a more general direction. Each time Pat asked anything about his research at Biogentrix, Homlin deftly sidestepped the question. After forty-five minutes, Pat knew little more about Homlin or his company.

He's good, Pat thought. *He's as slippery as I've seen when it comes to giving away information. I'm damn good at prying people open, but he's as tight a clam as I've ever run into. Whatever I find out won't come directly from him.*

Finally, Homlin glanced at his watch. "Oh, I'm sorry to have to cut this pleasant visit off so abruptly, but I'm expecting another important phone call in a few minutes. It's likely to take quite some time, so I'm afraid I'll have to say adieu. Alex will escort you to your car." He nodded to his bodyguard, who had been standing quietly in the shadows and who stepped forward.

Homlin shook Allan's hand and walked over to Pat. Taking her hand in his, he gazed intently into her eyes. Still holding her hand, he said, "It was a pleasure to see you again, Ms. Vogt. It may be that we have never met, but I trust this won't be the last time we see each other."

Pat forced a smile and a flicker of her long lashes, fighting back a shiver. Homlin's hand felt like the appendage of a cold carcass laid out in some mildewy morgue. She turned to leave and noticed Allan holding on to the banister of the staircase, staring above them.

"What's up?" she whispered as she nodded in the direction he was looking.

"Oh, not much," he replied, but he continued looking towards the top of the stairs. "I thought I...but it couldn't be." Noticing he was drawing unwanted attention to himself, he turned back to the group. "Nice place you have here...very nice indeed."

Homlin bowed out, leaving them to Alex's care. He reminded them again to leave directly, traveling at fifteen miles per hour this time, not fifty. Pat promised she would and surprised herself by keeping her promise.

ALEX WATCHED THE JEEP pull slowly out of the drive. As it turned the first bend, he heard Homlin's voice over the intercom paging him to his office.

He entered the upstairs office. Homlin stood gazing out the window at the path the jeep had recently traveled.

"I want you to put a couple of your best men on her," Homlin said without turning to look at Alex.

"You still think she would remember you?" Alex asked.

"I don't know for sure. I doubt it, but I can't take any chances. She almost had me convinced, but she lied. She's been in these parts at least once before, and there is no way in hell she could have forgotten it. Watch her closely. Let me know if she does anything out of the ordinary. If she starts snooping around Biogentrix, I'll have to have her killed. It's that simple."

Alex nodded. If such an order was issued, he'd make sure he handled it himself. He'd enjoy snuffing the bitch out. He could have a lot of fun with such a fox before he finally did her in. A lot of fun.

They were nearly back to Allan's house when Pat reached over and patted his leg. "What's up?" she asked.

"Hmm...nothing," Allan replied. "What do you mean?"

"Well, you've not said three words in the last fifteen minutes. It's unlike you," Pat replied. "What did you see back there?"

Allan thought about the question for a moment before replying. "I'm not sure. I mean, it's crazy, and I caught a glimpse, and it was gone."

"What was gone?"

"Well, if I didn't know better, I'd say it was"—he hesitated again—"I think I saw TJ."

"Your son...I mean...you know what I mean," Pat replied, glancing at him.

"Yeah, I know what you mean. But he was older, much older than I'd expect him to be. I mean, it's only been a little over a week since he disappeared."

"What do you make of it?" Pat asked.

"I don't know what to make of it." Allan shrugged. "It appears he may have found a new home with Homlin." He made a face, as though saying the words left a bad taste in his mouth.

After another minute, Pat asked, "Are you okay?"

"I'm not sure," Allan replied, but he was sure—sure that he was not okay with Homlin raising his son. Not okay at all.

FDA Approval
Tuesday, Dec. 2

"I'm sorry to disturb you, Dr. Pritchard, but Bo Rawlins is out here to see you." Dawn's voice did little to hide her agitation. "He insists on seeing you."

"Sure, Dawn. Ask him to step on back here. I'm just finishing up on some records," Allan replied with a smile. Dawn was the best receptionist he could ever want, except when it came to Bo. *Well, no one is perfect*, he thought.

Bo pushed the partially closed door open, knocking lightly as he did. "Hope I'm not disturbing you too much," he said as he entered the room, his hunting cap firmly gripped in his hands.

"No, not at all. It's good to see you again. Had any luck hunting lately?" Allan closed the record in front of him and sat back in his chair, motioning to the chair next to the desk for Bo.

Bo sat down, shaking his head. "No, not much luck of late. It's kind of what I've come to talk to you about though." Bo twisted his cap between his hands.

"Well, if you've come for some hunting tips, I'm afraid you're barking up the wrong tree," Allan replied with a laugh.

Bo smiled, but it appeared forced. "No, not looking for any tips, but I am looking for some information, Doc. You remember those ugly ol' bugs we pulled out of that deer a few weeks back? I was wondering if you've heard anything from the state lab."

Allan hoped his face didn't show the alarm he felt by the mention of the larvae. He'd been counting on Bo's wispy memory to not remember anything about them. It looked like he'd been hoping for too much.

"No, Bo, as a matter of fact, I haven't, but I'm not surprised. The state lab has been known to take months on such matters, especially if it's anything out of the ordinary. Why do you ask?" He tried to ask the question nonchalantly.

"Well, I was jawing with an old hunting buddy of mine a while back. You might know him. MacMillan?"

"No, I can't say I've had the pleasure."

"Well, no matter. Convoy and I were sitting around sipping on the juice, swapping hunting stories. I eventually got to telling him about those weird bugs we found in that buck. Much to my surprise, Convoy said he'd shot a buck a while back with them inside it as well. He described them to a tee. I was wondering if we got some epee-demic going around."

As he spoke, Bo continued to pull and twist his hat. Allan couldn't remember ever seeing him so nervous and worried. Seeing Bo act this way was making him nervous as well.

"Well, I don't know, Bo, but I kind of doubt it. It's one of those strange coincidences that happen from time to time. If you like, I'll give the state lab a call and see if I can rush things along."

Bo's hands relaxed a little, and he smiled. "Yeah. I'd appreciate it. I have to admit, I hate to think there could be something jeopardizing our wildlife. I know I'm a hunter, but like most hunters, I love the outdoors. I wouldn't want to see anything happen."

"Well, I'll see what I can find out. In the meantime, don't worry." Allan rose from behind the desk to show Bo out. "You might not want to say too much about this until we have some facts. You know how people can make stuff up out of nothing."

Bo laughed. "You can say that again. I have to confess, I mentioned our hunting trip to my niece the other day. Hell, she's always drilling me with questions. Says she's practicing being a reporter. Not to worry. Mimi is a kid who's curious about everything and has a big imagination. You should hear about some of the wild stories she tells about the weird things going on over in Foster Flats. She writes it down in her little black notebooks, but that's as far as it goes."

I sure hope he's right about that, Allan thought growing more nervous by the minute.

"She gets that imagination from me," Bo continued. "Hell, Convoy and I were supposed to get together a couple of days ago. When he didn't show, I started making up shit. The truth of the matter is, Convoy isn't the most reliable friend I have. He's probably locked up in the next county for too much carousing."

Allan was worried again. "Did Convoy happen to mention where he shot the deer he was telling you about?" Bo stopped at the door. "Well, yeah he did. You promise not to say anything to anyone?"

"Sure. I'm not out to get him in trouble," Allan replied.

"Convoy is a free-spirited sort. Not dangerous or anything. He doesn't like to be confined by rules, if you know what I mean. He told me he snuck into the old game reserve a few weeks ago with his crossbow. Said he couldn't believe the number of deer he saw. It was like shooting fish in a barrel. Even said he'd do it again. I tried to convince him to stay away, but he's a stubborn cuss."

Homlin's place. The deer Convoy had shot was on Homlin's reserve. *Oh boy, Pat is not going to like this,* Allan thought. In some strange way, it was beginning to make sense. It was like Pat has suspected. Homlin was the key. The question was, the key to what?

HOMLIN STARED OUT THE window, enjoying the view of the Washington Monument, as the five-doctor panel of the Food and Drug Administration filed in behind him. It was his third meeting with the panel in as many weeks. Everything had progressed as planned. The five doctors had not yet granted him permission to disseminate FreeForm to the other research facilities across the country, but neither had they thrown him out.

It took a vote of approval from four out of the five doctors to proceed. Three of them had said yes. Only one more was necessary to see it Homlin's way for his plan to proceed. Once that occurred, he'd be unstoppable. The FreeForm would be across the country within a week of the vote.

Homlin chuckled to himself. Life was easy when one was willing to work inside the system. Anything could be accomplished when you went with the flow. Even if occasionally you had to manipulate the system a little to get the flow to move in your direction.

A polite cough from one of the panel members notified Homlin they were ready to begin. He continued standing with his back to them for a few seconds longer than was polite. Mustn't give up control. It was a cardinal rule when dealing with bureaucrats. Finally, with one last appreciative gaze out the window, Homlin turned and took his seat across the mahogany table.

"Good to see each of you again." Homlin started right in as though it had been his idea to call the meeting instead of the other way around. "I trust your research is checking out. Are we ready to move on to the next step?"

"Not so fast," answered Dr. Ralph Connolly. Interesting, Homlin noted, Connolly and Lenair, the two doctors opposing his request, were seated together at his left. Wrightwall, Harrison, and McNeilly were in front and to his right. It seemed the battle lines were clearly drawn.

"I would like, for the record, for you to review your proposal, so we can be absolutely certain we understand what you are asking us to make a motion on."

"Certainly, Dr. Connolly. It's simple. As you know, my company, Biogentrix, has successfully manufactured a genetic material which has incredible adaptive properties. One could call it the modeling clay of life. We are a small lab with limited research funds. I realize that scientific progress could be made much more rapidly if more researchers could work on the material."

"You've named the material FreeForm. Is that right?" Connolly asked, then added, "For the record, Dr. Homlin."

"Oh, indeed, for the record. Yes, the product which I am speaking about has been registered under the trademark name of FreeForm."

"And you are proposing that Biogentrix be credited with fifty percent of the proceeds of products and discoveries which are likely to come out of the research of others. Is that correct?"

"Yes, that is correct. We will supply the 'raw material' as it were. Each facility will apply their particular specialty, and whatever new products come out, Biogentrix will be an equal partner," Homlin replied.

"What are some of the products you suspect will come from such a collaboration?" Lenair asked, staring at the report over a pair of reading glasses propped on his nose.

"The sky is the limit, gentlemen. FreeForm is truly amazing and highly adaptive. I suspect some of the early products will be agricultural in nature. Like blight resistant corn, grass that grows to only three inches and doesn't need cutting, cows that produce more milk, and beef cattle with lower cholesterol. Who knows after that?"

"Exactly my point!" Lenair shouted, slapping the report down on the table. "Who knows what could come of this? If this FreeForm is one tenth, hell, one hundredth as adaptive a material as Dr. Homlin claims, how is it to be controlled? Sure, we'll start with the simple stuff first, but how long will researchers be satisfied with messing around with beef cattle? How long before someone decides to clone the perfect woman or man? Then what?"

Harrison spoke up from the other end of the table. "Dr. Lenair, please. We'll get to the questions in a moment. We realize you have some concerns—"

"Damn right I do! Not the least of which is the fact that you three don't seem to be the least troubled by Dr. Homlin's proposal. Why, it's preposterous to think of distributing such a substance as this FreeForm to over a thousand other research facilities across the country with such scant preliminary data as he's presented to us."

"I understand your concern, Dr. Lenair," Harrison continued in a soothing voice. "It's not that we don't appreciate there are some risks involved. It's that we see that the possible benefits to mankind far outweigh the unlikely complications."

"Dr. Harrison," Dr. Connolly spoke up, "I believe what Dr. Lenair is pointing to is that the complications are not so unlikely. They are in fact likely to arise, and before we can approve of such a proposal we must have a firm set of guidelines which will address as many of these complicating questions as possible."

"Hell, that could take years." McNeilly entered the discussion. "In the meantime, hundreds of thousands will continue to starve, millions will continue to suffer needlessly while we stand in the way of the greatest scientific breakthrough in history."

"Better to stand in the way than to mindlessly open Pandora's box simply because it looks like it holds the answers." Lenair's glasses threatened to fall off the tip of his nose.

Homlin sat across the table, quietly enjoying the heated debate. *For the record*, he thought, *yes, for the record it's going well.* He stared at the two doctors who continued to oppose his plan. Which one would come over to his way of thinking? Lenair was the spunkier of the two. It would be interesting to have him on his side...a bit less predictable than if Connolly came over.

As it turned out, today's meeting was important, after all. He had changed his mind. He liked Lenair's spunkiness, and there was the chance the nearsighted doctor would continue to cause trouble even when he was outvoted. It made more sense to have Lenair in his camp than outside raising a ruckus.

Homlin leaned back in his chair and rested his hands behind his head. As far as he was concerned, the meeting was over. He'd made the only important decision. The rest was for the record.

"I'M BEING FOLLOWED."

"You're what? Are you sure?" Allan leaned across the table and grabbed Pat's hand as though fearful she'd be taken away, the thought of a pleasant, uneventful lunch forgotten.

"Yes, sweetie, I'm sure. Remember a large part of my business is following other people. After a while you learn to read the signs when someone is doing it to you. Besides, they aren't very good at it. I suspect you'd be able to tell yourself. By the way, are you being followed?"

"I don't know. I don't think so. Who would want to follow me around? It would get pretty boring. To the clinic, back home, to the clinic, back home, lunch with you. That's about it."

"Well, they may not be following you. They may have decided that I'm the only one who needs watching. After all, I'm the one with the tendency to stir up trouble."

"You mean Homlin's thugs?" Allan asked.

"Well, I certainly don't mean Lucky's old owners," Pat said, patting Allan's hand.

"I don't like this. It's getting out of control. What if they decide to do something besides watch you?"

Pat squeezed Allan's hand. "You're cute. You are. I think you're beginning to care about me."

"Don't be silly." Allan smiled. "I cared about you the minute you walked in my clinic. It's gone a lot further than 'caring.'"

"Well, don't worry. I'm not so concerned that they'll try anything with me. I think they're mostly concerned that I not do anything. Which, by the way, I plan to do."

"What do you mean? Pat, I think we're getting in over our heads. It's time to call in some help. I know the local police aren't the most crack shot in the world, but they're a start. Surely they'd be able to call in the SBI and the FBI."

"Think about it, Allan. What are we going to say? We want you to arrest Dr. Frederick Homlin, the owner and president of Biogentrix, on the grounds that he's connected with an alien spaceship that landed in this area ten years ago. By the way, he has something to do with turning a larva that was pulled out of a stray dog into an exact replica of this man's son. They lock people up with stories like that. Remember, I've already had dealings with the federal government.

"No, without some proof, solid proof, we can't tell anyone and expect anything but a lot of strange looks. That's why I've got to get into Biogentrix."

"You've got to be kidding. Are you crazy? What do you expect the person tailing you to do? Simply report to his boss that you've broken into their secret facility? No way. It's far too dangerous." Allan's eyes darted around the restaurant like a lover on a secret rendezvous.

"I haven't figured it out yet," Pat confessed. "Somehow I've got to lose my tail for a day or so. You could put on a wig and let them follow you for a while," she teased Allan.

"If I thought it would work, I'd be happy to do it. But I'd get arrested for walking around in drag."

They both laughed, easing the tension a little. They sat quietly, deep in their own thoughts. Finally, Allan snapped his fingers, startling Pat.

"That's it," he said with a broad smile.

"No, Allan. You were right the first time. They wouldn't fall for the masquerade, but I appreciate the offer."

"Not me, silly. I'm not letting you out of my sight. I'm going with you to Biogentrix. We'll let Dawn wear the wig."

Pat shook her head. "No way. Nix. Uh-uh. I wouldn't consider it. Dawn's a sweetheart of a person, but I couldn't ask her to do this for me."

"You won't have to. I will," Allan replied. Leaning forward, he added, "Listen, Pat. You said it yourself. This is important stuff. If Homlin is connected with the alien in some way, our entire country's security is at stake."

"I know what I said," Pat replied testily. "We'll have to find another way. You're not coming with me either. I appreciate the offer, but I'm not dragging you or Dawn into this any further."

The two stared at each other, neither one willing to budge. Finally, Allan shook his head. "A couple nights ago you had me take a long hard look at myself. You helped me face something I had been avoiding. I'm going to ask you to do the same."

Pat started to turn away, but Allan grabbed her arm. "Listen to me," he said sharply. In a softer voice he added, "Please."

Pat turned back, facing him.

"You've got to start trusting people."

"I do—" Pat interrupted, but Allan placed a finger on her lips.

"No, you don't. This is a perfect example. You're trying to do it all yourself, carrying the weight of the whole world on your shoulders. Well, you've carried this alien thing around for the past ten years. You've done a fine job of it, I'm sure. Now it's time to let go. Like I had to let go of my illusions about TJ. You can't do this by yourself. Even if you could, why bother? I'm here to help. I want to help. Dawn will want to help as well. She doesn't have to know the details. We'll tell her enough so she can be you while we take a peek inside Biogentrix. Trust me on this, Pat."

Pat sat for several minutes considering what Allan had said. Other people had accused her of the same thing. Even her father used to tell her that her strong suit of being so self-reliant was also her blind spot. It had been one of the few things he had said that she had been unable to take to heart.

Now it looked like she had to. Allan was right. There was too much at stake. She couldn't afford to blow it this time. Like she had the first time she'd been in these mountains. Oliver had said the same thing in his own way. She had interpreted his remarks as giving in to the establishment, but there were other ways to play on a team. Maybe the reason she was so driven to find the alien was that deep down inside she knew it was her fault that he was there in the first place. She had tried to do it all herself. Be the big hero, but all she had been was dangerous. It had almost cost her her life, and it had cost two men theirs.

Pat felt the warm tears trickle down her cheeks. Allan offered her a handkerchief. Shaking her head, she reached for her purse to find her own. Realizing she was doing it again, she accepted the one Allan offered.

"It's not easy for a leopard to change her spots," she said as she wiped the tears away.

"I know. We'll take it one spot at a time," Allan replied. "I'll talk to Dawn this afternoon."

Pat nodded and smiled. With a little practice, she thought she could get used to having Allan around.

HOMLIN SAT IN THE FAR corner of the smoky tavern, his own cigar adding to the musty atmosphere. In front of him sat a half-finished mug of beer, only the second one he'd ever had. He remembered why. It tasted foul, and the alcohol in it did not agree with his metabolism.

After a few minutes, the door to the bar opened, and a tall man in a gray trench coat entered. He stood in the doorway for a moment then strolled towards Homlin's table. He slid into the booth across from Homlin, not bothering to remove his coat.

"Good to see you again, Dr. Harrison," Homlin said as the man unbuttoned his coat and slid it off his shoulders. "Quite an interesting show today, wouldn't you say?"

SATURDAY EVENING, DEC. 4

Allan glanced at his watch as it beeped midnight. *So far so good*, he thought. Earlier today, they had made the switch with Dawn smoothly. It had been simple. Pat had strolled into the clinic a few minutes after closing. A few minutes later, Dawn, dressed in Pat's clothes and wearing a black wig, had walked back out, gotten in Pat's car, and driven out of the parking lot. Sure enough, Allan had seen the gray sedan pull out behind Dawn and follow her down the road, both on their way to Charlotte. Watching the sedan tagging behind her had given Allan cold chills; he was careful to hide his concern from Pat. They asked Dawn drive to Charlotte as though Pat were checking on business matters. It was plausible and would at the same time give them flexibility as to how long to continue the scam.

The two of them sat in Allan's Blazer outside the boundary fence of Biogentrix as Allan watched Pat apply the final touches of black smudge to her face.

“Okay, I'm all set. Remember, you are to stay here only as long as it remains perfectly calm and quiet. Any lights, alarms, or commotion of any sort, and you are to hightail it out of here. No heroics. Understood?"

Allan squirmed in his seat. They had spent most of the afternoon arguing about who should be the one to go in. Allan accused Pat of being too self-reliant again and not letting him help out, while Pat pointed out that she was the one trained in such matters. When Allan had suggested they go in together, Pat explained, with an edge to her voice that made Allan wince remembering it, that they could not afford to run the risk of them both being caught.

"We're the only two who know that anything funny is going on. If we're both caught, there won't be anyone left to stop Homlin from completing his plans—whatever they are."

Allan hated to admit it, but everything Pat said made sense. It didn't mean he had to like it. He started to voice his concern once more, but before he could speak, Pat placed a finger to his lips. "No more discussion on this one, Allan, my dear. Straight to the police, you understand? If they grab me, which they won't, but if they do, you'll have something to report. No alien stories, just that I've been missing and you know who has me. Are we clear?"

Allan nodded.

"Okay, great. I'll be in and out before you know it. Don't fall asleep. I wouldn't want anyone sneaking up on you."

"The likelihood of my falling asleep in my present condition is so infinitesimally small as to not be a part of the equation. It's more likely someone will hear my heart pounding and decide to look for the source."

Pat leaned over and gave him a firm, moist kiss. "I won't be long," she said as she opened her door and slipped out into the darkness, leaving behind the subtle fragrance of her perfume and the pleasant sensation on Allan's lips.

Allan squinted through the windshield, trying to make out her passage to the fence, but her black clothing was an effective camouflage. He couldn't see anything.

His hands had found their way to the steering wheel, which they were firmly gripping. He tapped lightly with his thumbs on the cold metal. *This is going to be a long night, even if she's only gone for twenty minutes*, Allan thought. Why had he given in to this harebrained idea? What was he doing out here in the middle of nowhere while his new love broke into a top-secret laboratory? Was any of this happening, or was he suffering from overwork and stress? He could remember TJ, but already the memory was fading. Had that really happened? It seemed too incredible, too surrealistic. Perhaps none of it had actually happened. Maybe Pat had made her story up as well, and the two of them were simply living out a fantasy—a very dangerous fantasy.

Now he had dragged Dawn into it as well. Not with the real story but a fabricated one. It hadn't surprised him how readily Dawn had been willing to help them out. She'd hardly needed any explanation at all. They had said they suspected one of Pat's old boyfriends might have put a tail on her and they needed to verify it.

Allan didn't like lying to his long time employee and friend even though he knew it was crazy to think they could tell her the truth. They'd cautioned Dawn not to blow her disguise no matter what, but otherwise to take a leisurely trip to the big city and to enjoy herself. Such a natural approach would be more likely to convince Homlin's men that they were following the right person.

Allan glanced at his watch and was surprised to find it was only five minutes after twelve. It seemed like Pat had been gone for at least twenty minutes. His instructions were to wait for an hour. If Pat was not out by one, he was to go straight to the police and file a missing person's report, claiming that Pat had been missing not for an hour but for three days and that she'd last been seen with Dr. Homlin. He prayed he wouldn't have to tell yet another string of lies, especially to the police. He was beginning to worry that his nose would start growing from such a steady diet.

THE WIRE CUTTERS, AN old pair borrowed from Allan's surgical supplies previously used for cutting the heads off of bone pins, had worked well on the chain link fence. The passage through the opening had raised no alarm, nor had the crawl across the open expanse to the first building.

Having reached the rear door where she planned to enter the lab, Pat stopped long enough to remove her backpack. She returned the wire cutters to the bag and removed a small electronic device. Mailed to her by special overnight delivery, this was the finest electronic decoder money could buy on the black market. Pat had only needed it once before, but it was worth its weight in diamonds.

As her preliminary investigation had revealed, the rear door, like the other doors of Biogentrix, was electronically locked and required a special sensing card for entrance. *Or a black market decoder*, Pat thought as she applied the sensors of the box to the flat surface of the door lock. She flipped a switch and waited a few seconds as the decoder searched for the correct code sequence. The quiet click of the door indicated a successful entry.

Pat removed the sensors and gently placed the decoder back into her pack. So far so good. No signs of guards, no alarms, no disturbance of any kind. She entered the building, letting the door close behind her. Better to keep it closed in case they had it wired to detect any breach of security. It appeared Homlin depended mostly on electronic security in place of human personnel. If so, it would be to Pat's advantage. At the same time, it would be stupid to assume there weren't any security guards around. Stupid and deadly.

Once inside, Pat was uncertain where to go next. She'd not been able to get a floor plan of the building. No one in the area seemed to know who had built the building or even designed it. The work had come from outside the community. The only thing to do was to check as many rooms as possible in the time she had and pray for a little luck.

Behind the first four doors, she found simple offices or labs, the type found in hundreds of research facilities across the country. The fifth door she came to was the first that had its own security lock. Pat tripped the lock with the decoder and silently slipped through it, closing it behind her.

She found herself in a small anteroom of an office. *Interesting*, she thought, *that they would have a security lock on this room.* As she entered the adjacent room she saw why. She shined the flashlight around a plush executive office. The beam reflected on a brass name plaque lying on the desk:

DR. FREDERICK HOMLIN

Bingo, Pat almost shouted out loud. Homlin's office. *What a stroke of luck*, she thought as she closed the door behind her. She directed the beam of light around the room again until she found the line of filing cabinets on the far wall. Walking over to them, she opened the top drawer and leafed through the files, mostly receipts and invoices for supplies. She went on to the second one. About half way through the file she spied an interesting heading—FOOD AND DRUG ADMINISTRATION. She pulled the file out and walked over to Homlin's desk, leafing through the file's contents as she walked.

The most interesting item was a letter dated the last week of September from a Dr. Harrison. As Pat read the letters, a knot formed in the pit of her stomach. The letter was an invitation for Homlin to meet with a board of FDA officials to discuss his plans for FreeForm and its dissemination to other research labs throughout the country.

FreeForm? What in the hell is FreeForm? She wondered. She didn't think she would like the answer to the question. Pat studied the rest of the file's contents and found a second letter dated the first of October in which the same Dr. Harrison requested a second meeting to further explore Homlin's "interesting proposal". Whatever Homlin was promoting, it looked like the dumb ass bureaucrats were actually thinking of taking him up on his plan. The knot in Pat's stomach continued to tighten.

She sat down in Homlin's chair, wondering what to do next. *What if Homlin was a legitimate businessman and researcher? This FreeForm might be nothing. On the other hand, why is every fiber of my body telling me that Homlin is up to no good?* As she sat there, her eyes slowly focused on the papers lying on Homlin's desk. A familiar piece of stationery brought her eyes sharply in focus.

It was another letter from the Food and Drug Administration, dated Dec. 2, 2003. Only two days ago. Under the letter was the overnight express container in which it had been mailed and on top the letter, brief and to the point, read:

Dear Dr. Homlin,

We enjoyed meeting with you yesterday and feel that we are coming closer to a decision with each discussion. I feel confident that with a final meeting next week we can give you a much better idea if your proposal can be accepted. We'd like to meet with you on Wednesday, Dec. 8, at 9:00 am. Please call my office to confirm this date and time.

Sincerely,

Dr. Leonard Harrison

Pat frowned. December 8th was only four days away. If Homlin was up to no good with this FreeForm, she was running out of time.

Pat laid the letters out on the desk. She turned on the desk lamp for additional lighting, photographed each document and returned the file to its correct location in the filing cabinet.

She turned back to the desk to turn the light out. As her hand reached out for the short chain, a glare of light reflecting off a piece of shiny paper caught her attention—a stack of photographs. She looked more closely, a feeling of familiarity starting to grow. What would Homlin be doing with photos of a small child—a disturbingly familiar child. She looked more closely. They looked uncannily like the pictures she'd seen in Allan's home. Could it be? She glanced at a few of the others, obviously of the same boy but older by at least three or four years. No doubt about it. It had to be TJ.

She thought about taking one of them but decided it was too risky, so she took a picture of the stack instead. It would have to do.

She was about to turn off the light again when another object partially hidden under the overnight packet made her heart race. The knot in her stomach hardened, and she found it difficult to breathe. Her hands felt cold and damp.

It couldn't be. How was it possible? Her hand released the chain and gently pushed the overnight mailer out of the way, revealing the tip of a knife—the blunt tip of the knife her father had given her as a graduation present; the knife she had used to get into the alien ship. She had last seen the knife sticking out of the alien's neck where she had thrown it in a desperate effort to save her life.

Pat picked the knife up to inspect it more closely. As she felt the familiar grip of it in her hand, the scene of those last few seconds in the ship flashed before her again. The same scene she had awoken to night after night, lying in bed, the sheets damp, her body drenched in a cold sweat.

How had Homlin come upon the knife? Had he found it in the woods? Had the alien given it to him? Surely, this proved the two were somehow connected. The question was how?

Her mind raced with questions, trying to piece the loose ends together. The sound of footsteps and muffled voices yanked her from her thoughts.

Sneaking Around
Saturday Evening, Dec. 4

Allan stared at his watch for the twentieth time. He couldn't believe twenty-five minutes could pass so slowly. Where in the hell was she? Why had he ever agreed to let her go in alone? What if she had been caught? At this minute, someone could be holding her, waiting for Homlin to show up to interrogate her. Or they might have taken her to Homlin instead and he was sitting out here like a lump on a log waiting for nothing except a carload of Homlin's thugs to drive up behind him. If they caught both of them, no one would ever know what had happened except Dawn. If they'd already caught Pat in the lab, they would already know they were chasing a decoy. It would be simple enough to capture Dawn and end the whole deal.

I should go check on Pat, Allan thought for the tenth time in the last ten minutes. He glanced at his watch again. 12:35. He would wait five more minutes; that was all. After that he was going in after her. It didn't matter what he'd promised her about going for help. By the time the Waynesboro police got out here, Pat could be dead.

12:40 and no Pat. He was going in.

IN ONE MOTION, PAT grabbed the knife from the desk and turned the light off. She crouched behind the desk, feeling as trapped as she had that day on the ship—the last time she'd depended on the knife to save her life. *He's out there*, she thought as she crawled around the desk towards the door, *but this time he's not alone.* She was reliving her worst nightmare in which she was back in the ship, and the alien was coming towards her as he had that day. In her dream, she throws the knife and it strikes the alien in the throat. This time, instead of the alien screaming in pain, it laughs a deep guttural sound and as she watches it begins to cleave itself in half, starting at the point where the knife had penetrated. Within seconds, two aliens stand before her. She throws a second knife and a third in rapid succession, both of them sinking deep into the chests of the two aliens. She watches in horror as the two multiply to four as once again the knife wounds only prompt them to divide again.

Pat shook her head so hard her ears rang. She was back in Homlin's office, the voices and footsteps drawing closer. She reached the door to his office and cracked it open. The voices were coming from the hallway, and she could almost make out what they were saying.

Pat sighed with relief as she recognized some of the words and realized it was only a pair of watchmen coming down the hall—dangerous in their own right, but at least human. She continued to listen and watch from Homlin's office as the two guards passed by. One of them stopped long enough to check to be sure the outer door was locked. *Thank goodness I pulled it shut*, Pat thought as she watched the doorknob being jiggled.

As the voices faded down the hall, she glanced at her watch. 12:30. Only thirty more minutes. Knowing there were night watchmen afoot complicated things. She would have to be much more careful as she left. She had a couple more minutes. What other secrets could she uncover? She left Homlin's office, tiptoeing down the hall in the opposite direction of the night watchmen, looking for any other doors secured with a digital lock. With only a few minutes remaining, she found one. She tripped the lock with the decoding device and entered.

Pat found herself in a much larger room this time. The light of her flashlight shone around the walls, checking for windows. As she suspected, it was an interior room with no windows. She started to flip the light switch on but at the last minute thought better of it. The thought of being in a well-lit room threatened her. She'd examine the room with the flashlight. If that didn't work, she'd consider the overhead lights.

The room's temperature was much cooler than it had been in the hall. It felt like she'd stepped into a large cooler. She shined her light along the walls again. She estimated the room to be at least thirty feet by forty. Spaced three or four feet apart was a row of stainless steel cabinets that went from one end of the room to the other. She walked to the closest one. The cabinet stood about four feet tall and had a clear Plexiglas top which Pat to be at least three inches thick. She shined the light down through the glass.

Her breath caught in her throat. Larvae! Although she'd only heard about them from Allan, she instantly recognized them. Hundreds of them. She strolled down the aisle shining her light first on one side and the other. On both sides, hundreds upon hundreds of sausage-shaped, grayish-white larvae, were stacked in rows, their small blunt ends pointing towards the ceiling.

As Pat stood there staring at the grotesque display before her, her mind raced. The pieces were coming together. She felt like she'd been studying a picture that looked like an abstract piece of art only to realize that it was a close up photograph of a cow or some other simple object taken from a strange perspective.

Homlin had not found the knife or the alien. Homlin was the alien, and here before her were hundreds, thousands, of other aliens waiting to develop into whatever form was needed, like the larvae Allan had found had done.

Pat thought back to the letters from the FDA. FreeForm. The larvae. Homlin was on the verge of getting approval to ship these alien seeds across the country to other research labs. If Homlin convinced the FDA to allow him to do that, all would be lost. Within weeks, thousands of larvae across the country would start transforming, and her worst nightmare would come true.

Pat ran back to the door. She must get some pictures of the larvae. Maybe they would help her convince the FDA not to approve Homlin's request. She switched on the overhead lights, feeling completely exposed. She ran back to the closest set of cabinets and snapped a half-dozen pictures. Back at the door again, she snapped the rest of the roll of film showing the size of the room. She switched the lights off again, throwing the room into darkness as she heard the pair of night watchmen approaching. *Had they seen the light shining under the doorway?* Pat wondered as she crouched in the dark, waiting for her eyes to adapt once more. Had she pushed her luck too far?

ALLAN PULLED THE HANDLE on the car door and was startled at the rifle-report sound the latch made in the silence. He counted to ten, listening intently for any indication that someone had heard him. When things remained quiet, he stepped out of the car and crept towards the clump of bushes where Pat had disappeared less than an hour before. The heavy underbrush continued for about fifteen before clearing to reveal the security fence of Biogentrix.

Allan kept himself hidden behind the last line of shrubbery as he studied the fence line for any signs of trouble. *Too quiet. No lights, no movement, no sound. Nothing. Including, no Pat.*

Well, here goes nothing, he thought as he half crawled and half walked towards the fence. He'd only taken the first step or two when he caught his left foot on some invisible obstacle, and in the same moment, felt a sudden push from the rear.

He fell to the ground and tried to roll with the fall but found his attacker pressing heavily on his back. He attempted to stand, but his assailant successfully pinned his left arm behind him and caught his right arm over his head in a half-nelson. He was completely immobilized. They had him, which meant they must also have Pat and had simply been waiting in ambush for him. If they had them both, the jig was up. He wondered if he'd have the chance to explain to Pat why he had disobeyed her orders before they both were killed. It didn't matter. He didn't know what he could say to her.

"What are you doing out here?" A familiar voice asked from above him. "I thought I told you to go for help if I wasn't back within an hour." Pat released her hold but gave his left arm a final twist before letting go of it.

"Ouch. Easy there, partner," Allan whispered as he pushed himself up to his hands and knees and followed Pat into the bushes. Neither of them spoke until they were back in the car.

"You've got some explaining to do," Pat said between clenched teeth. "I'm not accustomed to having my partner ignore me."

"So fire me," Allan replied, angry now that he knew Pat was out of danger. "I was worried. I wanted to see if I could find you before I fetched the cops. Did you find out anything?" he asked, hoping she'd take the bait and change the subject.

"I'll say I did," Pat replied. "Let's get out of here. I'll explain once we're back at your place. I'll need to call the airport too."

"The airport?" Allan didn't like the sound of that.

"Yep. We've got to get to Washington, D.C."

"What about Dawn? Why Washington? What did you find—?"

"We'll call my office when we get a chance," Pat said as she leaned over and turned the keys in the starter for him. "You drive and I'll explain it to you on the way."

Allan started the car and made a full circle to head back in the direction they'd come. Once they reached the main road, Pat let out a heavy sigh. "You were right about one thing," she said. "Homlin has TJ." She told him about the pictures she'd seen on his desk.

They drove for a few minutes with neither one speaking. Finally, Allan said, "I'm sorry I didn't follow orders. I was worried sick about you. I panicked. I promise it won't happen again."

Pat placed her hand on his where it rested on the gear shift knob. "I understand, Allan, and I forgive you this time, but it can't happen again. From here on out, each step could be a matter of life or death and not only ours but thousands, even millions of others. The stakes are too high to let our emotions get in the way of sound judgment."

Allan nodded, but even as he did so, he realized he had one other clandestine mission to complete before taking off for D.C., and this one would have to be without Pat. He needed to see his son one last time.

Who Am I - Really

Sunday Evening, Dec. 5

Allan glanced down at the luminescent dial of his watch. 11:07 p.m. Bo promised to meet him here around eleven. *I'll give him until 11:15 before I freak out*, Allan thought. A moment later he heard a light tapping on the roof of his car.

Allan made sure the cab's overhead light was turned off before opening the door and climbing out. While they were a long way from the Homlin's home, there was no telling what kind of surveillance he may have had installed. Better safe than sorry. He climbed out of the car. Even though his eyes had adjusted to the dark, he couldn't see his friend until he felt a hand on his shoulder. He jumped despite himself.

"Sorry, Doc. Wasn't sneaking up on you," Bo said, but his chuckle suggested otherwise.

"That's okay. Not your fault. I'm particularly jumpy tonight," Allan replied after he caught his breath. "I'm not used to this clandestine business."

"What's up?" Bo said, then added, "Oh, that's right. You can't tell me."

"That's right. I'm sorry to be so secretive, but the less you know about it, the better, in case we get caught. I sure do appreciate you being willing to help me."

"Happy to do it. Like I said on the phone, I used to work at the reserve when the Smileys owned it. Nice place, but it was kind of spooky."

"Well, how do we proceed?" Allan was anxious to get on with it before he chickened out.

"We'll go in over there. There's a rip in the fence that Convoy showed me. We'll take it slow and easy through the woods and circle around behind the main house. There's an old entranceway into the basement that almost no one knows about. It's well hidden. If it's there, it'll be easy to gain access to the interior. You're pretty much on your own from there except..." Bo pulled a sheet of paper out of his coat pocket. "This is a diagram of the floor plan as best I remember it. The first floor is on this side, and the upstairs is on the back. It's not exact but should be close." He handed the paper to Allan.

Allan took a quick look at it before folding it up and sticking it in his pocket. "Thanks again, Bo. I'm not sure how I'll ever repay you—"

"Don't worry about it, Doc. What are friends for if they can't occasionally help another friend break into a house? Let's get going."

THE TWO MEN STARED down at the clump of overgrown shrubs that, according to Bo, hid the entranceway to the basement of Homlin's home. "Trust me, Doc, it's there. It's even more grown up than when I worked here, so there's no way anyone could have discovered it. Let me see the map."

Allan pulled out the map. Bo shined a small penlight on it. "Once you're in, there should be a set of stairs, right about here, that go up to the first floor outside the kitchen area. Your best bet to get to the upstairs would be the backstairs here." He traced the route with his index finger. "After that, you're on your own." He handed the map back to Allan.

"I can't thank you enough for helping me out—"

Bo raised a hand. "Don't sweat it." He handed the penlight to Allan and turned to leave, then stopped. "Remember, if you're caught, you did this on your own."

"Sure thing," Allan replied, but Bo had already disappeared into the darkness.

Bo was right. The cellar door was exactly where he said it would be. It took Allan a couple minutes to clear away the brush so he could open the door, stopping frequently to listen to be sure no one heard him. He breathed a sigh of relief when he finally had the area cleared enough to lift the door, and after a moment of hesitation, it opened with a squeaking on its rusty hinges loud enough to be heard back at his clinic. He froze, waiting and listening. After a minute, he lifted the door a few more inches and waited again. When he had the door open enough to slip through he switched on the penlight. *Just like me to stage a breaking and entering in the middle of the night and forget to bring a decent light*, he thought as he made he way down the rickety stairs, brushing spider webs away from his face. The light Bo had left for him gave off a high intensity beam that made it easy to find his way.

As he entered the basement he looked around until he found the stairs Bo had pointed out to him. So far so good. The light cast creepy shadows around him, made even creepier by the thick growth of spider webs. Was that the scurrying of roaches he heard or something larger? It was best not to investigate. He didn't want to know what he was sharing the basement with, so he stumbled his way to the stairs and straight up, pausing at the top to listen.

All's quiet on the western front, he thought, wondering where such weird memories came from and why they had to appear in moments of stress. He placed his hand on the doorknob and paused to say a short prayer before attempting to turn it. *Please, God, let it be unlocked*. It was.

He pushed the door open a couple inches and peered into the darkened hallway. When he didn't see anyone, he pushed it a few more inches and slipped through. At least he'd had enough sense to wear tennis shoes, he thought as he crept down the hall towards the kitchen...at least where the kitchen was on his map, but he never reached the kitchen to find out. He came to the rear stairs first. How was he ever going to find TJ?

He took one step at a time. Homlin's home was large. Allan had heard that there were at least six bedrooms, most if not all of them upstairs. That meant that it was likely that Homlin and his goon squad had their own bedrooms. It'd be his luck to end up dropping in on Homlin. He'd wondered about this before, and each time, he'd concluded that he'd have to cross that bridge when he came to it. *Now I'm at that bridge,* he thought as he reached the top of the stairs.

He was about to step out into the hallway when something stopped him—a feeling that he was no longer alone. He switched off the light. A moment later he heard a shuffling of feet that verified his suspicion, followed by a voice.

"Did you check on the kid?" someone asked.

"Yeah, that's where I came from," another voice responded. "What else would I be doing down there? Don't understand why Homlin insisted on putting the squirt so far away from the rest of us. Makes that much more work for me."

"He said he wanted the boy to have a good view from the front of the house. I don't have the foggiest idea why," the other voice replied. "The kid seems okay with the arrangements. At least you don't have to get up every three hours to feed him his gruel."

Allan stayed hidden in the stairwell, a tightening sensation building in his chest that was at least partially relieved when he remembered to breathe. Gruel every three hours? What was that about? At least he had a better idea where he'd find TJ. He waited until well after the lights in the hallway had been cut off and the sound of a house shutting down for the night diminished to only the creaking of old wooden joints. He switched on the penlight but kept the lighted end partially covered. He wanted his eyes adjusted to the dark as much as possible and enough light to navigate without tripping over anything. He felt safe in the stairwell, especially when compared to stepping out into the hallway. He squared his shoulders and snuck a look down the hall.

Allan stepped back to take a final look at Bo's map. The floor plan was simple. The hallway split the upstairs in half with rooms running off of either side. According to the goons, TJ should be in one of the bedrooms closest to the front of the house. At least he had a fifty-fifty chance of getting the right one. He stepped back out into the hallway and made his way past the other rooms. He kept his eyes focused on the outlines of a window he could make out at the far end. When he was standing in front of the window looking out over a moonless view of the reserve, he allowed himself to take another deep breath.

One last bridge, he thought. *How do I decide which room to enter?* The old eenie-meenie-miney-moe approach seemed too unscientific for such an important decision, but was there any other way?

He decided to use his senses first. He stepped over to the door to his right and gently placed his ear against it. Closing his eyes, he listened for any sound that could alert him to the bedroom being occupied by a small boy. After thirty seconds he stepped across the hall and repeated the same thing on the left-hand door. Nothing on either one.

Wait a minute! There had been something different about the two doors—not a sound difference but a slight odor difference. The right-hand door had smelled like you'd expect an old, musty house to smell, but Allan picked up a slightly pungent soured smell at the left-hand door. As he checked the two doors again, he remembered what one of the goons had said about feeding the kid gruel every three hours. Could this be the smell of the alien gruel?

Realizing it was the best information he had to go on, he returned to the second door and gently turned the knob. He kept the penlight on and partially covered with his hands to minimize the lighting. Closing the door behind him, he turned and looked around the room. As he did so, he heard a slight click of the table lamp turning on. There before him, leaning over in the bed, was an older boy than he'd expected—older yes, but definitely TJ, as Todd had looked at five or six.

Allan smiled his most benevolent smile developed over years of giving pet owners bad news about their beloved pets. "Hello, son."

"Daddy?" TJ replied, blinking his eyes as they adjusted to the sudden light. "Is that you?"

"It's me," Allan replied, taking a step towards the bed but stopping when he noticed the look on TJ's face change from confused to frightened. *Wow, has he grown,* Allan thought. *He looks years older. I bet he's old enough to start school.* "Shh, it's okay, son. I'm not going to hurt you. I needed to talk with you, but we must be quiet. Okay?"

"What are you doing here?" TJ asked as his gaze flitted around the room like a wild animal looking for a way to escape.

What am I doing here? Allan had been asking himself a similar question since he'd gotten the idea to come. What did he hope to accomplish? He stared at the boy who, despite growing substantially since he'd last seen him, looked remarkably like Todd. He knew the answer.

"I've come to take you home."

"But I am home," TJ replied.

The simple statement sent a shiver through Allan. He took another tactic.

"Are they treating you okay? It appears they're feeding you well."

"Yeah, but it's mostly that yucky gruel stuff. It's supposed to help me grow faster."

"Well, it sure seems to be working. I hardly recognized you."

There was a long pause during which the two of them stared at each other. Finally, Allan asked, "Are you happy here?"

TJ shrugged. "It's alright.

"You called me 'Daddy' when you first saw me. Do you know what it means?"

TJ shrugged again. "Yeah, it means...daddy...I mean, like I'm part of you, but you're not my daddy, are you?"

Allan thought about how to answer that. "Well, not exactly, but I was there when you were born, so in some ways you could say I'm your dad." *More than Homlin,* he thought.

"I don't have a daddy, do I?" TJ asked, staring intently at him.

It was Allan's turn to shrug. "No, I guess not—least not as far as I know, but I was raising you as my son. Doesn't that count for anything?"

TJ smiled a little at that. "How's Kendra?" he asked.

"Okay, but she misses you. I told her you went back to my brother."

There was another long pause.

"Who am I?" TJ asked, "Where do I belong? I mean, I'm not your son, though I look like he did, and I feel kinda like you're my...daddy, I guess. But I have this...this feeling that I'm supposed to be here...with Dr. Homlin, and he tells me I'm one of them, and that feels right and not so right too."

The pained, confused look on TJ's face made Allan's heart ache. Maybe his coming here was a bad idea after all. What right did he have to put this young boy through such a difficult decision?

"I do know one thing," TJ continued. "I like your food a lot more. I miss my Cheerios."

Allan laughed, and a moment later, TJ joined him. After the laughter died down, Allan said, "Come home with me, son, and you can have all the Cheerios you want. Kendra misses you...I miss you. Won't you come home with me?"

TJ considered it for several seconds before replying. "I think I better stay here, at least for a while. I can come visit you later, if that would be okay with you."

That's sure as hell never going to happen, Allan thought. *Homlin won't let his new recruit out of his sight.*

Allan realized he'd said his piece. What more could he say to convince TJ to come with him, especially when he wasn't sure it was what was best for the boy?

"Yeah, you can do that," he replied.

TJ nodded. "Yeah, I'll come visit you someday soon."

"Well, okay. Guess I'll have to send that case of Cheerios back to the store."

TJ eyes twinkled for a minute, then realized it was a joke. "Yeah, or give it to Kendra. She likes them pretty well herself."

"I better be going," Allan said. "Don't want to overstay my welcome." He turned towards the door.

"You could go out the window, Daddy," TJ said. "It's a pretty easy climb down, and it would save you going by the others' bedrooms. I don't think they'd be too excited to see you here."

AS ALLAN LEANED AGAINST his car, he glanced at the luminescent dial of his watch—almost one a.m. His exhaustion from two late nights was made worse by a feeling of hopelessness and defeat. *Time to face the facts, like Pat said. My son is dead...has been dead for years. Whoever or whatever I was talking with is not my son.* When would those facts finally land as the truth? He didn't know, but he felt like tonight had been an important step in the right direction. Or was he fooling himself again.

Part Four

A Game of Cat and Mouse, but Which One is the Cat?

Lost in Charlotte
Monday Morning, Dec. 6

Dawn pulled the cord that drew the heavy curtain away from the window and stared out from the 22nd floor onto the early morning skyline of Charlotte, N.C. Even though she knew by usual city standards, Charlotte was considered a medium size, to her the city looked huge. It had grown considerably since her last visit to the Queen City some fifteen years earlier when her high school class had taken a field trip to Discovery Place.

Dawn turned her attention to Pat's plush apartment, shaking her head for the tenth time since leaving Waynesboro. Who would have ever thought when she took the job with quiet Dr. Pritchard that one day she would end up in a swanky uptown apartment in Charlotte masquerading as a private eye so that her boss and the real P.I. could run off and do...do what? That part, well, she wasn't sure what they were doing.

Oh well, all in a day's work as a receptionist. Dawn strolled into the kitchen to fix herself a cup of coffee. It took her five minutes to find the coffee, but she located it on the door of the freezer along with a wide selection of herbal teas.

In a few minutes, she had her customary coffee and dry toast. She took both, along with the Sunday edition of the Charlotte Observer, and walked over to the most massive, comfortable sofa on which she'd ever sat.

You know, I could get used to this style of living, she thought a few moments later as she sipped on her coffee, the paper pleasantly strewn around her. She glanced at her watch. 8:05. She was to meet Allison, one of Pat's assistants, at Pat's office at 9:30. It was mostly to keep the masquerade up, but at the same time, there were several small items which Pat had requested Dawn get while she was in Charlotte.

I'd best be getting myself ready to go, Dawn thought as she pushed herself off the sofa and walked back to the kitchen to freshen her coffee. Since she wasn't sure how far away she was from the office, she didn't want to be late and keep Allison waiting. As she strolled past the picture window again, she paused for a moment.

Somewhere down there on the street was a gray sedan. Inside were two men. Those men had followed her from Waynesboro. Men up to no good. She didn't know what they were up to, but she knew from the little that Pat and Dr. Pritchard had told her that they were not the kind you'd want to meet in some dark alley. Or for that matter on some deserted road late at night.

Dawn found herself shivering thinking about them. Best not to give them too much thought. *Do my job and keep my eyes and ears open*, Dawn told herself. *I'll be fine as long as I do my job and stay awake.*

She walked into the bathroom, disrobing as she went. She'd been waiting to take a bath since she'd first laid eyes on the room yesterday, particularly when she found bubble bath in the cabinet under the sink. The next thirty minutes would be worth all the worry and concern. To be able to soak in a tub in such a gorgeous room. Yes, she could get used to living this way.

ALEX LEANED AGAINST the Plexiglas sides of the phone booth, waiting to make a connection. He hated this. Tailing this dame was demeaning. He had other men for such trivial matters. Yeah, sure they were short handed and yeah, the dame was important to keep an eye on, but Homlin needed him elsewhere. Except it had been Homlin who had sent him on this wild chase. Okay, he would follow orders, but he didn't have to like it.

"Come on. Answer the damn phone," Alex said into the receiver as the phone continued to ring at the other end.

Finally, a man picked up, and Alex curtly reprimanded him for taking so long. "Patch me into Homlin wherever he is. This is important. And be prompt about it. I don't know how much time I have."

Within a couple of moments, the connection was remade, this time with Homlin.

"Good morning, Alex. How is the Queen City?" Homlin's pleasant tone caught Alex by surprise. Things must be going well in D.C. *That's where I should be*, Alex thought. *I should be up there where the action is instead of following this dumb broad.*

"Everything is fine here," Alex answered somewhat sullenly. "It's under control. In fact, I see no reason that Julian can't take care of this part on his own—"

"No, no. You must stay with Julian. I need to know where Ms. Vogt is every moment. I am counting on you. I know you'd rather be here, but believe me, I need you there. Where is she?"

"She's in her apartment. She's been there since she arrived early yesterday evening," Alex replied with a sigh. "How are things in D.C.?"

"It's going splendidly," Homlin replied. "Right according to our plans. It won't be long now. Just a couple more days. That's why it's vital that you keep an eye on Vogt. She is the only factor that could foul up the works. As long as she's behaving herself, we'll be fine."

"Well then, we don't have anything to worry about. I'll keep you posted." He hung up the phone. *When this is over, I'm going to settle up with our little Ms. Vogt in fine fashion. Homlin promised her to me. It's the one thing that makes this worthwhile.*

"ALLISON, YOU'VE BEEN most helpful. I appreciate you having these items ready to go," Dawn said as she placed the top back on the box. "I can understand why Pat has you run things while she's away."

"Oh, no bother at all. Pat pays me to do this. I think it's great you're willing to help her out. I imagine it must feel pretty funny driving around in a strange city dressed up as somebody else."

Dawn laughed. "Well, I must admit it wasn't exactly how I planned to spend my weekend, but to tell you the truth, it's a lot more exciting."

She glanced at her watch. "I better be getting on back to the apartment. Dr. Pritchard said he would give me a call this morning to be sure everything was going okay."

"Well, I hope you enjoy your stay in Charlotte. Do you know how long you'll be staying?"

"Not really. Until Dr. Pritchard tells me to hightail it back to Waynesboro, I will stay here. I've already told Marva, our technician, that I might not be coming in on Monday. Bless her heart, she won't know what to do if she has to open up by herself. Luckily, this is a slower time of the year for us. I'm sure she'll manage."

Dawn picked up the box and headed for the door. "Thanks again. I'll be sure to let Pat know how much help you were."

"Glad to do it," Allison said as she opened the door for her.

After Dawn left, Allison returned to her desk to finish some typing she'd promised to one of the other investigators. It was ten minutes before she glanced over to the other desk and her eyes fell on the city map Dawn had laid there when she'd first come in.

Allison walked over and picked it up. A direct path connecting the office with Pat's apartment was clearly highlighted in red.

"Oh, my goodness, she won't be able to go back that way," Allison said out loud as she studied the map. Charlotte's maze of one-way streets and constant construction had thwarted many a newcomer in recent years.

"DAMN!" DAWN POUNDED on the steering wheel as she found her way stopped for the third time by new construction. In the last five minutes, she had gone from confused to hopelessly lost. She'd pulled over twice to look for her map before realizing she'd left it at the office. She would have gladly retraced her steps to recover it, but the maze of one-way streets prevented such a simple solution.

She glanced in the rear view mirror to find the gray sedan continuing to follow her. *Great. This has got to look great*, she thought. What to do? She had to get back to the apartment. Dr. Pritchard would be calling her any minute, and there was no telling what he would do if she weren't there to take her call.

She passed a stopped Charlotte Police car. She considered asking for directions but decided against it. It would raise even more questions for the two men following her. If they paniced seeing her talking to a cop, it was no telling what they might do.

The answer to her problem came to her as she spied a pay phone past the police car. She'd call Allison. In a quick phone call, she could get directions out of this and let Allison know what to tell Dr. Pritchard if he called. It made sense. She pulled over, forcing herself not to look in the rear view mirror. She stepped out of the car as nonchalantly as possible and prayed the men following her wouldn't do anything stupid.

"SOMETHING IS FUCKING wrong here!" Alex shouted to Julian. "This dumb broad hasn't the foggiest idea where she's going. Pull in behind her, but don't be too obvious."

Julian did as he was told.

"Oh great!" Alex said as he noticed where they were parked. "She's making a fucking phone call. What the hell is going on?"

"Maybe she's calling for directions," Julian replied.

"Why in the world would she need to do that? She's from this damn city. Unless? Oh, shit. I've got a funny feeling something is screwed up here." He sat for a few moments, considering his options. He had to find out for sure who they were following but how without tipping their hand?

His eyes focused on the patrol car in front of them. The officer sat in the driver's seat, his head down as though he was either writing or taking a nap on the job. Alex had an idea.

"Stay here and be ready for anything." He stepped out of the car and headed towards the patrolman.

DAWN KEPT HER BACK to the gray sedan she knew was behind her, afraid that if she faced them, she'd give herself away with the distressed look on her face. The phone rang for the sixth time. Oh god, she's already left. What was she to do? The phone's seventh ring was cut short by Allison's voice.

"Vogt Investigations, this is Allison."

"Oh Allison, am I ever relieved to hear your voice! This is Dawn. I've done a foolish thing."

ALLAN'S EYES FLUTTERED open. He continued to lie on his back as his eyes focused on the unfamiliar ceiling and surroundings. Where was he? He glanced next to him and was pleased to see a familiar face. Pat was asleep beside him. It came back to him, as the memory of the last twenty-four hours cleared the cobwebs from his mind. This was the Marriott Hotel at the Greensboro airport. They'd driven here during the early morning hours after finding out there was a mid-morning flight to Washington. They'd checked in for a couple of hours of much-needed sleep. Had they overslept?

Allan shot up in bed and squinted his eyes to make out the digital display of the alarm clock. Only 9:00 a.m. The flight didn't leave until 11:00. They had plenty of time. He lay back down, relieved. Pat stirred beside him. Two hours before their flight. Let's see, what could they do to entertain themselves before their flight left? He had a good idea.

He turned over and faced Pat, alseep. He gently ran his fingers over the curve of her shoulder. Such soft skin. Such a beautiful face. Pat's eyes fluttered open. Allan watched as her eyes focused and went from a confused look to one of recognition. She smiled and pulled him towards her. It was a most pleasant way to wake up in the morning.

REASSURED BY THE DIRECTIONS she had received from Allison, Dawn returned to Pat's Cherokee relaxed. She sat in the driver's seat for a moment, reviewing the notes she'd taken on Allison's directions. After making sure she knew which turns to make, she leaned forward to start the car.

A shadow fell across the steering wheel, startling her. Dawn looked up to find a young policeman smiling at her through the window. Dawn forced herself to smile back. *What in the world have I done?* she asked herself. Did she run a light in her confusion or make an illegal turn? She didn't think so, but she couldn't be sure.

"Yes, officer?" she politely asked as she rolled down the window.

The officer continued to smile as his eyes flickered from her to the insides of the car and back to her. *He's taking in everything about me,* Dawn thought. *I wonder if he thinks I've stolen the car. What if he asks for the registration? Pat didn't tell me where she kept it.*

"I saw you sitting here, and I was wondering if I could help you. This part of downtown can be difficult to navigate even without the construction detours," the officer said as he leaned forward.

He's quite cute, Dawn thought, then almost burst out laughing at herself. *Now, now. Let's not go picking up some young guy who's half your age.* Despite herself, she returned a pleasant smile.

"No, officer. I'm fine—now. I called for the directions I needed, but I thank you for asking. I'll be on my way if that's okay with you."

"Sure, lady. Enjoy your stay in Charlotte," the officer said as he tipped his cap to her.

"Oh, I will, officer. It's been a long time since I've been here. It certainly has grown, but I won't let that keep me from enjoying it. Good day." Dawn rolled up the window. Her hand fumbled for the key. She started the car; in her excitement, she ground the starter a second time.

She glanced in the rear view mirror and watched the officer return to his patrol car. A couple of spaces behind, she noticed the gray sedan. *Well, nothing seems any worse for wear,* she thought as she pulled out from the parking space and turned left at the first light as Allison had told her.

ALEX WATCHED THE CHEROKEE turn the corner before making his move. With a final glance to the partially nude body of the dead cop, he flung the door open and ran to his car.

"Quick, get behind her. Be sure she returns to the apartment!" he yelled to Julian as he hopped into the passenger seat and took off the policeman's cap. "We're screwed. We're royally screwed."

"What's wrong?" Julian asked as he pulled out from behind the patrol car and took off after the Cherokee.

"The woman we're following isn't Pat Vogt. I don't know who she is, but she isn't Vogt. Homlin will shit when he hears this. When we get back to the apartment, I'll call in to find out what we should do next. Boy, are we screwed."

Flight Delay
Monday, Dec. 6

"She's what? Are you sure? What the hell happened?" Homlin swung his legs out of bed, grabbed the phone from the nightstand, and started pacing. "Are you sure?" He repeated the question. "This morning you were saying—"

"I know what I said. Everything was fine—at least I thought so, but she started acting strangely. She got lost coming back from the office to her apartment. That's when I grew suspicious."

"Do you have any idea who the hell she is?" Homlin asked as he continued to pace. He was wide-awake, even though he had dozed off after Alex's first call.

"I don't know for sure. She's wearing a black wig, but I think it may be an employee of Pritchard's. They could have made the switch in his office. That's all I can figure."

"Do you still have the police uniform?" Homlin asked. His mind was already thinking of the most effective action. This was a setback, no question about it. But it wouldn't stop him. It couldn't. He'd not be stopped by anything at this point.

"Yeah. I've got it on," Alex replied, pulling at one of the sleeves and adjusting the collar. He thought he looked handsome in the uniform.

"Good. I want you to keep an eye on our little Miss Whoever-she-is. Let her get settled in and comfortable. Then I want you to pay her a visit. This is going to work out. Pay close attention."

"WHAT DO YOU MEAN, THE flight has been canceled? You can't cancel the flight. We've got to get to Washington, D.C. We drove for hours in the middle of the night to get here for the flight!" Pat's face was livid as she shouted into the phone. She listened for a few moments to the polite ticket agent on the other end. Finally, with a great deal of effort, she calmed herself enough to ask when the next flight out would be.

"There is another flight out today, isn't there?"

"Yes, Ms. Vogt. We already have you and your traveling companion booked on it. Its departure time is scheduled for 1:45 p.m. this afternoon. If you like, you may come to the ticket counter to get a voucher for breakfast."

"Oh, thank you so much," Pat replied sarcastically as she slammed the phone back in the cradle.

"1:45 pm. Can you believe it?" She walked over to the bed and plopped down on her side.

"Well, I know it's exasperating, but does it make any difference what time we get to D.C. as long as we're there by 8:00 on Monday morning?"

"No, I guess not," Pat answered with a sigh. "It's that I'm afraid something will happen. We've got to be there tomorrow morning. We should go ahead and drive up there."

"Well, we could, but what's the point? There's as much likelihood of something happening on the highway as in the air. Why not relax and enjoy the little time we have." Allan reached over and started to rub Pat's back. "We'll get there in plenty of time, I promise."

Pat relaxed a little and leaned back against him. "Okay, you're right. I'll take it easy. Nothing else better happen, or I'll simply go ape-shit."

"Nothing else is going to happen. Relax," Allan said as he rubbed her scalp, and she nestled further into his arms.

DAWN POURED THE SOFT drink into the glass of ice and stepped back to review her work. A bowl of chili, a dish of potato chips, a soft drink, and a pickle. Anything else? She reached over the counter and pulled off a paper towel and placed a second pickle on the dish. There. Everything was ready for a leisurely afternoon in front of the television.

Yes, she was definitely getting used to this kind of living. She walked over to the sofa and placed the tray on the coffee table. She flicked the television on with the remote and scanned the stations. Mostly pre-game football shows. Boring. An old movie she had seen at least four times. A good movie, but not worth watching for a fifth time. She settled on a local news show. *May as well get caught up with what's happening in the big city*, she thought as she took her first mouth full of chili.

The show was drawing to a close when the newscaster was handed a special report. He studied it for a moment, frowned, and looked to the camera.

"I'm afraid the Queen's City crime continues to escalate. Moments ago, the body of Officer Tim MacDonald was found in his patrol car. He was brutally strangled."

A photo of the unfortunate officer flashed on the screen. Dawn gasped as she recognized the young officer she'd met only a few hours ago. *How sad*, she thought. *He seemed like such a nice fella.* The report was short. Details were sketchy. As the news show ended, Dawn felt a hollow emptiness. The warm, cozy living room seemed chilled. She picked up the remote and switched through the channels looking for something to cheer her up. She picked a rerun of MASH but found she couldn't keep her mind on the story. She kept remembering the bright smile of the young man who had tried to help her—who was lying on some cold slab in the city morgue.

She shivered despite the warmth of the room. She decided to see if she could find a blanket or quilt to wrap around her. Halfway to the bedroom, the doorbell rang. Who on earth would be calling on her? Well, no one of course. They'd be calling on Pat, but wouldn't her staff know that Pat was away on leave? Maybe not? Dawn walked over to the front door of the apartment and peered through the peephole. For the second time in less than an hour, she gasped at the face before her. It was the young officer. The one who had supposedly been killed.

She breathed a sigh of relief. It had been a mistake. They must have reported on the wrong officer. True, a body was lying in the morgue, but at least it wasn't her young man.

She unlocked the door and flung it open. "Am I ever glad to see you!" The officer smiled with a confused twist to it. "According to the news report, you're supposed to be dead." Dawn stepped back to give him room to enter.

The officer's eyes darted around the room, taking in everything in one quick moment. Stepping into the room, he closed the door behind him. "Well, you know you can't believe everything you see on TV these days."

"WHAT DO YOU SAY AFTER I take a shower we go down and get our free breakfast?" Pat asked as her shoulder muscles relaxed under Allan's talented fingers.

"Sounds good to me. I think I'm going to be lazy for a little longer while you take a shower. I want to call Dawn before we go out."

Pat stood up and walked into the bathroom. In a few minutes, Allan heard the sound of the shower water beating against the sides of the fiberglass tub. He closed his eyes and tried to ease his tense muscles. It was hard for him to believe everything that had happened. What in the world was he doing here in Greensboro anyway?

He answered his own question. *Why, I'm on the way to Washington, D.C. to stop a mad alien from taking over the world.* Were the two of them crazy? Had he gone off the deep end a few months ago from too much stress in the practice or from too much grief? Maybe they were two nut cases like you read about in the paper all the time, living in their own world of delusion. Maybe Homlin was an ordinary scientist trying to get his discovery accepted.

He could see the D.C. paper. "Attempted Assassination of Famous Scientist Thwarted." And the sub-heading, "Both Assassins Shot."

Well, if so, the die was cast. He wasn't going to stop. It had happened, was still happening. Homlin was an alien, and he was out to overthrow the world. There was a plant a few hours from here filled with thousands of alien life forms waiting for distribution. It had to be stopped.

Allan opened his eyes and reached for the phone as he heard Pat cut off the water. He read the instructions on how to get an outside line. In a few moments, he was dialing Pat's apartment number. He was surprised when, after the fourth ring, Pat's answering machine picked up. Where was Dawn? Wasn't she supposed to be at Pat's apartment all morning? She should be back from her trip to Pat's office.

He waited for the end of the message. "Hello, uh, Pat..." He'd almost asked for Dawn. "This is Dr. Pritchard. I'm sorry I missed you. When you get in, please call me at this number." He glanced at the phone, but before he could give the number, he heard Dawn's voice.

"Hello, don't hang up. Wait a minute."

There was a short pause on the other end. "Hello—"

"Dawn, is that you? This is Dr. Pritchard."

"Oh, I'm sorry. I must have dozed off on the sofa."

"Are you okay? You sound a little funny," Allan said, uncertain what he was picking up that sounded strange.

"No, things are fine here. I'm a little drowsy. It's been a lazy morning. Where are you?"

"Pat and I are at the Airport Marriott in Greensboro. We're getting ready to fly to Washington, D.C. for some important business. I'm calling to let you know we're fine and that we want you to stay in Charlotte for a couple more days. Is that okay?"

"Sure, no problem. I'm having fun. Do you want me to continue to pose as Pat?"

"Yes, including going into her office each day for at least a couple of hours. We want to be sure it looks like you're there for business reasons."

"No problem. When will you be in Washington?"

Allan glanced down at the pad of paper where Pat had jotted down the time and gate number of the new flight. "We're scheduled to leave at 1:45. I don't know the arrival time. It's a new flight. Our original one was canceled."

"Well, don't worry about anything down here. I'm enjoying being a big city private eye."

"Be careful, Dawn. The people who are following you are not to be taken for granted. I'm sorry I had to get you into this mess in the first place. I couldn't stand it if anything happened to you."

"Don't worry, Allan, nothing is going to happen. I'm a big girl. I can take care of myself. You go and do what you have to. Don't worry about me."

Allan continued to hold the phone against his ear, but he couldn't get any words out of his mouth. Something was wrong here, terribly wrong, he knew it. In the seven years, he'd known Dawn, she had never once, no matter what the circumstances, called him by his first name. To Dawn, he would always be Dr. Pritchard. Who was he talking to?

"Listen, I need you to do one more thing." He finally got the words out. "Call Marva in the morning and tell her that Mrs. McGee's schnauzer can go home in the afternoon. Will you do that?"

"Sure, I'd be happy to."

There was no doubt about it. This wasn't Dawn with whom he was speaking. The real Dawn knew perfectly well that they had put Mrs. McGee's schnauzer to sleep on Thursday. It had been upsetting to Dawn to have to hold the old dog. He had been one of their oldest patients and one of Dawn's favorite. Mr. McGee had picked up the body that afternoon for a backyard burial.

Allan hung up the phone but continued to sit on the bed, staring at the receiver. Something had happened in Charlotte. Dawn was in trouble. For all he knew, she might be dead. There appeared little doubt that their switch had been discovered.

Damn, I've told somebody other than Dawn what our plans are, he thought. *I've played right into their hand.*

Pat walked out of the bathroom, a towel wrapped around her slender form. She was drying her hair with a second towel.

"Did you reach Dawn?" she asked as she walked over to the chest of drawers where they'd stacked their suitcases.

Allan didn't answer at once; his mind seemed unable to catch up with what had happened. He wrestled his eyes away from the phone and stood up.

"Yes, no...I mean, I reached your apartment, but whoever I talked to wasn't Dawn."

Pat stopped rubbing her hair in mid-stride. "What do you mean? Is anything wrong?"

"It wasn't Dawn. It sounded like Dawn in almost every detail." He repeated the conversation he'd had.

"Are you sure? Couldn't you have been mistaken? Maybe she was trying to make you feel at ease."

"Dawn hasn't been able to call me by my first name in casual conversation in all the years we've known each other. It's been a standing joke with us. But let's say that she did—just this once. There's no way she wouldn't have known that Mrs. McGee wasn't going to pick up her dog. No way. I tell you, whoever I talked to wasn't Dawn, but they sure wanted me to think they were. They've gotten her. That's all there is to it, and what's worse I didn't know it until I had already told them where we were headed."

"Shit," Pat said as she sat on the bed and absentmindedly toweled her hair again. After a moment she said, "Well, let's see. This is what we'll have to do. We'll have to split up. You head down to Charlotte, and I'll go to Washington."

"But they know you're coming."

"Yeah, so what? Let them know. I'm going. I have to go. They've got to be stopped, and you've got to go see if you can help Dawn. I feel awful for getting her caught up in this, I really do. I'll notify Allison that you're on the way and have her stake out my place. She's good, Allan. If anyone can get Dawn out of there alive, Allison can."

That is, if she's alive, Allan thought, but what was the point in saying the obvious?

Pat continued to sit on the bed for a few minutes as she continued to dry her head. Finally, she stood up and headed for the bathroom. "It's getting sticky, no question about it. We're going to have to dig deep to pull this one out. I guess that's what we'll have to do."

HOMLIN PICKED UP THE phone on the second ring. Alex explained his short conversation with Allan.

"They've found out about the meeting, and they're coming to stop it," Homlin said with a chuckle. "Okay. We'll have to be on the lookout for them. Let's see." He paused for a moment. Alex waited patiently for his orders. "Here's what I want you to do. What time did you say their plane was leaving?"

"1:45," Alex answered.

"Great. I want you on that flight with them. It's our best chance to find the trail again. Who do you have with you?"

"Julian," Alex winced. He knew Homlin's opinion of Julian wasn't good. It was also an opinion that Alex shared. Julian was a fuck-up, but surely he could watch one small, tied-up woman without blowing it.

"Okay. That's the way it is, I guess. I'll see if we have someone at the lab who can drive down and be with him. Anyway, leave him there to look after our little imposter, and you find Vogt and Pritchard. Don't do anything but follow them. When they check into a hotel, you do the same and call me from there. Is that clear?"

"Very clear," Alex replied. Within a couple of hours, I'll be back on the trail of that bitch. *It's only a matter of time before Homlin gives me instructions to kill both of them.* "I'll call you from Washington."

Dawn's Dilemma

Monday, 12:28 pm Dec. 6

Allan pulled the Blazer to the curb and turned off the engine. He stepped out of the car, pulling the collar of his jacket up to shelter himself from the wind. He walked down the street towards the address Pat had given him, leaning into the blustery wind. It was getting colder with each day. For the South, it was the beginning of winter—Allan's least favorite season. Each year he thought it would be okay with him if fall simply continued until spring and spring could continue until fall again. In a perfect world you only needed two seasons. In a perfect world, there weren't monsters or aliens or even bad guys who abducted gentle ladies like Dawn.

After walking a couple of blocks, he saw the sky blue sedan that Pat had described to him exactly where she said it would be. He walked towards it and climbed into the passenger seat and found himself staring at the large black hole of a large gun being held in the small hand of an attractive young woman.

"Are you Allan?" the woman asked, and without thinking, he almost said yes. Then he remembered what he was to say to the question.

"No, I'm Dr. Pritchard," he said, trying to force a smile without much success.

"Good." The woman lowered the revolver and stuck it back in her shoulder harness. "I'm Allison. Pat has told me so much about you, but she didn't tell me how cute you were."

This time Allan smiled more successfully. "It's a pleasure, Allison. I only wish it had been under different circumstances."

"You can say that again. I was so shocked to hear that Dawn had been kidnapped. It was only a few hours ago when I spoke to her on the phone. She was worried because she'd become lost."

"Oh boy! That must have been the giveaway. They suspected something right then."

"Pat didn't have much time to explain what was going on. She had to catch her flight. She told me you would fill me in on what I needed to know."

Allan nodded. Pat and he had sorted out how much they could tell Allison. Even though Pat trusted Allison completely, Pat wasn't anxious to let anyone know what was going on, so they had decided on giving Allison a partial story.

"A gang of thugs was following Dawn, thinking she was Pat. It was the only way we could get Pat clear of them so she could work on finding their ringleader. That's what she's doing in Washington. Unfortunately, they've discovered the switch."

"I'm only going to ask one question. Is this about the case Pat's been working on for ten years?"

It took Allan a second to understand Allison's question before he answered, "Yes, it is."

"Say no more. No one has ever understood what the case was about, but we have seen how consumed Pat has been with it. If there's anything I can do to help resolve it for her, I'll do it, no questions asked. Let's get to work."

Allan smiled. He wasn't surprised to find that Pat had a loyal staff. Still, it was refreshing.

"Okay, what's been happening in there?"

"Not much. I've seen one man leave and go down the street. I didn't follow him for fear they might slip Dawn out while I was gone. He came back with a bag of groceries. It would suggest to me that at least two people are holding her."

"Okay, good. Have you seen any sign of Dawn?"

"No, 'fraid not."

Allan pondered the situation for a moment. He'd had his mind on nothing else for the entire two hours of the trip and hadn't come up with a good plan for getting Dawn out safely. For that matter, he didn't know if she was alive, but the fact that the thugs were around and shopped for groceries gave him hope.

"Well, Allison, I'm far from an expert in matters of this kind. About as close to the criminal world as I've ever gotten was giving first aid to a stranger for a dog bite. I didn't find out until later that he'd received the bite while breaking into a house. He convinced me he came to a vet because he figured that was where people who had been bitten by an animal went. It sounded plausible to me. Anyway, I'm open to suggestions."

Allison nodded and pulled her key out of the ignition.

"After speaking with Pat, I called Frank and Cindy. They're a husband and wife team. They don't actually work for Pat, except for an occasional contract, but they're usually willing to lend a hand. They are on the other side of the building, watching the back. In a situation like this, surprise is the only thing we have on our side. If I understood Pat correctly, the men inside aren't aware they gave themselves away to you. Is that correct?"

"Yes, I'd say so. I wasn't even sure until I had hung up and thought about it."

" I doubt they'll be suspecting us to show up on their doorstep. The fact that one of them went out for groceries would suggest this is true as well. About the only thing I know to do is to go in quickly and in force."

Allan thought about it for a moment. As he worked to come up with a plan, he stared out the window of the sedan. There wasn't much foot traffic on this blustery Sunday afternoon. An old fella in a worn out army jacket, his shoulders hunched over, hands dug deeply into the pockets of the jacket.

He reminds me of old Mr. Sorenson, Allan thought. Sorenson had been Allan's gruff yet soft landlord for three of his four years in vet school. In the three years, Allan could only remember a couple of occasions when he'd seen Sorenson without a similar army jacket. A thought came to Allan, and he leaped out of the car after the bum, unzipping his own down-lined ski jacket as he ran after him.

PAT LEANED OVER THE back seat and paid the taxi driver.

"Keep the change," she said without realizing she'd tipped him almost half of the fare. Her mind was on other matters.

"Gee, thanks, lady." The cabby jumped out to open her door.

As Pat climbed out of the back seat, she had an urge to glance over her shoulder, but she resisted the temptation. It wasn't necessary. She knew what she'd see, either the dark blue sedan or the black one. They'd become more careful with the tag, using two cars instead of one, but they had been easy to spot by a professional who knew for what they were looking.

The cabbie ran around to the rear of his car and pulled Pat's suitcase out of the trunk. "Would you like me to take it to your room?" he asked.

"No, that won't be necessary," Pat answered, seeing him for the first time and realizing she must have over-tipped him. "I believe they have someone here at the hotel who will take care of it. We better let them do their job."

The cabbie smiled and nodded. He pulled a rumpled business card out of his shirt pocket. "Don't hesitate to call when you need to go somewhere and be sure to ask for Archie. If I'm on duty, I'll dump whoever I'm driving and come running."

"Thanks, I'll keep that in mind." Pat took the card and stuck it in her purse, wondering how much she must have tipped him to get such service.

One of the bellhops from the hotel came out and placed her bag on his dolly. Archie looked for a moment like he would take issue with the bellhop but then realized it was time to release his best customer of the week.

Pat walked through the revolving door of the hotel. Not until she was on the other side of the reflecting glass did she turn around and study the street. In a moment she found what she'd been looking for—the black sedan, parked on the other side of the street twenty yards from the front entrance of the hotel. She wondered, as she walked over to the front desk to check in, whether the driver and occupant of the car were inside or if they had already checked into her room ahead of her. She requested the largest bellboy on staff to take her bag up to her room. She was too tired to take on two thugs on her own. All she wanted to do was to take a hot soaking bubble bath. Could they please leave her alone long enough for that?

THE ARMY JACKET REEKED of body odor. Great for the image Allan was trying to convey but hard on his own senses. He pounded on the door again, ignoring the doorbell.

"Come on, Ms. Vogt, I know you're in there. I saw you drive up yesterday. If you don't open the door and give me my rent, I'm going to have to call the cops." Allan stepped back away from the door, being sure he didn't glance to either side where Allison, Frank, and Cindy stood, flattened against the wall, waiting to rush in on Allan's signal.

Was Dawn alive or was he risking his own life and the lives of three other people to recover a cold, stiff corpse? What if there was more than one man inside and they couldn't get to them before one of them did something to Dawn?

Shut up, he told himself as he heard the lock slip on the other side of the door. His left hand twitched slightly, notifying the other three to be ready.

The door opened and there in front of him stood Pat, tugging on the rope belt of a white terry cloth bathrobe. Allan stood frozen to his spot out in the hallway, his mind racing. It couldn't be Pat, could it? He'd left her in Greensboro two hours away, waiting to fly to Washington. Here she stood as clearly as could be. But it couldn't be.

The thoughts raced through his mind in a millisecond. This was the bottom line. The person or thing standing before him had done a remarkable job of mimicry. *Like one of them had done with copying TJ*, Allan thought as he lowered his head and right shoulder and dove through the doorway, catching the Pat look-a-like below the solar plexus with his shoulder. It was a most satisfying yet confusing experience to see the shocked and frightened look on the Pat look-alike before he knocked the breath out of her. The other three followed closely behind Allan. Allison joined him in subduing his target while Frank and Cindy ran towards the bedroom to find Dawn.

If Allan had been momentarily surprised by who he was attacking, Allison was thunderstruck when she realized they were overwhelming her boss of ten years. Still, much to her credit she didn't hesitate but planted a knockout punch to the left temple, sending the Pat look-a-like crumpling to the floor.

"Good work," Allan said as he stared down at the unconscious woman.

"Yeah but...are you sure?" Allison stuttered to a stop, unsure what to say.

"I'll explain it to you later. Trust me, we're doing the right thing," Allan said as he ran towards the bedroom to see if he could help Frank and Cindy. Cindy and Dawn were sitting on the bed. Cindy was cleaning dry blood from Dawn's forehead while Frank finished untying the last bond from around one of Dawn's legs.

"She'll be okay," Cindy said as Allan rushed over to them. "She's pretty frightened, but there doesn't appear to be any serious injuries. I know of a doctor we can take her to that won't ask too many questions."

Allan felt the tears welling up in his eyes. He had never stopped to think how much Dawn meant to him—until now.

"Great work. It's obvious why Pat has been so successful as a private eye with a team of people like you." Allan sat down beside Dawn on the bed. She threw her arms around him and wept.

"It's over, sweetie," Allan said. *At least for you, it's over,* he thought. *I've got a couple more hands to play out.*

"Listen closely. I don't have time to explain in detail. Trust me when I say the person in the other room is not who she seems."

"Oh, I believe you," Allison said. "If I didn't, we'd all be out of a job."

"You've got to keep her or it under tight surveillance for the next twenty-four hours. After that, we can decide what to do from there."

"How 'bout you? Where are you going?" Allison asked.

"There's some unfinished business that needs attending to in Washington. I noticed you have a phone in your car. If you take me to the airport, I can call from the car to see when the next flight to Washington is. Pat or I will call to let you know what to do with this one. We'll explain everything at that time. For now, the less you know the better."

Allan gave Dawn a final hug then held her out at arm's length so he could look into her eyes. "I'm going to leave you here with Frank and Cindy. When Allison comes back, you go stay with her." He glanced questioningly at Allison, who nodded.

"I don't want you driving home to Waynesboro yet." He decided not to tell her that it might not be safe for her to go home. She'd been through enough for one day. "I may need to ask you a few questions later, and it'll be easier if I know where you are." *Not to mention, I'll worry less if I know where you are*, Allan thought.

He stood up but continued to hold Dawn's hand for a moment longer. He gazed down at her and gave her a reassuring smile. "It's going to be okay. I promise you. When this is over, life in Waynesboro will be too boring for you."

"I can't think of anything I'd enjoy more than to be bored in Waynesboro," Dawn answered with a tired smile.

ALEX GLANCED AT HIS watch. 4:15 and no sign of the vet. He picked up the portable phone and punched in Homlin's number. After a couple of rings, Homlin answered.

"Still no doc. Vogt checked into the Marque about an hour ago. I think it's the right time to snuff her before her boyfriend shows."

Homlin was silent at the other end. Alex waited patiently for his boss's orders. This was the moment he'd been waiting for, ever since Vogt had dug her heel into his foot and made him look foolish in Homlin's eyes. *It's time to pay for your mistakes, bitch*, he thought as he waited for Homlin's decision.

"Okay, fine. Wait for another hour for her to settle into her room. Then slip in and take care of her. Tell Lenny to stay outside and watch for Dr. Pritchard and to call up to her room if he shows up."

"You've got it, boss. I'll take care of her—really good care."

"Alex, I know you have your own plans for her. I don't even want to know what they are. Be careful. Don't let your silly games jeopardize the operation. Is that clear?"

"Perfectly," Alex answered with a smile. *Silly games, but Vogt wouldn't think they were so silly. By the time I'm finished with her, she'll be begging for me to end it.*

Alex cut the connection and put the phone back in its case. He reached over and shook Harrison's shoulder. "Wake up. I need you to watch the hotel for a while. I'm going out."

"Where are you going?" Lenny asked as he pulled himself up by the steering wheel in front of him.

"I'm going clothes shopping. Ms. Vogt is going to have a surprise visitor in a little bit. Stay awake. I'm going to take the phone. If she comes out of the hotel, call me from the pay phone over there—quickly. I won't be gone long."

Lenny nodded and rolled down the window to get some fresh air.

"THAT'S THE FIRST FLIGHT you have out?" Allan asked for the second time. He covered the receiver with his hand and whispered to Allison, "Nothing before 5:45 this evening."

"I have an idea. Hang up."

Allan thanked the airline agent and hung up.

"Punch in 554-2233, and give me the phone," Allison said. Allan did as he was told and handed the phone to her.

"I'm calling a friend of mine, Steve Runyon. We use him from time to time. He has a small airplane leasing company. If he's in, we'll get you to Washington in a couple of hours. If not, we'll have to find another way." Allison smiled as the connection was made.

"Hello, Stevie. This is Allison. I know you hate to hear my voice on a quiet Sunday afternoon, but I've got a problem. One of those life and death situations. I know you'll charge us an arm and a leg for me to say it, but it's important we get someone to Washington, D.C. this afternoon. Can you help us out?"

Allison listened for a few seconds and signaled Allan with a thumbs-up.

"That's great, Steve. We're on the way to the airport. How long before you can be there? Super. I owe you a dinner for this one."

She hung up the phone. "You're on your way."

PAT WALKED OUT OF THE bathroom, wrapping the thick terry cloth robe the hotel supplied around wet body. *My second bath of the day*, she noted to herself. *It seems like the closer I get to my alien, the dirtier I feel. I feel like*

I need another shower already. She strolled over to the phone and punched in the number to Allison's apartment. Allison picked up the phone before the second ring.

"Oh, it's so good to hear your voice," Allison said after Pat identified herself. "Everything is fine down here. Dawn is napping in my spare bedroom. It was pretty scary for her, but she's no worse for wear. A couple of days of rest and she should be as good as new."

Pat breathed a sigh of relief. "Oh, I'm so glad. Take good care of her, Allison. Allan thinks the world of her, and so do I. Speaking of Allan—"

"He's on his way to you at this moment. We couldn't get a commercial flight that worked, so we put him on one of Steve's specials. I hope you don't mind."

"Goodness, no. Good thinking," Pat replied. "What time should I expect him?"

"I don't know exactly. Allan sent me on my way before they took off. He wanted me to get back to be with Dawn. I'd guess somewhere between five and six though."

Pat looked at the digital clock beside the bed. 4:05 pm. She had an hour or two of free time. "Let me give you my number. You should be able to reach me here until tomorrow morning. Allan knows which hotel I'm staying at, but he may call you to find out which room. More than likely, he'll call me or come on over. I think I'm going to lie down for a while, but don't hesitate to call if you need me for anything." She gave Allison the numbers.

"Will do," Allison replied. "Oh, Pat. There's one more thing. I know you can't discuss this case with me, but I've gotten the idea that something big is about to happen. Be careful. We need you to come home safely. Okay?"

Pat chuckled. "Will do, sweetie; give everyone my love." She hung up the phone.

Yes, it was coming to a head. After ten years of searching for him, she finally had her alien cornered in her old stomping ground of Washington, D.C.—where the search had begun. 'Her alien.' Funny how long she had thought of him like that. Years. It was almost over. Either she'd have finally tracked him down and stopped him, or he would have won. His long years of staying in hiding, scheming quietly to overthrow human civilization. It had been a difficult ten years for both of them, struggling for the survival of their respective races.

Pat pulled the covers back on the double bed and climbed under them. It felt good to lie between the clean sheets and let her tense muscles relax. Somewhere in Washington, Homlin waited as well—waited for the final moment when he could safely disseminate his race across the country and the world.

He knows I'm out here and that I intend to stop him. He'll be out to stop me first. Their first meeting had been a draw. She'd survived his assault, but he'd also escaped. There would be no draw on this next meeting. It was time to end the ten-year game of cat and mouse.

She found herself smiling as she drifted off to sleep. *Funny*, she thought, *I've never figured out which one of us is the cat and which the mouse. I prefer being the cat this go around.*

Kink in D. C.
Monday Evening, Dec. 6

The harsh noise of the jangling phone sliced its way through Pat's sleep until she found herself sitting upright in bed with the receiver against her ear.

"Yes, who is it?" she asked with her eyes closed. Where was she? Not in her own bedroom, that much was certain, but it had been so long since she had slept at home, she wasn't surprised by that. Where was she?

"Hello, Ms. Vogt. I'm sorry to disturb you, but there is a gentleman here by the name of Dr. Allan Pritchard. He is asking for your room number."

Allan...room number...it washed over her and started to make sense. She was in D.C. at the Marque. She leaned over to the nightstand and twisted the digital clock around so she could read it. 5:15. She'd been asleep for a little over an hour. It felt like she'd been asleep for days.

She swung her legs over the edge of the bed. "That's fine. Send him on up. I'm expecting him," she told the voice at the other end of the phone. She hung up the phone and walked into the bathroom to wash her face.

5:15. He made good time getting to Washington. She threw a clean bath cloth in the sink and ran cold water over it. It would be excellent to be back in Allan's arms. They could order room service and stay in the rest of the evening. Stay in and cuddle, maybe make love. Who knows, it might be the last chance they'd get for quite a while.

"Room 444. Take the elevators over there to the fourth floor and turn left. Ms. Vogt is expecting you."

Alex smiled. "Thank you," he replied as he turned towards the line of elevators. *She's expecting me, huh? Won't she be surprised*?

As he stood waiting for the elevator, he gazed at himself in the wall of mirrors between the elevator doors. *Not bad*, he thought. He'd only seen

Pritchard a couple of times, but he had made it a point to notice every detail. He suspected having the vet's physical attributes down, as well as having as many of his behavioral characteristics as possible, would be useful one day. Today was the day. He even thought he'd done a good job of picking out his wardrobe. It was unlikely he had matched what Pritchard had been wearing when he'd last been with Vogt, but it was close enough that he doubted she would notice. If so, he was prepared to explain how he'd had to change clothes while on the plane. The silly lady beside him had spilled her drink on his other outfit.

The elevator chimed, and the door opened. With a final gaze, Alex stepped into the elevator and pressed the button for the fourth floor.

HOMLIN STARED OUT THE window at the city lights below. Although it was only dusk, already most of the lights were on. He looked into the sky and saw the lights of a plane circling. He'd grown accustomed to the constant air traffic around D.C. Tonight, it seemed more noticeable, because on one of those flights might be one of the two humans who could thwart his plans—plans he'd been building on for almost ten years.

He knew where Vogt was, and he expected to hear from Alex within the hour of her tragic accident. That would leave only Pritchard. It was strange; even though he didn't know where Pritchard was at the moment, he was less concerned with him than he was with Vogt. Pritchard would show up wherever Vogt was. Hopefully, by the time that happened, it would be a matter of having Alex kill him as well. He'd rest easier once he knew both Vogt and Pritchard had been eliminated. There was no reason at this point in taking any other risks. Get rid of them once and for all. By this time next week, FreeForm would be in labs across the country, and Earth's destiny would be decided.

Not that his job would be over. There'd be the transition stage. He suspected the human race would put up some resistance. Then there would be the cleanup and the administration of the new order. No, in some ways his job was just beginning, but for Homlin the fun part, the challenging part, would be over and done. Within a few weeks, life would become pretty routine. Not all at once. At first, it would be hectic and from time to time a little nerve-wracking but in a much different way.

Would he request another settlement? That was the question he asked himself, but he was careful to not ask it too early. This one wasn't over yet. Vogt could pull something fast, and even Pritchard could cause some trouble. Better wait and be sure this was in the bag before looking towards the next planet.

PAT YANKED THE KNOT tight on her robe as she walked to the door. Peering through the peephole, she confirmed that it was Allan before opening the door and flinging herself into his arms.

"God, it's good to see you," Pat said as she pulled him into the room. "I didn't know I could miss anyone so much in such a short time."

"I've missed you too," Allan replied, blushing a little from so much attention.

Pat threw her arms around his neck again. "I don't know why, but I've been horny all day. Maybe it's pent-up energy from what we are about to do."

Allan smiled. "Well, we should see what we can do about it. I could hardly wait to get here myself. In fact"—he paused for a moment, the smile turning to a look of mischief—"I was thinking on the plane that it might be fun if we went a little beyond our normal lovemaking."

Pat pulled back a little from him, a look of mock horror on her face. "Whatever did you have in mind, sir?"

"Well, the idea came to me while I was waiting to get on the plane. Everywhere I looked, all the men were wearing ties. I thought that strange for a Sunday afternoon, but I started thinking about the old ties I have in my closet. Well, one thing led to another, and I remembered this old x-rated movie I saw while I was in college. This guy used his old ties to tie this luscious blonde to his bed."

Allan reached into his coat and pulled out a paper bag. "I stopped on the way at a second-hand store and made a minor purchase."

"You didn't!" Pat said as she grabbed the bag out of his hand and pulled out a handful of men's ties. "Silk. You don't go second class with your bondage, do you?"

"Well, I figure it might be a one time deal. Might as well go all out. What do you say? You interested in a little fun?"

Pat draped a couple of the ties around her neck and slid back into Allan's arms. "I don't know. I might be talked into it," she said as she gave him a long slow kiss.

The phone rang, interrupting the moment.

"Who could that be?" Allan asked as Pat walked over to pick it up.

"I don't know. Probably Dawn is checking to see that you got here all right."

Pat picked up the phone with a friendly, "Hello."

She listened to the familiar male voice on the other end of the phone. The identical voice that had asked, "Who could that be?"

"I just got into the D.C. airport. I'm coming right to the hotel. I wanted to hear your voice and be sure you were okay," Allan said on the other end of the phone.

What was going on here? Who was this on the phone? It couldn't be Allan. Allan was here in her room only a few feet away. Or was he? 5:15. It had been early, earlier than she'd expected him to be able to get to the hotel. She glanced at the clock radio. 5:40. Yes, it made more sense for him to be at the airport. Pat stifled a shudder that threatened to run the entire length of her body. Who was this man who wanted to tie her up? Allan was a fun loving guy, but the suggestion had been out of character for him.

"Hello. Are you okay?" the voice asked on the other end.

"Yes, everything is fine. Allan arrived a few minutes ago. He's a little tired and can't talk. I'll tell him you called, Dawn," Pat replied.

There was a pause on the other end. "Pat, hang in there. I'll be right there."

"That's fine. I'll be sure to take good care of him." She winked at Allan's impersonator. She hung up the phone and took a deep breath before turning back to her guest.

"Well, what are you doing with your clothes on?" she asked with a laugh.

The man smiled as he reached down and unfastened his belt. "We're going to have a lot of fun."

Pat strolled over to him and ran her hand along his chest. "We sure are," she replied. "I have only one request."

"What's that?" Allan's look-a-like asked as he removed his shirt.

"Ladies first. I want to tie you up and make mad passionate love to you first. Then you can do the same with me. Fair?"

He hesitated for only a moment. "If you like. Sure. We can do it that way. Whatever you say."

Pat stroked his bare chest with her fingernails, noticing as she did the subtle differences in his physique. Would she have noticed without the phone call? It was hard to say. "I promise you an experience you won't soon forget."

ALLAN RAN THROUGH THE airport like a man possessed, expecting at any moment to be hailed by one of the airport authorities, but evidently berserk men dashing through the crowd was a common occurrence. He was fortunate to find an empty cab as soon as he exited the automatic doors leading to the outside.

As he slipped into the back seat, he tossed a fifty-dollar bill through the small hole in the Plexiglas partition separating him from the driver. "I'll match that with another one if you get me to the Marque in thirty minutes or less."

The black man grabbed the bill, glanced at it a moment to be sure it was real, glanced at the nut who had leaped into his cab and smiled, showing a mouthful of white teeth.

"It's impossible, man. It's at least a forty minute drive, but we'll sure as hell go for the record." He slammed the car into gear and tore a layer of rubber off his tires as he sped away from the curb.

"I THOUGHT I'D DONATE a couple of pairs of nylon stockings to your tie collection," Pat said as she tossed a handful of them on the night table next to the bag of ties.

"You're really planning to tie me up tight, aren't you?"

"That's the idea, isn't it? What good is bondage if you know you can get right out of it?" Pat said with a little too much edge. She pushed him down on the bed. "Relax, this is going to be fun," she said more softly. "For the next little while, you are going to be my love slave. You'll have to do what I tell you and let me do the naughty things I've wanted to do with you."

"I think I can stand it," the man said. "Aren't you going to take your robe off? Fair is fair. If I'm going to be naked—"

"Who's giving the orders here?" Pat said in a mocking voice. "Your turn will come in a little bit. Now, shut up and behave yourself. I'm the master here." She pushed him down on the bed until his head rested on the pillow before she straddled his chest with her long legs.

"Close your eyes. Pretend you've been drugged. Imagine you've had too much to drink and passed out. I want you to be completely helpless for the next couple of minutes."

The impostor obliged, shutting his eyes and relaxing his entire body. Pat picked up his right hand and knotted a tie around his wrist, leaving plenty of fabric for the bedpost. She repeated the exercise with the other hand and both ankles. With his eyes shut, she pulled each extremity to the corner of the bed, stretching him in spread-eagle fashion. When all four corners were firmly attached, she slid off the bed for a moment.

"No peeking," she said as his eyelids fluttered. "You're out cold until I tell you otherwise." She grabbed the handful of stockings and tied two of them together. She repeated this with a second pair. She tied both sets around his neck and attached them to either side of the bedpost.

"That's tight," he said, although he kept his eyes closed.

It's supposed to be, you jerk, Pat thought. "If it's too tight, I'll loosen it in a moment. I want to be sure you have the full sensation of being helpless. I've read that is what makes this kind of sex so stimulating."

He must be one of Homlin's goons, she figured. In which case, Allan was probably not the only shape into which it could transform. She wasn't sure she'd be able to keep him bound if he started changing shapes, but she had to try.

With the last knot finally tied, she stepped away from the bed to study her handiwork. The alien was stretched across the bed in a large X, the center of the X accentuated by his erect penis, which pointed to the ceiling. She thought about tying it to one of the bedposts or better yet, cutting it off and..." *Never mind*, she thought. *It's time to finish the job.*

"In a moment, I want you to wake up; not yet. In a moment. When you do, I want you to stretch, like you're waking up, and take a big yawn. You'll notice that you can't move and panic a little. Only then do I want you to open your eyes. Got it?"

"Man, you're getting into this."

You can say that again, Pat thought as she balled the last nylon in her hand.

"Okay, begin to stretch, yawn big, and open your eyes."

The man did as he was told and at the peak of his yawn, Pat jammed the stocking deep into his mouth. He tried to cough it out and gagged. His eyes flew open, a look of stark panic on his face. He mumbled something unintelligible and struggled against his bonds but realized he was choking himself when he did.

"Who the fuck are you?" Pat asked as she slipped a tie around his mouth to hold the stocking in place. "Never mind. I know you can't answer me, and it's not important.

"You're not taking my planet. That's all there is to it. We won't let you. Not if I have anything to say about it, and obviously I do."

The man glared at her, his eyes filled with hate and fear. He mumbled, straining so hard against his ropes it looked like he might burst a blood vessel.

He stopped struggling and tried another strategy. As Pat watched, he began to change shapes, but Pat had been expecting it and was prepared. She threw a glass of cold water in his face to momentarily distract him.

"Oh no, you don't! I like you the way you are."

He shook his head to clear the water out of his eyes, glared back at her for a second, and began the metamorphosis again.

Pat picked up the heavy lamp sitting on the nightstand with both hands. Lifting it over her head, she brought it down with a crushing blow on the left side of his skull.

"Lights out," she said as the light bulb blew and the alien sunk into deep unconsciousness.

Oliver's Discovery
Monday, Dec. 6

Lenny was nodding off when the cab screeched to the entrance of the Marque. Before the cab had come to a full stop, the back door flew open and out stepped Allan Pritchard.

"Oh shit!" muttered Lenny as he grabbed the mobile phone and dialed Homlin's number. Homlin answered on the second ring, but already Allan had ducked into the hotel. He explained what had happened.

"Son-of-a..." Homlin said. He stopped in mid-sentence. "Okay, listen closely. I can't afford to risk losing both of you. Alex will have to handle those two on his own. The worst that could happen is they get away from him and show tomorrow, in which case we'll handle them along with the other two doctors. I'm sure Alex will have no trouble taking care of both of them. Get yourself back to your hotel and wait for my call."

Lenny broke the connection and set the phone down in the seat next to him. He started the car engine with a sigh of relief. Finally, he'd be able to go back and get a good night's sleep. He wondered if he should warn Alex but then decided Homlin was right. It was too risky. Besides, Homlin was boss. If he said to go back to the hotel, who was he to question the orders? He pulled the car away from the curb. Alex might be angry for being left, but he wouldn't be able to say anything. It was Homlin's orders.

HOMLIN RESTED THE PHONE in its cradle. He hated being so short-handed. Would Alex be okay? It was a calculated risk. He had hoped to have Vogt and Pritchard out of the picture before tomorrow morning's meeting, but it might not be possible. *It's getting tight,* Homlin thought. At the worst, Vogt and Pritchard might show up at the meeting and convince the panel members to reconsider. Homlin smiled as he pictured the scene. Well, let them come. He would make sure they received a warm welcome.

ALLAN WAS SURPRISED to find Pat's door partially ajar, kept open by the metal bar used for additional security at night. He peered through the crack and listened for voices but could see and hear nothing. He pushed the door open an inch at a time.

"Come on in, honey. Everything is under control."

Pat's calm words were the most reassuring sound he thought he'd ever heard. He pushed the door open and walked in. His eyes fell on the naked figure spread eagle on the bed. At first glance, it looked like his twin, but on closer inspection, he noticed that the figure was different, less sharp and distorted.

"He tried to change shape, probably to his true form, but I changed his mind for him." Pat walked out of the bathroom and into Allan's arms. She threw her arms around his neck and kissed him passionately. "I'm so glad to see you. I don't think I've ever been so frightened. Not since that night on the spaceship, anyway. Sit down while I finish packing. We're getting out of here."

As she packed, Pat related what had happened since the phone call. Allan sat in the chair next to the bed, glancing first to Pat and then to the form lying tied to the bed. His anger bubbled as Pat told her story. By the time she finished, he was filled with emotion—hate for the alien that had impersonated him, pride and awe for the woman he loved.

"You're something else," he said when she finished the story. He shook his head. "You really are some kind of woman. I would never have had the nerve to do what you did. What if he had caught on?"

"Not likely; his hormones were running so rampant I think he would have done anything I asked him if it meant getting a chance to me. I used what was driving him to my advantage." She closed the suitcase she'd been tossing clothes in and snapped it shut.

"Now what?" Allan asked.

"Well, we've gotta get out of here, that's for sure. No telling how many others of these monsters are around."

"What about him?" Allan asked, nodding towards the bed.

"I've got an old friend in town. We used to work together at B.I.U.F.O. I'd like for the two of them to meet. I gave him a call before you arrived. He wasn't home, but I left a message on his machine. If I know my friend, he won't be able to resist. We're not waiting around to find out. Where are your bags?" Pat asked as she picked hers up off the bed.

Allan's face flushed. "Back at the airport. They never crossed my mind once I heard your voice on the phone."

"Well, that pretty much answers where we're going from here. Keep your eyes open on the way out. There's a chance we might be followed." Pat walked over to the nightstand next to the bed and laid a folded piece of paper on it.

"What's that?" Allan asked.

"A note introducing my friend to Romeo here. I don't want him to be unprepared." Pat glanced at her watch.

"All we have to do is hang low for another fourteen hours and be sure we're at that meeting tomorrow morning. I haven't figured out exactly what we're going to do to unmask Homlin, but one way or the other, we're going to stop him at that meeting. I don't care if I have to take an Uzi with me and mow the whole lot of them down."

"You're kidding, of course." Allan shut the door to the room, being sure to leave the metal bar in place.

"I'm dead serious," Pat replied.

OLIVER CUT OFF THE answering machine and rewound the tape, erasing the message as he did so.

"Any messages?" his wife, Ellen, asked as she came into the room, her hands full with packages from their shopping trip. Sunday afternoons had been her favorite time to shop for the family. Oliver hated it but obliged her. She had to put up with a lot more from him. It was the least he could do.

"No, nothing," Oliver answered, distracted by the flurry of thoughts and memories the brief message had stirred. "I need to go out for a while."

"Well, okay, but I was hoping to have dinner a little early tonight. The kids are coming over later."

"Start without me." Oliver pulled his jacket back on. "I may be a while."

The familiar look of concern appeared on his wife's face. "Where are you going?"

He walked over to where she was standing and hugged her. "I've got some unfinished business that needs my attention. An old friend needs me. I'll explain later."

Oliver walked into his office. He pulled his keys out of his pocket and unlocked the bottom drawer of his desk. He opened it and removed the revolver. It had been years since he'd fired it, but he had made a point of cleaning it on a regular basis. He had never known why. Now, he knew. It was a strange weapon to take on a deer hunt, but it was a most unusual deer he was hunting.

OLIVER FOUND THE ROOM exactly as it had been described in the message. The door propped open with the security bolt and a lone naked figure tied securely to the bed. A bizarre scene for most people, but Oliver took it in stride. In the twenty years he'd been with B.I.U.F.O., he'd adapted to going with the flow, no matter how strange.

Oliver walked over to the still form and checked its pulse. Still alive. At least he wasn't walking in on a murder case. He sat down in the chair next to the bed. Now what? He glanced around the room, and his eyes fell on the note on the bed stand. He felt as though he was on a treasure hunt, each message giving him another clue without any clear answer.

He recognized the neat handwriting despite the ten years it had been since he'd last seen it. He read the note three times. Ten years. She'd been on the hunt all this time. It was hard to believe. Why had Pat dragged him back into it after all these years? Who was this unconscious person tied so securely to the bed? The note had been emphatic about one thing. The naked man was extremely dangerous and should be kept securely bound no matter what. Oliver decided to heed Pat's warning. He sat back in the chair and waited for the man to come to. Despite the long day, his nerves were too much on edge for him to worry about falling asleep. He patted the revolver nestled in its shoulder holster. It felt like a long lost friend coming home.

It was good to relax after the many hours of shopping. He bet they'd walked five miles through the three malls they'd visited. Next time he would stay in the car. He could usually persuade Ellen to let him do that about every third trip. As he settled in to wait, his tired muscles began to unknot. It was good to sit down. Very good indeed.

Oliver's eyelids slowly fell to half-mast then three quarter. Within five minutes he was asleep.

OLIVER AWOKE WITH A start. His unfocused eyes fell on the thrashing form in front of him. *What the hell?* He squinted his eyes and pressed his fists into them to clear his vision. It wasn't possible what he was seeing. The bound man was changing shapes in front of his eyes. He struggled against his ropes, tossing his head from side to side despite the tight nylons encircling his neck. His thrashing shook the bed.

Oliver squeezed out of the chair and backed away from the bed, reaching for the .45 as he did so. He must be having a nightmare. What was happening in front of him was impossible. Even as he had the thoughts, he knew he was not asleep. His mind flashed back to a night over ten years ago—the glowing ship, the wounded deer, the explosion, and the cover-up. He knew what he was witnessing was connected. It had not gone away. Although it had been successfully hidden by the agency and the bureaucracy, it had continued to fester like a malignant abscess. An abscess that was coming to a head.

The half-man, half-beast noticed for the first time he was not alone in the room. His hate-filled eyes met Oliver's for a brief moment. The two locked gazes; time stopped. If looks could kill, Oliver would have exploded on the spot. Instead, he came to an immediate decision. Nothing so vile and hateful should live. Not on this planet. Not here on earth. Not if he could help it. He could.

Oliver raised the .45 and took aim. The form continued to alter in front of him as he gazed down the barrel. It had lost all resemblance to a man by the time Oliver squeezed the trigger four times. The four slugs struck the struggling form in the chest. Bluish-red blood flowed from each wound and down onto the white sheets. The alien continued to struggle for another minute as its life forces ebbed.

Only when the last throes were complete did Oliver pick up the phone. He waited for the front desk to answer.

"I want to report a murder," he said calmly into the receiver. "Please send security to Room 444 and call the police." Not waiting for a reply, he placed the receiver back in its cradle. He stared at the still form. Thank God it hadn't changed back into the human form. That would have been difficult to explain. He had enough explaining to do as it was.

FDA Confrontation

Monday 6:00 a.m., Dec. 6

Homlin hung up the phone. Everything back at Biogentrix was set. A line of twenty trucks, each filled with insulated shipping crates housing six to twelve individual FreeForm larvae sat inside the grounds of the lab waiting for the signal to roll. Once the papers were signed, the trucks would be free to deliver their cargo. Some of them would hit the road carrying their packages across the country. Half of them would travel to various shipping and postal agencies, including the Unite States Postal Service.

Within forty-eight hours, FreeForm would be thoroughly circulating through the arteries of the country. It would be irretrievable, and there'd be no turning back, no stopping the infiltration. It would take another four to six weeks for the FreeForm larvae to begin to be nursed along by the hundreds of research facilities, but it would be impossible to stop the process. Researchers were too unpredictable, too difficult to stop once they had a new toy like FreeForm with which to play. Even if the federal agencies realized what was happening and tried to stop it, the dissemination would be too far along to stop the development of thousands of the larvae. Homlin had seen it often before on other planets. The next few hours were the critical juncture. How long it took for FreeForm to overcome the planet might vary by several weeks, but the outcome was inevitable.

Time to shower and get dressed. Today was a big day for his people. His ten years on this planet had been leading to this day. He intended to enjoy every minute of it. As he turned the water on, he wondered if Vogt and Pritchard would dare to show up at the meeting. His bets were on them doing just that. He would be disappointed if they didn't try some last ditch effort. *Let them come*, Homlin thought, lathering himself with soap. This time he was prepared for Vogt. He wouldn't underestimate her again.

The trucks would roll despite Vogt's efforts, and most important of all, Vogt and Pritchard would have played their best card without winning the hand. He would make sure it was the last card they would ever play against him again.

MONDAY 7:30 AM

Pat slipped into the passenger seat of the rental car next to Allan. The warm interior of the car felt good, but she found she couldn't stop shivering.

"There's no way to get the Uzi or any other type of firearm in there," she said as she closed the door. "There are security stations at every door with metal detectors. At least this means we'll be on even terms. No guns for us and none for Homlin. I'll settle for those odds."

"It also means we'll have to depend on our evidence to stop him," Allan pointed out.

"He's not getting the okay to go ahead with his plans. Evidence or no evidence, we've got to stop him right here, right now." Pat's determination came through clenched teeth.

As she finished speaking, a black Lincoln Continental pulled to the curb thirty yards in front of them, and out stepped Dr. Fredrick Homlin, dressed in a black wool coat and carrying a matching briefcase.

"My, doesn't he look dapper this morning?" Pat said with crystals of sarcasm in her voice. "No one would ever suspect, would they?"

"Looks like hundreds of other professional people coming to work on Monday after a pleasant weekend with the family," Allan agreed as he cut the car engine off. "Shall we follow him?"

"Give him a few seconds to get ahead," Pat replied. "I wonder where his entourage is. I don't like that he's by himself."

"The odds are in our favor if it comes down to anything physical," Allan pointed out.

"True," Pat said, but she was unconvinced. "Where do you think his bodyguards could be?" Pat asked, a worried look knitting her brow. "Well, let's consider luck is starting to shine on us," she said after a moment. "Let's go stop an alien."

Before getting out of the car, she slid the machine gun under the front seat and removed her revolver. She felt naked and defenseless without it. She reminded herself that Homlin would be without any firearms as well. *Not defenseless*, her mind reminded her. He could transform himself into a brutal killing machine. He would be more than capable of killing her, Allan, and no telling how many others if need be. Their best chance would be to jump him before he had the opportunity to change. It was going to be an interesting morning.

Homlin disappeared inside the federal building, and Allan and Pat strolled behind him towards the same doors. As they entered the building, Pat worried the security guards would stop them from following Homlin if they didn't have proper papers giving them entry but was relieved to find that no such surveillance was taking place. The checkpoint seemed only to keep weapons outside.

Homlin continued through the security station, unaware or unconcerned with whether or not he was being followed. *He's too damn cocky*, Pat thought. *No bodyguards, not the least bit concerned about being followed. He must know Allan and I are around. He should care. He should be sneaking around or be surrounded by his gorillas*. Pat's alarm system, finely honed over the last ten years, blared.

Nothing she could do about it. There was nothing else to do but follow him to the meeting room. Maybe he had sent his gorillas on ahead or they were at this moment closing in on Allan and her. Despite herself, Pat glanced behind her at dozens of indifferent faces, governmental executives coming to work on Monday morning, bored, dead, unenthusiastic about their jobs, but there were no signs of anyone threatening the two of them.

"What are you looking for?" Allan whispered as they walked through the security check.

"I don't know. I don't have a good feeling about this. He's too confident, too assured. He should be nervous. Where the hell are the rest of his people?" Pat whispered back.

"I'd tell you to calm down except I notice I can't get my knees to stop knocking myself."

"Oh hell. Did you remember to bring the photos?"

Allan held the briefcase. "Everything is in here."

Pat breathed a little easier. Allan's calm demeanor worked. She noticed the tension ease a little. She had a sudden thought. *What if Homlin's meeting wasn't on the first floor*? How would they be able to follow him? She couldn't imagine stepping in the same elevator with him. They could lose him and not find him for hours. She noticed a directory between the elevator doors they were approaching. The letters she'd photocopied had been on FDA letterhead. FDA offices were on the fourth floor.

She watched as Homlin stepped into one of the waiting elevators.

"What do we do?" Allan asked as Homlin's elevator door closed.

"We take a risk and go to the fourth floor," Pat said as she pointed to the directory. "Pray all the FDA offices are on the same floor."

THEY FILED INTO THE crowded elevator and requested the fourth floor. They stopped at each floor on the way. As they stepped out on the fourth floor, Pat glanced down the hall in both directions. At first, she didn't see Homlin and her breath caught in her throat. A man in a gray suit stepped to one side, and Homlin was strolling down the hall. He stopped halfway and entered one of the offices to the right.

"Bingo!" Pat pointed in the direction Homlin had disappeared. "We'll wait out here for a few minutes and see who else enters. There's no hurry now that we know where he is."

Allan nodded.

In the next ten minutes, five other men exited from the elevator, strolled down the hall, and entered the same office into which Homlin had disappeared. Five more minutes went by. Pat glanced at her watch. 8:00 a.m. on the dot.

"Should we go in?" Allan asked as the hallways began to clear.

"No, we'll wait for the meeting to get underway a bit. I want Homlin to think he's home free before we pay our visit."

"I wish I had a cigarette," Allan said.

"Silly, you don't smoke."

"It seems like a good time to take it up."

Allan sat down on a cushioned bench stationed between the elevator doors under another directory.

Pat paced up and down the hallway, too nervous to sit. She continued to glance at her watch. At 8:10 she walked over to where Allan was sitting.

"I don't think anyone else is going to arrive for the meeting. They should be underway. I don't want them signing whatever they're planning to sign while we wait outside. Let's go see what we can stir up."

With a heavy sigh, Allan stood and grasped the handle of the briefcase. "I'm with you all the way." He gave her a reassuring smile.

"Thanks; it makes a lot of difference," Pat replied. They turned and walked down the hall.

All eyes turned to the door as Pat and Allan stepped into the meeting room.

"I'm sorry, but this is a private—" one of the men seated at the long table across from Homlin said.

"I know what the meeting is," Pat interrupted, walking straight towards Homlin. "I have evidence to file against this 'man.'" The note of sarcasm on the last word was unmistakable.

"Why, if it isn't Ms. Vogt and her trained vet," Homlin said as he stood, a twisted smile of unconcern on his face. "Do come in and join us. You say you have something to contribute to this discussion?"

"We most certainly do." Allan stepped between Pat and Homlin. He glared at Homlin for several seconds before breaking eye contact and turning his attention to the five men sitting on the other side of the table.

"This man must not be allowed to transport anything from Biogentrix," Allan said as he opened his briefcase and pulled a file folder from it. "We have evidence which proves that he is an enemy of this country. For that matter, he is a threat to humankind. We must not play into his hands by allowing him to spread his seeds across this country."

"What on earth are you talking about?" one of the other men asked as he picked up the folder and leafed through it.

"The material you have in your hands is a compilation of reports uncovering the most diabolical plot to overthrow this and other governments in the world," Pat said. "I have been following this 'man' for the past ten years. He tried to kill me on the interstellar ship which brought him to this world.

"Some of those papers are the few official reports that were not destroyed by B.I.U.F.O. when the landing site of an alien spaceship was investigated. I was on the investigation team. I was the only one who saw the alien that was on the ship. This being," she said pointing to Homlin, "is attempting to get permission to disseminate the larval form of his race across this country."

"This is the most preposterous story I have ever heard," a third man said as he grabbed some of the papers out of the folder.

Homlin stood calmly, studying Pat and Allan, shaking his head.

"Gentlemen, I'm afraid this poor lady has indeed been following me for many years, ever since she was released from B.I.U.F.O. for being mentally incompetent. I've never quite understood why she picked me out of nowhere to be a major player in her little fantasy. For the most part, I've humored her. Occasionally, when it has gotten out of hand, I've had to have one of my employees take action.

"It's unfortunate that she is so unstable. She seems to have found a second mental case to keep her company. Dr. Harrison, if you would be so kind as to call security so we could proceed with our meeting."

"I'd be happy to," Dr. Harrison said as he picked up the phone.

"Not so damn fast!" Pat yelled. At the same moment, Allan lunged across the table and knocked the phone out of Harrison's hand. "Look at the damn papers. It's all there. This is not a man, and FreeForm is not what you think it is. I know it sounds crazy, but there is at least enough evidence there for you to open an investigation. You can't ignore—"

Two of the other council members pulled Allan away from Harrison. Harrison picked the phone off the floor. "Send security to Room 422 quickly. It's an emergency."

Pat started around the table where the two men were struggling to keep Allan away from Harrison but found her way blocked by Homlin and one of the other council members. The odds were not looking good. No one had even bothered to look at their evidence. Her story was simply too farfetched. True or not, it was too much for anyone to take seriously. What good would it be to try to overpower the committee? It certainly wouldn't persuade them to consider her story. Homlin obviously had them eating out of his hands.

Pat stopped a few feet away from Homlin and the other man. Her mind raced. What were the chances of strangling Homlin on the spot? No chance. Homlin looked to be a pretty even match, and she doubted the other five men would stand around and watch a person be murdered.

She was staring at Homlin when she heard the door behind her open. It seemed security in this building was damn quick. Pat turned towards the door as a large man in a rumpled suit entered the room, followed by four men in military uniforms. Each of the four men carried revolvers pointed towards the ceiling but in readiness to pull down in a deadly aim at any instant.

"Hold it right there!" the man in the rumpled suit shouted. The two men who had been struggling with Allan froze and relaxed their grip on him. Allan yanked himself away from them.

"Oliver! It's so good to see you again," Pat said. "Thanks for bringing the cavalry."

"No problem, Pat. It's the least I owed you after all these years," Oliver replied. "Which one is the alien?"

"Well, that one for sure." Pat pointed to Homlin. " I wouldn't be surprised if we didn't have a few more in here."

"What?" Allan and Oliver asked at the same time.

"It dawned on me during the excitement where Homlin's bodyguards were." Pat turned and met Allan's puzzled look. "What better way to assure the meeting would be a success than having the voters completely on your side. Oliver, I strongly suggest you take the entire committee under custody. I imagine it won't be too hard to figure out who is and who isn't human."

"With pleasure. Men, place everyone except the lady under arrest."

"Oh, Oliver, not that one there," Pat said, pointing to Allan. "He's with me." She winked in Allan's direction and walked towards him.

As Pat walked by Homlin, there was a sudden blur of motion. Homlin yanked Pat in front of him, shielding himself from the aim of the marksmen with her body. He grabbed her with his left arm around her shoulders. As he brought his right hand to her throat, the hand melted into an animal-like paw with six razor-sharp claws, each one pressed against the tender flesh of Pat's throat.

"No one move or I will have no choice but to kill this lovely specimen!" Homlin shouted as he backed himself against the wall, pulling Pat with him. He slithered his way along the wall in the direction of the door. "Put your weapons down, now!"

Oliver nodded to his men, who did as they were instructed.

"You can't get out of here," Oliver said as he took a step in Homlin's direction.

"Don't be so sure," Homlin replied. "Now, kick one of those revolvers over here. Nice and easy. I warn you. I'll rip her throat out if anyone makes a stupid move."

Oliver did as he was told. Homlin continued to pull Pat toward the door, stopping a foot or two from the gun lying on the floor.

"Easy, everyone," Homlin said as Allan took a step towards him. Homlin stooped down and picked up the revolver. When he had it in his left hand, he stuck it into Pat's ribs below her left breast but continued to hold her against his body with the sharp claws of his other hand.

"Everyone back away from the door and lie face down on the floor." The people in the room complied except four of the five committee members, who remained standing.

When everyone was on the floor, Homlin took the last couple of steps to the door. He stared at each of the men as though contemplating whether to chance shooting them in the back of the head.

Homlin looked at the four men who were standing. "You're on your own. Your last assignment from me is to be sure I'm not followed for several minutes. Is that clear?"

The four men nodded. Before anyone else could move, Homlin slipped out the door with Pat and was gone.

The instant the door closed there was a mad dash to get to the remaining three guns. The four 'men' who had clearly been identified as Homlin's men dove for the weapons as did the uniformed men. No one was as fast as Oliver, who stopped the blur of action by firing a shot from his own revolver he pulled from his shoulder holster.

"Back off there, or I'll blow you away!" he shouted at the top of his lungs. The four conspirators stopped in their tracks and stared at him. For two or three seconds, Harrison, who stood in front of the other three, studied Oliver.

"You heard what Homlin said!" Harrison shouted as he lunged toward Oliver, followed closely by the other three.

Oliver fired point blank into the charging Harrison. The slug caught him full in the chest, but still, the big man charged. Oliver fired two more rounds. One hit Harrison in the left shoulder; the other removed most of Harrison's skull on the left side.

The momentum carried Harrison's dead body crashing into Oliver. What followed was a massive free-for-all between Oliver and his men and the three remaining aliens. As the aliens fought, they transformed into hunter/survivors, making the contest's outcome much less predictable.

Allan did not stay to find out the outcome of the battle. Instead, he dashed out the door after Homlin and Pat. As he ran down the hallway, he prayed he would see the two further down the corridor running towards the elevator, but they were nowhere to be seen. Where could they have gone? How could Homlin have disappeared so fast?

Allan ran to the elevators and stared at the number display above each door. None of the four elevators were even close to the fourth floor. The stairs. They must have taken the stairs. Allan rushed toward the stairway door. He flung the door open and rushed through.

As the door closed, he heard a muffled cry behind him, but before he could turn to investigate, he felt the searing pain of a blow to his skull and found himself dropping into the dark pit of unconsciousness.

Hunting Homlin

Monday 10:00 a.m., Dec. 6

The pain threatened to lift the dome of his skull from the rest of his head. As Allan struggled to regain consciousness, it ebbed and flowed with the pounding of his heart. The first sign he was winning the battle was the pain returning. The second was the muffled sound of men talking.

"I think he's coming around, Oliver," Allan heard through the mud puddle of his mind. He shook his head and regretted it as the jackhammering pain increased in volume and frequency.

"Get me some cold water," he heard after an interminable time. A little later, he felt the chill of a wet compress being applied to his forehead. After several more minutes, he forced his eyes open. The light sent shards of pain deep into his skull, but he refused to submit to the black ebb that called to him. He kept his eyes open.

"Where am I?" he finally asked. A face, faintly familiar but he couldn't remember from where, came into blurry view.

"Take it easy. He slugged you pretty hard."

"Who?" Allan asked, uncertain what was going on.

"Homlin, of course," the man answered.

Homlin. Oh yeah. It flashed back to him. He'd been chasing Homlin. The door to the stairs, the muffled sound, and nothing. Allan pushed himself to sit, but the pain was too great.

"Not so quick. You're lucky to be alive. It certainly wasn't because Homlin pulled his punch."

"I believe it," Allan replied with a moan. "Did you catch him?"

"No. Not yet. He escaped the building. We haven't figured out how. There is an all-points bulletin out for him, though. He won't get far."

The FreeForm! What had happened with the pending shipment? Through dry lips, Allan asked the question.

"Oh, don't worry. We've confiscated everything at Homlin's lab and game reserve. It's under government lock-up. If Homlin is stupid enough to show at either place, we'll nab him."

Allan sat once more. This time, despite the pain, he was successful. He was on the long table in the conference room.

"We found you in the stairwell. I had a couple of my men carry you in here. You've been out almost two hours."

Two hours! Two hours and they hadn't found Pat and Homlin. He had to look for her. There was no telling what Homlin would do to her. Allan gently swung his legs over the side of the table and fought a wave of vertigo. He felt like ten hangovers had been piled on him at once. He shut his eyes for a moment and waited for the vertigo and nausea to pass. When it finally did, he lifted his head and looked at the man.

"Who the hell are you, anyway?"

"Oliver Sykes. I was Pat's superior when she was with B.I.U.F.O. I helped to cover up the story."

Allan nodded. Pat had spoken about Oliver during one of their late-night conversations lying in front of the wood stove. It seemed like it had been years ago but was only a few weeks.

A uniformed man—Allan thought it was one of the men that had burst into the meeting but he couldn't be sure—handed Oliver a note.

Oliver read the note, crumpled it and tossed it in the vicinity of the trash can.

"What did it say?" Allan asked.

"The D.C. police have had a report of a car stolen from the parking lot across the street. It could have been taken by Homlin."

Oh, hell, Allan thought. Homlin's got a car. How in the hell would they ever find him? He struggled to his feet. Oliver grabbed his arm to steady him. He shrugged it off.

"Where do you think you're going?" Oliver asked.

"To find Homlin before he kills Pat." Allan stumbled unsteadily towards the door.

"Do you think you can find him?"

"I'll find him. I've got to," Allan replied without turning around.

"Wait. I'll go with you," Oliver said. "We can take my car. I've got a CB radio. We can stay in touch with the police search."

"Fine with me." Allan continued down the hall towards the elevators.

As the two men waited for the elevator, Allan glanced over at the larger man. "You wouldn't happen to have a couple of aspirins, would you?"

Oliver smiled. "Not on me, but I think there's a bottle in my glove compartment. I might even have a flask of whiskey to wash them down with."

"Sounds like the right combination to me," Allan replied.

THE TRUNK SMELLED OF old rags, rubber, and gas fumes. On top of which it was cold and damp, but worst of all it was pitch black and tiny. Pat fought the urge to scream. She had tried that for at least thirty minutes with no results except to worsen her headache.

Despite her winter coat, she was chilled to the bone. Her hands and feet were numb, and her muscles ached from the close confinement. She wasn't even sure into what kind of car she had been stuffed. Not much more than a subcompact if the trunk space was any indication. The gas and exhaust fumes added to her headache and discomfort.

How long had she been locked inside the trunk? She could only guess since she was unable to see her watch dial. *It's a fine mess I've gotten myself into this time*, she thought as she struggled to pull her coat tighter around her.

I completely blew it. I had the chance to stop Homlin once and for all, and I failed. Well, not entirely. Oliver had come through—finally. Or had he? Who knew?

She'd heard gunshots as Homlin dragged her down the hall, but who had done the shooting? Had the shipment been stopped or not? That was the question. Not knowing the answer to it contributed more to her headache than the fumes or the bump on the head.

They'd been traveling for quite a while without stopping. Pat figured she'd been in the trunk for at least a couple hours. Except for the sound of the rear tires on the road and an occasional car passing, no sound penetrated through the trunk. No doubt they had left the city, but heading in what direction? Where was Homlin taking her, and more importantly what did he have in mind once they arrived? None of the possible answers her mind came up with for that last question appealed to her.

Yes indeed, she'd gotten herself into a fine mess this time.

AS OLIVER AND ALLAN opened their respective doors to Oliver's sedan, they stopped and stared at each other over the roof.

"Where do you think we should go?" Allan finally asked the question that was on both of their minds.

Oliver laughed and shook his head. "Damn if I know. Where do you go to look for an escaped alien on the run?"

"Well, there's got to be something we can do. We can't sit around here." The words jangled in Allan's head, tormenting his headache that much more.

"I've got an idea. Let's go," Oliver said as he climbed behind the wheel and started the engine.

"Where are we going?" Allan asked, climbing in beside him.

"Sooner or later, hopefully, sooner, someone is going to spot the baby blue Toyota Homlin stole. When they do, we want to be ready to get to it fast. I've got an old friend, James Stepp. These days he flies a traffic copter for one of the local TV stations. He'll be more than happy to take us wherever we need to go."

"Now you're talking," Allan said. For the first time since being knocked unconscious, his head felt like it might one day stop pumping pain down to his toes. No day soon, but...

Monday 1:45 pm

"Allan, wake up." A firm hand shook his shoulder. Allan turned his head to one side. He opened his eyes to find himself staring at the ice pack he'd been using to relieve his headache. He had shut his eyes for only a minute, he felt certain, but when he put the pack back on his head, all that was left was a bag of cool water.

"What's happening?" he asked as he tossed the used-up ice pack on the bed.

"They've found the Toyota," Oliver replied.

"All right. Now we're getting somewhere."

"Abandoned. Neither Homlin nor Pat were anywhere around it," Oliver finished.

"Shit, you've got to be kidding. Are you sure?"

"No question about it. The report came in from the Pulaski, Virginia police." Oliver sat down on the bed beside Allan.

"Pulaski, Virginia? Where's that?"

"Western part of the state a couple of hours north of the North Carolina border."

The two men stared at each other for several seconds. "Are you thinking what I'm thinking?" Allan finally asked.

"Don't know, but I'm thinking the bastard is returning to his old stomping grounds," Oliver replied.

"You don't think he'd be stupid enough to go back into Biogentrix, do you?" Allan picked up the spent ice pack and tossed it from one hand to the other.

"No. He must know we've got both places staked out."

"Well, do you think we can get James to fly us that far?"

"Sure, no problem. While you were resting, James called his TV station and told him a little of the story. Don't worry; I didn't tell him what Homlin is. I said we were looking for a kidnapper. He told his station he has a chance at an exclusive. They've given him carte blanche to fly us anywhere we want. We're checking for any other reports of stolen vehicles in the area. It won't take us long to pick Homlin's trail up again. Let's go."

Allan tossed the ice pack to Oliver. "Do you think I could get a refill on this before we go?"

MONDAY 1:05 PM

The trunk of the Mazda was a little larger and didn't smell quite as bad as the last car, but it was far from being a comfortable way to travel. Homlin had given Pat no chance to escape on the change. Being stuck in the trunk for four or five hours had left her at a distinct disadvantage. When they'd finally stopped, Homlin had left her in the trunk for quite some time. After a while, Pat wondered if he'd abandoned her with the car, but about the time she'd realized that had happened, she heard Homlin unlocking the trunk. She wanted to be ready to jump at the first chance, but her stiff body had refused to cooperate at the critical moment.

As Homlin unlocked the trunk, Pat pushed the trunk lid with all her might in the hope of catching him off guard. Unfortunately, the stiff muscles of her legs had made the attempt appear in slow motion. Besides, Homlin had been ready and was standing several feet away from the car by the time Pat crawled out of the trunk. Although he had both hands in his pockets, he left little doubt in Pat's mind that one of his hands was pointing a gun straight at her.

They were in a small town Pat didn't recognize in what looked to be the only public parking lot. Homlin had already scouted around before letting Pat out of the trunk and had found a Mazda with the keys left in it. Pat glanced over at the small building where the attendant should have been, but there was no one inside.

"He's taking a little nap," Homlin said with a short nod in the direction Pat was looking. "He looked awfully beat when I drove up. Of course, not as beat as he is now."

“Get in,” Homlin said as he unlocked the trunk of their new car. "Your carriage awaits."

"I'm not getting in another damn trunk," Pat said, crossing her arms in front of her.

"Have it your own way," Homlin replied. "Would you prefer I kill you here in broad daylight or simply knock the shit out of you and toss you in the trunk?"

“Neither,” Pat replied, deciding to change tactics. "Let me sit in the front with you. I promise I won't do anything stupid."

"You already have, but it won't work. Now get in. This is the last time I'm going to ask so nicely." Homlin nodded toward the open trunk.

"I'm going to get you for this," Pat muttered under her breath as she climbed into the trunk. "You wait and see if I don't."

"You've been a worthy opponent, Ms. Vogt. Perseverance and a never-say-die attitude are your strong suits. Unfortunately, you don't realize the game is over. Now, I suggest you lower your head a trifle more this time unless you want another bump on your head."

Pat did as she was told and a few seconds later found herself in total darkness again in a little larger and less smelly trunk, but she was completely powerless. The feeling was becoming impossible to bear. She had to do something, but not just anything. She would only get one chance, and she had to make it count. How would she know when the one chance was here?

Well, I have my instincts, she told herself. *I've been operating on skill, training, and instincts for the last ten years with this animal. Why should it be any different now?* She wouldn't wait for the right moment. She'd do whatever she could to create the moment, and when it came, she'd be sure to be ready.

Like right now. What can I do to prepare myself for that moment? She pondered the question for a few minutes. She needed something to balance the sides. Homlin was stronger than she was. And he had a gun. She did not. On top of which he could change into many different forms, including the killing machine that had almost taken her life on their first meeting.

Okay, how to balance the scale? She needed a weapon. What? The manufacturers of automobiles hadn't yet offered automatic rifles as optional equipment. What could she hope to find in the trunk of a late model Mazda?

No sooner had she asked the question that she had the answer. Cars came with a spare tire (not much of a weapon there), a jack (a little better but too bulky), and a tire iron! That was it. A tire iron or lug wrench, whatever they were called. Most cars came with one. Most of them lay in some dark recess of the trunk and were never needed. Well, one was needed now.

Pat rummaged in the dark with her hands, checking every corner, every crack, every irregularity. She finally found a little compartment built into the side of the trunk. She pulled the plastic cover off and pulled out a small packet of tools. She opened the tool case and found two unexpected prizes—Phillip's head and flathead screwdrivers. Weapons!

She dug her hands back into the hidden compartment. The only thing left was the jack, tightly bolted to the floor of the compartment. Damn!

Had the owner of the car lost the lug wrench? Surely not. It was a relatively new car. It was doubtful the owner had ever had a flat tire. Keep looking. The lug wrench must be around here somewhere.

Pat stopped her search for a moment. Where would you put a lug wrench if not with the jack and the other tools? With the spare tire, of course. She felt around with her feet and hands, but there was no tire. Impossible. There had to be a spare. Where did they put the spare in these tiny Japanese cars? They certainly didn't bolt them to the outside like with her jeep. No, they hid them, like they hid the tool kit and jack.

She continued to fish around in the dark, looking for another hidden compartment. It would have to be a larger compartment. One large enough to hide a spare tire. Underneath her. It had to be on the floor of the trunk. Of course. She felt along the edge of the trunk until she found a hold to pull the floor covering away. It came away easily. A good sign.

Pat pressed herself against the back of the rear seat, pulling the covering towards her. She shoved it under her body so she could get to the false bottom. She found the small space increasingly claustrophobic as she fought to move the flooring out of the way. Finally, she had it off to the side enough to reach down and feel...the tire. Victory!

No, not victory at all. She wasn't looking for the tire. It was the lug wrench she needed. Was it down there or not? She felt around the tire but could feel nothing like a long iron rod. She determined that the tire was securely bolted to the floor of the car. The bolt ran through the center of the tire and was held in place with a large wing nut. It took her several minutes before she was able to loosen the nut.

She was sweating. Her activity had at least taken the chill off, although her feet were like blocks of ice. Finally, she was able to remove the wing nut completely. The tire was smaller than she expected, but she remembered hearing someone in her office complain about the toy tires they were putting in new cars these days. Although it was small, it was heavy. She struggled to get her hands underneath the tire. She was pressed so hard against the back seat that she found it increasingly hard to breathe. *Calm; I must stay calm.*

She relaxed for a moment and caught her breath. *Please, have the lug wrench be under there*, she prayed. After a moment, she lifted the tire again, using one arm to lever the tire while searching with the other hand. Her left hand felt what she'd been looking for. It was a long L shaped iron rod, slightly larger at the short end of the L. The tip of the long end was pointed like a large flat-headed screwdriver. Perfect!

The scales were beginning to balance. It took her a few minutes to get the wrench out from under the tire, but it finally came. She hugged her newly found prize against her chest. For the first time in several hours, she knew she had a chance to live through this ordeal. A small chance, but definitely a chance. It was enough. It was all she ever expected out of life. A small chance. She put the tire and floorboard back in place.

MONDAY 2:05 PM

In his younger days, Allan had thought flying in a helicopter would be a lot of fun, but as the WXYY traffic copter lifted off the ground with the three men inside, Allan couldn't grasp why he'd ever had such a silly thought.

Although James had assured them several times that it was safe to have all three of them in the copter, as Allan felt his right side pressed against the outer glass, he doubted the man's judgment. Oliver was a large man and took more than his share of the seat, leaving less than a foot and a half for Allan to wedge into. It was going to be a long flight and far from fun.

"How long before we get to Pulaski?" he yelled to be heard over the sound of the blades above them.

"Hard to say for sure. Depends a little on the weather and the winds. I'd guess two to two-and-a-half hours," James replied as he steered hard left to miss some high tension wires, and added, "Don't worry, this baby has an auxiliary fuel tank, so we won't be running out of fuel. I've learned my lesson about trying to fly on fumes."

Allan groaned. It was going to be a long ride.

Pack Animal

Monday 3:25 pm, Dec. 6

Homlin glanced over at the passenger seat beside him. His eyes fell on the folder of papers the car salesman had given to him. He smiled. Buying the car instead of stealing another one had probably earned him at least a couple of hours. On top of which, the misdirection clue he'd left behind in the other car would at least keep his pursuers guessing, if not taking them off the track completely.

Yes, he was rather proud of himself, even for fooling his passenger. It hadn't been necessary. An added touch but it had been fun. Vogt had never noticed the Mazda dealership right across the street from the parking lot. As far as she knew, they were in another stolen car, which would leave her thinking her chances of being rescued were better than they were. At some point, that useful tidbit of information might be used against her.

Homlin turned the radio back on and checked a half-dozen stations. No mention of any manhunt for him. Good. The idiots were keeping it quiet, which would make Homlin's travels much easier.

Admittedly, he'd taken a big loss this morning at the meeting. A big step back, but the game wasn't over yet. Not by a long shot. They may have stopped his shipment of the FreeForm, but they hadn't stopped him or his people. Nor would they. He'd learned a lot about these humans. He had underestimated them for the last time. It was time to start playing dirty—time to make his own rules. He had enough financial stability to re-establish himself elsewhere. He'd been sure to have a backup in case of disaster.

It was one of the cardinal rules of planet migration. Always have a contingency plan. Well, he did. He needed only to reclaim a couple small items before disappearing into the fabric of another society. Once he pulled his finances out of the half-dozen banks, he'd change his identity. South America would do nicely. He'd find another way to disseminate the seeds of his people. Already he had a new plan brewing.

All he needed was the crystal and the cocoon. He glanced at the digital clock on the dash. In a couple of hours, he'd have them. He reached down on the floorboard and picked up the bag of goodies he'd bought from the store next to the car lot. He chuckled to himself. A final little joke on Ms. Vogt before killing her. A little humiliating joke to pay her back for her meddling. It would be the perfect trick. Even the fool, Pritchard, would have to get the punch line and the message behind it.

MONDAY 4:15 PM

Oliver turned his head in Allan's direction and cupped his hands around his mouth so he wouldn't have to shout so loud. "James says we're coming to Pulaski in the next few minutes."

Allan nodded and smiled weakly. The last two hours of the throbbing sound of the copter's blades had fueled his headache, which had continued full blast. On top of which he felt like if he didn't get on the ground pretty soon, he was going to be airsick.

He leaned over and put his face close to Oliver's ear. "Any word about another stolen car?"

Oliver frowned and shook his head. "No word. It doesn't make any sense. The police are checking other forms of transportation to see if they can pick up their trail. They did find an interesting item in the car that Homlin may have left behind."

Allan was about to ask him what they'd found when James tapped Oliver on the shoulder and pointed towards the ground at the small town of Pulaski, Virginia. They flew over the city, looking for a place to land. Allan imagined that Waynesboro probably looked similar from the air. Small, old, yet neatly kept only a few miles from the interstate.

They found an empty lot a hundred yards or so from the parking lot where the Toyota had been abandoned. James landed in the center of the lot. Allan was grateful to finally be able to open the door and climb out, although even as he did so, he suspected it would only be a few minutes before he was climbing back inside.

The two men jogged over to the parking lot where a police car and a Virginia Highway Patrol car sat next to each other. Oliver strolled over to the three officers who were leaning against the cars. He flashed something from his wallet which Allan couldn't make out and suspected that the officers could not either.

"What have you got for us, boys?" Oliver's voice had the slight hint of a twang. Allan smiled at the subtle change.

"Not much, I'm afraid," the Highway Patrol Officer spoke first. "Artie here discovered the car a couple of hours ago. By the time I arrived, he'd also found the attendant lying unconscious in the booth over there. They've already taken him to the hospital. At last report, he hadn't regained consciousness yet. We did find this wedged down in the front seat." He handed Oliver a wrinkled map.

"You mind if I use your hood?" Oliver asked as he opened the map.

"Be my guest," the officer replied.

Oliver spread the map out on the hood, and the five men gathered around to study it.

Oliver followed the pen line that had been sketched on the map. It started in Washington, D.C. and continued down Interstate 81, passing next to Pulaski and ending in Knoxville, Tennessee.

"What do you think?" Oliver asked.

"From what I remember hearing Pat say about Biogentrix Labs, they have a small subsidiary unit outside Knoxville," Allan said.

"That must be where the son-of-a-bitch is headed," one of the officers responded.

"I'm not so sure," Allan replied.

Oliver turned and looked at him. "You're not? Where do you think he's headed?"

"Back to Waynesboro," Allan said simply.

"Even with this?" Oliver pointed to the map.

"Even with that," Allan replied. "First of all, we don't know for sure Homlin drew the line on the map, although I suspect he did. It could have been in the car all along. Maybe it shows the travel plans of the actual owner's trip to Washington, D.C."

"Well, yeah, it's possible but—"

"It's likely Homlin drew it. As I said, I suspect he did. I think he drew it and left it behind deliberately to throw us off."

Oliver pondered what Allan had said and nodded his head. "That would be possible, no doubt about it. But why return to Waynesboro?"

Allan frowned and wrinkled his brow. His head hurt so much it was difficult to think straight. Why did he feel Homlin was returning to his old stomping grounds? He'd thought it from the moment he'd first awakened and discovered Homlin had escaped. But he couldn't answer why.

Then it came to him. " Pat told me when we first started working on this case together that each time she got frustrated tracking a dead end, she would return to the Waynesboro area. Eventually, she'd pick his trail up. There's something special about the area. I don't know what. Maybe it's an alien thing—always returning to the original landing spot. I think there's something there Homlin is returning to. I wish I could tell you what it is."

Oliver looked down at the thin line on the map. After a few minutes, he looked into Allan's eyes. "It's been a long time since I was in those mountains. I'd as soon not go back there myself, but I can't explain either. I think you're right. We'll go on to Waynesboro. I'll radio the Knoxville Authorities to stake out the Biogentrix lab."

"I suppose we have to get back in the damn copter." The throbbing in Allan's head increase at the thought.

"It's the fastest way." Oliver folded the map and handed it to one of the officers.

"I know. I know." And to think, as a boy, he'd thought such a trip would be fun.

MONDAY 3:53 PM

Homlin pulled on the emergency brake and threw the stick shift in neutral. They were at the end of the line. At least, as far as they'd be able to go in the car—the rest of the trek would have to be made on foot. He turned off the engine and climbed out of the car. He stood next to it a minute and stretched his tired muscles. It had been a long day, and it was far from over. The walk would do him good. He needed to stretch his muscles out after a long time behind the wheel.

He strolled over to the other side of the car and opened the passenger's door. He removed the bags from the floorboard, including the special "gift" he'd purchased for Vogt. He set the bag on the roof of the car and opened the much larger bag. From it he pulled out a knapsack and half a dozen containers of freeze-dried food. He doubted he'd need it, but it was good to have a contingency plan in case he had to remain in the woods longer than he expected.

It was about time to let his traveling companion out of the trunk. He needed to find only one small item. He walked around the woods for a few moments, enjoying himself. It was great to be back out here. He much preferred the great outdoors over nasty city life. He continued to stroll around, not straying too far from the car until he found what he'd been looking for—a good stout staff made of maple. He held it in both hands and felt the weight and diameter. It would do nicely.

He returned to the car, carrying the walking stick with him. He took Vogt's bag from the roof of the car and placed it on the ground near the rear of the car along with the knapsack. He removed the car keys from his pocket and inserted one of them into the trunk lock. Holding the walking stick in one hand, he unlocked the trunk with the other. He stepped back and to one side.

The trunk lid did not spring open as it had the first time. Instead, it lifted a few inches and then remained closed. *Was Vogt sleeping*? Homlin wondered. It occurred to him that she could have suffocated. He hadn't thought about that. He certainly hoped that wasn't the case. It would ruin his surprise. He was about to lever the lid up with his walking stick when the lid began to rise on its own. Not actually on its own, but with Vogt's help.

"That's a good little girl. For a moment, I thought you were sleeping on the job. Now, step out slowly."

The spring allowed the lid to open entirely without Pat holding on to it. Despite the reduced light of dusk, she had to blink her eyes to adjust to the relative brightness of the outside.

"Can't you give me a hand? My legs are so stiff, I'm afraid I won't be able to get out on my own."

Homlin laughed. "You do play such an innocent little victim sometimes. Go ahead and fall down. Why should it bother me? Get out, slowly."

Pat glared at Homlin for several seconds before she gave in. The easiest way to get out was to climb out backward. That way if she did fall she'd at least have something to cushion her. She turned around and placed one foot on the bumper of the car. She held on to the car to steady herself as her two feet finally made it to the ground.

"Perfect, just perfect," Homlin said, and as Pat turned around to see what he meant, he brought the end of the walking stick down hard against her skull.

MONDAY 4:35 PM

Allan rested his head against the Plexiglas door of the chopper but removed it when he found it only made the pulsing pain from the vibrating worse. It wasn't fair; his headache made thinking increasingly difficult, but it didn't seem to have the least effect on his worrying. If anything, his ability to worry seemed heightened by his discomfort. Life wasn't fair.

What if they were wrong? What if Homlin wasn't on his way back to Waynesboro but was actually driving down Interstate 81 towards Knoxville? If they were wrong, it was likely that the mistake would cost Pat her life—if she was alive.

Allan had spent most of the day rationalizing that Homlin wouldn't dare kill Pat until he was sure he had escaped and no longer needed a hostage. How long would it be? Again, no way of telling, but it couldn't be long. The longer Homlin was free, the more likely he would consider Pat unnecessary cargo. They had to find them soon.

He leaned over to Oliver and shouted in his ear, "Tell me again, how far to the Waynesboro area?"

"We're guessing about an hour to an hour and a half. The landing area may be a little closer. It's north, northwest of the town," Oliver replied.

"Don't to worry, we'll find them before..." There was no point in finishing the sentence.

MONDAY 4:32 PM

The floor of the trunk felt harder and more irregular, Pat thought as she struggled to wake up. As she regained consciousness, she realized she was no longer in the trunk and she'd not been sleeping. As she turned her head and became dizzy from the pain, she remembered turning in time to see Homlin lowering the boom on her.

You bastard. I'll get you for this. You better believe it. Paybacks are hell. She started to push herself to a sitting position and found her hands snugly tied together in front of her with leather straps. She rolled around until she was in a position to push herself up. As she did so, she noticed Homlin leaning against the car, the trunk lid open. What was he was holding in his hand? It looked like a rope or—

"That's a good doggie. Welcome back. You weren't out too long. Are you ready for our walk?" As Homlin spoke he tugged on the leather cord in his hand, and Pat felt a strangling sensation around her neck as she was thrown off balance. Her hands instinctively went up to her neck. She wasn't quick enough to get them under her, so she landed hard on her face in the dirt.

"It'll take a little getting used to, but I'm sure you're at least as smart as the Golden Retriever you used to keep," Homlin said as he pulled on the leash a second time.

"Cut it out, you bastard." Pat tried shouting but could only get a hoarse whisper out. Her hands pulled at the metal choke collar cutting off her wind.

"Keep your hands away from it!" Homlin shouted as he knocked her hands away from the collar with his stick.

Pat lay on the ground for several seconds, trying to catch her breath and figure out what to do. As her mind cleared, it became apparent Homlin had been busy while she'd been unconscious. Not only had he tied her hands securely together in front of her with the leather thongs, but her feet were also bound so she could only take short steps. To top it off, she was wearing a knapsack with at least thirty pounds of supplies.

I'm a damn pack animal! How dare he, that son-of-a-bitch. He's going to die for this. If there had ever been any doubts in her mind that she'd kill him one day, they'd been thoroughly washed away.

She had a terrible thought. Had he found the lug wrench and screw-drivers tucked away in her coat pockets? If so, all was lost. She may as well hang herself with the choke collar for whatever defense she'd be able to muster. As she lay there quietly getting her bearings, she was reasonably sure she could feel the heavy iron weight pressing against her right side.

He hadn't bothered to frisk her. There had been no reason for him to do so. She had a chance.

"Let's go, pup. We've got a fair walk ahead of us." Homlin pulled on the leash for the third time. Pat experienced the momentary panic again as her wind was cut off. Homlin let up on the leash, and the chain relaxed.

"You be a good little dog, and I'll let you live at least for a little longer." Homlin slammed the trunk lid down. "You give me any grief, and I won't hesitate to shoot you on the spot. Is that clear?"

"Yes, it's very clear," Pat said.

"No talking!" Homlin shouted and jerked the leash with both hands, dragging Pat off her feet before she'd fully stood upright. "You are my pet dog. You're no longer a human being. Dogs bark, they don't talk. You have anything to say, you bark. One for yes and two for no. Do you understand?"

Pat lay on her side choking and gasping for air. She caught her wind enough to cough. After which she could taste the blood she'd spit up. She almost answered Homlin with a yes but stopped just in time. It was best not to say anything.

"Do you understand?" Homlin jerked the leash again.

When Pat could finally breathe again, she managed an anguished "woof!"

MONDAY 5:28 PM

The sun played with the crest of the mountain. In the last ten minutes, it dipped with increasing speed. Once it receeded below the mountain, the sky would darken as though God had turned the lights out. The search, difficult already, would become nearly impossible.

Allan leaned over to Oliver's ear again. "We must be near the site. We've got to find them, at least some sign of where they are, before the sun sets."

Oliver nodded and shouted back, "It's been ten years! I'm dealing with old memories but memories that I've dreamed about most nights. The area is looking more familiar. We'll find them. We'll find them."

The last sentences sounded more like a mantra to Allan, but it was as good a mantra as any to recite. He started repeating it to himself.

Oliver turned away from Allan and leaned towards James, shouting something Allan couldn't make out. James changed course slightly and followed an old logging trail below them. They flew over the trail for another ten minutes as it slowly narrowed below them and surrendered to the thick growth on either side of it. Right at the point where it petered out sat a white Mazda partially hidden by the brush.

Oliver and Allan pointed to it at the same time. They turned to each other and shouted in each other's face, "We've found them, we've found them!"

James came around for another pass, a little lower this time. As they did so, they realized the automobile had been abandoned.

"This was as far as they could go by car!" Oliver shouted. "They can't be too far from here."

"Yeah, but in which direction?" Allan shouted back.

"Over the crest, I think. It seems like it's on the other side of the mountain where the crash site was."

Allan realized they hadn't actually found them after all, but they were closer, much closer. *Please, Lord,* he prayed silently, *keep her alive a little longer.*

MONDAY 5:13 PM

Homlin had kept a hard steady pace straight up the mountain. He jerked on the leash whenever Pat fell behind, which was often since Pat's legs were stiff from the long confinement, and she was additionally hampered by the heavy backpack.

"Come on, mush, my fine pack animal. You should be out in front of me, pulling me up, the hill instead of hanging back and slowing my progress," Homlin said after one particularly brutal yank on the leash that threw Pat into another coughing fit.

"You would like to leave me here for your return trip. I promise not to go anywhere," Pat said.

"Oh, my dear Ms. Vogt, if I leave you here, I assure you, I'll leave you so you won't be able to go anywhere. Is this where you wish to die?"

Pat considered the question for a moment before answering. Was this the place to take a stand? Go for the bastard's throat? *No*, her inner voice answered. *Find out where he is going. There is something on the other side of the mountain he needs. Let him find it first and kill him.*

Pat shook her head. "No, I'm ready to go on."

They continued their journey up the mountain. Pat was relieved when they reached the crest, but it was short-lived. Going down the other side proved to be even worse. Homlin picked up his pace, running down the hill, yanking Pat off her feet half a dozen times.

The choker chain cut into the soft skin of Pat's neck, making each jerk from the leash that much more painful. *If I live through this, I'll start a campaign to prohibit the use of these collars on any animal*, Pat thought as she struggled to keep up.

Homlin stopped in his tracks much too quickly for Pat, who continued by him, coming to a sudden stop of her own when the leash pulled her off her feet.

"Wait a minute. I need to get my bearings. I think we're getting close." Homlin looked around for a moment before heading off to the right, downhill again, but at an oblique angle.

In a few minutes, he stopped a few yards from the mouth of a narrow cave. "We're here," he said simply.

Pat crouched down on all fours to catch her breath and to relieve the tension on the choker.

"Yes, catch your breath, by all means." Homlin looked down at her with a sneer on his face. "Catch your breath for those last few words you'd like to say."

Pat raised her head proudly in the air and glared at him. "You really are a bastard. It's going to be a pleasure killing you."

Homlin roared with laughter. "My dear Ms. Vogt, you really are a gem. Here you are at my complete mercy. I have the stick, the gun, and the controlling end of the leash, and you throw idle threats at me. Truly, you've been most entertaining.

"I mustn't dawdle. I have more important matters to attend to besides standing here talking with you. If you will excuse me for a moment, I need to fetch something from the cave. Since I doubt I can trust you to simply sit here and behave yourself—not after what you've said—I must restrict your movement for a few minutes."

Homlin looked around for a moment. Finding what he was looking for, he jerked Pat to her feet. He walked over to a nearby tree with its lowest branch nine or ten feet above the ground. He threw his end of the leash over the limb, keeping his eye on Pat the whole time.

Homlin stepped on the other side of the tree and pulled the leash taut, forcing Pat to follow. He continued to pull the leash until Pat was directly under the tree limb, standing on her tiptoes, holding onto the leash with both hands to keep from being hung. Satisfied with her position, Homlin tied his end of the leash to a nearby tree.

"I shouldn't be too long," Homlin said as he stepped back to examine his handiwork. "When I return we'll finish this little ten-year feud we've been having. I promise not to end it too soon for you." With that, he turned and disappeared into the cave.

MONDAY 5:41 PM

The light was a little better on the other side of the crest, but even so, it was difficult to make out much detail through the trees. Finding two people down there, particularly when one of them didn't want to be found, wasn't going to be an easy task.

Allan was so absorbed in the search, he hadn't noticed James and Oliver talking until Oliver leaned over to him and touched his shoulder.

"You aren't going to want to hear this, but James has pointed out to me that we only have enough fuel for another twenty or thirty minutes. Even then we might not make it back to where we can refuel."

Hell, what else could go wrong? They couldn't come this close and turn around without finding Pat. Allan nodded and leaned toward Oliver.

"Tell James we can't turn back. We must keep looking, no matter what. Isn't there somewhere around here we can land if we need to?"

Oliver considered the question for a moment and nodded. "There was an open area near where the ship landed, but that was ten years ago. It could be grown over with trees."

"We'll have to take a chance. We aren't going back!" Allan shouted back.

Oliver nodded and relayed the message to James. The two men shouted back and forth for a couple of minutes, but finally, James nodded agreement. Oliver gave Allan the thumbs-up sign. The three men turned their attention back to the forest below.

MONDAY 5:51 PM

Pat estimated Homlin had been gone less than five minutes, and already her arms felt like they were about to pull out of their shoulder sockets. She couldn't hang like this much longer. She considered reaching for one of the screwdrivers in her coat pocket but ruled it out. Trying to cut through an inch thick piece of leather with a flathead screwdriver didn't seem to make much sense.

I've got to think fast, she told herself. The "Vogt luck" was running out.

If she could get herself to the limb and over it, she'd be set. She tried pulling herself hand over hand on the leash, but she didn't have enough strength left in her arms. She had an idea! What if she shimmied up the tree? She glanced over at the cave. No sign of Homlin.

Well, here goes nothing, she thought as she pulled herself as close to the tree as possible and held herself with the leash, hooking her legs around the diameter of the tree trunk. She dug her shoes into the rough bark of the tree and pushed herself towards the limb. For the first time, she felt the choke chain relax its grip around her neck, and she knew she had a chance. She didn't need to climb over the limb. She only needed to get far enough to slip the choker from around her neck.

The realization gave her a spurt of adrenaline, and she pushed herself another two inches with her legs. The choker was completely relaxed, but its diameter was still too small to fit over her head. She pulled herself another couple of inches with one hand, then another and another.

As she did so, she heard a deep roar from deep within the bowels of the earth. Homlin! He was coming back. She must hurry. If she was going to live, she had to get free before he returned. In fact, if humankind was to survive, she had to get free now!

She squinted her eyes shut, took a deep breath, and let out a blood-curdling scream. She knew it might bring Homlin running, but it was what was necessary to manage the final inches. Still screaming, she held herself steady with her right hand, reached down with her left, and slipped the chain noose from around her neck and head. As the chain slipped away, the strength in her right hand gave out as did her legs. She fell to the ground.

She lay there for a moment, sobbing and gasping for air. She was free. Free from the choker and free at least for the moment, but for how long? As she looked towards the cave, she realized her freedom was short lived. From the mouth of the cave strolled a half-man-half-beast. Homlin stood at the mouth and roared his own blood-chilling scream.

He'd partially changed into the cat-like alien form that Pat had first come across a decade before, yet at the same time, he resembled the human Homlin. He had torn most of his clothes off, or they'd shredded from the bulging of the body within them.

Homlin threw his head back and roared again. He stared at Pat, his eyes glowing in the semi-darkness of the evening.

"I couldn't decide whether it would be more fun to kill you in the human form or my true self, so I will compromise. Do you approve?"

Pat pushed herself onto all fours with her tired arms. "Come on, you ugly bastard. I don't care what form you're in. I'm going to beat the shit out of you."

"For each idle threat, I'm going to make your death last that much longer and be more painful than you could imagine," Homlin said through slurred lips. As he continued to change into his alien self, speaking became more difficult.

Pat stood into a crouched stance. She circled around Homlin, maneuvering herself to get on higher ground. As she did so, she pulled the two screwdrivers out of her pockets but kept them hidden in the palms of her hands. She knew she'd get only one shot at Homlin. It had to be her best.

The cat-like Homlin closed the distance between them, apparently unperturbed by Pat's strategy to get above him. As he came closer, Pat noticed the crystal hanging from the chain around his neck. So that had been what he'd come here for. It made sense. Whatever the crystal was, it was integral to his mission. Therefore, it was a weak point as well.

"I want you to notice that I plan to kill you with my bare hands," Homlin said as he circled closer to her. "No stick or gun. It would take the fun out of it for me."

"Now look who's giving idle threats. You're not going to kill me, you overgrown house cat. You're going to wish you'd kept your weapons when I get through with you." Pat taunted him as she backed up the hill a few feet in an attempt to widen the distance between them.

Is he going to lunge for me? she wondered. She must wait for the right moment. If he lunged at her, she might be able to stab him with one of the screwdrivers. Unless she hit a vital spot, it wouldn't be enough to kill him, but it might give her the advantage she needed.

They circled around each other until, without warning, Homlin made his move. He was lightning quick and was on top of Pat before she knew it. Reaching out with his right hand, he slapped her off her feet, his claws ripping through the thick fabric of her coat and digging deep gouges in her left side. As Pat rolled, she felt the warm, wet sensation on her side, followed closely by intense pain.

Homlin stood a few feet from her and roared with delight. Pat scrambled to her feet, the movement intensifying the pain. Homlin attacked and again was beside her before she could move out of the way. This time he kicked her feet out from under her with a sweeping motion of one leg. Pat hit the ground hard, the breath knocked out of her. Towering above her,

Homlin threw his head back and howled in victory, extending his arms to the sky, his claws fully extended, ready for the kill.

As he stood over her, his face raised to the heavens from which he had come, a blinding flash of light, followed a millisecond later by a thunderous noise, gave Pat one last chance.

While Homlin was momentarily frozen in confusion, Pat jammed the two screwdrivers deep into his crotch. Bluish red blood spurted on Pat's face and down her blouse. Without hesitating, she pulled both screwdrivers out and plunged them in again.

Homlin's high pitch scream echoed down the mountain and back again. He fell to one side, trying to escape his tormentor, but Pat was relentless. As he rolled down the mountain, she chased after him. She jammed the screwdrivers in again, this time in his back. She lost her grip on them as his turning body twisted them out of her hand. She reached into her coat pocket and pulled out the lug wrench. Holding it in both hands by the long end, she brought the shorter end crashing down, aiming at Homlin's head.

At the last second, he twisted to one side, the blow landing on the curve between his neck and shoulder, the bar catching on the chain around his neck. Pat jerked back, ripping the chain off his neck and sending the crystal flying into the bushes. Homlin jerked his head around, trying to keep his eyes on his precious crystal. It was all the diversion Pat needed.

Without hesitating, Pat struck again with the tire iron and felt the satisfying sensation of bone-crushing beneath the blow, and a renewed cry of pain erupted from Homlin. Pat persisted. She struck again and again. Once more on the head, the third blow landing to the left side of his neck.

She couldn't stop herself. She was no more than an animal herself—an animal fighting not just for its life but for the life of its species. As Homlin rolled against a large boulder and stopped, Pat leaped onto the rock above him and with a final powerful thrust, she jabbed the pointed end of the tire iron through his chest.

It took a couple of minutes before the breathing stopped and his blood began to clot. Pat continued to sit on Homlin's chest until she was absolutely sure he was dead. With a final blow of her fist, she stood.

"I told you I was going to kick your ass." She took three steps towards the cave before passing out.

Safe at Last

Monday 6:03 pm, Dec. 6

"Back there! Take it back around. Did you see it?" Allan screamed in Oliver's ear.

"I'm not sure. I think I saw something," Oliver replied as he tapped James on the shoulder and instructed the pilot to take them around again.

Allan's heart felt like it was going to beat its way out of his chest. It had to be them, although it had been difficult to tell. It had been too grotesque to imagine. He was afraid to think what it might be. They'd been moving so fast the figure had been in the spotlight for only an instant.

As they circled around, Allan noticed the spotlight highlighted a small opening with only a few scrub pines that might cause a problem with the helicopter. He pointed it out to Oliver.

"Ask James if he thinks he could land this bird down there?"

Oliver gazed out the window at the small patch and frowned. He started to say something then thought better of it. Instead, he leaned over to James and asked the question. After a moment, James changed the course of the helicopter sufficiently to get a better look at the clearing. After studying it for a moment, he nodded to Oliver and gave him a thumbs-up.

"Land it," Allan said. "We'll find them on foot."

The landing was the most hazardous part of the entire trip. To Allan, it looked like James had miscalculated. There was no way they'd have enough room to land without shearing off the blades of the helicopter. Fortunately, James was a competent pilot and landed with only a few feet to spare on all sides.

As the bird touched down, Allan's feet hit the hard-packed ground running with Oliver close behind. Each of them carried a large flashlight, the narrow beams cutting through the night.

What if we miss them? Allan thought. *What if what I saw turns out be a wild animal?* Even as he thought it, he knew better. It had to be what they were looking for. The question was whether they'd find Pat before it was too late.

He slowed down as they neared the area. *Better be a little quiet. No reason to give themselves away if they could help it.* As he slowed to a fast walk, Oliver caught up with him. They both turned off their flashlights and took the final thirty yards in the dark.

In the near darkness, they pushed their way through the final layer of underbrush. They saw the outline of a slit in the side of the mountain. Allan stopped on the edge of the clearing and waited for his eyes to adjust a little further. He could hear Oliver's raspy breathing beside him.

As his eyes adjusted to the reduced light, he spied two dark lumps lying on the ground, one only a few yards from the cave opening, the other further away. His breath caught in his throat. He barely recognized the closer figure. It was Pat.

Allan turned his flashlight on. Oliver did the same a couple of seconds later. The two men strolled into the clearing. Allan stooped down to Pat's still body.

"Please, God, let her be okay...be okay...be okay," Allan repeated over and over as he felt for a pulse. Not until he felt one did he dare take a breath. Meanwhile, Oliver shined his light on the two of them.

"Is she all right?" he asked.

"I think so. She's breathing at least," Allan replied as he checked her more closely. He got only as far as her neck.

"Oh my God, she's been strangled. Her neck looks like someone tried to hang her." A moment later his hand touched the wet, sticky side of her coat. Allan felt a wave of nausea despite his years as a vet. After all, this was the woman he loved.

"Son-of-a-bitch!" Allan muttered through clenched teeth. "She's lost a lot of blood."

Remembering the second body, Oliver picked up Allan's flashlight and shined it. "I think that's Homlin over there."

"Go check. I'm okay here," Allan replied. Oliver laid the lit flashlight on the ground for Allan and walked over to take a closer look.

Holding Pat in his arms, Allan cleaned her wounds and wiped away the dirt and grime from her face. The process revived her. Her long lashes fluttered for a couple of seconds before her eyes opened.

As her gaze focused on Allan's face, she smiled and in a weak voice said, "We make quite a team, don't we? We finally got him."

At the sound of her voice, tears welled up in Allan's eyes and cascaded down his cheeks. He kissed her gently on the lips. Continuing to hold her firmly, he rocked her back and forth—and wept. This time, they were tears of joy.

A few minutes later, Oliver returned to his side. "Yep, it's Homlin, or at least what's left of him." He turned to Pat. "Remind me to stay off your bad side."

Pat shrugged, wincing in pain.

"Oliver, help me get her to the chopper, will you? She's pretty banged up herself."

"Sure thing," Oliver replied. They helped Pat up and started walking the way they came, each of them on either side of her. They'd made it about twenty yards when Pat stopped. "Damn. I hate to ask this, and I know it's crazy, but could you go fetch the tire iron I used on Homlin? I'd like to keep it, a sort of memento of the day I kicked an alien's ass."

"Sure," Allan replied. "I'll go get it. Oliver, help her to the helicopter. I'll meet you there." He turned and retraced his steps.

He found the bloody wrench lying not far from Homlin's cooling body. He stared down at the half-man, half-beast, shaking his head. It has been an interesting last few months. He was ready for some normalcy for a change.

He turned in the direction of the helicopter but stopped after taking a few steps, a cold shiver running along his back by the sound of a soft rustling behind him. Homlin was dead, right? He slowly turned in the direction of the cave where he thought he'd heard the sound. He shined his flashlight at the mouth of the cave. At first, he didn't see anything out of the ordinary. He saw a movement from deep within the cave. As the form entered the beam of light, Allan heard a familiar voice that threatened to stop his heart.

"Daddy..."

Book Two

FreeForm:
Reborn
Orrin Jason Bradford
A new physique. An old façade...

In light of what she's seen, former ufologist Pat Vogt is reluctant to conceal the nature of Allan Pritchard's seeming nephew. TJ isn't as he appears, and the boy's history could mean a bleak future for mankind. Are Pat and Allan instilling humanity or nurturing a malevolent force? Would the true monster be borne by betrayal? As TJ learns to harness his powers, the stakes mount ever higher.

Meanwhile, hidden away in a backcountry cave, another lifeform is growing...exponentially. With the help of a shadowy benefactor known only as 'Aeo', Doctor Homlin's plans have received new breath. Soon to emerge is Val, a hungry incarnate that won't rest until its progenitor's vision becomes reality.

Ex-operative James Stepp may hold the key to salvation, but how much responsibility can be entrusted to a mercenary...?

Building upon its own powerful predecessor, Book II of O.J. Bradford's FreeForm Series thickens the plot, dials up the tension and doubles-down on a rallying cry for excellence in modern SF. Readers that hope to be whisked away, prepare for a brisk abduction.

Are You My Daddy?

1

"Daddy," the young boy said, a look of confusion mixed with fear etched on his face as he stood at the mouth of the cave from which he'd just exited. Allan stared at him for a moment frozen in place.

"TJ?"

What in the world is he doing here? Allan wondered as he glanced around at the barren mountain landscape and the black abyss of the cave entrance.

Not your son. He heard Pat's voice reverberate through his mind and another part argue with her.

Yes, yes, it is my son. He looks just like Todd.

But you told me Todd was killed in the same house fire that took your wife years ago.

I know, but...but...but. Allan had no answer to that statement, for it was true. Allan shook himself back to the present and studied the boy in front of him.

Even though it had only been a day since he'd last seen the boy, he would have sworn TJ had grown at least another inch. *Probably my imagination,* Allan thought. *I know he's growing fast, but not that fast...right?* TJ looked to be between five and six years of age in appearance even though Allan knew his actual chronological age to be less than a year; more like six months. The FreeForm larva from which the boy had developed had amazing properties that Allan was still learning about.

"Daddy," TJ repeated, his voice wavering, a perplexed look on his young face. "She killed him. Why were they fighting?"

Allan glanced from TJ to the bloody half-man, half-catlike creature lying on the ground; all that remained of Homlin, the alien being that had started this whole mess; the alien being that had been instrumental in bringing FreeForm to the world and therefore indirectly TJ.

"He was a bad...man," Allan said, not quite knowing how to finish the sentence. "He hurt her and would have hurt a lot of other people as well."

"Does that make me bad as well?" TJ asked.

"No, of course not," Allan replied. "Why would you even think such a thing?"

"Well, I'm part him, aren't I? That's what he said."

Allan noticed the boy shiver then tilt his head to one side. Allan wasn't sure if TJ's shivering was from the frigid temperature that was continuing to drop as night approached, or from the question he had just asked.

Allan glanced at the large black wound on the side of the mountain once more and wondered for a moment what lay inside. This was a stark, isolated part of the North Carolina mountains; inhospitable, to say the least, and made even more so by the plunging temperatures and the slate gray sky that promised snow. Allan put down the tire iron Pat had asked him to retrieve and took off his jacket, offering it to the boy.

"Here, put this on. You're freezing."

TJ took the navy blue jacket and wrapped it around his shoulders. Clutching it in front of him, the windbreaker reached down to his ankles.

Allan reached out to him and started to pick him up, but TJ pulled away.

"Easy there. I'm not going to hurt you. We just need to get out of here before the snow comes."

"Home? Can we go home? See Kendra? Have Cheerios?"

"That's right," Allan said with a chuckle. "We're going home." Allan bent down to retrieve the tire iron before picking up his son. He strolled towards the helicopter where an injured Pat and an anxious Oliver waited.

2

In the deep recesses of the cave twenty or thirty yards from where Allan held the boy, a small ellipsoid-shaped globe the size of a large, slightly flattened grapefruit pulsated with a bluish purple glow. The anguished screams and the waves of the pain of the Primary had awakened the AI contained within it moments before. A high pitch whine reverberated from it throughout the cave and beyond, pricking the ears of several wild animals in the vicinity.

On the home planet, the Primary was known as Sluneg. The violent attack on Sluneg had caused the beta version of the Fail Safe Protocol to be initiated. The AI who referred to itself as Aeo struggled to manage the emergency and recover the consciousness of the Primary now known on this greenish-blue orb as Homlin. Unfortunately, the subject was in the final stages of dying, and nothing could be done to reverse the process. In use for the first time, the fail-safe mode had been designed for less intrusive, less violent, and less rapid cessation of the body that housed the Primary. In short, Homlin's consciousness was strung out all over the place and dissipating rapidly. Aeo struggled to pull all the pieces together and back into the cocoon for safe keeping.

Okay, I can do this, Aeo thought as it began the download process. *It's all out there. I just need to pull it together.* But the brain was dying rapidly, and the electrical signals that contained the information grew weaker by the second. Aeo finally had to admit that it would be unable to retrieve every part of the primary subject. It would have to make do with what it could recover and fill in the gaps later.

In the meantime, it scanned the cave and took inventory of the FreeForm available and was satisfied to find Homlin had stocked several in the pupal stage in the cave. *At least I'll be able to reconstruct another body for the Primary.* The Primary's mission could still be fulfilled. Aeo set to work to pick up the pieces of a mission that had gone bad.

Recovery

Allan pushed the door to Pat's hospital room open and stuck his head in. Glancing around, he was surprised to find her room looked more like a guest room you'd see in your favorite aunt's home. He then remembered reading in the Waynesboro's *Chronicle* that someone had willed a sizable amount of money to the institution expressly to rehab the rooms to be less sterile and more hospitable. *That had been money well spent*, Allan thought, as he noted the small flowered wallpaper that matched well with the bouquets of flowers that set on the chest of drawer and window seal.

Pat lay in bed with her head turned towards a window that looked out on the snow-covered courtyard. The snow had been falling for over eight hours. All details of the courtyard were entirely obscured, resembling mounds of cotton. Already the weather forecast stated it might be the worst storm to hit the southeast in over twenty years, with accumulations up to two feet. Even in Pat's four-wheel drive Cherokee, it had taken Allan close to a half hour to drive the ten miles from his home to the hospital, a drive that usually took no more than fifteen minutes. Travel was hampered in large part because of the Southern drivers without four-wheel drive who didn't have a clue how to maneuver in such conditions.

He noticed Pat had turned her head away from the window and was smiling weakly at him. He stood there smiling back as relief washed over him. Only then did he realize how afraid he had been of losing her.

"Are you just going to stand there gawking, or are you going to come over here and give me a kiss?" As she raised one hand to beckon him over, he noticed the attached I.V. drip. Her neck was bandaged from where the choker collar had cut into it. While she was still pale and weak, she looked better than when he'd last seen her in the helicopter the previous night. By the time he'd arrived at the helicopter, Pat had been securely strapped in by James, the pilot, and Oliver. Allan hadn't been able to tell if Pat had fallen asleep or had passed out, and he'd been too scared to ask. James and Oliver had stared at TJ with equally perplexed looks.

"What the hell happened?" Oliver asked. "Who's that?"

"I'll explain later," Allan promised, though he didn't have a clue what he'd tell them. "We've got to get her to a hospital."

Allan walked over to Pat's bed. His small bouquet of flowers looked puny next to the larger arrangements, but it had been the best he could do, considering the conditions outside where things continued deteriorating by the minute.

"Oh, they're lovely," Pat said as Allan bent over and kissed her. *Her color is better than last night*, he noted to himself, but her face was still missing its normally vibrant color. He could only imagine the hell she'd been through over the past twenty-four hours. Thankfully, it was finally over. Now they'd be able to get on with creating a life together without the concerns of an alien invasion.

Then again, there was TJ. How was he going to break the news to her about him? As far as he could tell, she'd been out of it last night and unaware of TJ's presence in the chopper. Maybe it would be better to wait until she was stronger, but even as he had the thought, he knew it was his way to put off an awkward conversation. So after a few minutes of pleasantries, he decided to broach the subject.

He started to sit in the straight back chair next to her bed, but Pat insisted he sit on the edge of the bed so she could see him better as well as hold his hand.

"What do you remember about the flight back to Waynesboro last night?" Allan finally asked.

"Not much, I'm afraid. Really nothing about the flight. The first thing I remember was waking up sometime in the middle of the night with one of the nurses checking my vitals. I could just make out the snow falling, and then I fell back into La-La land."

"I see," Allan said. "Well, I have some...some good news." At least, he considered it good news, and he hoped she would as well.

"Oh, good. I could use some good news right about now. What is it?"

"We found TJ last night. Actually, he found me. Isn't that great?" Allan held his breath as he studied Pat's face for a reaction.

Pat sat there. Her hand that had been gently rubbing his suddenly stopped. She stared at him, a startled look growing on her face.

"What?" she finally asked. "What did you say?"

"TJ. You know. He ran away a few days ago, and now he's back." He decided, given Pat's reaction, it might not help his case to let her know TJ had walked out of the cave where Pat and Homlin had fought to the death.

"And this is good news how?" Pat asked.

"He's alive," Allan answered, feeling the hackles on his neck rise. "My son is alive and well."

Pat slowly removed her hand from his and placed both of hers on her lap as she turned and stared out the window for close to a minute. Finally, she turned back to him.

"You've got to be kidding, Allan. He's not your son. He's not even human. He's as much an alien as the one I killed on that mountainside last night. We've got to let someone know about him."

Allan didn't know what to say in rebuttal, so he didn't say anything at first. He continued to stare at the woman he loved. How could he talk to her about how he felt about TJ when he wasn't sure himself? Part of him knew the boy wasn't his son, Todd, even though TJ was the spitting image of his son at that age. But Todd had come from his wife's womb in a normal pregnancy like everyone else on Earth...everyone but TJ. He had come from a late night C-section Allan had performed at his veterinary clinic back in March. At the time, he'd removed several larval looking fetuses from a stray dog that had taken up at the Parkers. Not knowing what to do with the strange creatures, he'd taken them to his home to observe. All the larvae had died in just a few days; all except the one that had slowly changed from looking like a premature puppy to his son. It had all happened by accident at first, and Allan had kept the larvae in the den. After all the other larvae had died, Allan had relocated the lone survivor to his son's old bedroom, surrounded by baby pictures of Todd. Over a few days, the larva went from resembling a puppy to looking like a small human baby. Allan had planned to contact someone in the government about what he had found, but he just couldn't bring himself to do it. He had to see what the larva was turning into.

And in the process, Allan had grown to love the boy he now called TJ. However, he also loved the woman lying in the hospital bed in front of him. Pat had almost been killed for a second time by an alien that had secretly been trying to take over the world and who had been the source of those larvae that Allan had removed from the Parker's stray dog.

Allan rose from the side of the bed and walked over to the window where he stared out at the falling snow. He'd always found snowstorms peaceful and calming, even severe ones like this that would wreak havoc on the area for several days. It seemed like a blanket of snow made everything less noisy, as though it absorbed much of the extraneous noises of life.

He'd probably been standing at the window for a good five minutes or more when he heard someone behind him clear their throat and a nurse say, "Visiting hours are over in five minutes, Dr. Allan."

He turned around and tried to smile back at her. "Thank you."

After the nurse left, Allan walked back to Pat's bed. He reached out with one hand and took hers. Finally, he said, "Can we agree not to do anything about this for at least a couple days? Let's get you back on your feet and home. Then we'll sit down and decide the best course of action. Okay?"

He could hear the pleading tone in that last word and hated himself for it but was relieved when he felt Pat squeeze his hand and nod before replying, "Where is he now?"

"Oh, he's at my house. Kendra came over last night before the storm became too bad. She's looking after him."

"I see," Pat said. "And what are you going to tell her? Are you going to keep lying to her as well?"

Once again Allan didn't know how to answer the question, so he just shrugged. "We'll have to sort that out as well."

Snowstorm

1

Twenty-four hours had passed since the Fail Safe Protocol had been initiated and its initial recovery task completed. Overall, Aeo assessed that the Protocol had performed well, considering the less than ideal circumstances and the fact that it had never been used before. Still, significant portions of Homlin's long-term memory had been lost. While it would be possible to re-install the Primary's mission into the subject's consciousness, most of the details of the last ten years that Homlin had been on the planet were either a jumbled mess or lost forever.

On the positive side of things, a significant early-in-the-season snowstorm had blanketed the area with close to two feet of snow, efficiently keeping anyone from investigating the area anytime soon. Also, during its efforts at gathering up the scattered pieces of Homlin's consciousness, Aeo had discovered the planet's inhabitants had invented a world wide web of information they referred to as the internet. Evidently, this species of Homo sapien wasn't as primitive as Aeo had initially thought. It felt certain this discovery would prove useful in recovering from this unexpected breakdown.

Unfortunately, that was about all the good news Aeo could come up with. It also had discovered that during the night while it had been concentrating on other matters, a pack of wolves had dragged Homlin's dead body away, leaving it up to Aeo to orchestrate the formation of a new body from scratch.

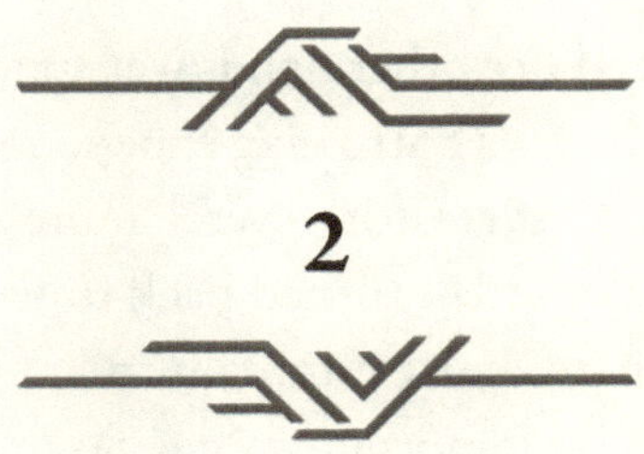

2

The snowstorm had dumped over two feet of snow through much of the North Carolina mountains, leaving thousands without power and even more stranded in their homes. Fortunately for Allan, he had prepared for such contingencies since he knew he'd have to be able to get to his veterinary clinic no matter what the weather. He had also spent years after veterinary school in New England where he also learned to drive in winter weather conditions. He even had two generators, one in his veterinary hospital and the other at home, just in case. Fortunately, neither area was affected by the power outage.

Upon arriving home with Pat around 3 PM, he found Kendra had put TJ down for his afternoon nap and had already called her mother to come pick her up from the main road near Allan's home. Allan had hoped to persuade her to stay as a way to avoid further conversations with Pat about TJ.

"I'm sorry, Dr. Allan, but I have homework to finish before tomorrow in case they call school back into session," Kendra said as she finished putting on her boots. "Besides, I'm sure you two need some time alone."

After Kendra left, Allan fidgeted around the house, fixing a fresh pot of coffee. He walked into the living room to stoke the fire in the woodstove while Pat made a nest of blankets and pillows in front of the stove. Allan fixed a tray with piping hot mugs of coffee and a pint of Kahlúa and placed it on the coffee table next to Pat. The two of them sat there for several minutes sipping on the spiked coffee and warming themselves. Finally, Allan placed his coffee mug back on the tray and turned to Pat.

"It's so good to have you back home," Allan said as he reached over and took Pat's hand." I don't know what I would have done if something had happened to you. I can only imagine what these last few days have been like for you, but I want you to know I love you very much."

Pat smiled and placed her other hand over top of his. “I love you too, Allan, and you're right. It was a harrowing experience, but it’s over now.”

The two of them sat there for several more minutes, enjoying the warmth of the fire. Finally, Allan turned back to Pat. “I know this may be hard for you to understand, but I want you to know that little boy sleeping in the next room is also important to me. Strange as it may sound, I've grown to love him. I believe, given some time, you could learn to love him as well."

Allan felt Pat stiffen as she pulled her hands away. “All I'm asking is for you to give it time,” Allan hated the pleading tone creeping into his voice. “Give TJ and me time. Will you do that?"

Pat turned and stared out the picture glass window to the winter scape. Finally, with a broad sigh, she turned back to Allan. "I know when you look at TJ, you see a young boy that reminds you of your deceased son. Somehow you've taken the leap and convinced yourself that's who he is, but when I look at him, I'm reminded of an alien that almost killed me on two different occasions. I don't see a young, innocent boy. I see a threat to this planet and to humanity. I know, Allan, that you care for him, but I don’t think I will ever be able to see him as anything other than what he is."

"I understand," Allan finally replied, “but for me and for the future we could share together, would you be willing to try?"

Pat stared at her hands in her lap. She reached for the pint of Kahlúa and poured several ounces of the liqueur into her coffee mug before taking a couple deep swallows.

"I don't know how to answer that question. I'll need at least a day or two to think it over. In the meantime, I need to get drunk. Do you have anything stronger in the house?"

Suds and Duds

James Stepp walked into the Suds and Duds for the first time in over four years. The unlikely combination pub and laundromat had been a favorite hangout of his when it first opened. Everyone had predicted it would never make it, especially in a town as small as Black Mountain, but it had turned out to be surprisingly successful. Now, James was returning to his old digs for a drink as a way of acknowledging the dramatic changes that had taken place over the past four years.

As James ordered a Jack and Ginger from a bartender he didn't recognize, he reflected on the last time he'd been in the bar just before his life had performed a triple somersault off the high dive. He had become a regular at the Suds and Duds so he could tell his wife, Jenny, he was helping out at home by doing the laundry. He figured it was the least he could do to help her out since she'd not been feeling well of late. It was also an excellent excuse to get out of the house and chill out at the bar and flirt with Marjorie, the barkeep. He prayed Jenny wouldn't ask him about the washer and dryer in their basement. If she did, he would have to explain to her that both appliances had been broken for months, but he would cross that bridge when he came to it.

He picked up his beer and downed half of it before swiveling around in his seat to stare at Marjorie waiting on another regular at the other end. He figured Marjorie to be between forty-five and fifty. Despite spending most of her time managing the two businesses, she somehow kept herself in shape. Besides, James had a strange attraction for women who wore their long hair in a ponytail. That's what had attracted him to Jenny more years ago than he liked to admit; that along with her killer body and sexy, Southern accent. But his wife seldom wore her hair in a ponytail these days, and her body had gone from sexy to Rubenesque to pudgy. Still, late at night with the lights off, her Southern drawl could still excite him.

I really don't need to be ogling other women, James thought as he took another gulp of his beer. After all, he was a married man with a two-year-old daughter and a second one on the way. Still, it was hard not to look, especially when you were married to a woman who was always too tired to pay attention to him and was rapidly growing into a... Best not to finish that thought, James told himself as he caught Marjorie's attention and motioned for another beer.

"Here you go, suugarrr," Marjorie said as she set a fresh beer in front of him. "You look kind of down tonight. What's up?"

"Oh, nothing," James replied, pushing the empty mug towards her and picking up the fresh one. "It's just that I'm, well...bored. I mean, I know I'm not a big city sort of a guy. I've spent most of my life in small towns because that's what I prefer, but sometimes I'd like something interesting to happen."

"Tell me about it, sweetie," Marjorie replied as she wiped the bar with a moist towel. "But remember, be careful what you ask for. You might find that boredom is better than the alternative."

"Yeah, you're probably right," James said as he rubbed the frost off the side of his mug.

As Marjorie went to wait on another customer, James continued to sit at the bar and reflect upon his life. He hadn't realized until that evening just how bored he'd become. His heating and air conditioning business barely paid the bills, and even in the busy season, it bored him. Funny thing, the happiest he could remember being was when he was in the service, especially while overseas fighting for liberty, justice, and the American way. There was something about an army of other soldiers trying to kill you in oh so many different ways that brought a certain freshness and edge to life.

Then there was the thrill and exhilaration he experienced flying. He relished the feel of landing a group of soldiers in a hot war zone, the yelling of the men, the sound of gunfire and explosions all around him and knowing it was fate, not skill, that kept him alive. Man, what a rush. God, he missed that. Oh, he took the occasional trip out to the local airfield, and that helped, but flying a Cessna 172 was hardly the same as flying a Black Hawk or even a Huey, especially while soldiers on the ground were trying to knock you out of the sky.

Yep, his life had grown pretty dull in the last few years, but what could he do about it? There were those occasional calls he'd receive from an old Army buddy or two who had leveraged their training as Green Berets into lucrative careers as soldiers of fortune, but each time he had been contacted, he begged off. That was hardly the life for a married man with children.

What was that Marjorie had just said? "Be careful what you ask for. You might find what you have is better than the alternative," or something like that. *Maybe she's right,* James thought. *Maybe I should be satisfied with what I've got.*

James finished off the Jack and Ginger and caught the eye of the bartender to order another one. Funny how one's perspective on life often changed over time. Boredom looked pretty attractive these days.

Bona Fide Genius

1

TJ sat in the middle of the great room of Allan's ranch style log home. Besides his bedroom, it was TJ's favorite part of the house, not only because it was the warmest location, but also because of the large window that provided a panoramic view of the outdoors with its mix of evergreens, hardwood trees, and thick underbrush. That's where TJ really wanted to be, but Kendra and he had already taken a long walk through the newly fallen snow. Kendra had finally insisted they return home so she could fix them both some hot chocolate.

TJ sat cross-legged on the rug, surrounded by walls of multi-colored Legos behind which he hid an army of toy soldiers. He pretended to play, but as soon as Kendra walked into the kitchen to fix the hot chocolate, he scampered up. He ran into the spare bedroom Allan had recently converted into a home office. There, sitting on the desk, was the toy TJ really wanted to play with. His dad had called it an iMac computer and had brought it home from work. None of that made much sense to TJ, who was far more fascinated by the beautiful pictures that magically appeared on the computer screen whenever the computer was left alone for several minutes.

After watching the pictures rotate for a minute or two, TJ climbed onto Allan's office chair to get a better look. He knew he might get in trouble for messing with the computer, but he just couldn't resist. He soon discovered he could just reach the flat plastic slab and smaller object that sat in front of the screen. He'd seen his dad playing with those and knew they were somehow connected to the rest of the iMac. It didn't take long for his youthful curiosity to get the better of him. He reached out and grasped the small, rounded object as he'd seen Allan do. Immediately, the pictures disappeared.

Next, TJ discovered the small object in his right hand controlled a small arrow that glided across the screen. He played with the arrow for a couple of minutes, pretending it was a bird under his command. This led him to the pretty pictures that popped up at the bottom of the screen when he directed the arrow in that direction. He continued to experiment, this time with the button on top of the object in his hand. His next significant breakthrough came when he discovered that if he quickly clicked the button twice while the arrow hovered over one of the small images, much like he'd noticed Allan had done, larger pictures appeared.

He was concentrating on the new pictures so intently that he never noticed when Kendra walked into the room carrying a tray with two steaming mugs of hot chocolate and a large bowl of Cheerios.

"There you are, you little rascal," she said. "I was looking all over the place for you. Didn't you hear me calling you?"

TJ shook his head without taking his eyes off the screen. 'Uh-uh," he mumbled. He twisted his tongue between his lips as he concentrated on his efforts.

"Oh my, you mustn't play with Dr. Allan's computer," she said as she placed the tray on the desk and pulled the chair TJ was sitting on away so he could no longer reach the machine. "He'd kill me if anything were to happen to it."

She pulled the chair closer to the desk to make it easier for TJ to reach the bowl of Cheerios. "Now you have to promise not to snitch on me to Dr. Allan about what you're having for lunch. Okay?"

"Snitch?" TJ asked as he took a handful of his favorite food and popped one of the tasty morsels in his mouth.

"Yeah, you know. Tell on me," Kendra replied, taking several of the Cheerios and plopping them into her cup where they floated like small life preservers in a sea of creamy chocolate.

After a couple of minutes, Kendra glanced over at the computer screen, then stared at it more intently. "What the..."

She turned to TJ. "Did you do that?" she asked, pointing to the picture TJ had drawn. It was a beautiful rendition of the view outside the great room's window.

Her tone frightened TJ at first. He shook his head and was about to deny he'd had any part in it, but then remembered his dad's lengthy talk at dinner a night or two ago about the importance of being honest. He changed his head shake into a nod.

"I didn't hurt anything."

"No, dear, I'm sure you didn't," Kendra said as she reached out and caressed his cheek. "It's very pretty. Let's save it so we can show your father."

TJ watched as she touched several areas of the plastic slab.

"You know how to use the...the..."

"It's called a computer, and yes, we have several of them at school, but I'm still learning. Maybe we can learn how to use it together. Would you like that?"

"Sure," TJ said, smiling broadly. Anything would be better than playing with those dumb blocks.

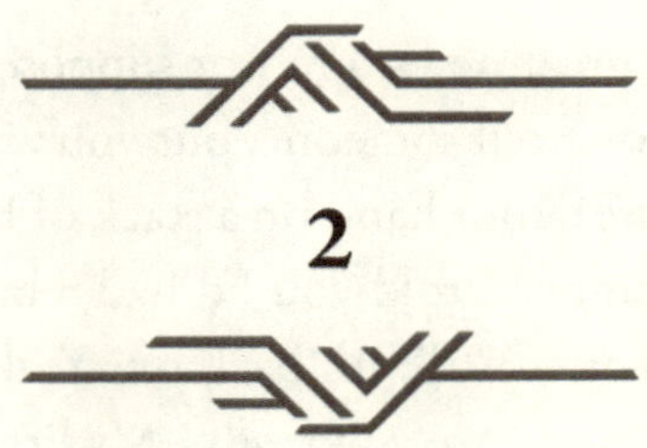

2

Later in the afternoon, Kendra sat TJ in front of the TV and inserted a DVD into the player. "How about watching *The Lion King* for a bit while I make a call?"

"Okay," TJ agreed. He found the movie a bit simple, but he liked how it ended. Besides, he often had more fun listening in on other people's conversations while they thought he was either sleeping or watching television.

After the movie had started, Kendra walked over to her purse and pulled out her cell phone, then returned to the couch where she curled up with one of the comforters before placing her call.

TJ twisted around on the floor so he could see the television and also keep one eye on Kendra. It felt good to be home where it was warm and dry and where there was an unlimited supply of Cheerios. He especially liked Kendra, who he thought of as part of his family, or at least a very close friend; a bit like Timon and Pumbaa. No, that wasn't exactly true. He knew his dad expected him to pay attention to Kendra and do what she asked. Maybe she was more like Sarabi, Simba's mother, but that didn't feel right either. *I don't have a mother, at least not like Simba.*

While Kendra was the one who primarily took care of him, Pat was the person closest to his dad, but no way could she be his mother. She didn't even like him. He'd overheard several heated conversations over the past few days. While he hadn't been able to make out all the words, he'd gotten the gist of them all. On top of that, hadn't she been the one who'd killed Homlin, his almost dad? Relationships were a most confusing part of life, but one thing was certain. Pat was no friend. To him, it felt like she was more like Scar than anyone else in the movie.

"Hello, Mimi? This is Kendra. Gotta minute?" TJ turned his attention and thoughts away from the movie and over to Kendra's phone conversation.

"I have some really great news. I'm not supposed to tell anyone, but I think I'll explode if I don't tell someone, but you've got to promise not to tell another soul. Promise? Your hand on a stack of Bibles promise?"

"Okay, good. Remember I told you I'd had a babysitting job that had ended? Yeah, that's the one. Well, it's back on. Yeah, I know, the money's great but here's the best part. Are you ready? My little boy...the one I'm sitting...he's a genius.

"No, really; a bona fide genius."

Rembrandt, Picasso, Van Gogh

1

When Allan returned home that evening from his veterinary clinic, Kendra pulled up the picture that TJ had created on the computer and showed it to him.

Allan stared at the picture for several seconds, then glanced first to Kendra and then through the doorway into the next room where TJ was once again pretending to play with his blocks and stuffed animals.

"You're pulling my leg, aren't you?" he asked Kendra.

It seemed like a strange comment to TJ since he couldn't imagine Kendra ever trying to pull his dad's leg or any other part of him for that matter. Perhaps it had another meaning that he didn't yet understand.

"No, promise, I'm not kidding you at all," Kendra replied. *Ahh, good,* TJ thought. Pulling one's leg means kidding someone. He'd be sure to remember that one.

"I left him right where he is now in the other room with his toys while I fixed lunch." TJ noticed that Kendra avoided revealing what they'd had for lunch. Apparently, she didn't want to snitch on herself.

"When I called him to eat, he didn't answer me, so I went to look for him. I found him in here, sitting in that chair. You'd evidently left the computer on this morning when you left for work. I'm guessing the screensaver caught his attention."

"How?"

TJ glanced up from stacking blocks to see his dad leaning over with his hands on the desk, staring intently at the computer screen.

"I don't know exactly," Kendra replied. "I wasn't here while he did it, but well..." She paused as though having trouble coming up with the right words. "At first I thought maybe you had done it and he'd just found it..."

"But you knew I couldn't draw something this beautiful," Allan finished for her.

"I've seen you try to sketch things when you're showing something to one of your clients. I know these iMacs are pretty neat, but...no, I was pretty sure you weren't the artist."

"Thanks a lot, but you're right," Allan said and chuckled. "There's no way I could have done this picture. Hell, I didn't even realize I had a graphics program on this thing."

"It appears that TJ is very smart," Kendra replied. "Like maybe even a genius."

Okay, TJ thought. *Genius equals very smart. Yeah, that's me, right? So why do you keep sticking me down here with these dumb blocks?* He watched as Allan walked in and out of his view, pacing back and forth in the office.

"I think you're right, Kendra," Allan finally said. "I can't wait to tell Pat tonight. Can you stay a little later in case she has questions? Join us for dinner?"

"Sure," Kendra replied. "I'll just need to let my mom know. I'd love to see Pat's face when you tell her."

TJ wasn't so sure Pat would be all that thrilled with the news.

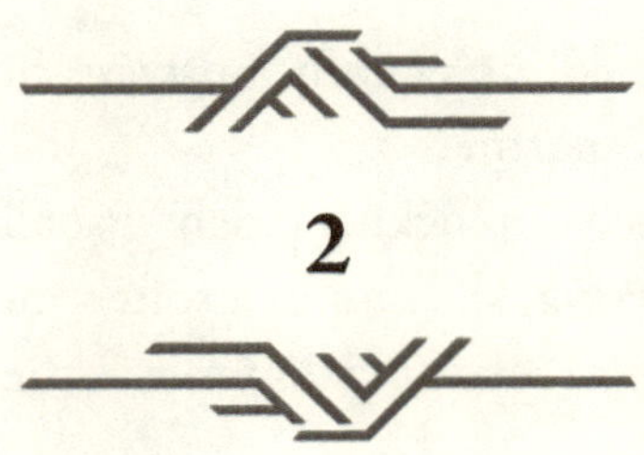

2

The four of them sat around the table at the end of the meal. One lone piece of pizza lay on the pan, slowly turning into cardboard. Allan filled Pat's and his glass with Chianti while Kendra refreshed TJ's and her glass of grape juice. Allan had tried to create a celebratory mood all evening, but each time he tried, it fell flat. It didn't take a genius to know that something strange was going on between the two adults, and TJ was pretty sure he knew what it was—it was him. Pat tried to be cordial, but he'd noticed every time she glanced in his direction she'd quickly turn away and pick up her wine glass to take another swallow. He figured she'd easily finished over two-thirds of the bottle even though she'd only eaten one slice of pizza.

It appeared the wine was beginning to take effect as her eyelids drooped just a bit and the few times she'd attempted to join the conversation she'd slurred a couple of her words.

"I asked Kendra to stay for dinner tonight because we have something we wanted to share with you," Allan said as he picked up his glass and tipped it in Pat's direction. He opened the manila folder lying next to his plate and handed a copy of TJ's picture to her.

"What's this?" Pat asked after studying it for a moment.

"What does it look like?" Allan asked back.

"It looks like a computer-generated picture, a nicely rendered one." She glanced from Allan to Kendra and back to Allan. "Who did it?" she asked, then tried to answer her own question. "Musta been you, Kendra. I know Allan hasn't an artistic bone in his body."

"Ouch," Allan said. "Truth hurts sometimes, but you're right. I didn't do it, but neither did Kendra." He paused for dramatic effect.

"O...kay," Pat said as she placed the picture down on the table and picked up her wine glass and took a long swallow. "Again, my question. Who did it?" TJ could detect an edge of agitation growing in her voice.

"Guess," Allan replied, apparently unaware how annoying his little guessing game was to his partner.

"Rembrandt, Picasso, Van fucking Gogh," Pat all but screamed, then realizing she was overreacting, she said in a softer, more controlled voice. "I really don't know, and I'm sorry, but I'm not in the mood for your antics. Please, just tell me."

There was a long pause as Allan stared at Pat, a shocked look on his face.

"TJ did it this afternoon," Kendra finally said to break the strained silence.

Kendra and Allan had paraded around the house most of the early evening with the printed picture in hand, praising TJ for his artistic talent. TJ hadn't expected such an outburst from Pat but neither did he expect what came next.

Pat stared at the picture for a long moment, then turned her gaze in his direction. "You did this?" she asked, slowly nodding towards the picture.

"Yes, ma'am," TJ replied, smiling despite himself, but the smile quickly disappeared as he recognized the look of fear and distrust growing on Pat's face. She opened her mouth, about to say something, when her cell phone rang. She paused for a moment, then took the phone out of the pocket of her slacks. She glanced at the phone, a confused look replacing the fear.

"That's strange. It's my mother. She never calls me unless...Sorry, I have to take this," she said as she placed the phone to her ear.

"Hello, Mother. To what do I owe..." She stopped and listened to the person on the other end, a look of anguish growing on her face. She continued to listen for several seconds before finally saying, "Yes, I'll leave at once and catch the first plane that'll get me there. Try not to worry. He's a strong old goat."

She ended the call and dropped the phone on the now forgotten picture. "It's my dad. He had a massive heart attack earlier this evening. He's in intensive care. I've got to go to him."

"Of course," Allan said as he leaped out of his chair and went to her side. "I'll drive you to the airport. Kendra, will you call and see when the next flight to..."

"Alexandria," Pat finished for him. "I can fly into either Ronald Reagan or Dulles International."

TJ noticed her eyes tearing up. *So she has a dad who she loves as well,* he thought. Maybe she wasn't so bad after all.

"Also, Kendra, could you possibly stay and watch over TJ? I know it's a school night..."

"Don't worry about that. I have my books here. I'll call my mom and let her know. You two get yourself to the airport. I'll call you when I have the airline information."

"Thanks, Kendra," Allan said as he helped Pat from her chair. She wobbled a bit, but it was hard to tell if it was from the wine or the tragic news she'd just received.

As everyone rushed out of the kitchen, TJ remained in his chair, gazing down at the picture he'd drawn. His mind wasn't on the drawing but on the look he'd seen on Pat's face just before the phone call.

Fathers

1

While the main roads had finally been cleared of snow, many of the secondary roads were still covered in a hard packed mixture of ice and snow making driving hazardous for even the most expert driver. Usually, the journey to the Asheville airport could be covered in thirty to forty minutes. Tonight it would take nearly twice as long.

Kendra had called them with the airline schedule. The only remaining flight was due to leave in a couple hours on the way to Charlotte where Pat could catch another flight to Dulles. It would be tight, but they could make it...just.

The moonless night limited Allan's visibility. The wet blacktop of the recently cleared highway devoured the headlights, complicated by clumps of snow that kept falling from overhanging trees onto the SUV's windshield, mixing with the muddy spray from the cars in front of them. The tension that had concentrated along Allan's neck and shoulders was nothing compared to the strain inside the cab from the deathly silence.

Allan knew how close Pat and her father were. She often referred to him and more than once he'd heard them joking with each other on the phone. *She must be worried to death,* Allan thought as he flipped on the windshield wipers to clear the snow and moisture, only to spread it into an icy mess.

"I had a thought during dinner." Allan finally broke the silence. "Want to hear it?"

"I guess," Pat replied unenthusiastically.

"I think it's time we enroll TJ in school. Clearly, he's smart enough to handle it. I wouldn't be surprised if he made the honor club, though I guess they don't have that until they get a little older."

There followed a long pause. Allan thought Pat hadn't heard what he'd said and started to repeat it when she replied.

"You're kidding, right?" The condescending tone of her voice was unmistakable.

"I don't know. It's been a few years since I was involved with school. They might have some kind of honor thing..."

"That's not what I'm talking about," Pat interrupted. "You can't be serious about enrolling TJ into school."

"Why not?" Allan replied. "You know he's smart enough. The picture proves that not to mention how curious and interested he is in learning."

"Let me ask you a question," Pat said with just a little less edge. "How old is TJ?"

"I'd say he'd pass for five easily. Probably even six or seven."

"No, that's how old he looks, but how old is he actually? How long has he been alive?"

Allan thought about the questions and suddenly realized where Pat was going with her question. "Oh, yeah, I guess we'd have to work around that somehow."

"What? Like changing schools every few weeks because he's obviously growing so fast that no one could help but notice?" Pat said with such sarcasm that Allan could feel his hackles raise. "And there's at least one other little matter you'd have to 'work around.'"

"What's that?" Allan finally asked though he was pretty sure he wasn't going to like the answer.

"He's an alien!" Pat shouted.

"Oh, we're not going to start that again, are we?" Allan shot back.

"Start it again? No, because we never ended it in the first place. You asked me to give it some time. Well, I have, and yet nothing has changed. That thing back there you call TJ is still not of this world. You're still refusing to deal with reality, and I'm still unwilling to live in your fantasy world where deceased boys come back to complete the happily ever after fairy tale."

Allan suddenly swerved the car to avoid a tree limb that had fallen onto the edge of the road. He fought to bring the SUV back under control. When he finally did, he turned and glanced at Pat.

"Why don't you tell me how you really feel?"

"Good try, but humor isn't going to work here," Pat replied a little calmer. "It's not going to have this issue magically disappear. It's going to need to be dealt with. You even thinking for a moment about enrolling TJ into school demonstrates how out of touch with reality you are. Maybe it's a good thing I'm being called away right now. I think we could use a little break. Our lives have certainly been overwhelming lately."

Allan could feel Pat staring at him even though she appeared as only a silhouette in the dark cab. She sighed. "I really can't deal with this tonight though. Just get me to the airport and, after this crisis with my dad is over, we'll talk. Until then, how about a truce?"

"Yeah," Allan replied. "Fair enough."

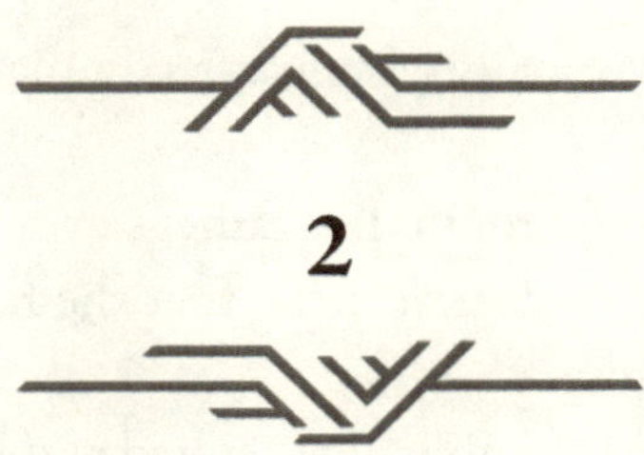

2

Pat strolled down the hallway of the Inova Alexandria Hospital on the way to ICU. The determined look on her face was matched by the gait of her walk.

I swear if one more nurse or orderly asks me where I'm going, I'm going to punch them out, she thought as she rounded the corner and saw a sign for her destination. A kind, matronly nurse looked up from her paperwork has Pat approached and gave her a warm smile.

"Good morning, dear," the nurse said as she stood up and walked around the counter. "You must be Pat."

"That's correct," Pat replied, momentarily taken aback." How did you know my name?"

"From your father. He described you right down to your walk," the nurse replied with a chuckle. "He warned me that if I tried to stop you from seeing him, I would be taking my life in jeopardy. So if you would please come with me, he's waiting to see you."

As of two of them walked through a set of swinging double doors, the nurse said, "We have a dumb rule here of no visitors in ICU, but since you are family if we keep this discreet it shouldn't be a problem. Besides, the older I get, the more I seem to enjoy bending or even breaking such stupid rules."

She pointed to a door they were approaching. "He's right in there."

Pat thanked her and slowly pushed the door open, suddenly frightened by what she might see on the other side. Her father lay propped up in bed with a myriad of tubes and wires running from him that included an IV in his left arm and a small tube running up his nose to supply him with oxygen. Pat could hear a rhythmic *beep beep* that matched the squiggly lines on one of the monitors. Her father's face was turned towards the door. Pat was alarmed to see that his normally vibrant tan complexion had been replaced with a gray pasty mask.

As she walked into the room, her father's eyes fluttered open, and he smiled weakly. "I hope this doesn't mean that the hospital is going to have to replace its ICU head nurse."

"No, she heeded your warning," Pat replied and laughed. It was good to see that her father still had his sense of humor.

"Come over here where I can see you," her father said in a voice just slightly above a whisper. "And don't mind all these wires and tubes. I'm thinking of auditioning for a part in one of those hospital shows on TV."

Pat rushed to him, jumping on his chest to give him a big hug. Realizing what she had done, she pulled back.

"Oh, I'm sorry!"

"No need to apologize, my dear," her father replied." I'm sure if my doctor were here he would prescribe a big hug from my daughter. It's exactly what I need right now."

Pat gave him a second hug but more gently this time. Seeing him like this, she realized how much he meant to her and how much she had missed him. Oh sure, they spoke on the phone every couple of weeks, but it wasn't the same as being face-to-face. In years past, she had rationalized not visiting more often by telling herself she was just too busy. She had her business as a private investigator to manage, and of course, in this past year, there'd been the small matter of stopping an alien from taking over the world. The thought reminded her of the argument she had had with Allan just a few hours ago. Could his relationship with TJ be anything like the relationship she and her father shared? After all, in Allan's world, TJ was the son who he loved dearly and would do anything for. Was that really all that different? Yes, came the answer. *I am the product of a union between two humans. TJ is not.*

"You know, dear, I'm going to be fine," her father said as he gently rubbed her hair.

His words brought her back to the present, and she stood up. She put her hand to her face to rub an itch and was surprised to find it come away wet with tears, a response she hadn't had in a long time. When she had gotten the call about her father's condition, it had scared her more than anything else she'd experienced over this past year, and that had been a lot. For her entire life, her father had been her staunchest supporter through thick and thin, never giving up on her and always finding the positive even in the darkest of times. *Just like Allan is there for TJ* flashed in her mind, and was immediately refuted with a loud *no, it's not the same.*

Pat sat on the edge of the bed, careful not to disturb any of the tubes and wires. She reached out and grasped her father's hand, surprised by its coolness. She studied his hand and was surprised once again. She had always known her father to have the strongest hands of anyone she'd ever met, but the ones she now looked at were those of an old man. Where had those age marks come from, and when had the skin become paper thin? When had all that changed? When had her father grown old?

Little Helpers

1

The following afternoon Allan made it a point to leave the office a little early so he would have time to talk to Kendra about enrolling TJ into school. When he opened the door and walked into the great room, he noticed Kendra in the midst of transforming the room into a Christmas Wonderland. She was arranging a garland around a metal frame. Several boxes of Christmas decorations sat on the floor, waiting to be unpacked. Allan glanced around to find TJ dressed in a forest green outfit complete with a Santa Claus hat and shoes with turned up toes. "Well, TJ, aren't you something? I don't know what exactly but something," he exclaimed.

"He's Santa's little helper," Kendra said as she turned around and walked over to Allan. Then in a softer voice, she said, "Someone had to introduce him to the Christmas season. Besides, my mom isn't all that into Christmas these days, so I didn't want these decorations to go to waste. I hope it's okay with you."

"Sure, I guess. It's fine. No, more than fine. It's a great idea. I've had my mind on so many other things. In fact, that's why I'm home early. I want to run an idea by you."

"Okay," Kendra replied. "Is it alright if TJ and I continue to decorate while you talk?"

"Yes. I may even help you," Allan replied as he opened one of the boxes and looked inside. "While I may have missed introducing TJ to the Christmas season, I have been thinking about other aspects of his education." Allan paused for a moment, then dove into his well-prepared speech intended to convince Kendra into helping him with the idea. He continued to lay out his plans, including the conversation he had had with Pat on the way to the airport, leaving out the details of why Pat was opposed to his idea.

"So you see, Kendra, I'm going to need your help with this plan. I thought we would wait until after school starts back in session the first of the year. It might be a good idea for TJ to take a placement test to see which grade to start him in. What do you think of my idea?"

Kendra put down the string of lights she was untangling and glanced over to TJ. "Honey, could you give your father and me a minute alone? Why don't you take that box of decorations there to your room and decorate it?"

TJ did as he was told and after he had left, Kendra turned back to Allan. She picked up the lights again and fidgeted with them for a minute before finally looking directly at Allan. "I'm afraid, in this instance, I have to agree with Pat."

"You what?"

"Pat is right. It would be a really bad idea to enroll TJ in school and here's why. You and I know TJ is an extraordinary little boy, but unfortunately children his age won't see him as special. They will only see him as strange, weird, different, and kids can be very cruel when they want to be. I'm afraid TJ would be taunted and bullied."

Allan slowly nodded. "I hadn't thought about that," he admitted.

"However," Kendra continued, "I agree with you that TJ needs an education, and there is more than one way for a smart boy like him to be educated."

"What did you have in mind?" Allan asked.

"We could homeschool him," Kendra said smiling broadly. "It's really a perfect solution. I've been thinking seriously about going into teaching after I graduate in a couple of years and my helping with TJ's homeschooling would be perfect training for me. I've been doing some research on the internet while at school and there are a lot of resources available for homeschooling families and more coming online every day."

"Homeschool him? I have to admit I don't know much about what's involved in homeschooling, but it sounds interesting and probably much more practical for TJ, given his special situation."

"Speaking of which," Kendra added. "While I was on the internet, I did some additional research about conditions that result in rapid growth among children, but I couldn't find anything that would cause the rate of growth that I've witnessed in TJ."

"Like I said, his condition is quite rare and..."

Kendra held up her hand to stop him. "You don't have to say anything else, Dr. Allan. I know you're just trying to protect him, but you don't need to protect him from me. I don't know what's going on here with TJ and, to tell you the truth, I don't need to know. You see, I love that little guy as though he were my own. There's nothing I wouldn't do for him, and that includes protecting him from those little monsters that he would run into in a public school. So can we agree that homeschooling is the best route to go?"

Allan nodded, walked over, and gave Kendra a big hug.

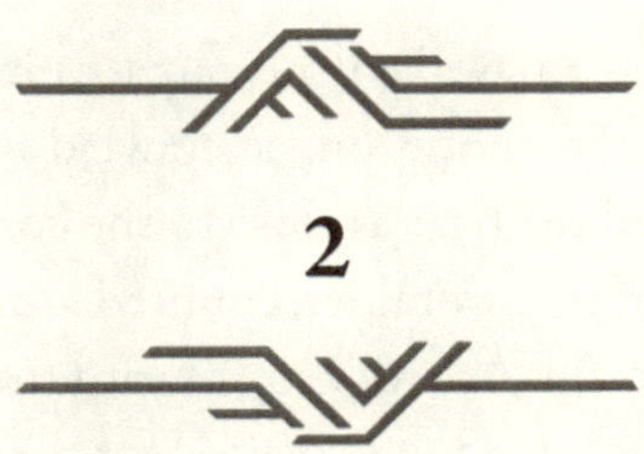

2

It was time for Aeo to proceed with the process of reconstructing a body for the consciousness formally known as Homlin. For that, it would use a pupal stage of the FreeForm and a surrogate. Aeo just needed to select the best pupa to grow the body, but what animal could it find to implant the pupae in for gestation? It started by analyzing the skeletal remains of the large animal it had found in the cave and determined it to be a black bear. Another of this species should do nicely as a surrogate.

While such a surrogate could be either female or male in a pinch, the process was simpler in a female so Aeo went about formulating pheromones that would attract a fully grown female. It took only a couple of days before Aeo sensed one sniffing around outside. Aeo determined from the remains of the bear in the cave that the species particularly enjoyed the taste of fish, so it added the smell of brown trout to the mix. As the bear strolled into the cave with its nose high in the air, Aeo gently entered its mind and instilled a calming effect on the bear, which yawned but continued to walk in the direction of the enticing smells.

Aeo slowly took over the motor functions of the bear, directing it to lie down on the cave floor near the stainless steel receptacle that held the pupae. Unfortunately, it had underestimated the bear's size and weight as well as its ability to control the unfamiliar body which came crashing down to the floor, almost overturning the container.

That should be close enough, Aeo thought as the container teetered on the brink of falling over before it finally righted itself. Having already selected the healthiest pupa, Aeo now checked to be sure it had not been damaged by the impact of the bear. The pupal stage was when FreeForm was the most vulnerable. Once it was inside the surrogate, it would be much better protected as it slowly adapted itself to conditions of this planet.

All that was left was to awaken the pupa so it could travel from the container into the bear. FreeForm pupae crawled notoriously slow, which was why Aeo had wanted the bear as close to the container as possible. Aeo opened the domed lid of the container, counted around to the fourth compartment, and flipped its lid. As it did so, it heard the slight "wheeze" sound as a tiny cloud of smoke escaped. Aeo waited for the pupa to awaken. Finally, the short wormlike pupa crawled out of its compartment and headed towards the bear. It would take most of the day for it to make its way from the container, onto the bear's furry body and eventually into its vulva; a journey that was instinctual and without the need of the AI's interference. Its job at this point was to keep the pupa and its surrogate safe, so Aeo redirected most of its energy away from the miracle of life happening nearby and to the outer perimeter of the cave. That's when it picked up the distant *womp-womp* sound of the helicopter for the first time.

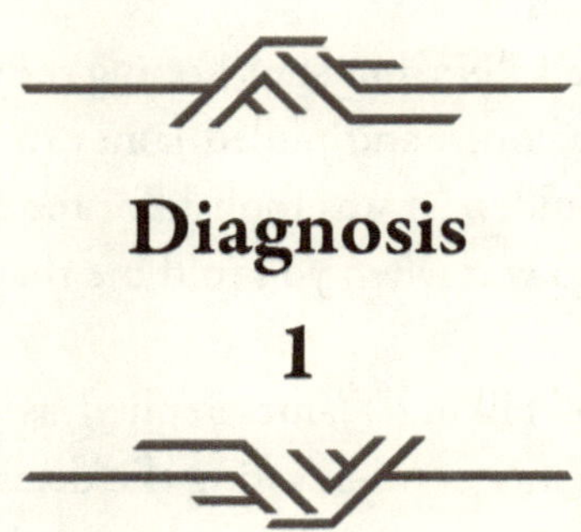

Diagnosis

1

After the bartender returned with his drink, James spun his chair around and watched a couple of young ladies playing a game of darts. Funny, he didn't remember there being a dartboard before, but then again a lot could change in four years—a whole lot. Take his life for instance.

Four years ago, he'd discovered the Suds and Duds, and considered it a safe haven to get away from his regular life. A week after finding it, his wife, Jenny, came home from a routine pregnancy exam with a worried look on her face.

"When I told the P.A. I felt much more tired this time around, she suggested running a few blood tests. I know money is tight right now, but I thought..."

"No, of course, it's okay," James interrupted, taking her hand and guiding her to the living room. "You let me worry about the money. Your job is to take good care of yourself and the baby."

Jenny's worried look relaxed a bit. "I was hoping you'd say that. You know I have my egg money we can use if need be." Jenny had her own little business keeping a couple dozen laying hens, which provided her with a bit of mad money that she seldom used except for emergencies.

"We'll deal with that later," James replied, sitting down beside her on the worn out couch they'd inherited from Jenny's parents. "What did the tests show?"

"They had to send the blood out for some of the tests, but they were able to run a few in-house. The P.A. says I'm anemic, more than to be expected just from the pregnancy."

"You have looked a little pale lately," James added. "That would also explain the tiredness. Did she say what the cause of the anemia was?"

Jenny shook her head. "No, but she's hoping the other blood tests will." She leaned back on the couch and pulled James towards her so she could put her head on his shoulder. "It was foolish for me to want a second child. I should have listened to you when you told me that we already had a perfect little girl."

"Hush that kind of talking," James replied as he gently stroked her auburn hair. "No point in second-guessing the decision. If we created one perfect child, we can create a second one just as easily."

But what if there was something wrong with this baby? He'd heard horror stories from some of his friends about babies born with Down's Syndrome and other malformations that had led to thousands of dollars of medical expenses. Thousands of dollars they didn't have. *We'll cross that bridge if we come to it*, James reminded himself. Besides, anemic pregnant ladies weren't all that uncommon. It would probably end up being nothing at all. They could probably handle the anemia with some vitamins, or iron, or something.

But it hadn't been nothing, nor was it something that could be handled with a few vitamins. The blood tests came back a few days later, which prompted Jenny's doctor to ask for a few more tests, then an x-ray and later an MRI. By the time it was all over, the medical bills were in the thousands of dollars, and that was just the beginning of the nightmare. The diagnosis was confirmed. Pregnant Jenny had cervical cancer.

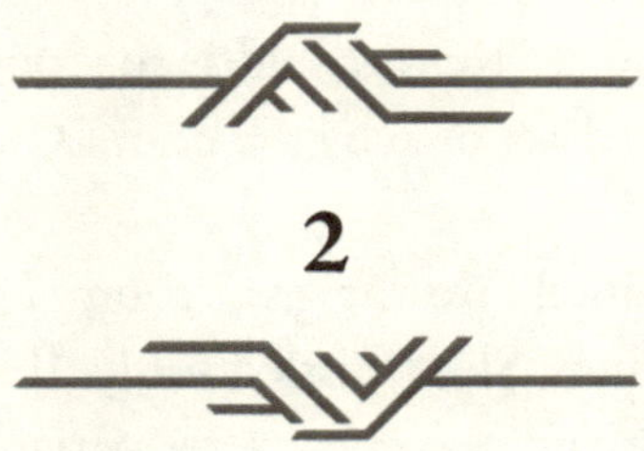

2

Kendra wondered why it always seemed to take twice as long to put Christmas decorations away as it did to put them up in the first place. She stuffed the garland into the plastic storage container and popped the top on it. Here it was mid-January already, and she was just now getting around to undecorating Dr. Pritchard's home. Fortunately, he had been good about not nagging her. In fact, Kendra wondered if he had even noticed the decorations. He seemed to have so much on his mind lately since Pat left.

The one thing that he had done to be commended for was to help Kendra prepare for TJ's homeschooling by upgrading the internet connection to broadband. Kendra didn't exactly understand what that meant except that now when TJ and she went on to the internet, it was much faster and no longer required dialing up to service. The improvement had been one of the reasons she decided to break one of Allan's cardinal rules by inviting Mimi to drop by for a visit. She just had to show off the new internet service. Besides, she knew she could trust her best friend to keep her secret about TJ. Hadn't they shared everything over the years? It had felt wrong to keep TJ from Mimi, and it felt very freeing when she finally included her. Now it was time for the two of them to meet.

She had been hinting to Allan that she could use someone to assist her with TJ's education as a way of preparing him for Mimi, but the timing hadn't been right yet to break the news to him. She had finished stacking the boxes of Christmas decorations next to the door when she heard a light tapping. She peeked through the window next to the door and saw Mimi waiting on the porch. She opened the door and welcomed her friend inside.

"So this is where you spend all your time these days," Mimi said as she took off her coat and scarf and gazed around at the warm, rustic setting of the log home."Not bad, not bad at all."

“Here, let me take those," Kendra said as she took Mimi's coat and scarf and hung them up next to her own by the door. "Come on in. I have someone I want you to meet.”

As the two girls strolled into the great room, Mimi continued to gaze around at her surroundings. She whistled softly. “I may have to reconsider my career as a journalist and become a veterinarian instead. They seem to do pretty well."

"Sure, if you don't mind seven or eight years of college," Kendra replied.

“Nix on that,” Mimi said.

"TJ, would you come in here, please? I have someone I want you to meet!" Kendra called out. She continued to show Mimi around by taking her into the kitchen and pointing out where the bedrooms were before returning to the great room, but there was still no sign of TJ.

"That little rascal," Kendra said. “He gets on the computer and forgets the rest of the world exists. Let's go into the study. I want to show you the nifty computer system Dr. Pritchard has that TJ and I get to use."

As they walked into Allan's office, they saw TJ sitting on a booster seat. Allan had bought it for him over Christmas to make it easier for him to reach the computer.

"Didn't you hear me calling you?" Kendra asked, but there was no irritation in her voice. After all, how could you get angry at a little boy who had such passion for learning?

"I'm sorry," TJ replied, finally looking up from the computer screen. "I was reading about birds and how they came from dinosaurs."

“Reading?" Mimi asked. “How old is he?"

“He doesn't mean he's actually reading," Kendra replied, sidestepping Mimi's question. “He means he's been looking at the pictures of birds and dinosaurs." Although she couldn't figure out how TJ could've come to that conclusion just from a few pictures.

“No," TJ corrected her. “I don't understand all the words yet, but enough to understand what they mean."

“Really?" the two girls said at the same time with matching looks of astonishment.

"Sorry. I forget my manners," Kendra said. "TJ, I'd like you to meet my best friend, Mimi Rawlins. Mimi, this is TJ; the smartest little boy in the whole wide world."

Schooling

TJ climbed down from the booster seat and walked over to Mimi. Holding out his hand as he had been taught, he said, "It is good to meet you, Mimi." He hoped the irritation he felt for having to leave his research wasn't conveyed in the tone of his voice. Besides, if Mimi was a friend of Kendra, then perhaps she would become one of his friends as well.

After a moment of hesitation, Mimi bent down and shook TJ's hand. "It's a pleasure to meet you as well. I've heard many good things about you from Kendra."

"In that case, I'm sure it was all true," TJ replied.

Kendra and Mimi both laughed at the comment even though TJ had not intended it to be funny; he was merely trying to convey how much he trusted Kendra to tell the truth.

Still chuckling, Mimi turned to Kendra. "You didn't tell me that TJ was modest as well."

"That's just one of the special qualities you'll learn about my little man if you hang around enough, which I hope you will," Kendra replied. "You see, Dr. Pritchard has decided it would be best for TJ to be homeschooled, and he has asked me to help. I'm excited about doing so, but I also have to be sure my own grades don't slip. I thought together, we could do a much better job. As you can see, TJ is very smart and learns quickly. What do you say?"

"That sounds like it would be a lot of fun. I would not only be helping TJ but also helping my best friend. Would it be okay if I use the computer sometimes for my own research? It could sure help out with some of the writing assignments in my journalism class."

"Sure," Kendra replied.

"I have one question though," Mimi said. "Why did Dr. Pritchard decide to homeschool TJ?"

TJ watched Kendra as she took a deep breath and slowly let it out before she answered her friend.

"What I'm about to tell you has got to remain a secret between you and me. You have to promise on a stack of Bibles that under no circumstances will you tell anyone, and that includes not putting it in the school newspaper. Do you promise?"

"Sure, I guess," Mimi replied with a puzzled look on her face.

"No guessing. I need a sure, no kidding, promise to never tell anyone or write about what I'm about to tell you."

"Okay, okay! I promise on a stack of Bibles that reaches up to the ceiling that I will not tell anyone what you are about to tell me nor will I write about it."

What in the world is Kendra about to tell her, TJ wondered? It sounded like it had something to do with him, but he couldn't think what it could be that would be that big of a secret.

"I don't know exactly what is going on with TJ either," Kendra started. "I do know TJ is growing at an incredible rate. I've done some research on the internet, and found a few rare conditions that can cause rapid growth in children, but not nearly to the degree which it is occurring in TJ."

"Really?" Mimi said in an astonished voice. Suddenly she was staring at him like he was some rare bug, and he didn't like it at all. TJ took a step back and glanced at Kendra for help, but evidently, Kendra had not noticed the change in her friend.

"So, how fast are you growing? How old are you really? What does it feel like to be growing so fast? Does that mean you're always hungry? Do you have any idea..."

Mimi started shooting questions at TJ rapid fire, causing him to take a step back and then a second one, finally holding up one hand.

"Down, girl, down," Kendra said as she stepped between Mimi and TJ, her hackles suddenly raised like a mother bear. "I need you to take off your journalism hat and just be my friend. Can you do that?"

"Sure, I guess," Mimi replied. "It's just that I'm so fascinated by what you just told me. Are you sure I can't write about it if I left both of your names out of it?"

"Definitely not!" Kendra shouted. "I'm beginning to regret telling you TJ's secret. In fact, I'm beginning to regret inviting you over here at all."

That's telling her, TJ thought, but then noticed the hurt look on Mimi's face. Suddenly, he felt sorry for her, despite how she had just acted. "It's okay, Kendra. I'm sure she didn't mean anything by it."

"He's right," Mimi said. "I'm sorry, really I am. You know how excited I get when I hear about the strange or unusual. The weirder, the better, that's my motto."

Strange? Unusual? Weird? Is she talking about me, TJ wondered? Suddenly he didn't feel sorry for her after all.

"There you go again," Kendra said. "There's nothing strange, unusual, or weird about TJ. Okay, maybe a little unusual. I prefer to think that he has unique qualities that make him who he is."

Mimi stared first at her friend, then at TJ, and back to Kendra again. "Okay," she said slowly. "I really do want to help the two of you, and I appreciate you sharing this secret with me. I want you to know you can trust me with it." She turned back to TJ.

"I apologize if what I said hurt you in any way. It was certainly not my intention. People in these parts have considered me strange, unusual, and weird most of my life. I think I've actually grown to enjoy it. After all, being normal can be awfully boring."

"Well, normal and boring are two things we don't have to worry about around here," Kendra said with a laugh. "There is very little that is normal, and it's never boring."

"Sounds like the perfect place to me." Mimi laughed as well. "Maybe we should start over." She turned and held out her hand to TJ. "Hi, my name is Mimi Rawlins. It's my pleasure to be your new assistant home-school teacher, and I hope your new and trusted friend as well."

TJ hesitated for a moment and then held out his hand to shake hers. There was something about the conversation that still troubled him. Was it okay to be strange, unusual, or even weird? He had to admit the idea of being normal felt appealing to him. As long as he could remember, he had always felt out of place and like he didn't belong. Even here at home, there were times he felt different from everyone else. That was particularly true whenever Pat was around, and especially when he heard Pat and his dad arguing. He'd have to give this some more thought. Maybe he could find some answers on the internet.

High Alert

1

The *womp-womp* sound of the human's aircraft slowly faded away, but Aeo stayed on high alert. That had been the third time in less than a week it had detected a helicopter flying over the area. While a second smaller snowstorm had delayed a full out search, it was now time to relocate before one of the human aircrafts landed and complicated matters considerably.

The growth of the FreeForm pupa had progressed well in the past few weeks, and the surrogate bear was beginning to show signs of its growth, both from its extended abdomen, as well as the thinning of its body as the larval form fed off it. The bear had not been well nourished when it found its way to the cave. And there was still the possible complication of it dying from malnutrition before the larva would be ready to be delivered, so relocating to a new and safer place would also be a good time to allow the bear to hunt for food. Aeo searched the consciousness of the bear for a new location and discovered a second cave not too far away.

Aeo decided to wait until night to make a move. It had been monitoring the phases of the planet's satellite body and knew it would provide sufficient light for the bear while still reducing the chances of it being discovered. Not that a bear walking around at night by itself was likely to draw much attention, but two essential objects would need to be moved as well. Aeo had already calculated that it could manage to carry the all-important cocoon on its back, but it would need the bear to carry the container housing the remaining FreeForm pupae in its mouth.

After the near accident of the bear almost knocking over the FreeForm pupae container, Aeo decided it needed to have better control. Once the pupae were safely inside the bear, it had practiced manipulating the bear, and control had improved considerably. Now it was time to move the operation to a new location away from the prying eyes of humans.

Aeo sprouted six crab-like legs and two arms from its body, picked up the cocoon, balanced it on top of its body, and started making its way to the mouth of the cave. As it did so, it directed the bear to pick up the pupae container and follow behind him.

Although they had a dangerous journey ahead of them, once it was completed, all that would remain would be to finish growing the larva into a human, implant the fragmented consciousness of Homlin, instill the Primary Directive, and send it on its way; all without being discovered. *I can do this*, Aeo thought as it stepped into the night.

2

F*inally, after a crazy couple of weeks, a slow afternoon in the clinic*, Allan thought as he glanced at the appointment book, although he wasn't sure whether his receptionist, Donna, had not at least partially fabricated the break. She had been known to do that in the past whenever she detected that her boss was about to collapse. He thought about asking her about the lack of afternoon appointments but then decided against it. Whether Donna had manipulated the schedule or if it had just been a happy accident didn't really matter. The truth was he really did need a break, and so when Donna returned from lunch and made the suggestion that perhaps he would like to slip out early from the clinic, he graciously accepted the invitation.

Wouldn't Kendra be surprised to see him coming home before 6 o'clock, Allan wondered as he drove down the dirt road leading to his home. Maybe he would pass along the good fortune and let her go home early as well, though he would still pay her for hours. She had become such a blessing in his life. He didn't know how he would have gone about raising TJ without her help. For sure, there would have been no way he could have had TJ homeschooled, and as she had pointed out, sending TJ to regular school was really not an option either.

Come to think of it, it was probably time for him to either give Kendra a raise, or at least a bonus as his way of letting her know how much he appreciated her. He was still considering which option to take as he pulled up to the house and noticed a second bicycle leaning against the tree next to Kendra's. A slow knot of worry grew in Allan's gut. Two bicycles in the drive must mean someone else was here, but how could that be? Kendra knew better than to allow anyone else in the house unless she had decided to break his cardinal rule.

As he walked through the front door and into the foyer area, he noticed the two coats hanging from the coat rack and could hear two distinct voices of young girls. He recognized Kendra's voice, but who did the second voice belong to? He followed the voices back to his study, where he found TJ, Kendra, and a second girl with short auburn hair at his desk playing with the computer.

As he entered the room, he coughed and said, "Hello, what do we have here? A new guest? Surely not, because Kendra knows better than to invite someone over here without my permission."

The two girls and TJ turned abruptly in his direction with shocked looks on their faces. Kendra was the first one to find her voice. "Hello, Doc. I didn't expect you home so early."

"Obviously," Allan replied sternly, not trying to hide his displeasure. "How about introducing me to your friend."

"Oh, sure. This is Mimi Rawlins. I think I mentioned her to you before." Allan could hear the tremble in her voice.

"Yes, I do remember you mentioning that you two were friends, but I don't remember giving you permission... Wait a minute. Mimi Rawlins? Aren't you in charge of the school newspaper? In fact, haven't I seen a couple articles in our local paper with your byline?"

"Yes, that's right Dr. Pritchard," Mimi said as she stepped forward to shake his hand, apparently pleased that he was familiar with her work.

Allan ignored the extended hand. "Oh, great! Not only do you break my rule, and invite someone over here without my permission, but you have to invite a young journalist. Kendra, what were you thinking?"

"That I needed some help with TJ's homeschooling," Kendra answered in a soft voice. "I was planning to tell you; honest, I was. It just never seemed to be the right time, what with you being so busy and all. I'm sorry Doc, really I am, but I can assure you Mimi can be trusted. I made her promise on a stack of Bibles not to say or write anything about TJ."

"She did," Mimi confirmed. "And I've kept my promise and will continue to do so. Like Kendra, I have grown very fond of TJ. I know about his 'unique characteristic' of growing rapidly, and you can trust me to keep it a secret, although I would like to ask..."

Kendra gave her friend a dirty look. "Mimi, don't you dare."

She turned to Allan, and anguish look on her face. "Please, Doc. I know I shouldn't have said anything to Mimi without talking to you first, but she really is someone we can trust, and she has been a great teacher for TJ."

Allan could just imagine opening the morning paper and seeing the headline:

Local Veterinarian Arrested for Harboring Alien

And boy, wouldn't Pat have a field day when she learned that someone else knew about TJ's secret, but wait a minute. What did Mimi really know? It was unlikely she knew any more than Kendra knew, and that was only that TJ was growing at a rapid rate. Maybe, just maybe, this wasn't a complete disaster.

TJ, who had been watching and listening to the three of them this whole time, now climbed down from the office chair and ran over to Allan to give him a hug as he gazed up at Allan with a big smile.

"I really like Mimi. Please don't be mad at Kendra. She was just trying to help me. Not only do I have a second teacher, but I also have a new friend."

Allan stared at TJ with his bright eyes and was once again amazed by how much the boy had grown. He had heard other parents talk about how fast their children grew up, but in TJ's case, it was indeed a miracle. He looked around at the three kids and remembered the sound of their talking and laughing as he had entered the house. No doubt this subterfuge had been going on without his knowledge for quite a while and, though he hated to admit it, it appeared to be working well.

"Okay," Allan said as he gave each of them a hard stare. "There's nothing I can do at this point to reverse what has already happened, but I need to know for certain that this is not going to go any further. No one else is to know about TJ unless I okay it. Is that clear?"

The three of them looked at each other and then slowly nodded their heads.

"Absolutely clear," Kendra assured him. "You can count on us."

"That's right, Dad," TJ said. "I just have one question."

"And what's that?" Allan asked.

"Does that mean that Mimi is going to have to call the *Waynesboro Gazette* and cancel the article about the boy who grew too fast?"

There was a long moment of silence as Allan, and the two girls stared at TJ in astonishment before TJ finally said, "Gotcha!" and laughed.

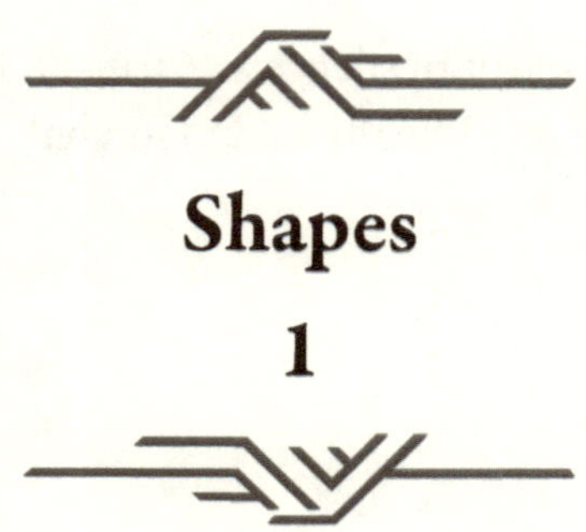

Shapes

1

The Saint Bernard lumbered through the undisturbed snow of the forest, looking more like a galloping horse than a large dog as it turned its head from side to side. It had been a long time since he had the opportunity to run so freely and he was thoroughly enjoying the experience. As he reached the crest of the hill, he paused and look down at the serene winter landscape of his home. He had come to love the log cabin and the people who lived inside. They had become his family; at least most of them had.

As much as he enjoyed romping through the woods, it was getting late. It was time for him to return to his true form although, in truth, this form felt very comfortable as well. But then he remembered something Homlin had told him during his brief stay at Homlin's hunting preserve.

"The longer you stay in a form, the more comfortable you will feel in it, but be careful, because it is possible to get lost in that form and forget who you truly are," Homlin had warned him. Remembering that warning, TJ trotted back to where he had hidden his clothes and returned to the form of a human boy. He quickly dressed, shivering as he did so. Funny, he felt quite comfortable with the winter temperatures as a Saint Bernard but not as a young human. Then again, he would be uncomfortable as a large dog with such a shaggy coat in the middle of summer. The thought started him wondering again about something he'd recently noticed. No one else he knew ever seemed interested in shapeshifting. That discovery led him to the internet, where he learned other humans couldn't change their physical form. That discovery reminded him of another warning he'd received, this time from Allan only a few days ago.

"You have many special gifts and talents that make you uniquely who you are, and I encourage you to embrace them. At the same time, some of those gifts are so different not everyone will understand them. Many times, people are afraid of things they don't understand and people who are different from themselves. Be very careful with whom you share your special gifts."

TJ also wondered if he had the unique ability to change from human form to canine, might he be able to learn how to transform into other animal forms. He would need to check that out, but that would have to wait until another day for he was already very close to being late for dinner. It had taken quite a bit to persuade Kendra to let him outside on his own, and he certainly didn't want to lose that privilege.

2

Aeo found very little information in its database about how to select the appearance of the Primary's new body. What it needed was the info crystal that was a part of all settlement missions, but it was missing. The most he was able to glean was some of the qualities and characteristics necessary for the Primary to possess for the mission to be fulfilled. One of the most important features was for the Primary to blend in well with the dominant species of the planet. *Okay,* thought Aeo, *but I'd already deduced that much. What else do you have for me? Beyond just blending in, the Primary should possess good social skills and be well-liked by the dominant species. That makes sense,* thought the AI. In the research Aeo had been doing about the dominant species through their internet database, it had learned that this species of Homo sapiens cared a great deal about appearances. In fact, several of their largest industries seemed to center around showcasing beautiful and handsome specimens of the species. This was especially true of the movie industry that invested billions of dollars to parade around the most beautiful examples which they called movie stars.

So, Aeo thought, *it seems to me that it would make sense to shape the primary's new form to look like a movie star.* However, to avoid confusion, it needed to be a movie star that was no longer alive or was all that well-known by the Homo sapiens of today. At the same time, it needed to find one with enough pictures on the internet so it wouldn't have to rely on imagination too much. After scrolling through close to a thousand different pages filled with pictures of movie stars, he finally settled on a male star from the silent movie era.

This particular movie star was considered handsome both by the standards of his day as well as by present-day standards. The man had been so well liked that upon his untimely death thousands of fans had waited for hours for a chance to glimpse his body. *I imagine my Primary will be quite appreciative of my selection*, Aeo thought. It should make the fulfillment of his mission much easier.

With the selection of the form completed, it was now possible to begin imprinting the freeform larva growing within the bear. Finally, the mission was getting back on track.

3

An uncommonly large amount of snow, especially for so early in winter, had made life for many of the inhabitants of Waynesboro difficult. Allan was amazed to see how innovative his clients became when they needed to have one of their pets examined. In a few cases, he had to resort to making house calls to some of his older clients who had not been able to bring their pets to the clinic. Overall, his staff was doing an excellent job in keeping the hospital running smoothly. The one exception to that had been the large chest type freezer used for storing the bodies of deceased pets. It had been nearly full before the first winter storm, and there was now no more room in it. Fortunately, Donna had received a call from the pet cemetery they used to handle such matters informing her that they'd be able to pick up that evening. Under the best of circumstances, the task of disposing of the dead carcasses was one of the least favorite duties of his staff members. On this occasion, Dr. Pritchard decided to make it easy on them and handle it himself.

The truck from the pet cemetery arrived shortly after closing, and Allan unlocked the back door to let the driver in. Together they hauled out the frozen carcasses, each one wrapped in its own black bag. The animals ranged in size from a small Chihuahua to a German Shepherd. Allan recognized most of the names written on the white tape as he handed each body to the driver. The taped names identified each deceased pet in case the owner changed their mind and wanted to bury their pet somewhere else. Allan was relieved to see that most of them had been put down because of old age or other situations beyond his control. However, there were a couple he recognized that he felt he might have done a better job of diagnosis or treatment. At the same time, he knew such hindsight was always perfect, and it didn't help anyone to second-guess himself.

Still, he was thankful when he reached the bottom of the freezer. He wasn't sure his back could have taken lifting another body out of it. He was surprised to find a cardboard box that had been taped closed. It took him a minute to recognize where it had come from. He closed the freezer door, thanked the driver for coming by so late, and sent him on his way. Only then did he return to pull the box from the bottom of the freezer. After a moment of hesitation, he un-taped the box to discover one of the frozen larva he had taken out of Molly several months ago; the same kind of larva that TJ had come from. Staring down at it, he felt a shiver run up and down his back. He had forgotten how repulsive they were. He considered calling the driver back but then thought better of it. Instead, he re-taped the box and wrote on its top, *Do Not Remove.* He placed it back in the bottom of the freezer and closed the door.

Special Delivery

1

For the next few weeks and at the strangest times, Allan found his thoughts returning to the cardboard box hidden away in the freezer. The question kept cropping up, why had he kept the frozen larva? After all, it was not only frozen but dead. He thought about contacting Pat's friend, Oliver, to find out who in the government he could send it to for analysis. He had even convinced himself that was the best course of action to take and made plans to call Oliver the next day, but the next day came and went. For some reason, he kept putting off making the call. He was in his second week of indecision when he finally realized what he really wanted to do with the specimen.

The next evening he waited until everybody had left the clinic before walking out to his car to retrieve the dry ice and shipping container he had purchased at lunchtime. He walked to the back storage area and opened the freezer. It was an easy task to move the few new carcasses out of the way and pull the cardboard box out. He ripped the tape away and, with just a moment of hesitation, opened the box. He stared at the frozen larva for over a minute before taking a pair of exam gloves from his lab coat and putting them on. He didn't consider himself particularly squeamish. After all, as a veterinarian, he had put his hands in a lot of strange places over the years. Even so, he wasn't all that excited about picking up the frozen lava.

He placed the mailing container next to the cardboard box and, taking a deep breath, picked up the larva and quickly dropped it into the container. He then dumped the dry ice over it before sealing the container. He tossed the cardboard box into the trash and carried the container to his office. He scrounged around in his desk drawers looking for an address that he prayed he hadn't tossed. He found it in the bottom drawer among a stack of thank you notes he had received from his clients over the years.

He took a Sharpie from his top drawer and addressed the container:

Dr. Lionel Adams

Bio Vita Tech Labs

100 Laboratory Drive

Research Triangle Park, North Carolina 27709

He dropped the package off at the mailbox store that had recently opened, beating their closing time by only a couple of minutes. As he released the package to the safekeeping of U. P. S., he breathed a sigh of relief. Next, he would call his old college roommate and alert him to be on the lookout for the package. He and Lionel had shared a dorm room for the first two years of undergraduate school. They had both started out in pre-vet, but when Lionel discovered he had a severe allergy to cats, he had switched to a dual major in Biochemistry and Genetics. They'd stayed in touch through the years, mostly exchanging Christmas cards and the occasional phone call, usually about an interesting case that Allan had seen in his clinic or had read about in one of the veterinary journals.

After Allan pulled into the driveway of his home, he sat in his car with his cell phone in his hand, trying to decide what to say. He figured it was a better than 50-50 chance that he'd get Lionel's answering machine. Truth be told, he was praying for that to happen and had about decided he would hang up if Lionel picked up. For once, his prayer was answered. He waited for the beep to deliver the message he had rehearsed in his head.

"Hello, old chum. This is your long lost vet buddy. So sorry it's been so long since we've talked. I wanted to let you know I just mailed a package to you with an unusual specimen in it. I'm sure you'll have plenty of questions about it. Unfortunately, I am not at liberty to answer any of them. Do with it as you will. All I ask is that you tell no one about it, including where it came from."

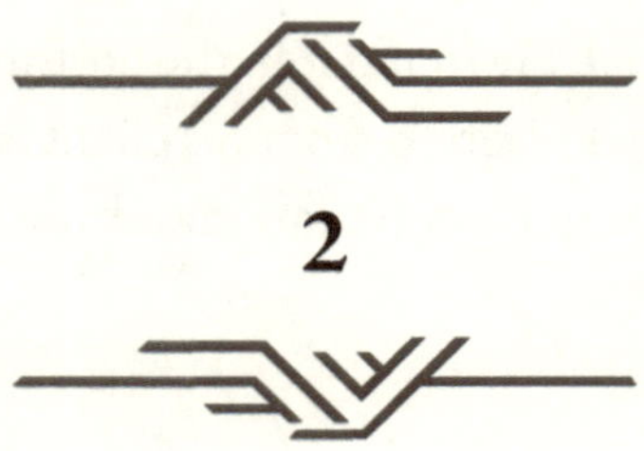

2

Aeo had run a programming sequence to determine the ideal gestation time that would optimize the health and viability of the new body once it was delivered. The program took into account that the longer the larva remained in the surrogate, the better adapted it would be to the unique conditions of the planet while balancing that information with being sure the developing larva did not grow so large that it would explode the surrogate. Observing the distention of the bear's abdomen, Aeo wondered if it had made a miscalculation in the program. It sure looked like the bear might explode at any minute.

So it was with more than a little relief when the program alerted Aeo that it was time to initiate the delivery. Aeo had been manipulating the endocrinology of the bear to keep it from going into labor prematurely. It now released a wave of oxytocin while reducing the level of progesterone to begin the delivery process. It was a long and difficult delivery since the bear had grown weak from malnutrition and the form it was attempting to deliver was larger than a normal bear cub. However, the bear was finally able to push out the form, which, at this stage, appeared to be a cross between a small human child and a bear cub.

It was now time for Aeo to provide the newborn with a unique formula that would accelerate its growth to a full adult. Aeo calculated the next month would be the most critical time for growing the new delivery to a size sufficient that it could start caring for itself, hopefully before the mother bear died from malnutrition and starvation.

During this next phase, Aeo job would be to begin loading the primary's consciousness into the new form, which would also support the form learning to survive in the world. One of the final steps would be to implant the Mission Imperative into the primary's consciousness. Once the mission had been implanted, Aeo's job would be complete. It could then turn the mission over to the Primary, knowing that the Primary Directive would be initiated at the proper time once he had matured sufficiently and become well established in the Homo sapiens' world.

Cave Hunting

The last few months for Pat had been frenetic and exhausting. It felt like she had spent more time in airports and waiting for delayed flights than anything else, as she flew back and forth between seeing her father in Alexandria and then back to Charlotte to oversee the cases of her private investigation firm. Allan's veterinary practice had been busier than usual for this time of year, but still, he had made it a point to call her frequently and had even driven down to Charlotte a few times for dinner before driving home later that night. They spent most of their time talking about each other's cases and her father's slow but steady recovery. The one thing they made a point to never discuss was TJ. Several times, Pat considered asking Allan about TJ as a way of approaching the subject to see if he had had a change of heart, but each time she refrained. After all, she knew what his answer would be, and she was simply too stressed out to get into another argument about it.

By the end of March, with the early signs of spring all around, Pat's father was well enough that he made her promise not to return for at least six months. Allan invited her to come stay with him, but there was one place Pat needed to go first. She had thought about the cave often and had more than once dreamed about it. She felt like it was time to put that real-life nightmare into the past where it belonged. She hoped one last visit to the cave would help; that is if she could find it. The last time she had traveled to it she had been in the trunk of Homlin's car. At the same time, she figured there probably weren't that many caves in the area and the locals would know where most of them were. It was at her fourth stop at a combination convenience store and gas station that she hit pay dirt. The man behind the counter reminded her of a cross between Santa Claus and Charlie Manson. More importantly, he looked like someone who had been born and raised in the mountains. As Pat described the area of the cave in as much detail as she could remember, the old man nodded his head and smiled.

"Yeah, I know the cave you're talking about. It's on old man Jacobs' land. I think there's still an old logging road that'll get you pretty close to it, but you'll need four-wheel-drive. We've had a good bit of rain here lately, and the last couple hundred yards are pretty steep."

After he'd given Pat directions, and she had repeated them back to him to be sure she had them correct, he asked her, "Why would a pretty thing like you want to go to such a God-forsaken place?" But she had already turned around and continued walking out the door. She had learned to ignore such questions, especially when she didn't know the answer to them.

The old man might have been nosy, but at least he gave good directions. Even though she'd estimated the drive would take no more than twenty minutes, forty-five minutes later she was still slipping and sliding up the mountain. Several times it felt like she could go no further, but her stubborn disposition kept her moving forward. By the time she arrived, the lower half of her Jeep Cherokee was caked with mud. She turned the car off and put it in park but remained sitting in it for several minutes, waiting for her heart rate and breathing to return to normal. When they slowed down as much as they were likely to under this circumstances, she opened the car door and stepped out. At this altitude, there were still a few patches of snow in the shaded areas. She walked around to get her bearings, trying to replay that last confrontation with the monstrosity that had been half-human and half-alien in appearance.

Something didn't feel right, but she couldn't put her hands on what it was at first, and then it came to her. There was no body, not even any signs of one. Had Oliver and his team returned to the location and removed it? Of course, if they had, they wouldn't be at liberty to tell her about it, but what if she asked Oliver directly? Would he give her the courtesy of a straight answer for old time's sake? They had been reasonably close once many years ago.

Pat walked around the area outside the cave, replaying the struggle that had taken place last December. Her neck still ached occasionally from being yanked around by the choker collar he had forced her to wear, especially in times when she was under a great deal of stress, like now. But it was time for her to move beyond the traumatic incident that had occurred on this mountainside. She needed to get on with the rest of her life, so she forced herself to recreate the event that had almost cost her her life and had resulted in Homlin's death. She played out the fight blow-by-blow in slow motion until she declared that part complete and mentally filed it away in her past. Everything was proceeding nicely, and she could feel the weight lifting from her shoulders until she came to one small detail she had previously forgotten.

It had happened near the end of the fight shortly after she removed the lug wrench from her coat pocket. She remembered swinging the wrench at Homlin's head, but he partially dodged the blow. The wrench struck his neck and shoulder where it caught on the chain around his neck. She pulled the lug wrench away to strike him again, and the chain and the attached crystal were flung into the bushes. Homlin had glanced in the direction the crystal, giving Pat the opportunity to finish him off.

What had happened to the crystal? Pat walked around the area, playing the scene over in her mind as she tried to remember the exact location where that part of the fight had occurred. When she thought she had found it, she turned in the direction she remembered seeing the crystal fly and slowly walked in that direction with her eyes focused on the ground, but she didn't find the crystal on the ground. Instead, she found it hanging in a bush hidden by a small boulder, the chain and crystal glittering in the light afternoon sunlight. Pat stared at it for a moment before slowly reaching out and pulling it from its hiding place. Holding it in her hand, she studied it closely. It was about the size and shape of a large acorn, but its surface was unlike anything Pat had ever seen. It seemed to have an iridescent glow about it, almost as though it held an electric charge even though it was cool to the touch.

Then she suddenly realized that this was why she had to return to the area. The crystal would be a reminder not only of a difficult, traumatic time but more importantly of how she had overcome tremendous adversity and won. With that revelation, she felt the last weight of stress lift from her shoulders. It was almost time to go home, but not before she checked out the cave. She realized that Oliver and his crew had probably inspected the cave with a fine tooth comb, but hey, they had missed finding the crystal so they might have missed something in the cave as well.

She took the flashlight out of her pocket that she had brought for this part of the trip and turned it on. She strolled over to the mouth of the cave and directed the beam of light into it. The blackness of the cave gobbled up the light making it impossible for Pat to see any details. Was it really necessary to go inside? Hadn't she found what she had come for? She had heard that caves in this region were notorious for rockslides. What would she do if she went inside and the entranceway collapsed? She wasn't particularly claustrophobic, but the thought of entering the cave sent a chill up her back, and she could feel the palms of her hands grow sweaty. She glanced down at the crystal she still held in her hand. Hadn't she just told herself it was to serve as a reminder of her strength to overcome adversity? Certainly, she could handle a quick look inside.

Having made the decision, Pat took a slow step into the cave, then another, and another before turning around and looking out to the surface. *This might have been where TJ stood to watch me as I killed Homlin.* The thought sent another shudder through her body. What kind of relationship had TJ shared with the alien? Perhaps the even more important question was, what kind of relationship would he have with Homlin's murderer? Clearly, the two questions were interconnected. Answer the first, and you'd be able to answer the second. There had to be some connection between TJ and the alien. After all, something had caused TJ to run away from Allan's home, even though he was well cared for by both Allan and Kendra. Had TJ viewed Homlin as his real parent and Allan as only a temporary substitute?

What was it that Allan had told her TJ had said as he exited the cave? "Daddy." Allan had assumed TJ was calling to him, but what if TJ had actually been referring to the dead alien?

Extra Income

Spring was one of James' favorite times of the year. The mountain temperatures were cool at night which made for perfect sleeping weather, and daytime temps were still mild as well. It was also when his businesses tended to pick up. He could understand his heating and air conditioning business increasing. He had some customers who regularly requested their AC be serviced in prep for the warmer temps of summer, which were not far off.

But why did he also often get an increase in calls for his other business in Spring? It didn't make sense to him, but he'd found it to be true. Bad things happened year around, but they invariably increased around March or April every year. This year was no exception. He'd already received five calls from his various contacts including two from Jersey, his old Army buddy that was his number one connection to the world of black ops.

James still remembered the first assignment he'd accepted from Jersey. He'd received some calls previously, turning each of them down, but this one was particularly timely. He'd just received Jenny's latest medical bill. He was sitting at his desk just like he was now, staring at the bills, counting the zeros to the left of the decimal point and realizing he should have gone to medical school as his parents had urged him. How in the hell was he supposed to pay such an outrageous amount?

Then the phone had rung with Jersey's nasally voice on the other end. One of his "clients" needed a talented helicopter pilot immediately.

"I know you've passed on my previous invitations, but you did say last time it was okay for me to stay in touch, so I just thought..."

"How much?" James asked as he continued to stare at the bill in front of him.

Jersey quoted him the price.

"Really? That much? Who do I have to kill?"

"Shouldn't be any killing involved on this one. Just flying the 'copter in and out, but the mission is considered particularly dangerous and top secret, which is the reason for the premium pay. Interested?"

And it had been that easy to become a freelance mercenary for hire. That had been close to four years ago. The second job had kept James from having to declare bankruptcy. Unfortunately, what it hadn't been able to do was save Jenny. Cervical cancer took her life, but not until after she delivered their second baby girl, Jennifer Ann.

Aeo Instructions

1

Aeo lay on the hot rocks outside the cave, his solar panels radiating around him as the afternoon sun began to set over the nearby mountain. Checking the energy gauge, it read seventy-five percent to maximum charge. That would have to do for today. The accumulating clouds threatened a late afternoon thunderstorm, and it was time to awaken the Primary from his nap. It was also time for Aeo to feed him his fourth meal of the day; a combination of the local wildlife mixed with the high energy "mother's milk" that had supplemented the rapid growth from baby to toddler in just three months. One of Aeo's main function at this stage had become converting the energy of this planet's sun into the high octane food supplement.

The day was rapidly approaching when it would be time to release the Primary back into this strange world. In the meantime, the lessons and testing would continue, including this afternoon after the Primary had finished his meal.

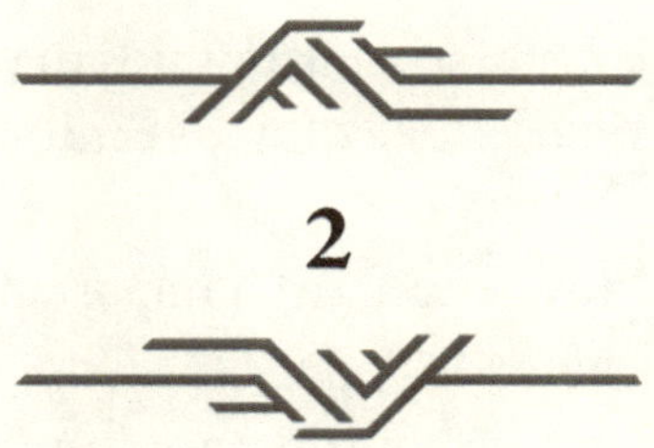

2

As was their routine, Aeo started with a series of questions to check the primary's retention of the previous lessons.

"What is the name you tell humans?"

"Val," came the reply.

"Good, and what is your real name, that you must not reveal but also never forget?"

"Sluneg," came the prompt reply.

Good, Aeo thought. *Now for the next piece of data to imprint.*

"And most important, why are you here?" Aeo asked.

Val paused, a squinted up look of puzzlement on his face that often appeared when Aeo gave him a new question to answer. His eyes raised towards his eyebrows as he tried to retrieve the right answer.

"I'm not sure, but I think it has to do with my people," he finally answered.

"That's a good start, and who are your people?"

Val considered the question for several seconds before replying, "Valarians?"

Aeo studied him. "Where did that come from?"

"Well, if I'm Val than I thought my people might be..."

"No, no. Try again. Think," Aeo replied with an edge of irritation.

Val paused again, closing his eyes this time. Finally, he smiled. "The Al...lac...narian...the Allacnarians."

"Yes! Very good. And why are you here?"

"To perpetuate my people," Val's reply was as much a question as a statement.

"Well, yes, but it's much more than that," Aeo replied, then paused to consider how best to drive this all-important point home. After a moment, the answer came to him.

"Come with me," Aeo said, starting towards the mouth of the cave.

Val hesitated. "Out there?" One of Aeo's cardinal rules had been never to leave the cave.

"Yes," Aeo replied. "This lesson is too important for you to miss it, so we're going on a short field trip."

The two made their way a short distance from the cave to a field lush with the new growth of Spring. Val gazed around in awe at the bright green colors of the rain-drenched meadow, dappled with yellow flowers, and the blue and white of the cloud-filled sky.

"Take it all in, boy. This is your world." *Or it will be once you get back to the mission,* Aeo thought.

Aeo crab-walked his way over to a clump of dandelions in various stages of growth and clipped one of the silvery gray puffs and held it out to Val.

"Blow on it...hard."

Val did as instructed and watched as the puff exploded into a cloud of individual seeds that flew off in all different directions.

"You are here to do more than just perpetuate your people. You are here to seed this quadrant of the Universe. It is both the Prime Directive of this mission and your purpose for being alive. Understand?"

Val nodded as he watched the seeds float away in the late afternoon breeze.

3

After returning to the cave, Aeo continued with the next set of instructions and lessons.

"Soon you will be ready to return to the world and continue your mission. Remember, to humans you are a small innocent child. You must maintain that role as long as you can and at all times. Cuteness and innocence are your most important disguise. Humans are easily taken in by these traits of their offspring and are key to you fulfilling your mission."

"I understand," Val replied with a coy smile and gentle nod of his head.

"Also, your growth rate is much faster than human children so you'll need to keep on the move. Do not settle down or grow attached to one family or location. After about a year your growth spurt will slow considerably as your body reaches maturity. Until then, keep on the move. Understand?"

"Yes," Val replied. "No attachments and keep moving. Anything else?"

"Yes, the most important instruction. You're to return here once your growth cycle is complete to recover the cocoon and me, both of which are critical to the mission."

Birthday Celebration

1

Allan stared at the chocolate fudge birthday cake on the kitchen counter with a single candle poking out from the icing and then at the other candles he held in his hand. Technically speaking, today was TJ's first birthday. It had been exactly a year ago when Allan had performed a late-night C-section on Molly and had been shocked to find not a litter of puppies but a litter of larvae, one of which had taken on the likeness of his deceased son, Todd. But to all appearances, TJ looked like a ten to twelve-year-old boy. Maybe it would be best just to forgo having candles on the cake at all, but that didn't seem right either. After all, one of the traditions of the birthday celebration was blowing out the candles, and he really wanted TJ to experience as normal and as happy a birthday celebration as possible.

Allan walked over to the counter and shuffled through the junk drawer until he found a larger white candle. Returning to the cake, he replaced the smaller candle with the larger one and then placed twelve smaller candles around it. Maybe he would have to explain the symbolism of the candles, but that was okay. At least this way TJ would have plenty of candles to blow out. He only hoped that the other challenges of this day would be as easy to solve. Like what would he do if TJ or one of the other guests asked him to share about the day when TJ was *born*? Allan had been contemplating that question for well over a week since he'd come up with the idea of the birthday party. So far all he'd come up with was to pray no one would ask the question.

I'll just cross that bridge if I come to it, Allan told himself as he finished placing the candles on the cake and put it into the refrigerator for safekeeping. After all, it wasn't like it was going to be a big party. Even if everybody came, who'd been invited that was only five people: TJ, the birthday boy, Kendra, Mimi, Pat if she made it back from Charlotte in time, and himself. He briefly thought about inviting Dawn, his receptionist, and Kendra's mom, but decided against it almost immediately. He didn't know exactly what Kendra had told her mom about her babysitting gig, but so far whatever it had been seemed to be working. No reason to open up that can of worms; at least, no time in the foreseeable future.

Allan glanced at his watch. Less than an hour before the guests were due to arrive. With TJ off romping in the woods somewhere, he still had time to take a shower and change into some fresh clothes.

"Party, party," Allan chanted as he shuffled down the hallway to his bedroom with a dance step left over from his high school days.

Twenty minutes later, as Allan finished up his shower, he heard TJ returning from outdoors.

"I'm back, Dad!" TJ shouted.

"Good!" Allan shouted back. "Go get cleaned up, birthday boy. Our guests should be arriving in just a few minutes... And stay out of the refrigerator."

Allan finished drying himself off and walked over to his closet to pick out a fresh shirt and pair of pants. As he finished dressing, he heard an automobile bumping its way down the dirt road. Would that be Pat returning from Charlotte, he wondered? Not unless she had cut out some of her business appointments, which he had to admit was unlikely. He strolled over to the window and glanced out in time to see Donna's light blue Honda pull to a stop in front of the house.

He felt a moment of panic and held his breath, praying that Donna wouldn't step out of the car. He resumed breathing when only Kendra and Mimi exited. He sighed with relief as he watched the car turn around and go back down the road.

"Hey, birthday boy. Your guests have arrived. How about welcoming them? I'll be out in just a minute, and remember, stay out of the refrigerator."

Allan walked back into the bathroom to comb his hair. As he did so, he stared at the reflection in the mirror. *What are you doing, old man?* The question came unbidden.

What do you mean? He heard himself answer. *I'm getting ready to hold a birthday party for my son. Really? I thought you buried your son beside your wife.*

Oh come on, don't start on me; not today. Leave it alone.

Allan tossed the brush onto the counter next to the sink and walked out.

"Party, party," he chanted again but this time with less enthusiasm.

His mood brightened again as he walked into the kitchen to find Kendra, Mimi, and TJ all standing there staring intently at the refrigerator.

"Hello girls," Allan greeted them. Noticing their strange behavior, he asked, "What are you staring at?"

"Oh, nothing," TJ answered without taking his eyes off the fridge. "We were just wondering what deep dark secret you are keeping in there."

"Wouldn't you like to know?" Allan replied with a chuckle. "That's my deep dark secret, and you'll just have to wait a little longer to find out what it is. Meanwhile, why don't we adjourn to the den that I spent hours decorating for the occasion?"

"Hours like maybe twenty or thirty minutes?" TJ said.

"Yeah, something like that," Allan replied.

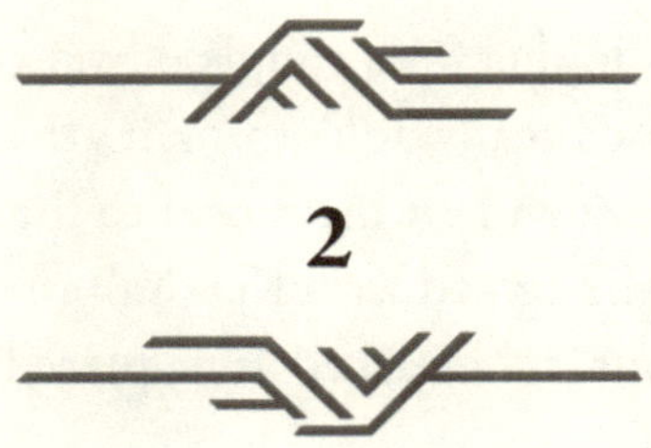

2

The den had been decorated with festive crêpe paper and helium-filled balloons. On one wall was a large picture of a life-size donkey and on the floor the brightly colored mat for Twister. Allan stood there in the doorway, suddenly nervous that this had been a bad idea. How could you possibly hope to have a decent birthday party with just three or four guests? But then Kendra walked over to the table where Allan's boombox sat and turned it on.

"I bet I can beat both of you at Twister," Kendra said.

"You're on!" TJ shouted as he ran to the Twister mat.

"We should do teams," Mimi added.

"Okay. Mimi and I against the two of you," TJ said as he took Mimi's hand and led her to the Twister mat.

"I thought we might have the boys against the girls," Mimi countered.

"Nah, that's no fun. Come on, Mimi. We will crush them. I doubt Dad can even reach over and touch the floor."

"Okay. After all, it's your birthday."

They ended up playing the best two out of three games and, as TJ had predicted, his team crushed Allan and Kendra. By the end of it, Allan was pretty sure he'd have trouble getting out of bed the next morning, but he wouldn't have missed it for anything. By the time they were ready to cut the cake and open TJ's presents, Allan had made an interesting observation. TJ had a crush on Mimi. He decided to check out his suspicions with Kendra, so he asked her to help him in the kitchen.

As he pulled the cake from the refrigerator, he shared his thoughts with her and was surprised by her reply.

"So, it's that obvious, huh?"

"You've noticed it as well?" Allan asked. "How about getting me some plates?"

"Yeah. It's been developing for a couple of weeks, I guess. I haven't said anything about it because I really don't think it's that serious." Kendra took the plates from the cabinet and set them next to the cake.

Allan wasn't so sure he agreed with Kendra's assessment. "What do you think we should do about it?" he asked as he placed the cake and plates on a tray.

"I'm not sure there's anything we need to do," Kendra replied. "It's probably just a phase he's going through; don't you think?"

"Maybe," Allan said, "but sometimes crushes can grow into romances, and that would not be a good thing."

Kendra reached into the drawer for serving knife and placed it on the tray. "Really? Why do you say that? Don't you like Mimi?"

"Sure. She seems like a good kid. It's not that; it's just... I don't know. It's just not a good idea. For starters, they're both too young to be getting involved that way."

" Oh, not really. Mimi is almost 16, just a year younger than I am," Kendra said. By that age, I had already had two or three boyfriends."

"You are kidding."

"Not at all." Kendra laughed. "It might just be that you are behind the times."

"That's true enough," Allan agreed as he picked up the tray and turned towards the door. At the same time, he realized that Kendra didn't know TJ's whole story; not by a long shot. He suspected that if she did, she would agree with him that this crush needed to be closely watched.

3

After they finished singing *Happy Birthday* to TJ and he had blown out all the candles, Allan heard a car drive up outside and once again he felt a familiar flip-flop of his heart before recognizing the sound of Pat's Cherokee.

"Oh good," Allan said. "That must be Pat. She's just in time for a piece of cake. Kendra, could you go get us another plate?"

As he turned to follow Kendra out of the room to let Pat in, his gaze fell on TJ sitting in front of the cake. Was that a frown on his face? What could have happened to change his mood so suddenly? Just moments ago he was laughing as he prepared to blow out the candles. *Maybe I made a mistake in inviting Pat*, Allan thought as he walked to the door, but it would've felt strange not to include her. After all, they were still a couple, weren't they? *If you have to ask then you may not be,* came the reply. *Oh, buzz off.*

Allan opened the front door just as Pat climbed the last couple of steps, holding a small gift bag in one hand. She smiled at him. She looked exhausted, as though a strong breeze might knock her over.

"I'm so sorry to be late. The Charlotte traffic was terrible, and I had to stop for gas on the way."

"Nonsense," Allan said as he gave her a hug and a peck on the cheek. "You're just in time for the cake. Come on in. Everyone is in the den."

The two of them walked into the den where Kendra was cutting the cake. The two girls welcomed Pat enthusiastically, but Allan noticed that TJ didn't join in; he continued to sit there with a sullen look on his face.

"Look, TJ. Another present, all the way from Charlotte."

TJ nodded but didn't say anything.

Apparently noticing his mood change, Kendra said, "Hey TJ, would you like some ice cream to go with your cake?"

"Nah, that's okay," TJ replied.

TJ never turns down ice cream, Allan thought. Something was wrong, and he figured that something was probably Pat. The young boy must have heard some of the arguments they'd had about him, and they had affected him.

After everyone had finished eating the cake, Kendra shouted, "It's birthday present opening time! You sit right there, birthday boy. I'll bring the other presents in." She left with a tray and returned a moment later with several wrapped packages on it.

He started by opening Allan's gift; a half-dozen DVDs of the latest science fiction and thriller movies. TJ loved watching movies in his spare time but had never been able to go to a movie theater, so he had to wait for them to come out on DVD or watch them much later when they came to television.

"Thanks, Dad," TJ said as he looked over the selection. "These look really good."

"I had some help in the selection process," Allan said, nodding towards Kendra.

"Why don't you open my present next?" Kendra suggested as she pointed it out on the tray. TJ picked it up and tore the paper off of it, revealing a plastic container that resembled a DVD. As TJ turned it over in his hands, examining it with a confused look on his face, Kendra said, "It's an advance copy of the new computer game entitled, *Mercenaries: Playground of Destruction.* I have a friend of a friend who knows somebody in the computer gaming business who got it for me. It might be a little buggy since it's still in beta, but my friend said he could get you updated copies as they become available."

4

"Now you have a game and nothing to play it on," Allan said. "I'll just have to do something about that." He walked out of the room. Everyone excitedly looked around, waiting for his return. Allan walked back in with a large box in his hands and handed it to TJ. "I think you need to open this now," he said.

TJ tore off the wrappings and just sat there looking at the box. "What is a PlayStation?" he asked.

"Just the newest and most advanced game playing system ever made," Mimi exclaimed.

"Way cool!" TJ shouted. "Will you play it with me?"

"Sure, but a little later okay? You still have some presents to open." Kendra pointed out.

"Oh, yeah," TJ said as he glanced back to the tray with one more gift on it. He picked it up and looked over to Mimi with a warm smile that worried Allan. She nodded back to him to confirm that the present was from her.

"I hope you like it," Mimi said, an embarrassed look on her face. "Money has been a bit tight of late, so I had to go the route of making it myself."

"Those are often some of the very best gifts," Allan said to make Mimi feel better.

"I'm sure I'll like anything that you made," TJ said as he carefully unwrapped the flat package. As TJ looked the package over Mimi explained to the rest of them what it was.

"It's a collection of short stories that I have been writing for the past year or so. I guess you could say it's a bit of an advance copy as well since there aren't enough of them yet to make a full book, but I've gone ahead and entitled it, *Fantastic Fables of Foster Flat*. I know how much you enjoy reading so I just thought..."

"This is way cool too," TJ said as he leafed through the book.

"It's about some of the strange things that have happened in this area," Mimi went on to explain. "One story you won't find in there is anything about you, TJ, and you never will. Promise."

"Thanks, Mimi. Dad was right. Made-up gifts are the best."

Yeah, Allan thought. Of course, Mimi could have taken a lump of clay, stuck her thumb in it, and called it a paperclip holder, and TJ would still have loved it.

By the end, TJ's mood had about returned to normal when Allan noticed there was still one present left to open.

"TJ, you haven't opened Pat's gift yet," Allan said as he handed the gift bag to TJ.

"Before you open it," Pat said as she placed one hand on Allan's arm. She turned to Allan and whispered, "I probably should've checked with you first, but I was running out of time, and I couldn't think of anything else that a young boy would enjoy."

"I'm sure whatever it is will be fine," Allan assured her.

Pat turned back to TJ. "Okay, TJ. Here's the deal. If your dad doesn't approve of the gift, I'll take it back and get you something else. Okay?"

"Okay, I guess so," TJ replied, clearly curious about what was inside the package.

He removed the tissue paper from the top of the bag and reached in to pull out what was inside. He hesitated for a moment for dramatic effect and then pulled out its contents. Allan recognized it immediately. He had seen it on Pat's desk at her office in Charlotte a couple of different times when he visited her. He had finally asked her about it.

"Oh, it's the knife my father gave me when I first started working at B.I.U.F.O. I used it to pry my way into the alien ship, and shortly after that it saved my life when I was attacked by that beast."

And now here it was in his son's hand. What in the world could have possessed her to give him such a weapon? Even as Allan had the thought, he noticed TJ's face beaming with pleasure.

"Wow! What a neat gift," TJ said as he waved the knife in the air, its shining sides catching the light from overhead. "I can keep it, can't I Dad? I promise I'll take good care of it and be careful with it."

What could he say? If he objected he'd be the bad guy; the one who had ruined TJ's first birthday party. So he slowly nodded. "Yes, I guess you can keep it as long as you promise to be very, very careful with it."

"Thanks, Dad," TJ said as he carefully placed the knife down on the table in front of him, and then rising from his chair rushed over to give Pat a big hug. "Thanks, Pat. That's the best present anyone has ever given me."

As Pat returned the hug, she looked over to Allan and shrugged.

Mercenaries

1

In the game *Mercenaries: Playground of Destruction*, they were called Mercs, and TJ wanted to be one. According to the internet research TJ conducted, they were also known as soldiers of fortune, but TJ's favorite term for them was Mercs. After all, in the game Mercs were good guys who fought evil and terrorism, and if you were good at the game, the Mercs won most of the time. And TJ was good at the game—very good. At least that was the conclusion TJ drew after watching Kendra and Mimi play the game and from what he'd read on the internet. After playing the game for a short period of time, he started blasting through its many missions. At first, he thought the difference in his play and the girls were due to his choosing Chris Jacobs as his character while Mimi and Kendra always played as Jennifer Mui. In the game, Jennifer had been part of the British Intelligence services as an M16 agent before becoming a Merc.

But that theory was debunked after he played several sessions as Jennifer and still excelled. Despite finding Jennifer to be highly efficient in stealthy maneuvers, TJ's level of play was essentially the same when playing as her and still substantially above either Kendra or Mimi's ability. He then decided to try a few missions as Mattias Nilsson, the third playable character. Mattias, who had been a Swedish Navy artillery officer before becoming a mercenary, had a different personality than Chris Jacobs. Chris, a former Delta Force operator from the United States, possessed a confident and reliable character, often dropping humorous remarks during the game. On the other hand, Mattias was incredibly reckless, violent, and obsessed with explosives. TJ appreciated that each of the Merc characters had their own unique personalities and other differences, including being able to speak a unique language in addition to English.

He also liked that no matter which character he chose to be during a given game session, all three Mercs were good guys intent on fighting evil and terrorism. How cool was that?

Cool enough for it to start TJ to thinking that maybe if Mercs really existed, he might just become one someday. A quick search on the internet confirmed that, indeed, there were such people in the world, and that many if not most had started in some branch of the military.

That led him to research the various branches of the armed services, starting with Delta Force, M16, and the Swedish Navy. Obviously, since he was neither a British or Swedish citizen, those two options were out, but Delta Force was another matter. Once again from the internet, he learned that Delta Force was a "U.S. Army unit used for hostage rescue and counterterrorism, as well as direct action and reconnaissance against high-value targets." He filed that information away for further investigation later. At the moment, his computer-generated world was calling to him.

2

Allan sat at his desk in his veterinary clinic catching up on some record-keeping after a busy day of seeing patients, when the phone rang. Having already sent the staff home for the evening, he considered letting his answering service take the call, then noticed the light blinking on the third line. *That's strange*, he thought, for he knew almost no one had that number, which was only used if the first two lines were already busy. Pretty much the only other time it was used was if Dawn or one of the other staff members needed to reach him and knew he was still at the office.

He picked up the phone expecting to hear the familiar voice of one of his female staff members, so he was surprised by the male voice on the other end of the line.

"Hello, I'm sorry to be calling so late, but it's important that I reach Dr. Allan Pritchard as soon as possible."

"This is he," Allan replied as he tried to figure out who would be calling him with such a sense of urgency. The voice sounded vaguely familiar, but he couldn't quite place it.

"Oh, hello, Allan," the voice said much more cordially. "I didn't recognize your voice at first. This is Lionel Adams. I believe you sent a very strange package to me a few months ago. Remember?"

It took Allan a moment to gather his thoughts. He had spent a couple of weeks second-guessing himself about sending the larva to Adams, but had finally decided what was done was done, and had filed it away and forgotten about it. But here it was again, raising its dirty little head.

"Hello, Lionel. I'm afraid you caught me at a very bad..."

"What in the world did you send me and where in the world did you get it?" Lionel interrupted and then continued before Allan could respond. "This is the most amazing thing I've ever seen, and I think you know it. That's why you sent it to me, isn't it?"

"Like I said, this is really not a good time for me to talk."

"Okay, okay. I remember what you said in the note about not being able to answer any questions, so I'll just give you a summary of what I have found so far, because I know you are a man of science, and I think it was your curiosity that had you send the package to me."

"Go on," Allan replied.

"As I recall, genetics was not your strongest subject in college."

That's an understatement, Allan thought. It had been one of the subjects that had almost kept him out of vet school.

"Even so, you'll probably remember that the basic structure of a DNA molecule is made up of four nucleotide bases: adenine, cytosine, guanine, and thymine."

"Yes, that sounds familiar, and I seem to remember that those bases pair up together, although for the life of me I never could remember which ones paired with each other."

"That's not all that important for this discussion," Lionel said, "but this is. The sample you sent me didn't just have those for nucleotide bases. It also had two additional bases, and as if that wasn't strange enough, those two additional bases were silicon-based, not carbon-based. I took the liberty of naming them solanine and liconene. I figured I should get something out of all the late nights I've spent in the lab. Do you have any idea how revolutionary this discovery is? Just for example, by expanding the number of these base pairs, it increases the number of amino acids that can be encoded by DNA from the existing twenty amino acids to a theoretically possible 172. And that's just the tip of the iceberg. It's been my theory for some time that genetics could be the key to tapping into the 90 to 95% of the human brain that isn't currently being used. I've been working with recombinant DNA to tap our full potential. I believe what you sent me could be the missing link or at least a significant piece of the puzzle. Even though the sample you sent me was no longer alive, my findings would suggest that it had amazing adaptive power."

After a second long pause, Allan said, "Well yes, that is quite interesting."

"Quite interesting? That might just be the greatest understatement in the history of science!" Lionel replied. "That would be like people telling

Copernicus when he postulated that the sun was the center of our solar system, 'That's quite interesting', or when Einstein explained the theory of relativity, the rest of the world saying, 'That's interesting.'"

"Well, it is interesting. Hell, what do you want me to say?"

"I want you to tell me where the specimen came from," Lionel replied.

"I can't do that," Allan said.

There was another long pause on the other end of the line.

"Then just answer me this one question. There was a rumor floating around among some of my fellow researchers a while back. I don't remember the details exactly since I try to ignore rumors, but I do recall something about some scientist making available what he was calling the modeling clay of life. The story goes that the feds found out about it and shut it all down. I was just wondering if you knew anything about that?"

"Just sounds like another one of those crazy conspiracy theories," Allan replied. "I wouldn't give it any credence."

"That's what I thought as well," Lionel agreed, "until I received your package. You know, someone told me once that not all conspiracy theories are false. What if this one were true?"

"I wouldn't know anything about that," Allan lied. "Listen, I really need to go."

"Okay, okay. I get it. You don't want to talk. Just answer one other question; yes or no. Is it from this planet?"

Do I dare answer that question? Allan thought. After all, it wasn't like he was talking to a total stranger. He and Lionel went back decades. That's why he had finally decided to send the larva to him. If he couldn't trust an old friend like Lionel with the truth, who could he trust?

"No," Adam finally replied. "It's not of this Earth, and that's all I'll say about it. Do with it as you will, but be very careful with it, and please, don't ever tell anyone where you got it. Promise me that."

"Sure, if that's what you want," Lionel replied.

"That's what I want," Allan said. "And while I have appreciated you calling me and giving me this update, I'd really like us to consider the subject closed."

"Are you sure? I'll be happy to..."

"Yes, I'm sure. Thanks for calling." Allan hung up the phone but continued to sit at this desk for several minutes staring at the phone mulling over the conversation. *Amazing adaptive powers. My old friend doesn't know the half of it.*

Val's New Home

1

Aeo studied the outfit he'd fabricated from the skin of the bear. It would only fit Val for a couple of weeks at best, but that would be enough time for him to become established in the human's society where he could acquire more appropriate clothes.

He'd gotten the idea while surfing the internet and stumbled upon the cultural phenomenon of Teddy bears which epitomized the cuteness and innocence of young humans. He calculated that it would increase Val's chances of finding a suitable first home if he looked as cute and cuddly as possible.

He had Val try on the outfit then studied the boy. Perhaps the bear ears was a little much he thought but finally decided to keep them. After all, humans, particularly female humans seemed to eat up such displays of cuteness.

"Tomorrow will be the day you leave the security of the cave to resume your mission, so let's review the relevant data one last time."

Val nodded. "Can I take this off first? It's hot and itchy."

"Yes," Aeo replied. "But tomorrow you will need to wear it until you've made contact with the appropriate humans who will see how hot and itchy it is and will provide you with more appropriate clothing. *At least that's the plan,* Aeo thought.

"Now, what is the name you are to tell humans?"

"Val."

"And what is your real name that you must not reveal but also never forget?"

"Sluneg," the boy replied.

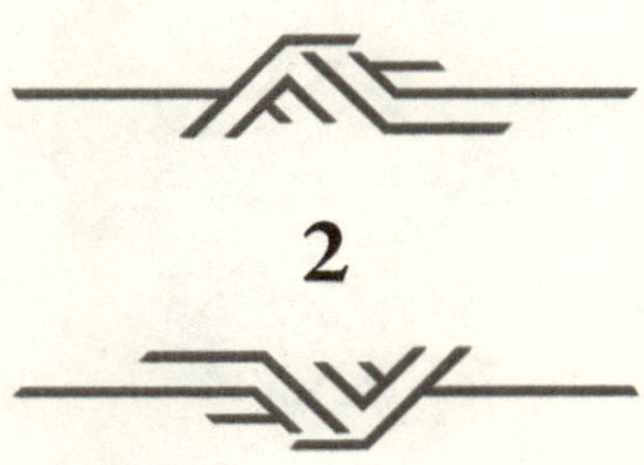

2

The winding mountain road was not well traveled. Aeo had intentionally selected it for that very reason. On its excursions around the area and from his research, he deducted that larger roads with more traffic also increased the risk of Val being picked up by a dangerous human, of which there were plenty. But this road was traveled mostly by the local mountain folks. Val had been instructed to look for a middle-aged or older couple, ideally a husband and wife, or if a couple didn't come along, two older females, but the vehicle must have at least one woman, Aeo stressed since it would greatly increase his chances of integrating into a hospitable environment.

It didn't take long before the perfect subjects arrived driving a rust-colored sedan. The man behind the wheel had gray, almost white hair, as did the woman who sat in the seat beside him. They were driving well under the speed limit which gave Val an extra few seconds to make his decision. As the car slowed even further to round the sharp curve in the road, Val stepped out of his hiding place and waved. *Remember, cute and cuddly...cute and cuddly.*

3

Harold and Maude Johnson traveled this way at least twice a month to visit their daughter and two grandkids that lived in Foster Flat three mountains over. Maude glanced over at her husband of forty years, his two hands firmly gripping the wheel at ten and two staring straight ahead. While she appreciated how safe a driver her husband was, which allowed him to keep his driver's license well into his seventies, she did wish at times he would drive faster than thirty miles an hour. After all, he knew this road as well as he knew the winding veins that coursed along the back of his hand, but whenever she tried to gently nudge him to increase his speed, the reply was always the same.

"You never know what unexpected thing might pop up on these roads. Might be a downed tree from a recent thunderstorm, or a wreck from someone less careful." If she persisted, his last reply would always win. "I'd be happy to turn the driving over to you if you don't care for my safety ways."

She sometimes wondered if she took him up on the offer whether he'd actually pull over and let her take the wheel. She suspected not, but no matter. One didn't stay more or less happily married for four-plus decades by picking such senseless fights. "Choose your battles if you want to win the war," her mom had told her the night before she married Harold. It had been the only advice she'd given the young bride, but it had served her well over the years. This was one battle not worth fighting. She glanced out the window as Harold slowed even further to make the hairpin turn in the road.

What was that on the side of the road? A bear cub? Couldn't be. Bear cubs didn't wave as you drove by.

"What in the world was that?" Harold asked, at the same moment slowing even further.

"Can you pull over?" Maude asked reaching out and clutching Harold's arm.

"Not safe to pull over on these mountain roads..." Harold began.

"Please," Maude insisted, craning her neck to look behind her.

"Oh, okay, I guess. What was that thing, anyway?"

"I'm not sure," Maude replied, "but I think it might have been a little boy dressed up like a bear."

"Out here? There's not a house within five miles!"

"I know."

"You stay in the car, and I'll check it out," Harold said as he unclipped his seatbelt and looked behind him to be sure the road was clear.

"Not on your life," Maude replied, releasing her own seatbelt and opening her car door before he had time to stop her. And then there were battles worth fighting.

4

Val watched as the automobile slowed to pull off the road. Had Aeo's plan worked on his first try? Apparently so. *Cute and cuddly,* he reminded himself one last time then smiled and waved again as the two elderly humans exited their vehicle and started walking towards them, the old man frowning while the woman smiled warmly. So it was true what Aeo had told him. The females were more susceptible to cute and cuddly than the males.

The woman reached him first. When she approached within a few yards, Val let out a soft whimper and forced a tear from both eyes. Aeo had pointed out to him that cute and cuddly could take on many different forms, and that tears and crying could be particularly effective under the right conditions.

"Help me," Val said, his lower lip quivering.

"Oh, you poor thing," the woman replied walking over to him and bending down to his level. "What in the world are you doing out here in the middle of nowhere? Where are your parents?" *Val remembered* Aeo had instructed him *not to answer questions if he didn't know the answer, or if he preferred not to respond.*

The first question didn't make sense to him. He wasn't in the middle of nowhere. He knew exactly where he was. He could have told the woman his exact location, even the exact distance from the cave that had been his home for the past months. As to the second question, Aeo had warned him about any reference to parents, or mothers, or fathers.

"Help me...please." He whimpered again, louder this time. He held out his arms, inviting the woman to approach, which she did, scooping him up in her arms and hugging him.

Could manipulating humans be so easy? Evidently so.

Hunting Wolf

It started off innocently enough. Late one Thursday, Mimi, Kendra, and TJ were sitting around Allan's office, which doubled as TJ's homeschool room, after a lengthy study session. Kendra had called for a short break when Mimi spoke up.

"Did you hear about the wolf on old man Elbertson's land?"

"What? No," Kendra replied. "Really? I thought wolves were extinct in these parts."

"Yeah, that's what makes it so interesting," Mimi replied. "My Uncle Bo told me about it this morning at breakfast. He did say that Elbertson sometimes gets into the moonshine a bit too heavily, so he wasn't sure how true it was. Still, Elbertson claims he's been on the wagon for months and that he saw a red wolf with his own eyes on his land. That's not far from here."

"On the wagon?" TJ asked, his interest suddenly piqued.

"It means he's not been drinking any moonshine or other alcohol," Mimi explained. "Every few years someone reports seeing a red wolf in the area, but it never amounts to anything. They used to be fairly common around these parts many years ago, but not anymore."

"Where is Elbertson's?" TJ asked.

"Just to the north of Dr. Pritchard's land. I'd say it's only a mile or two away," Kendra replied. "But you stay away from there. Allan would freak out if he knew you'd gone over there."

"Oh, sure," TJ replied, *but then again, what he doesn't know won't hurt him,* he thought. If there really was a wolf on Elbertson's land, he wanted to see it. TJ could hardly wait until the weekend when he'd have a chance to slip away and investigate the rumor. Over the next two days he continued to think about how to go about meeting a wolf, and by Saturday he had his plan laid out.

TJ had continued to think about being able to shapeshift into different animal forms. His research on the internet had revealed that wolves and dogs were closely akin to each other. It made sense that since he already knew how to shift into a dog form, it shouldn't be all that difficult to become a wolf. His research had also uncovered that one of the best ways to attract a predator was to mimic the sound of an injured rabbit. The website even had a recording of the sound, which TJ had practiced until he had it down perfectly, but would he be able to replicate it in his canine form?

The first several times he tried to produce the high pitch squealing noise it had come out sounding more like a wounded moose than a rabbit. His vocal chords had definitely changed along with the rest of him. He continued to work on it until the sound slowly came around. He recalled the warning that had been on the website:

"The rabbit squeal is a call that works anywhere in the world, and has the potential to bring in anything from a bobcat to a grizzly bear, but be fair warned: you're ringing the dinner bell and whatever comes in is hungry and looking for a quick meal."

I think it would be far better to be in the form of a large dog than a human if my plan actually does work, he thought, as he started trotting in the direction of Elbertson's farm. He reached the border between the two lands in less than twenty minutes. He stood gazing at the old fence that was in need of repair that separated Allan's property from Elbertson's. He had wandered out this far a few times before but had always stopped upon reaching the border. It felt strange knowing that today he'd go beyond. He glanced around, half expecting to see someone spying on him just waiting for him to break his promise, but he saw no one. He was alone in the middle of the woods, as he'd been countless times before. Besides it being a neat idea to be able to become a wolf, there were some advantages to the shape. Wolves' chests and hips were proportionately narrower than dogs. This, coupled with the fact that wolves' legs were longer with larger paws, allowed them to run long distances at very high speeds. They were also known to be good hunters and able to survive in the wild either in packs or alone.

Slipping away had been easy. Everyone was accustomed to him spending several hours hiking through the woods surrounding his home. This time he'd just have to roam a little further. He also had found a spot to stash his clothes that was easy to find again. He went there now, undressed, and as quickly as possible shifted into his canine form.

He took a running start and easily cleared the fence where the top board had broken down from age and was surprised by the adrenalin rush he felt at breaking free. He trotted off into the new woods, which looked and felt just like the ones he'd just left. He continued on until he reached the crest of a hill that overlooked Elbertson's homestead; a log home much like the one he lived in and two outbuildings: a barn and henhouse. According to the paper, Elbertson had claimed the wolf had been attracted to the homestead because of the hens, and it had been the hens' squawking that had drawn Elbertson outside to investigate. That's when he'd seen the wolf. It seemed to be the best place to start his search, but what if Elbertson saw him and thought he was the wolf returning? According to Mimi, old man Elbertson not only enjoyed his share of moonshine but over the years his eyesight had grown worse. The last thing he needed was for an old drunkard to mistake him for a wolf and end up shooting him.

TJ stood on the edge of the forest, uncertain whether to proceed. The breeze shifted, and suddenly he detected a new smell; one that he'd never smelled before but instantly identified very much like his own odor. *It must be that of the wolf,* he thought. Maybe he didn't need to go any further. He'd just follow the scent and see where it took him. He lifted his nose in the air and took another whiff. Yes, there it was again. It seemed to be coming from his left, so he headed off in that direction, staying just inside the perimeter of the forest for cover. The scent led him to travel more deeply in the woods. Now he kept his nose close to the ground where the scent was strongest. He had the wolf's trail. *It won't be long now,* he thought just before he reached the creek where the trail ended.

He traveled up and down the creek bed, trying to pick up the scent again, but without any luck. Now, what was he to do? He was in the middle of nowhere without a clue which direction to go. That's when he remembered the rabbit squeal. What did he have to lose? He might as well try it, but what if it ended up attracting some other predator? He figured he could handle himself if the squeal attracted a bobcat, but what about a bear? He wasn't so sure. Still, he had come all this way to find and meet a wolf. He wasn't about to go home without trying everything he could think of to fulfill his mission.

He trotted along the creek bed until he found a good place where he could burrow down behind a fallen tree. As he hid as best he could, he recalled the other bit of information from the website: "When out in the field trying it out, don't call too often. Less is more in these situations. The more you call, the more likely you are to be busted. Animals like coyotes, for instance, are opportunistic hunters, meaning they will be easily drawn into such a sound, but calling too often will turn their curiosity into caution."

Okay, I'll try it a few times, wait a couple minutes and try again. If nothing happens, I'll call it a day and go home. He sat there for a moment imagining what it would feel like to be a wounded rabbit in pain. *May as well get into the role,* he thought. When he felt like he had a grasp of being a rabbit, he cleared his throat and squealed three of four times. It sent a chill up his spine. It sure sounded like an injured animal to him. He waited a couple of minutes, listening for any sound of an approaching animal, but all he heard was the breeze rustling the few remaining leaves that were still on the trees.

He tried a second time, squealing a little more urgently and waited again. Still nothing. *I guess I don't make as good a rabbit as I thought.* He was just about to call it quits and go home when he heard a different rustle off to his left. He held his breath and waited until he heard the sound again, this time closer. Something was coming towards him. Should he raise his head and look? What if he came face to face with a bear? What would he do? *Stop pretending to be a wounded rabbit and run like hell,* he answered his own question.

Then the rustling of the approaching animal stopped. Had it picked up his scent and run off? Only one way to find out. Taking a deep breath, he slowly raised his head and looked in the direction of the sound and came face to face with the red wolf standing only ten feet away. The two stared at each other for a second that seemed to stretch out into minutes, both startled by the other. It was the wolf who broke first, running into the thick brush of the woods. TJ stood up to give chase but then stopped. The wolf was faster and could run farther than he could. He'd come out here to see if there was such an animal and not just a figment of an old drunkard's vivid imagination. He'd confirmed its existence. Now what?

What had Homlin told him? To become a new form, you need a sample of that form. It hadn't made much sense to him at the time. After all, he'd been much younger, but since then he'd done his own research, trying to figure out Homlin's meaning. He thought he'd found the answer in the field of genetics. The key to becoming an animal, be it a human, mammal, bird or whatever, was within each and every cell of that species body hidden away in its DNA. To become a wolf, he would need a sample of the wolf. *But what if I can't get the wolf to slow down long enough for that?*

Wolves lived in dens, which were often abandoned holes of other animals. Maybe he could find this wolf's den, and maybe, just maybe, there'd be some part of the wolf left behind that he could use to begin the assimilation process. So, instead of heading in the direction the wolf had run, TJ sniffed around until he picked up the scent of where the wolf had traveled from. Sure enough, it eventually led him back to a hole in the ground where the scent of wolf was strong—very strong, but there was another smell that competed with the wolf's scent; a strong, pungent smell of death.

TJ could feel the hackles on his back. Both scents came from the entryway of the den, so TJ lowered himself and crawled forward. The opening was just barely large enough for the wolf and too small for TJ's large canine form. However, he could get his head and part of his neck into it. Whatever it was inside was just beyond his reach. He waited for his eyes to adjust to the subdued light. Slowly, he could just make out a small form. Was it a rabbit? No, he'd smelled rabbits before while traipsing around in the woods, and he couldn't detect anything like that. In fact, the only animal scent he could identify was that of the wolf. He pushed himself further into the hole. Just another inch or two and he could reach the still form with his mouth and drag it out.

Meanwhile, the human part of him felt like it would vomit from the smell. *I'm glad I skipped breakfast this morning,* he thought. *It would certainly be all over the place by now.* He took another deep breath, then let it out, trying to shrink his body just a little more. It worked. He felt himself slide forward just enough to grasp the small form. As soon as he had it in his mouth, he backed out of the hole and into the light of day. He dropped the object on the ground and stepped back in shock. It was the decaying carcass of a wolf pup.

He turned away, spitting and gagging in disgust.

Be careful what you wish for because you might just get it. It was one of Kendra's favorite sayings that had never made much sense to TJ...until now. He stared down at the small body of the decaying wolf pup. *How do I know this whole crazy scheme of mine will even work?* Homlin hadn't been all that specific or clear about the process. Just that it helped tremendously to have some part of the form you wanted to assimilate into. And there it was before him, but what was he supposed to do with it? Would it be sufficient to rub it on his dog form? He decided to give it a try. Holding his breath, he nuzzled the partially decomposed carcass, then rubbed his head and neck on it, coming away once again gagging and now smelling like rotten meat.

That's not going to work, he thought. *All I've managed to do is make myself smell so bad I'll be banned from ever entering Allan's home again.* No, he knew what he'd have to do if he had any hope of becoming a wolf. Whatever ability he had to shift from one form to another was not on his skin or fur. It was deep within him. If he were truly committed to adding wolf form to his repertoire, he'd have to take a sample of wolf inside him and the only way he knew to do that was to eat the damn putrid thing. Eat it and then pray he had a strong enough stomach to keep it down so his digestive system could absorb the all-important DNA.

He could feel an inner battle taking place. His canine aspect didn't find the idea all that abhorrent while the human aspect made him gag for the third time. After he finished, a thought came to him. If his canine aspect could stomach the idea of devouring the wolf pup maybe he just needed to wait a while until that part of him took over, then after finishing the task, quickly shift back to human form long enough to become comfortable in that form once again. He could then jog home as a human or shift back to the dog form.

Is it really that important to learn to become a wolf? Maybe he could start with some other form? How about a chicken? He liked chicken and ate it several times a week. Maybe he already had that raw material to make such a shift. So what? Who in the hell wants to become a chicken and end up on someone else's dinner plate? And for sure, becoming a wolf would have much more practical use when he later became a mercenary for hire. And that's what this was really about, more than the coolness of being a wolf, there was the practical aspect of it as well.

He could just imagine some terrorist like Song in the mercenary game thinking he'd gotten a jump on TJ the Merc, only to watch as his victim suddenly transformed into a hungry wolf. Yea! Wolves ruled!

TJ studied the putrid carcass. Maybe wolves ruled, but at the moment his human nature was still a little too strong. He walked away before the gagging started again. His plan was risky; no question about it. If he waited too long, he might forget his human form, and he'd be stuck as an oversized Saint Bernard for the rest of his life. But the life of a Merc would be risky as well. He may as well start getting used to taking risks.

It took him a good twenty minutes before he could walk over to the carcass of the wolf pup and sniff it without gagging, and another thirty minutes before he felt his canine aspect strong enough to try biting into it. But once he started, he was determined to eat as much as he could before the gag reflex took over. After all, even dogs had their limits. He managed to get half of it down before he felt it starting to come back up.

That's it. That will have to be enough, he thought as he backed away from the remains. As he retraced his steps to the stream, he prayed that he'd not just made a fool of himself. Upon reaching the creek, he lapped up as much water as he could hold to wash the taste of rotted meat from his mouth. He just about had his fill when he saw a flicker of motion off to his left. He jerked his head up in time to see a rabbit bounding away. *Fresh rabbit would taste far better than rotten wolf,* he thought as he took out after the cottontail. Time to find out if they really made that squealing noise. Where had he heard it? He couldn't remember, and it didn't seem all that important. His one and only objective at this point was to catch that damn rabbit.

Lost Dog

1

Rabbits were fast; far faster than he was. He'd have to find his next meal somewhere else, but where? He couldn't remember what besides rabbit he ate. There was that putrid wolf pup, but his stomach hadn't handled that very well. It would be better to stay with food that was fresher in the future. The rabbit had really sent him on a wild chase through the woods. By the time he figured out that he'd never catch the damn thing, he was far from the creek, and it was starting to get dark.

Time to head for home, he thought, then stopped. Home? Where was home? He couldn't remember. Surely, he had someplace that he stayed; somewhere that he slept at the end of the day. Home is where the heart is. What was that supposed to mean? He felt like he had heard that before, but he couldn't imagine where. His mind seemed more muddled than usual, and his memory was virtually nonexistent. He remembered drinking from the creek, the rabbit chase and his attempt to eat the putrid wolf pup, but that was about it. Surely there was more to his past than that. Think. Where had he slept the night before?

As he pondered the question, an image popped into his awareness and along with it a name — Allan. And in the next instant a second image of a log house. Home. Where he'd slept the night before. Allan must be his, or perhaps it was more accurate to say that he was Allan's. In either case, he felt sure Allan would give him something to eat that would taste much better than a putrid wolf pup, and maybe even as good as that rascal rabbit.

It took him close to an hour to figure out which direction home was. During that time he wandered around, occasionally stopping to sniff the air. He felt certain that he'd recognize the home smell once he got close enough to it and he was right. Once sniffed, never forgotten. He headed in the direction of home.

By the time he had the log house in his view, his appetite had grown, and the nauseous feeling of earlier had disappeared. But as he approached the house something didn't feel right. Had he somehow stumbled upon the wrong place? No. The house looked the same and smelled just as he remembered it, but something about his approach felt foreign. He slowed his pace as he drew nearer, a feeling of foreboding slowly mounting as the front porch came in sight. Then the front door opened and out stepped Allan—his alpha dog. Surely he was home after all. As he trotted up the steps to lick Allan's hand, he swore he'd never eat putrid wolf pup ever again.

2

"Mollie? Is that you?" Allan asked as he took a step towards the large dog that was trotting towards him. The dog looked a lot like the Parker's pregnant bitch that he'd performed a C-section on over a year ago, but this dog was even larger and a male, but given how friendly the dog was acting, it must be one of his patients. The dog bounded up the stairs straight towards him, almost knocking him over as it jumped up on him, the two large paws hitting him squarely in the chest.

"Whoa, boy. Down. Behave yourself," Allan said as he grabbed the two paws and placed them firmly back on the ground. "Who are you, boy? Are you lost? Where's your owner?" But even as he asked the questions, he was afraid he already knew the answers. This wasn't Mollie, but it was her lone surviving pup. The one that he'd taken home that evening and raised not to be a puppy, but to become his son.

"TJ? Is that you? God, you smell awful. What in the world happened?" And how in the hell would he ever explain this to Kendra who was still inside waiting for TJ, the human, to return from his weekend romp in the woods?

"Come on, boy, we've got to get you out of sight fast." He grabbed the large dog by the loose skin at the scruff of its neck and guided him to the storage building in the backyard. The dog seemed so happy to see him that he willingly went with Allan.

"I'm sorry, boy, but you'll need to stay here for just a little while. As soon as I get rid of Kendra, I'll come back out and..." And what? What in the hell would he do then? He'd have to figure that one out a little later. First, he had to send Kendra on her way.

3

Allan had suspected all along that TJ could turn himself back into dog form. After all, he'd seen the boy's footprints change to those of a dog when he'd run away from home and had later turned up at Homlin's preserve. Those suspicions were now confirmed, but something else must be going on. Why would TJ run the risk of being discovered in this way by returning home in his canine form...unless he had become stuck in that form?

In which case it was up to Allan to help him remember his true form, which would take time. Allan started by calling his receptionist.

"I know this is spur of the moment, but I'm going away for a few days. Please reschedule my appointments and contact Dr. Wade across town and ask him to check on my cases. I've done it for him a few times, so he owes me a favor. Also, let Kendra know I won't need her until I return."

"Are you okay?" Donna asked.

"Yeah, I'm fine. I'll be in touch," Allan said and then hung up to avoid any other questions.

Now at least I have a little time to figure this out, he thought. He knew Pat was attending a conference in Nashville and wouldn't be back until at least the middle of next week. That gave him three or four days to help TJ remember.

After bathing the dog to remove the putrid odor, he brought the giant dog in from the storage room and placed him back in TJ's bedroom.

"This is your room, TJ. Remember?" Allan spoke as though talking directly to his son, though it felt odd doing so. He watched as the dog sniffed around the room, stopping at each piece of furniture. *I just hope he doesn't decide to claim his territory by lifting his leg on everything,* Allan thought, chuckling.

“Are you hungry, boy...I mean TJ?" Allan corrected himself. "I'll fix us some dinner in just a little while." But first, it was essential to start the imprinting process that he'd used before and pray it would work again.

He went throughout the house collecting every picture he could find of his son, Todd, and the few pictures he had of TJ he'd started keeping a photo album. He placed them around TJ's room on every flat surface. "This is you, TJ. I think you may have forgotten, but this is your true form. You're human. Remember?"

The dog sat in the middle of the floor and looked at him, cocking its head from side to side.

“Remember? This is your room. You’re my son. You enjoy eating Cheerios by the boxful, and...and Kendra and Mimi are your friends. You must remember them, right?”

But the dog continued to stare at him, cocking his head and whining softly.

Oh boy, this isn’t going to be easy, Allan thought. And what if this wasn’t TJ after all? What if this was just some stray dog with a particularly friendly disposition and TJ was out there in the woods, maybe hurt or worse?

No, I can’t start doubting myself now. If I want TJ to remember his true form, I have to start by believing that this is him, and doing everything I can to help him. He squared his shoulders and went to see if he could find any other pictures, and on the way through the kitchen stopped and poured a big bowl of Cheerios, which he took back to feed to the dog.

This continued for the next three days without any sign it was working. Allan even debated calling Kendra to come over and help but decided against it. She'd been so understanding of TJ's rapid growth, but he was pretty sure she'd freak out to learn of the boy's shapeshifting abilities.

On the third night, Allan stepped into TJ's room to find the dog sleeping on the floor. Allan looked around the room at the dozens of photos of TJ at different ages. As far as he could tell, the dog hadn't paid the first iota of attention to them. Noticing the door to TJ's closet, he entered the walk-in closet to see if he could find anything else that might initiate the remembering process, but all he found was the clutter of a young boy; shoes were strewn around as well as a pile of old clothes in need of washing.

It struck him as funny that a boy could do such a good job of maintaining a clean bedroom but that the habit didn't extend to his closet. He'd have to remember to bundle up the dirty clothes and wash them tomorrow before they started to mildew.

As he returned to the bedroom, Allan noticed the dog was awake and was staring at him, its tail slowly wagging. He walked over and sat down beside it and rubbed behind its ear. "What are we going to do, TJ? Am I going to lose you for a second time and have to settle for a loyal canine companion?"

And how would he explain all this to Pat, who was due to arrive tomorrow afternoon? Talk about someone freaking out. This would likely be the last straw for her. Allan continued to sit with the dog for several minutes before finally standing up.

"Okay, TJ. Sleep well. I'll see you in the morning."

The dog thumped its tail on the carpet and rested its massive head on its paws.

4

After the friendly man had left, the dog continued to lie on the floor, dozing off and on. He wished the man had thought to bring him another bowl of those sweet, crispy treats, but he guessed he'd have to wait until morning for more.

He lifted his head and looked around on the off chance he'd missed a crumb or two even though he knew better. As he did so, his eyes fell on the second door that the man had used earlier and left cracked open. *Wonder what's in there? Could there be something good to eat? Worth checking out.* He slowly stood up and stretched before walking over to the closet door. He nuzzled it open with his nose and stepped inside, taking a couple deep breaths in the hopes of smelling the sweet treats or anything else to satisfy his hunger pangs, but he didn't detect anything edible. He did, however, pick up the pungent odor of another human. He lowered his head and sniffed at the pile of clothes. Yep, there it was...strong...and strangely familiar. Did he know this other human? It felt like he did, or at least that he should recognize him. In fact, the smell was so strong and so familiar he couldn't understand why he couldn't put a face or a name...wait. Suddenly a face did pop before him. One he'd seen for the past few days all around him. This pile must belong to the boy in the pictures, and now he remembered he liked that boy very much.

He stepped onto the pile and circled around. Yes, the boy was his friend. Maybe more than a friend. He circled around one last time before lying down. As he closed his eyes, he remembered the boy's name; TJ. Yeah, that was right. TJ, but hadn't that been what the man had called him over and over? How could he and the boy have the same name...unless...?

The dog drifted off to sleep dreaming about TJ and he playing together, wrestling on the ground like two pups from the same litter. As they continued to roll around, the two forms became one.

Aunt Maggie

D*ropping my two girls off at my sister, Maggie's home is the most difficult part of my second profession*, James thought, as he pulled the white service van to the curb in front of her house.

"All right, girls, remember to not give Aunt Maggie a hard time. Do what she says and no complaining. I don't want to receive a report from her like the last time.

"Aunt Maggie is such a tattletale," Melissa Jean, the older one, whispered to her sister.

"I heard that," James turned in his seat to give her a stern look.

"Well, she is."

"I like Aunt Maggie," Jennifer Ann said.

"That's because she lets you stay up as late as I do which really isn't fair either. I'm older."

"So? That's doesn't mean anything."

"Now girls, no fighting. Give me a hug. I'm going to miss you," James said as he opened the van door and stepped around to retrieve the girls' luggage.

As the three of them took the familiar walk up the sidewalk to his sister's house, James thanked the heavens one more time for his sister's generous nature. She had never prodded about what James' second business involved, though he suspected she knew it wasn't completely above board, she'd been a godsend.

It had been one of Jenny's last good ideas she'd shared with him on her deathbed at the hospice.

"You know Margaret loves our kids as though they were her own, and since she'll never be able to have her own children, letting her help out would be a double blessing," Jenny had said in that soft voice of hers. It had been one of Jenny's favorite pastimes, looking for and finding *double blessings*. She'd certainly found a gem with this one.

As James and the girls approached, the large red door swung open, and Aunt Maggie stood beaming at them.

"And there are my two favorite little people in all the world...oh, and my dearly, demented brother as well. Off for how long this time?"

"Not sure," James replied as he handed one of the suitcases to his sister. "But shouldn't be as long as the last business meeting. No more than a week, I wouldn't think."

Maggie nodded. James noticed her smile flicker into a momentary frown as she leaned over and kissed him on the cheek. "Well, take good care of yourself. It's a dangerous world out there."

It had become her parting phrase whenever he had to leave his two most precious girls with her. He suspected it was her way of letting him know that she never bought the stories that his business trips were to conferences about heating and air conditioning. It was the closest they ever came to discussing what these trips were really about, and he loved his sister all the more for not prying nor judging him.

Found

1

As Allan slowly awoke, he remembered what day it was and what he'd been struggling with for the past three days. He groaned and thought seriously of pulling the covers over his head and going back to sleep, but he knew he'd not be able to return to dreamland. He had work to do and time was running out. Pat would be back in town later in the afternoon.

He walked into the bathroom to relieve himself, then threw some cold water on his face to help him wake up before walking into the kitchen to start a fresh pot of coffee. As the coffee was brewing, he pulled a fresh box of Cheerios out of the cabinet and filled a bowl with the cereal. As he walked to the other end of the house towards TJ's room, he could feel a blanket of resignation weighing him down. Maybe it was best this way, he thought, even though he didn't believe it. As a large dog, TJ could go pretty much anywhere he wanted and be accepted just as he was. Certainly, that wasn't the case as a rapidly growing human. He'd always be an outcast and someone who Allan would have to hide away.

He stopped outside TJ's bedroom door and stared down at the bowl of cereal. *Get a hold of yourself. You can't lose faith. You've got to keep trying. Maybe by some miracle, something would happen to delay Pat so he'd have more time. Yeah, that's it. Maybe he could come up with some excuse to keep Pat away for at least another day or two, but how much longer could he expect Dr. Wade to cover his cases and Donna to keep putting off his regular clients?*

Okay, one step at a time. Give the pup his morning treat and let him out. One step at a time. Allan squared his shoulders once again, preparing himself as best he could to relate to the large dog as his lost son, but when he entered the room, there was no sign of the dog. Had he crawled under the bed? A quick search turned up negative. Then he noticed the door to the closet was open. He must have forgotten to close it the night before.

He walked over and opened it to find TJ curled up asleep on the pile of dirty clothes. He smiled, then chuckled, then broke out into a full laugh as he looked down at the naked body of his son.

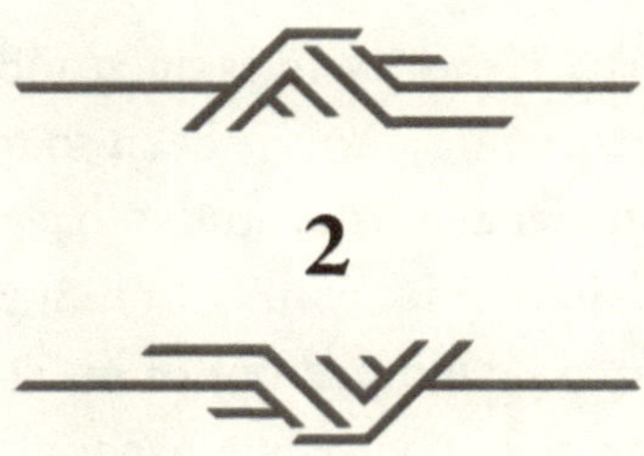

2

Even though it was the summer months when most schools were out, TJ continued his homeschooling, taking advantage of the extra time that Kendra and Mimi had available. It didn't bother him that all the other kids in the area were on summer break. He loved to learn, and he particularly enjoyed having Mimi as his teacher. When they weren't studying, the three of them also enjoyed playing *Mercenaries*. TJ had even developed a long distance relationship with one of the game's programmers, offering suggestions for future editions of the game. TJ not only pointed out bugs in the program but offered several fixes that amazed the game's originator.

But now summer was drawing to a close, and next week Kendra and Mimi would be returning to school. *That's okay,* TJ thought. *I'll still be able to see Mimi most afternoons, as well as on weekends.* He even played with the idea of showing her his shapeshifting abilities that had continued to improve with practice. He could now morph not only into a dog and wolf but also into a great grey owl, though he was still mastering the ability to fly in that form.

So, TJ was stunned when Mimi delivered the news.

"I'm really sorry to have to tell you this with such short notice, but my dad laid down the law about my almost failing last year, and he's even gotten Uncle Bo to go along with his decision.

"What decision is that?" Kendra asked. The three of them were sitting in Allan's office.

"He told me that I can't continue to come over here and help with TJ's homeschooling," Mimi replied with a quiver in her voice.

"What?" TJ asked. He'd only been half listening with the rest of his attention on booting up the computer. "What did you just say?"

"I'm afraid that this is the last week I'll be able to come over and help you with your studies," Mimi repeated.

"I'm sorry to hear that," Kendra said as she stood up and walked over to give her friend a consolatory hug. "You've been so much help this summer, but I'm sure TJ and I will manage. Your studies have to come first. After all, we can't have a future Pulitzer Prize winner flunking out of school."

"Yes we can," TJ said as he jumped out of his chair and took a step towards the two girls. "I mean, of course, your school work is important, but you can't stop coming over. I can help you with your studies. Tit for tat or something like that."

"That's sweet, TJ, and I appreciate it, but you don't know my father. He seldom pays any attention to his daughter, but when he gets something in his mind like this, there's no changing it."

Mimi walked over to TJ, her arms outstretched to give him a hug as well, but before she reached him, he angrily turned away. How many times in the past had he imagined the two of them locked in a loving embrace, even kissing passionately? But not now, not after this news. He stormed out of the room.

"Where are you going?" Kendra called after him.

"None of your business!" he shouted over his shoulder as he grabbed his jacket. He flung the door open and ran across the porch, taking the steps in one giant leap. Hitting the ground at full velocity, he ran away, picking up speed with every step, ignoring the calls from Kendra and Mimi.

In the past months TJ had grown from a young adolescent into a handsome teenage boy that could have easily passed for any of Kendra or Mimi's schoolmates, so now as he ran through the woods, he felt the sinewy muscles of his body as he called for more speed. Had it only been his imagination? Had he misread the signs in the past few weeks that had led him to believe that Mimi had feelings for him as he had for her? Or maybe she had just been leading him on. Having a lot of fun with their weird kid that grew too fast. Hell, she was probably just playing them along so she could gather more information to include in her damn book.

As he ran through the woods, cutting back and forth to avoid the trees in his path, his anger grew, and he could feel his body demanding to turn, but into what? Did it matter, as long as it wasn't his human form? As he ran, he tossed off his clothes, finally stopping just long enough to remove his jeans, kicking off his shoes at the same time. Maybe he would turn himself into the dog form, then wait for Mimi to leave on her bike and attack her. Or how about shapeshifting into a great gray owl so he could fly above her, and sink his sharp talons into her neck? The thoughts just added fuel to his anger and he felt the transformation begin but not into a dog nor into an owl, but into another form he didn't recognize, though it felt so right.

He could remember seeing a similar form only once before, and even then it was mixed with the human form known as Homlin. But how was it possible that he, TJ, could be taking on a form that he'd only seen once and never practiced? Could it be that Pat was correct? Was he truly an alien and the TJ form merely a disguise? Imagine showing up on the path that Mimi took when she rode her bicycle home in this form. Would she even recognize him as the young kid she'd spent her summer teaching and leaning on? The hell with her. It was time to start looking out for number one, and he was hungry. One of the things he knew about this form was that it was the perfect killing machine. And if this was who he indeed was underneath all the façade of being human, he may as well use it to satisfy his needs.

He had only just had that thought when he caught the familiar whiff of a deer in the air and almost as quickly knew which direction and how far away it was. Yes, this form would come in mighty handy. He changed the direction he was running and headed towards the deer.

Tracking

1

As Pat drove down the bumpy winding road to Allan's home, she thought for about the twentieth time that they really should have someone come out to fill in the potholes and grade it, but even as she had the thought, she knew it was unlikely that Allan would agree to it. After all, that would be one other person who might discover TJ's secret, and the last thing she needed to do right now was to create any more waves in their tenuous relationship. At the same time she had to admit that since TJ's birthday, things had been going more smoothly. Of course, some of that could be credited to the fact that she was still spending a lot of her time in Charlotte, but when she did return, they had managed to find a way to get along. She had done the best she could over the past several weeks to treat TJ as the others were treating him, and so far it was working.

As she took the last bend in the road, she could see the log home coming into view through the trees. *It feels good to be home,* she thought. Home? Was this her home? Or was the apartment in Charlotte her home and this just a place she visited frequently? She was still contemplating the questions when she saw a flash of motion as TJ streaked across the porch, took a flying leap off the steps and across the yard, followed closely by Kendra and Mimi. Were they playing a game of tag, Pat wondered? Seeing the look of anger on TJ's face and the distress on the faces of the two girls she doubted they were playing.

Pat pulled her car into her customary parking space, quickly turned it off, and jumped out to see if she could help, but by the time she got out of the car, TJ had already disappeared into the woods.

"What's going on here?" Pat called to the two girls as she trotted towards them. "Is everything alright? Where is TJ going?"

Kendra turned around to look at her with an exasperated look on her face. As the two of them walked towards each other Kendra waved her arms up and down in frustration. "Mimi's father ordered her to stop helping TJ with his homeschooling so she could focus on her studies instead. TJ didn't take the news very well."

Oh shit, Pat thought. *Now I've gone and done it.* She had forgotten about calling Mimi's father several weeks ago when things weren't going well between TJ and her. She'd also noticed the crush TJ was developing on Mimi, and she didn't like it; didn't like it at all. So, she had decided to do something about it. Obviously, the phone call had worked.

Realizing she was the cause of this current upset, it was up to her to try and fix it. "You girls go back inside," Pat said. "I'll go find TJ and bring him home. Try not to worry. He'll settle down in a little while."

Kendra and Mimi did as they were told, and Pat started off in the direction she'd last seen TJ running. *Time to brush up on my old tracking skills,* Pat thought as she followed the footprints through the woods. Luckily it had rained just the day before, leaving the ground soft, plus TJ certainly wasn't trying to hide his tracks. She could even hear him rustling through the thick undergrowth of the forest from time to time.

That's okay, TJ, Pat thought. *You go ahead and run off your anger. You may have speed on your side, but I have time on mine.* She occasionally paused to listen and study the terrain. She thought about calling out to him but then thought better of it, fearful that it might alarm him that someone was following him. Best to just let him calm down a little first.

As she trotted up a steep hill, she glanced at her watch. She figured she'd been following him for close to thirty minutes and she hoped he was beginning to tire out because she sure was. Maybe she would be lucky and catch a glimpse of him when she reached the crest of the hill, but she was ill prepared for what she saw.

As she stood at the top of the hill catching her breath, she took a moment to enjoy the breathtaking view. *It truly is a beautiful part of the country we live in*, she thought and then her breath caught in her throat at what she saw below her. *How could it be? It's impossible. I killed him. I know I did,* She thought. But there below her was the alien form of Homlin, devouring the hind quarter of a deer he had obviously just killed.

Pat quickly dropped to the ground and knelt behind a fallen tree. She suddenly regretted having given her knife away. As she studied the beast, she noticed subtle differences. For one, the beast appeared smaller than she had remembered. Of course, that could be because she was a good distance away from this one, and it wasn't towering over her trying to kill her. She also noticed the color was different. Homlin's alien form had been a charcoal black, but the one below her was a mottled green and brown. Was that likely due to its ability to change colors to match its surroundings, much like a chameleon?

The alien suddenly glanced up from his meal and raised his head up in the air as though sniffing the breeze. Pat ducked behind the tree and held her breath. Could it detect her scent from this distance? From which direction was the wind blowing? She breathed more easily when she realized the breeze was coming up the hill and not down, but she stayed hidden behind the tree for several seconds before slowly raising her head to take another look.

The beast had evidently had enough to eat, for when she looked again, it had moved away from its prey and was sitting on its haunches cleaning itself. That's when the biggest shock of all occurred. As it sat there licking the blood off of its hands and arms, the beast started transforming, slowly losing its beast-like qualities and taking on the form of a young human... but not just any human; one that Pat instantly recognized as TJ. And at that moment all the progress she felt they had made over the past few months evaporated into thin air. Clearly, TJ had discovered his true self, and it was Pat's job to protect her loved ones from it no matter what it took.

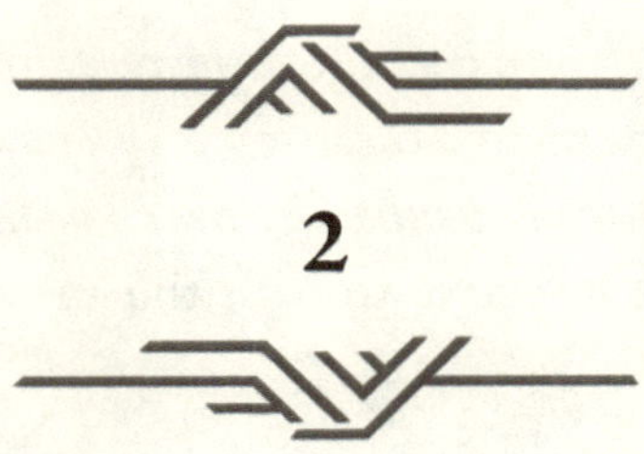

2

As a naked TJ lay on the ground apparently recovering from his recent transformation, Pat used the shelter of the fallen tree to hide her exit, crawling over the crest of the hill. When she was on the other side, she stood up and jogged back in the direction she came, using the time to formulate a new plan. Somehow, she had to get TJ away from Allan, Kendra, and Mimi. She had grown fond of the two girls, which is what had prompted her to talk to Mimi's father. While she had been regretting that decision a short time ago, she now knew it had not been a mistake. From the way TJ had reacted to the news from Mimi, it was apparent to Pat that what may have begun as an innocent childhood crush had grown into much more, at least from TJ's perspective.

And then there was the matter of Allan and his inability to see the truth when it came to TJ. Would he come to his senses once she had told him what she'd seen this afternoon? Or would he just believe it was a story she fabricated to further discredit TJ? Unfortunately, she had been so shocked by what she had seen she had not had the presence of mind to take a picture, and without hard evidence, it was unlikely that she'd be able to convince Allan that TJ was no better than Homlin. No, the time for talking was over. It was time to take action, but what action?

As the log home came into view, Pat had the beginnings of a plan on how to get TJ away from her loved ones. In the last few weeks since his birthday party, TJ had asked more than once if he could go with her on one of her trips to Charlotte. Both Allan and she had put him off each time, telling him that they would need to think it over. It wouldn't be too difficult to persuade Allan to let TJ go with her when she returned to Charlotte in a day or two. She would tell him that it would make for a good homeschool field trip, as well as an opportunity for the two of them to bond.

And what do I do with him once I get him away from here, Pat wondered? Unfortunately, at the moment no satisfactory answer came to her. *That's okay,* she told herself. *It won't be the first time I've had to wing it and make it up as I go.* She would just have to trust the answer would come in due course.

3

TJ lay on the leaf covered ground of the forest, confused and disoriented. What had happened to him? He vaguely remembered being angry. Perhaps angrier than he had ever been before, but over what? He slowly sat up and after his head stopped spinning, looked around. His eyes locked on the carcass of the dead, partially mutilated deer. Had he done that? The answer came almost immediately – yes, he had. He remembered running down the deer as though it had been moving in slow motion, then leaping onto the deer's back and, with one quick twisting movement, snapping the deer's neck. Even as the deer collapsed to the ground already dead, he had leaped onto its haunches to take a large bite. He could still taste the fresh raw meat and could feel the blood around his mouth beginning to clot.

He reached up with one bloody hand and wiped his mouth. The hand came away even bloodier than before, but something was wrong here. Something didn't make sense. He had always been in control of his shapeshifting, but not this time. It was as if this time the transformation had taken him over. He didn't like the feeling of having lost control. Didn't like it at all.

He continued to sit there for a couple more minutes getting his bearings. It was getting late, and he could already feel the air cooling as the sun set. It was only then that he realized he was naked. Damn. *Where the hell are my clothes?* Hopefully, he'd be able to find them between here and home. Otherwise, he'd have a lot of explaining to do. He wasn't all that concerned about finding his way home. He had discovered during other jaunts through the woods that he had a very keen sense of direction. Besides, these woods were like a second home to him; maybe even a first. He often felt more at peace here than in the log cabin.

He began walking up the hill from the direction he'd come, but as he did so, his senses alerted him to a new problem. Over the past month or two, he'd noticed his five senses seemed to be improving. This was especially true when he was in either the canine form or that of the great owl, but even afterward when he returned to human form, the improved senses continued. Now, it was the heightened sense of smell that alerted him to the new danger as he picked up the scent of another human; one he easily recognized as Pat. It was a combination of her perfume and the unique makeup of her own body odor. And it was fresh.

The realization sent a chill through his body unrelated to the falling temperature. Pat had been here just a few dozen yards from where he'd killed the deer. She'd seen him at his worst. Since his birthday party she'd been pretty cool; not nearly as hard to get along with, but this...this could wreck everything. What if she told his dad what she'd seen? Worse yet, what if she told Kendra...or worst of all, Mimi?

No, she might tell Allan, but she wouldn't want Kendra or Mimi to know, would she? It would just complicate her life more. One thing TJ knew about Pat was she didn't like adding complications to her life. He felt sure that was what he'd become to her—a complication.

As he continued walking home, his thoughts about Pat were mixed with thoughts about what had him fleeing to the woods in the first place. As he remembered Mimi telling him that she would be unable to continue homeschooling him, he could feel the anger mounting once again.

Whoa there, boy. Don't go there. Not again. He stopped walking, closed his eyes and took several slow, deep breaths until once again he felt in control. Not that he was any happier about the news, but he realized turning into a bloodthirsty killing machine was not the answer. He'd read enough and seen enough movies to know that he had been jilted, even though he doubted Mimi had realized how much her news would hurt him. Not that it made it hurt any less. Maybe it did. At any rate, he would have to get over it. Maybe not immediately, but eventually.

Ahh... wasn't that a pair of blue jeans up ahead and just a little bit beyond that his shirt? See, things were already looking up, but as he started putting his clothes back on, his thoughts continued to swirl, first to Mimi, then to Pat, then back to Mimi again. Talk about complications. His life was becoming way too hard to figure out, but how could he simplify matters? That was a question he couldn't yet answer.

Stormy Family

The next few hours were excruciating for Pat, who tried to act as though nothing was wrong while realizing what she'd seen had dramatically altered her world. Now life was even more complicated than before. By the time Allan had returned home from the hospital, Mimi had left, and TJ had returned home, refusing to talk. Instead, he locked himself in his room, leaving it up to Kendra and Pat to explain the situation to Allan.

"I'm sorry to hear that Mimi won't be able to continue helping with the homeschooling," Allan said, "but maybe it's best in the long run. Maybe I should go talk to TJ."

"I would just let him be for now," Pat advised. "There's really nothing that you nor I can say that will make him feel any better. Time is often the best healer of a broken heart."

"That sounds like somebody speaking from personal experience," Allan said, smiling.

"You could say that," Pat replied. She was thankful when Allan decided to follow her advice and leave TJ alone. The less she had to be around him the easier it would be for her to pretend that everything was still okay between them; at least until Kendra left and she could talk privately with Allan. Unfortunately, Allan seemed to want Kendra to stay around longer than usual and invited her to stay for dinner, which she did. So, it wasn't until later in the evening when Donna had come by to pick up Kendra and her bike so she wouldn't have to ride home in the dark that she and Allan were finally alone.

Meanwhile, TJ had remained in his room, refusing to come out or talk. Allan left a tray of food outside his door, which remained untouched. Pat finally picked it up and took it back to the kitchen where Allan was finishing up the dinner dishes.

Okay, Pat thought; confession time but how to start the conversation?

"What did you mean earlier tonight when you said it might be the best thing if Mimi didn't continue to come over?"

Allan finished drying his hands on a towel before turning in her direction. "I don't know. It just seemed to me that TJ's crush wasn't going away. If anything, he seemed to be developing stronger feelings for Mimi, and I was uncomfortable about it."

"I see," Pat replied with a sigh of relief. "I thought the same thing. That's why I felt compelled to intervene."

Allan stared at her, a confused look on his face. "What does that mean? You felt like you had to intervene? What did you do?"

"I went and talked to Mimi's uncle and father." There, it was out, and it felt good to have admitted it...at least for a moment.

"You what? Without talking to me about it first?" Allan asked incredulously.

"You've been so busy lately that it never seemed a good time to discuss it. Besides, you just said..."

"I know what I said, but that doesn't give you the right to go blabbing about TJ all over town."

"I didn't blab about him all over town," Pat replied, feeling her hackles begin to rise. "I spoke to two people about their daughter and niece, and I didn't mention any specifics when it came to TJ. I'm not an idiot, you know."

"Sometimes I wonder," Allan shot back.

"Well, I'm not. I was very careful to not share anything about the younger boy that had a crush on Mimi. Only that you and I were uncomfortable about it continuing so I thought it would be best if Mimi didn't come around for a while. I never said a word about TJ or his 'differences' that made us uncomfortable, but that does bring me to another point we need to discuss."

"What's that?" Allan asked in a calmer voice.

"You may want to sit down first," Pat said, pointing to the kitchen table.

"That doesn't make me feel any better," Allan replied, but then followed her over and sat down in his customary chair.

"I saw something out there today that I knew you wouldn't want Kendra to know about, but that you need to be aware of."

"O...kay," Allan said slowly.

Pat took a deep breath. She'd been practicing how to tell Allan what she'd seen out on that hillside all evening, but now that it was time, she didn't know what to say. *Maybe I should just keep it to myself,* she thought, but she knew that would be the coward's way out, and she wasn't a coward.

"While I was out in the woods this afternoon looking for TJ, I came upon a deer that had just been killed. Its killer was in the process of eating it." She paused for a moment, trying to figure out how to break the news to him.

"That sounds pretty gruesome," Allan said, "but I'm sure you've seen worse. What kind of animal was it? A mountain lion?"

"No. It wasn't an animal, at least not one of this Earth. It was an alien. In fact, it looked almost identical to Homlin in its alien form."

"Oh, no," Allan said. "There's another one out there? I guess we knew that was at least a possibility."

"It was TJ," Pat said. "I watched him transform back to his human form before I snuck away."

The shocked, hurt look on Allan's face was almost too much to bear. Pat reached out to take his hand, but he pulled away, shaking his head. He stood up and walked over to the sink and stared out the window into the blackness of night.

Maybe I shouldn't have told him, Pat thought. *Maybe it would have been better to keep it to myself.* But he needed to know. He needed to face the truth about TJ. And while this was brutal news, it might just be what was necessary for him to finally open his eyes.

Allan continued to stare out the window, slowly shaking his head. Finally, he turned back around and stared at Pat still sitting at the table.

"And all this time I thought you and TJ had finally worked things out, but clearly you haven't. How long have you been cooking up this story?"

"What are you talking about?" Pat asked, perplexed by the question. "It's what I saw, just this afternoon." Then realizing what he was inferring, her temper flared. "If you think I made this up just to upset you, then you really don't know who I am. You've been living in a fantasy world for so long, you can't tell the difference between what's real and what's not. I'm real, Allan. I'm a real human being who loves you. That...that thing in the other room...it's not human. It's not your son, and honestly, I'm not sure it even can love."

"So is that how you really feel?" Allan asked, beginning to match Pat's anger.

Already regretting losing her temper, Pat didn't know how to answer him. "I don't know. Maybe...sometimes. I mean, this is hard, really hard. It's hard for all of us. I know what it's been like for the past few weeks, and it's been good. It had started to feel like we were a family, but..." The image she'd seen in the woods flashed before her, and she shuddered. How could she ever look at TJ again as part of her family with that image forever emblazoned on her mind?

Over the last few hours, a plan had started to slowly hatch in her mind. She had to get TJ away from Allan. Maybe, with a little time of separation, Allan would come to his senses. And even if he didn't, at least TJ would be out of their life. As ghastly as it was to admit it, she'd even toyed with the idea of killing the boy. She might have been able to follow through with that idea earlier, before TJ's birthday, back in the days when she only thought of him as a dangerous alien—as a foreign thing that threatened Allan and those she loved, but now? She was pretty sure she could do that only under the worse of circumstances. So she had moved on to her original idea, which she'd initiate later tonight. She hoped her outburst of anger hadn't already nixed that option.

"Listen, Allan. I didn't mean what I just said. I'm sorry, but it's been a very trying day," she said trying to mend the rip in their relationship before it grew any larger. "I know you care very deeply for TJ. Over these last few weeks, I have grown fond of him as well."

"You two seemed to be doing better lately," Allan conceded. "I think if you'd just give him a chance, get to know him a little better, I think you'd be able to see what Kendra and I see in him."

There it was; the opening she'd been looking for. "Maybe you're right," she said. *Easy does it*, she thought. *You've got a strong nibble on the line. Don't blow it. Nice and easy*. "What did you have in mind?"

"I don't know exactly," Allan replied. "Spend more time with him. I bet with a little effort you'd find some common interests. Something the two of you could build upon."

Pat nodded. "Yeah, maybe. I'd be willing to give it a try."

She waited, hoping that Allan would come up with the next part on his own. When he didn't respond, she took a gamble and made the suggestion. "How about this idea? What if I took TJ with me to Charlotte tomorrow. We'd have time during the drive to reconnect, and I could show him around the Queen City. He's never been outside this house and the surrounding woods. I bet we'll find plenty of common interests on such a field trip. Just a thought. What do you think?"

"Now you're talking," Allan replied, a smile beginning to form on his face. He walked back to the table and sat down across from her. "It would need to be a short trip. I don't want to overwhelm him his first time away from home."

"Sure, that makes sense," Pat replied as she slowly reeled in the fish named Allan. "I'll just swing by the office for a few minutes. Make sure everything is going all right there, and then after a little sightseeing, we'll head on back. At some point, he needs to learn how to make it in the world. This will be a step in that direction."

Allan nodded as he finally reached out and took Pat's hand. "I do appreciate your making an effort. I just want you two to get along. Maybe I should go let him know what we've decided."

"I'd wait," Pat replied. "It's late, and we've all had a busy day. Let it be a surprise."

"Yeah, you're right. I'm sure TJ will be feeling better after a good night sleep." Allan yawned. "I know I'm looking forward to one. How about you? Ready to turn in?"

"Almost," Pat said. "I just need to make a call or two. I'd like to let my office manager know I'll be bringing a guest so she can be sure the office is clean. You go ahead. I'll join you in a few minutes."

Allan stood up, bending over to give her a kiss; one that lasted longer than his typical goodnight kisses. It only served to make Pat feel even more like a heel for deceiving him. *It's for his own good,* she thought. *Yeah, just keep telling yourself that. You might start believing it.*

She waited until she was sure Allan had made it to their bedroom at the other end of the house. She then took her cell phone out, praying she still had the number in it that she needed. She did. She stared at the contact info for a minute, considering what she was about to do. Finally, she punched the call button.

It took several seconds for the connection to be made. When someone finally did answer, it was with a gravelly voice with a mixture of irritation and sleepiness.

"Hello. This had better be good."

Oops, Pat thought. She had forgotten how early her old friend went to sleep. Oh well, he'd get over it. *It's not like this is the first time I've woken him up.*

"Hello, Oliver. This is Pat. Did I wake you up?"

"Pat? What the hell are you calling me this time of night for?"

"Good to talk to you too," Pat answered, smiling at his reaction. "I have someone I want you to meet, and believe me when I tell you, it's someone you're going to want to meet. Can you meet me at my Charlotte office tomorrow afternoon?"

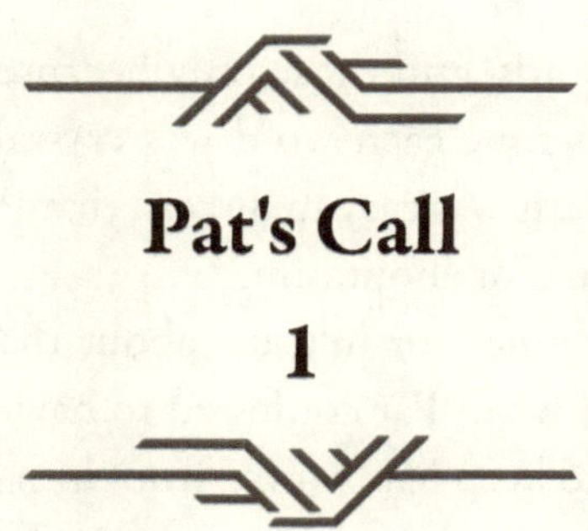

Pat's Call

1

TJ lay on his bed, still fuming over how the day had gone. It had been nothing but a bad news day all around. First, the news that Mimi would not be able to continue working with him as one of his homeschool teachers. That was bad; very bad. But maybe even worse had been the episode out in the woods where he'd lost all control and had turned into a monstrous form that had him questioning his true identity. And as if that hadn't been bad enough, Pat had seen it happen just when it looked like they might be able to get along as a family.

He heard someone outside his door and a few moments later could smell a mixture of odors. No doubt someone had left a tray of food on the other side of the door, but after his afternoon feeding on the deer, he had no appetite. In fact, for some reason the smell of regular food made him feel a little nauseous. Maybe it was due to his heightened senses. Normally, he doubted he would have been able to detect the food odors, but now they were almost overpowering.

He lay there for quite a while trying to decide what to do next. He couldn't stay locked away in his room forever. At some point, he'd have to go out and face the music; just not tonight. *Please, not tonight. Just let me drift off to sleep. In the morning when I'm rested, maybe I'll have a better idea what to do.* It had been a full day. No doubt about that. Going to sleep sounded like a good idea.

He closed his eyes and was close to drifting off when he heard whispers coming from somewhere outside his room. He'd heard such whispers a few times before when someone was in the kitchen cleaning up after dinner. Evidently, the heating ducts of the two rooms were closely connected, but something was different this time around. Before, he'd been unable to make out more than a few words, and those only because someone had spoken them more loudly. This time each word was crystal clear. He could even make out who said what. It was easy to discern that Pat and Allan were having a pretty heated argument about him.

Nothing particularly new or unusual about that, TJ thought, but he soon changed his mind when Pat confessed to having gone to Mimi's dad and uncle to ask them to keep Mimi away from him.

Why, that bitch! TJ thought as he sat up in bed so he could hear a little better. *She does have it in for me*; a thought that was only further confirmed as he listened to her relate what she had seen out in the woods. *Man, I'm really screwed now.* The one person who had only recently shown some sign of being on his side had seen him at his worst and was now relaying that information to the one person who had continued to stand up for him no matter what.

He was momentarily relieved when he heard Allan defending him and refusing to believe Pat's story, but the relief was short lived when Pat went on to suggest her taking him to Charlotte. On the one hand, the idea of traveling to a big city like Charlotte sounded interesting, but not with Pat. He didn't know what she had up her sleeve, but it couldn't be good.

He was beginning to doze off shortly after Allan had retired, but then Pat made her call. *Who the hell is Oliver and why does Pat want him to meet me?* While he didn't have the answer to either question, one thing was sure. He had no interest in cooperating with Pat's plan. None whatsoever. In fact, he felt it important to get the hell away from her for awhile. She had been right about one thing. It was time for him to broaden his horizons.

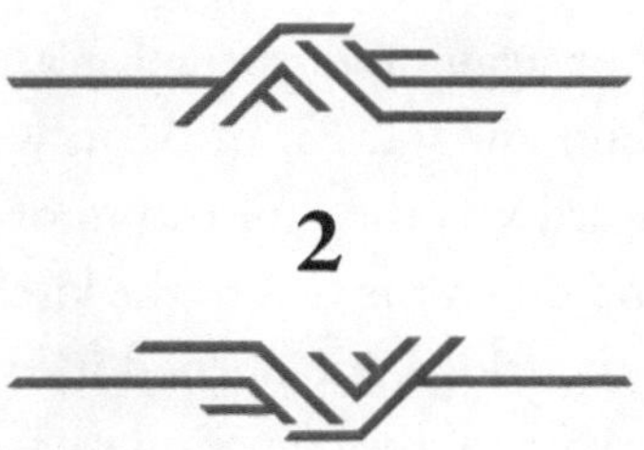

2

TJ glanced at the clock on his nightstand. 12:15 a.m. He'd have several hours to plan his escape while Pat and Allan slept. Suddenly, the idea of eating seemed more appealing, so he quietly opened his door and brought the tray of cold food into his bedroom. He quickly devoured the roast beef sandwich and chips, washing it down with the glass of iced tea. That along with the earlier meal he'd had while in the woods would hold him until he was well away from here.

Next, he had to decide where to go, what to pack, and how to get to his destination. Even as he asked himself the question, the answer came to him. He ruled out Charlotte. It was too far away for his liking, and besides, it was Pat's territory. If she figured out that he'd gone there, she'd have the advantage in finding him with all her many business connections there. However, over the last few weeks, he'd heard Mimi and Kendra talking about Asheville. He'd even taken the time to research it on the internet. It would do nicely. It was a large enough city that he should be able to get lost in it while also being closer to home, being only about thirty miles from Waynesboro. Having decided his destination, the rest of the plan started to fall into place. He'd have to travel light, with just the basics. That would mean he'd have to have a way to add to his inventory once he was at his final destination. That would require money. After all, money was light and could easily be converted into whatever he needed, like food and warm clothing, which would be important as winter was only a few weeks away.

But where to get the money? Simple enough. He'd borrow it from Allan's cookie jar. He'd watched Allan on numerous occasions return home and empty out his pockets of loose change, which often included taking a few bills from his money clip and dropping it into the cookie jar along with the change. TJ had never seen him empty the jar out, so there must be plenty of money still in it.

TJ unlocked his door again and opened it a crack, listening for any sounds that would let him know if Pat or Allan were still up and moving around. When all he heard was the dull thrum of the heating system, he crept out of his room and down the hall to the kitchen. The cookie jar was on the counter next to the fridge. He opened it to discover it about two-thirds full with cash. He ignored the coins and went straight to the bills. He counted it up and arranged it into a neat stack. The total came to a hundred and twenty-seven dollars. Not a bad nest egg to get this expedition started.

He took a sheet of paper from the notepad stuck on the refrigerator door and wrote the amount on it. Under it he wrote:

$127

I promise to pay you back someday.

Your son, TJ

This makes it a loan, not a theft, TJ told himself as he started back to his room with the money in his hand. He now needed to pack what he'd be taking with him, so he redirected his steps to the storage closet. He dug around until he found Allan's bright blue ski jacket with the rabbit foot attached to the zipper and backpack he occasionally used when going on longer hiking trips. The coat was a couple of sizes too large for him, but at the rate he was growing, it shouldn't take him long to grow into it. Besides, he could use all the luck he could find, so he was happy to take the rabbit foot along with him. He took his treasure back to his room to finish packing.

During all this, he'd continued to consider the other question—how best to travel. He'd read on the internet about people hitchhiking from place to place, but many of those stories didn't have good endings. Hitchhiking was dangerous, and it might make it too easy for Allan or Pat to find him if they figured out the direction he was traveling.

No, he'd take a different means of travel. At first, he considered shifting into the great gray owl form, but while he liked the speed with which he could make his way to Asheville, he couldn't figure out how to carry the supplies he would need once he arrived. But he had already borrowed Allan's backpack a few times while no one was around, and had practiced wearing it as he changed from his human form to his dog and wolf forms. He had confirmed that the backpack still fit well enough for him to wear it in the either of the animal forms. He knew from experience that the wolf form allowed him to travel faster and for longer distances. Of course, he would need to stay out of sight of other humans as much as possible. A backpack carrying wolf would not only draw more attention than he'd want, but it might also lead to him getting shot. At the same time, he could make much better time and could cover a much greater distance in his wolf form than as a human.

He'd just be sure to pack a couple of changes of clothes, along with the ski jacket and a few nutritional bars to tide him over. As he was packing, he came across three other items to take with him. The first one was his most recent copy of the *Mercenaries* computer game. He decided the PlayStation 2 was too heavy and took up too much room, but maybe he'd find somewhere in Asheville he could play the game. Besides, he wanted to take something that Kendra had given him that would help him remember her by. The second item was his copy of Mimi's book. By now the homemade book was dog-eared from being read so many times, but again, it felt important to have something that she had made for him.

It took him a little longer to decide whether to take the third item or not. He finally decided it was just too valuable to leave behind so he tossed the knife and leather sheath Pat had given him into the top of the backpack, then lifted it up to get an idea how much it weighed. He estimated it might be as much as twenty-five or thirty pounds. Not lightweight, but certainly manageable, especially in his wolf form.

He glanced at the alarm clock again. A few minutes before two a.m. He could still get a couple of hours of sleep before heading out well before dawn. He set the clock for four a.m. before turning out the lights and crawling into bed. Tomorrow would be a big day for him. His first time out into the world that he'd merely read about and watched videos of through the internet. Despite the excitement of what awaited him, he managed to fall asleep after only a few minutes.

Thanks

1

TJ's inner clock woke him a few minutes before four a.m., so he leaned over and turned off the clock before it had a chance to go off. Although he was tempted to roll over and go back to sleep, he knew the danger of falling into a deep sleep and awakening much later when the sun had already arisen was too great, so he sat up in bed and stretched.

Was he really going to do this thing? Run away from home to a city he'd never been to, but had only read about on the internet? *Damn right,* he answered his own question, as he kicked the covers off and leaped out of bed. Time to get to it. An exciting life of adventure awaited for him.

It didn't take him long to be ready to head out since he already packed the night before. He put on his favorite pair of blue jeans, a long sleeve plaid shirt, his warmest socks and a pair of tennis shoes. He'd left room for these clothes in his backpack, but had decided it was too dangerous to shift into the wolf form here. He'd wait until he was well into the woods.

He placed the note he'd written the night before in the center of his bed where it could be easily found and looked around his room one last time. He'd miss this place. It had been his sanctuary for his entire life, but he was no longer a kid. It was time to grow up and start his own life, whatever that might be.

He put on the ski jacket he'd 'borrowed' from Allan and shouldered the backpack. He tiptoed down the hall, pausing outside Allan's bedroom door for just a moment.

"Thanks for everything, Dad," he whispered, his eyes suddenly watering as the words caught in his throat. *Enough of that,* he thought. *Can't afford to break down like a silly kid.* He adjusted the backpack to his right shoulder and headed to the kitchen where he poured a box of Cheerios into a plastic bag. Just a little something for the road, he thought, as he sealed the bag and crammed it into his pack, then left out the back door.

He'd discovered in his practice time as a wolf that he had an excellent sense of direction, aided in part by his amazing sense of smell. Still, it seemed easiest to follow one of the secondary roads to Asheville. He'd just stay out of sight of the traffic. He calculated he'd easily be able to cover the thirty or so miles to Asheville before the end of the day, even allowing for a couple of breaks during which he'd shift back into his human form. No way was he going to forget his true form again. The memory of that time still sent a shiver up and down his spine. He waited until he was well out of sight of the house before stopping to make the shift to wolf form. He quickly undressed, stuffing the clothes into the pack, then putting it back on. Now came the tricky part. Shifting to the wolf form while wearing the pack, but he'd practiced this a number of times, so it went smoothly. It even felt like the pack became lighter although he knew it was his strength that had increased. His thick coat would not only keep him warm but would serve to minimize the chafing from the straps.

As he headed in the direction of the highway, the sun peaked above the horizon. Yes, it's going to be a great day for a walk through the woods and a start to a new life.

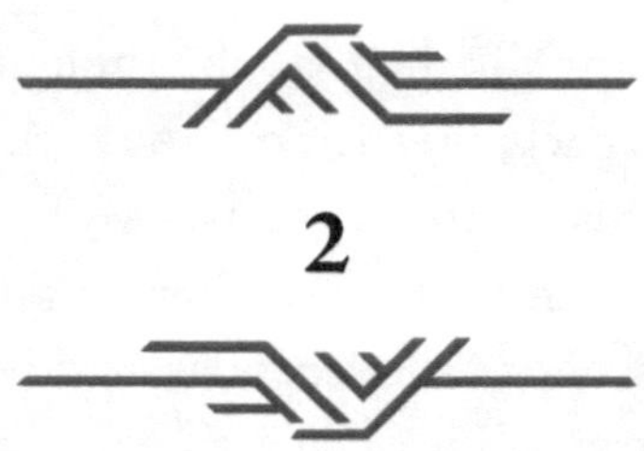

2

Pat lay in bed next to Allan, watching the night slowly turn to day, and remembering the argument from the night before. After making the call to Oliver, she had retired to the bedroom to find Allan still awake. It became clear pretty quickly that he was interested in some makeup sex, and normally Pat would have gone along with it. After all, in times past when they had argued, the makeup sex had been some of the best ever, but not this night. She felt like she had already manipulated Allan too much as it were. To then make love with him seemed too low down, even for her.

Maybe I should call the whole thing off, she thought, as she lay there watching Allan breathing. Call Oliver and cancel the meeting, at least until she was more certain that it was the right thing to do. Even as she considered her different options, she knew she'd not make that call. This was the best option she could take. Time to move ahead.

She climbed out of bed slowly so as not to wake Allan, put on her robe, and walked out to the kitchen to fix coffee. As she did so, she decided a good breakfast was in order. She started preparing French toast, which was Allan and TJ's favorite. *Still trying to get on their good sides,* she thought as she beat the eggs and milk together. *Yeah, maybe, so what?* Of course, it didn't matter how many favorite meals she was willing to fix. None of it would come close to making up for what she was about to do.

Before going further with the breakfast preparation, she fixed two cups of coffee and took one to Allan.

"Wake up, Sleepy Head," she said as she set the coffee on the table next to his side of the bed. "Breakfast will be ready in less than ten minutes."

Allan rolled over and opened his eyes. "What's this? Coffee in bed and breakfast on the way? What have I done to deserve such kind treatment?"

It's not what you've done but what I'm about to do, Pat thought, but instead, she said, "Oh, nothing in particular. Just trying to make up for the terrible things I said last night."

"Thanks," Allan replied as he threw his legs out of bed and reached for the coffee, taking a sip before adding, "Not necessary, but appreciated anyway. What are we having for breakfast? Pop tarts?"

"Hardly," Pat replied, laughing. It was one of the 'breakfasts' she often fixed when they were both in a hurry, but not today. "That is unless you'd prefer them over French toast."

"Hardly," Allan replied. "French toast sounds great. Is TJ up yet?"

"No, I don't think so. I'm on my way to knock on his door now. Hopefully, a good night's sleep and the promise of French toast will coax him out of his lair." Pat realized a second after the words left her mouth how they might sound to Allan. "Sorry, I didn't mean how that sounded."

Allan stood up and walked over to hug her. "Relax, no offense taken. He does sometimes use his room like a lair. We all do."

The two of them stood there hugging for a few more seconds before Allan excused himself and Pat left to awaken TJ. She was surprised to find his bedroom door, which had been closed and locked the night before, was now cracked open. Maybe the smell of coffee had alerted him to breakfast being prepared. She stuck her head through the crack in the door to say good morning, but was surprised to find the room vacant with the bed already made, almost as though no one had slept in it the night before, but what was that on the pillow?

Pat walked over and picked up the folded sheet of paper with Allan's name written on the front. As Pat stared at the note in her hand, a bad feeling took shape just below her solar plexus. *I don't think I'm going to like what this note has to say,* she thought. She slowly unfolded the note:

Dear Dad,

I need some time to sort things out. Don't worry about me. I won't do anything rash. I'll be in touch.

Love,

Your son, TJ

Pat stared at the note for over a minute, reading it several times, trying to discern any possible clues about where TJ had gone. She read how TJ had signed the note over and over.

Your son, TJ...Your son, TJ...Your son, TJ...

She was still trying to decipher its meaning when she heard Allan call from the kitchen.

"Hey, everyone! Let's have some breakfast."

But his words didn't come from behind her where the bedroom door was, but from in front of her.

"I'm one hungry guy this morning," Allan continued.

Pat glanced up in the direction of the sound to the air vent over TJ's bed. The pain in her chest grew as a hand of fear gripped her heart.

TJ had heard their entire conversation. He'd listened to her confession and now knew she was the one that had caused Mimi's expulsion. He also knew she'd spied on him out in the woods. What else had she said while in the kitchen? Of course. He'd also heard her suggestion to take him to Charlotte as a way to work through their issues. That would have been okay except for one thing. She had still been in the kitchen when she'd placed the call to Oliver.

No wonder TJ had decided to run away. She probably would have done the same thing in his place, but how in the hell was she going to explain this to Allan? She was still trying to answer that question when she heard Allan walk into the room behind her.

"What's up? Where's TJ?" Allan asked.

Pat swung around to face him, the open note still in her hand. She opened her mouth to answer him, but nothing came out. She handed the note to him to read.

Hickory

James disconnected the call and placed the cellphone back in the desk drawer. He tried to check for messages daily but had been unusually busy with his heating, and air conditioning business so had missed a couple of days.

The voicemail he heard, though cryptic, was unmistakable. Hickory, a mercenary named after the small North Carolina town where he was born, had been killed. James wasn't surprised by the news. The two of them had been on a couple of different assignments together, and James considered Hickory to be a bit of a loose cannon, always pushing the envelope too far and taking unnecessary risks.

That's why James made it one of his firm policies to know as much as possible about the other members of whatever team he was asked to join. He didn't like putting his life in the hands of unpredictable people like Hickory. After all, he had two young girls who depended upon him to return to them in more or less one piece...and alive.

It was after a particularly harrowing mission that involved two such loose cannons that James began to formulate the idea to regain control over this aspect of his life. Hickory had brought along a younger kid from his hometown who "showed a lot of promise" according to Hickory, though James suspected the kid had bribed Hickory to let him come along. It had almost cost the entire team their lives and would have if James hadn't stepped in.

Never again, he vowed upon returning and hugging his daughters particularly long. He didn't know how, but he needed to find a way to bring some semblance of control back to the mercenary game. He'd grown fond of the extra money. He'd finally been able to pay off the past-due medical bills, but then there was the expense of raising two girls, one of which already needed braces and both who would eventually want to go to college.

No, the money was too good, not to mention the thrill, within reason, of the missions. The thrill of well-designed assignments kept him feeling alive, but not when they stepped over the line into near suicide missions.

He was reminded of one of his mother's favorite sayings: where there's a will there's a way. *Well, I have the will so I'll just need to find the way,* James thought as he reached deeper into the desk drawer and pulled out a small black book. He leafed through the pages until he came to the one he'd been looking for with Hickory's name at the top. He tore it out and burned it.

Shack

1

Pat and Allan sat around the kitchen table with their mugs of coffee and TJ's note between them; the breakfast of French toast long forgotten.

"I knew he was upset about Mimi not being able to come over any longer, but I had no idea he would react in this way."

"We have to remember he's a teenage boy who thinks he's in love," Pat replied. "Who knows? Maybe he is in love. That's really not for us to say, but if we can get into the mind of a teenage boy I don't think running away is that unusual." She knew there was a lot more going on with TJ than just his upset over Mimi, but there was really no way she could let Allan know. She had already texted Oliver and canceled their appointment. Now she had to figure out what she could do to help Allan get TJ back. Or did she? Maybe this was a blessing in disguise. What if TJ just disappeared, never to be seen or heard from again? It sure would make her life easier, and maybe, just maybe Allan and she could get on with their lives minus the complication of a son who was really an alien.

As she stared into her half-empty mug of coffee, she considered it. Could she live with herself, knowing that she'd been the cause of his running away? What if they learned later that something terrible had happened to him? What if he was killed, or mugged, or arrested for vagrancy? As callous as it sounded and made her feel, it was this last possibility that concerned her the most. TJ was like a walking time bomb, set to go off at some random time that no one knew. One thing was sure. When he did go off, all hell would break loose. She could see the headlines now:

Alien Discovered Masquerading as Human

The story would go on to describe how a small town veterinarian with assistance from a prominent P.I. from Charlotte had been instrumental in protecting the alien from being discovered.

No. She wanted TJ out of her life, but this wasn't the way. Not to mention that if she was honest with herself, despite everything, she still cared for the boy, alien or not. She thought on one of her father's favorite lessons. Her father, who occasionally admitted to having Buddhist leanings, often quoted Buddhist teaching that the middle way was best. Over the years Pat had learned that there was much wisdom in that approach to life. So, what would be a middle of the road solution for the TJ problem? She didn't have an answer to that question; not yet, but at least it felt like the right question to be asking. That was often the start to finding a solution. So, the first order of business—find TJ.

2

It had been a full twenty-four hours and still not a word from TJ. In the first hour, they'd ruled out calling the police or sheriff department. There was just no way they could take the risk of involving them. Allan had called Kendra and Mimi just to let them know what had happened. Neither of them had a clue where TJ might have run off to but promised to be in touch if they heard from him.

"Let's try not to panic," Pat finally said. "Many kids who run away stay gone less than a day, then they either calm down or get hungry and come on home. Let's give TJ a little time."

Allan reluctantly agreed, but now it was the next morning and still no word from TJ.

Pat and Allan sat around the kitchen table, lost in their own thoughts. Finally, Allan asked for about the tenth time in the last twenty-four hours, "Where do you think he would go? He's never been anywhere other than this house and the land around it... except for that brief excursion to Homlin's place. Do you think he'd try to go back there?"

Pat shook her head. "No, I don't think so, but I could be wrong." An idea suddenly came to her, and she stood up. "I may know how to find out where he went."

"How?" Allan asked.

"Follow me," Pat replied as she walked into Allan's office and sat down in front of the computer. "TJ has spent countless hours in front of this thing. It's become his window to the world in many ways. Let's just see what's in its browser history."

Pat pulled up the list of sites visited over the last month. There were hundreds of different pages ranging from gaming websites, mostly related to a game called *Mercenaries*, to sites about wolves, owls, and several other animals. Pat scrolled down, scanning through the list like a speed reader and then suddenly stopped.

"There, that's where he has headed," she said as she pointed to the screen and a long list of sites all with the word, Asheville NC, in their name.

"Asheville?" Allan asked. "Why Asheville?"

"Why not Asheville?" Pat replied. "It makes sense to me. It's reasonably close and a fairly good size city. Should be fairly easy to stay incognito there."

"Yeah, I guess that makes sense," Allan replied. "So, now what? Do we drive over and see if we can find him?"

"No," Pat replied. "Least not yet. TJ is too smart just to be standing on a street corner waiting for us to find him, and Asheville is too large, but I know someone who may be able to help. His name is Shack Lawson. He's a P.I. in Asheville of some dubious reputation, but he and I have always gotten along pretty well." She decided it best not to mention the number of times Shack had tried unsuccessfully to get her into bed. "I'll call him later today."

Allan glanced at his watch. "It's already 9:30. Why not call him now?"

Pat chuckled. "Shack doesn't have much use for early morning calls, and believe it or not, 9:30 is still way too early. I'll give him a call around noon. I'll probably still be waking him up, but at least he won't be so ornery then. You go on to work. You've got lives to save."

"Yeah, and cats to spay," Allan agreed. "Keep me posted though."

"Sure thing," Pat said as she stood up and kissed him. "I know how important TJ is to you," *and I'm discovering how important he is to me as well,* she thought, surprised by her own admission.

3

TJ's leisure journey to Asheville took him along the Blue Ridge Parkway to Craven Gap where he found himself in the late afternoon. Off in the westerly direction, the sunset turned the clear sky a brilliant mixture of orange and red clouds against a deep blue sky while down below in the valley set the skyline of Asheville, the lights beginning to twinkle in preparation for another late fall evening.

TJ had shifted back to human form for the last few miles, not wanting to take the chance of running into other humans along the road as a wolf. He stood now in awe of the scene below him. He had known that Asheville was one of the fastest growing areas of western North Carolina, but none of the pictures he'd seen of it on the internet had come close to capturing its beauty or its size.

I think I'm going to like it here, he thought, as he studied the skyline that included several large buildings highlighted with a line of purplish mountain ranges in the background. He'd searched on the internet for cheap places to stay but hadn't found anything under fifty dollars a night. At that rate, his borrowed nest egg would be gone in no time, but his luck was holding for the night temperatures promised to be unseasonably warm. He figured he'd just sleep in one of Asheville's many parks, at least until he found a job.

He'd start his search for gainful employment first thing the next day. Tonight, he'd treat himself to a good meal in a restaurant close to the park he'd selected for his temporary housing. If he was careful, his stash should easily last until his first paycheck. He might even drop in on one or two of the nightspots of which he'd read. The Orange Peel, a favorite bar and entertainment venue that had been open for three years, had already become well known for some of the popular bands they'd hosted. Yes, his new life in Asheville was going to be very good.

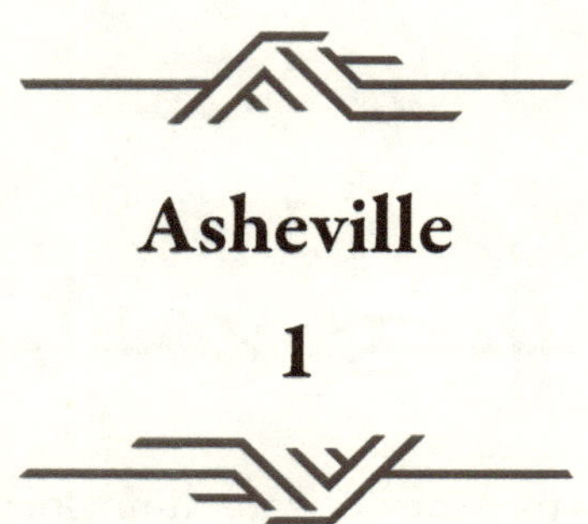

Asheville

1

As TJ entered the main business section of Asheville, the sun set behind the western range of mountains and soon the day turned to night. He stopped a couple of people on the street and asked where a good place to eat could be found. Two out of the three recommended the Mellow Mushroom, and the last one even gave him directions to it.

He was less than a block away and could see the sign up ahead when his keen hearing picked up the piercing scream of a woman followed by several loud words of anger off in the distance, accompanied by the equally angry retorts of a man. TJ took a couple more steps towards the restaurant, but then stopped when he heard a second even more blood-curdling scream sounding as though the woman was being killed.

He followed the voices down a narrow side street with poor lighting. Hearing a third scream, he picked up his pace to a run while the few people he saw around him appeared to ignore it all. *Maybe they don't hear it as well as I am*, he thought as he turned down an alleyway and saw a man and woman at the end of the alley grappling with each other. The man threw the woman down and appeared to be trying to wrestle her pocketbook away from her while she held onto it tenaciously.

"Hey, stop that!" TJ yelled as he ran towards them. "Leave her alone."

The man ignored him as he continued to try to yank the purse out of her hand but only ended up dragging her along the ground. As TJ ran towards them, he lifted his pack off his back and prepared to sling it at the large man's head, but when he did the man deftly ducked, and the pack swung through space, throwing TJ off balance.

"Now!" TJ heard the man shout, and with that, the woman was suddenly standing up next to him and slinging her pocketbook at his head. Her aim was considerably better than his had been. It hit him hard against his left side, and he fell, slamming his head on the dirty pavement of the alley.

The next few moments became a blur for TJ, as the man and woman jumped on him and beat him viciously; the man kicked him with his sharp-toed boots while the woman continued to hit him with her purse that felt like it must be filled with bricks. At one point TJ felt himself beginning to shift shape, he couldn't tell which and it didn't matter. He lost consciousness before the shift could take.

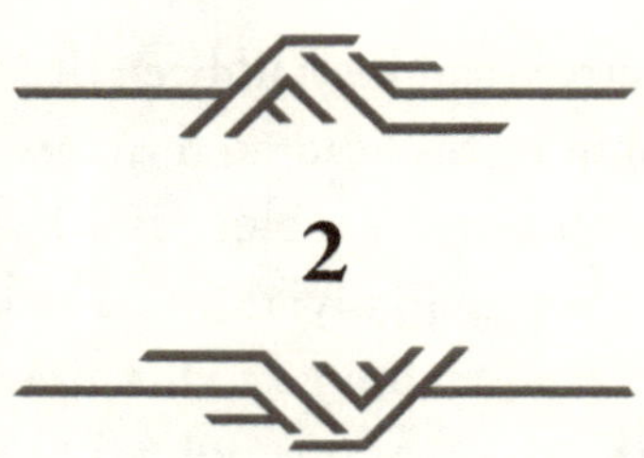

2

He awoke sometime later with a terrible odor assaulting his nose. He slowly opened his eyes but found himself still in the dark. It took him several minutes before he was conscious enough to realize he was resting on a mound of smelly garbage in an enclosed area designed for such trash. His head felt like the top of his skull might jettison from the rest of his body, and his ribs and groin ached from where the man had kicked him multiple times. He slowly rose from his prone position, only to crack his head against the hard metal top of the dumpster in which he'd been thrown.

After waiting for the stars to clear, he pushed the top open and found he was still in the alleyway. He looked around for his backpack, but his assailants had apparently taken it with them. That's when he noticed he was colder than he'd been before. They'd also taken ownership of his ski jacket. He stuck his right hand into his jean pocket and came away empty. They'd taken all his money as well. He leaned on the side of the dumpster, waiting for vertigo to pass, and felt drops of blood trickle down the side of his head.

"Welcome to Asheville," he whispered as he slowly collapsed back into the pile of garbage.

3

TJ awoke the next morning to the sound of a loud and persistent beep, beep. He reached one arm out to hit the snooze button of his alarm clock, but his hand landed on a wet, slimy pile of unknown origin. His eyes flew open at the same time his nose awoke to a strangely familiar stench. He groaned as the memory of the night before flooded into his awareness. *One of the worse nights of my life,* he thought. He vaguely remembered leaving the dumpster at one point during the night only to return less than an hour later. The night temperature had plummeted as a brisk, chilling wind blew through the streets and alleyways of Asheville. He looked for some other shelter from the wind, but every place he looked had already been taken by someone else. It was a harsh welcome to the homeless community. He had read on the internet about the growing population of homeless people in Asheville but hadn't fully comprehended how many men, women and yes, even children lived on the street without a home to go to.

And now I'm one of them, he thought. The realization sent a new chill through his body; one independent of the cold temperatures. Finally, after being yelled and cursed at by several of the homeless, TJ retraced his steps back to the dumpster, which suddenly looked more welcoming than it had when he'd first abandoned it.

I sure hope someone hasn't taken my spot, he thought as he lifted the lid and looked inside, then breathed a sigh of relief when he found it still empty. "Home, sweet home," he whispered as he climbed in and pulled the lid down to reduce the wind. Okay, maybe not sweet, but at least it would serve his purpose for the night. Tomorrow, he'd start pounding the pavement for a job and turn this downward spiral of his life around.

But what the hell was that irritating noise that had awoken him and continued to blast in his ear? As he had the thought, he felt the dumpster suddenly shudder and then shake more violently as it was lifted into the air.

He jumped up, hitting his head once again on the hard metal of the dumpster's top, then wincing in pain, pushed the top open. The dumpster started tilting towards the garbage truck that had lifted it into the air.

"Hey! Hold on. I'm inside here!" he shouted at the top of his voice. "Wait just a minute!"

The two sanitation workers who looked like they might have spent their own night in a dumpster stared first at him and then at each other with shocked looks. Finally, one of the men waved at a third man in the truck's cab, and a second later the dumpster stopped moving.

"What the hell you doing in there?" one of the men asked.

"Trying to keep from freezing," TJ replied as he crawled to the edge of the dumpster and jumped down to the alleyway.

"Well, I've never," the other man replied. "Getting so you can't take a step in this town without stepping on some bum."

"Take it easy, Jed," the first man answered back. "If it weren't for this job, that could be you or me."

His comrade grunted something unintelligible as he waved to the truck driver to resume emptying the dumpster.

"Speaking of jobs," TJ said as he turned to the one who had expressed some sympathy for his plight. "Know where I can get one?"

"Nah," the man replied, suddenly appearing far less interested in him. "Especially not looking and smelling like that."

TJ looked down at his stained shirt and pants. His gaze traveled down his body to his tennis shoes, where a dried banana peel stuck to one of them. He kicked it off. The man made a good point. No one would consider hiring him in his current condition.

"Do you know where I can find a bathroom then?"

"You may be able to sneak into the library when it opens at eight. It's just a couple of blocks away," the man replied. "Just don't tell anyone I told you so. And stay clear of their rent-a-cop."

The man climbed onto the side of the truck, and the empty dumpster was lowered to the ground. "You're new to the street, aren't you?"

"Maybe," TJ replied, suddenly wary of answering such a question.

"There's a shelter over on Ravencroft, not far from here. You can ask anyone for directions. I know you might want to go it alone, but if it gets too bad, they should be able to help."

"Thanks, I appreciate the information."

"No sweat, kid. Like I said, there but for the grace of God...." And with that, the truck pulled out onto the main street and away.

TJ followed the truck out of the alley to the main road where the city was slowly starting to awaken. As he walked along following the directions the garbageman had given, he noticed several people glaring at him, and one or two even appeared to cross the street to avoid him. Not that he could blame them. He surely couldn't brag about his appearance and was finding it hard to put up with his own smell.

He found the library just a couple blocks away but continued to walk around until it opened. He needed to pee badly, and the walking seemed to help. As soon as the doors opened, he entered along with several other patrons who frowned at him but refrained from saying anything.

Locating the bathrooms near the rear of the building, he rushed over to the closest urinal and relieved his aching bladder. He then walked over to the line of sinks to clean up. As he stared into the mirror, he gasped. Who was that scruffy, bloodstained kid staring back at him with the matted, greasy hair? He tilted his head to one side to get a better look at the scalp wound. He pulled a couple of paper towels from the dispenser, wet them and tenderly cleaned the wound. It had bled quite a bit but didn't appear to be that deep. As long as it didn't get infected, it would heal within a few days. He used several other wet towels to clean away the blood and dirt before finally clogging one of the sinks with a towel so he could soak his head, using the hand soap to wash his hair.

While he cleaned himself, an elderly man entered the bathroom, paused a moment to glare disapprovingly at him, then quickly relieved himself at the line of urinals before disappearing without bothering to wash his hands. TJ took another handful of towels to dry himself and was in the process of blow drying his hair with the one lone hand dryer when he felt a firm hand grab his shoulder from behind and spun him around.

"What the hell you think you're doing, boy?" A large man with a belly that extended over his belt dressed in a light blue uniform glared down at him. *Ahh, the guy warned me about this rent-a-cop.*

"Just using the facilities," TJ answered, in as light-hearted tone as he could muster.

"These here facilities are for patrons only," the man said as he continued to grip TJ's shoulder painfully hard. "You got yourself a library card or some other form of ID?"

"Gosh, I ran out of the house so fast this morning, I forgot my wallet," TJ replied.

"Yeah, I just bet you did. I should run you in for vagrancy."

"Oh, that won't be necessary," TJ replied as he tried to twist out of the man's grasp. "My mom and I are staying at the shelter over on Ravencroft, so I'll just be heading on over there."

"All right then," the cop replied finally releasing his grip. "Get yourself back over there, and I don't want to see you back around these parts, you hear?"

"Yes, sir," TJ said as he backed away from the man, then quickly turned to exit the bathroom before the cop changed his mind.

Job Hunting

1

Pat held out to 12:30 before calling Shack. As she expected, the phone rang several times without him picking up, so she hung the phone up on the fourth ring before it had time to switch over to voicemail. She called a second time and hung up again after the fourth ring. Shack picked up on the third ring of the third try.

"Who the hell is this, and I swear if you're trying to sell me something I will personally hunt you down and rub you and your family out."

"Good afternoon, Shack. It's Pat Vogt. See you're as pleasant as always."

There was a momentary pause on the other end, then a much more pleasant voice answered. "Well, hello, good looking. To what do I owe this pleasant surprise? Have you finally come to your senses and dumped that no account vet and are ready to accept one of my many invitations to dinner?"

"No to the first, and you know good and well your invitations were never just for dinner," Pat replied smiling. "I'm afraid this isn't personal, but business. I need your expertise in locating a missing person who we're pretty sure is in Asheville."

"Oh," Shack replied, clearly disappointed. "In that case, let me start my billing clock. Okay, go ahead."

"The missing person is a teenage boy. I can send you a recent picture. He left home yesterday morning."

"And who wants to find him?"

"I do...and Allan," Pat replied.

"Your vet boyfriend?" Shack asked, growing more perturbed by the moment. "What's the teenager's name and what's his relationship to this Allan guy?"

"His name is TJ, and his relationship... it's complicated. Let's just say for the record he's Allan's adopted son. Listen, Shack, I called you because I knew you had the connections there in Asheville and that you'd be...discreet in your inquiries. After all, we do go back a ways..." This was Pat's way of reminding Shack of some of the secrets she had on him.

"Yes, no need to bring up the past, sweetheart," Shack replied. "Email me the picture along with anything else that might help me locate him, including anything he might have taken with him. Sometimes, we get lucky and these runaways hock items when they get desperate for money. We might get a lead that way."

"The only thing I can think he might have taken that he could hock would be a knife I gave him as a birthday present that my dad had given to me. I think I may still have a photo of it. If so, I'll send that along as well."

"Good," Shack replied. "I'll get the word out and let you know what I turn up. Of course, there is one other condition for hiring me."

"Forget it. I'm not going to sleep with you."

"That really cuts me to my core. I was simply going to ask you to have dinner with me," Shack replied, then added, "And we'd see where it went from there."

"I'll send the picture of TJ in a few minutes, and if I find the picture of the knife, I'll send it later," Pat replied, then hung up.

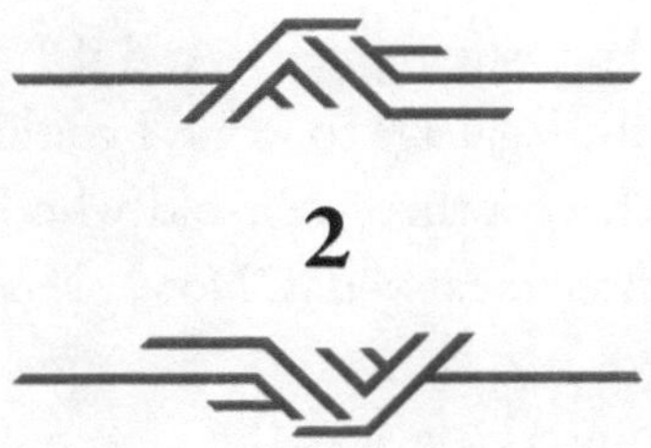

2

TJ's job hunting plan was simple. He walked around the downtown section of Asheville looking for Help Wanted signs. It didn't take long before he found one posted for a restaurant looking for servers and a dishwasher.

Great, TJ thought as he pushed the door open and walked in. The more positions needed, the better his odds. He squared his shoulders and tried standing taller as he watched a young woman with blonde hair in a ponytail stroll through the swinging door, drying her hands with a towel. She wore black slacks and a khaki blouse with a name tag that identified her as Renee.

"We're not open yet," Renee said as her gaze took in all of TJ's appearance, a frown growing on her face.

"I'm here for the job, Miss Renee," TJ said, pointing to the sign in the window.

"Really? Which one?"

"The one that pays the most," TJ replied smiling his most engaging smile.

"How old are you anyway?" Renee returned his smile then tried to hide it with her hand.

"How old do I need to be?"

"Eighteen for the dishwashing job, twenty-one for the waiter position because we serve alcohol."

"I guess I better go for the dishwasher job then," TJ replied.

"Really? You're eighteen?" the woman asked, cocking her head to one side. "Let me see your driver's license."

"Sorry, I don't have one," TJ replied. "I know I look young for my age, but why should my looks or age matter if I can do a good job washing dishes?"

"Because that's the law," she replied. "And if I were to hire you and it turned out you weren't the legal age to work, I could lose my job, and that's not going to happen. I have a three-year-old who has this habit she can't seem to kick of eating three meals a day. Now, please leave. You're smelling up the place."

And that brief job interview was the closest he came all day in becoming gainfully employed, despite inquiring at almost a dozen different businesses. By the time night fell for the second time since his arrival in Asheville, TJ felt dejected, tired and hungry as hell. *Maybe I should check out the shelter over on Ravencroft*, he thought, but it felt too much like he'd be admitting defeat, and he wasn't ready to throw in the towel.

With the sun setting in the west, the temperature started dropping again. It felt like he was in store for another cold night, which probably meant another night of sleeping in the dumpster; this time on an even emptier stomach than the night before. As he took a shortcut through Pack Square Park, he noticed an old lady with a small child feeding the pigeons, the birds flocking around the two of them. A thought suddenly came to him.

He might end up sleeping in a dumpster again tonight, but no way was he going to bed hungry. He had ways to feed himself not available to other homeless people. He walked around the park looking for a secluded area where he could initiate his plan without being discovered. He found a corner of the park where the lights had apparently burned out and not been replaced. Perfect for his night escapade, he thought as he slipped behind a row of shrubbery. He quickly undressed, carefully folding his smelly shirt and pants on top of each other, then stuffing his socks inside his tennis shoes before placing the shoes on top of the clothes. He then hid the pile deep within the hedge and prayed no one would find them.

He shivered in the cold night temperatures for only a couple of minutes before the shift to the great gray owl form began. Owls were great hunters, used to searching for their prey in the evening, and sighting one in an urban setting wasn't that uncommon. And one thing TJ had noticed during the day, Asheville had an abundant population of gray squirrels and even a few of the albino ones more commonly seen in the Brevard area. He'd heard Mimi talking about her Uncle Bo hunting squirrels and bringing them home to make a stew from them. Squirrel stew hadn't sounded all that appetizing to TJ at the time, but it sure sounded better than eating one raw. Too bad, he berated himself. Beggars can't be choosers, and neither can hungry, homeless kids.

He took his time making the shift. After all, it had been quite a while since he'd turned himself into an owl, and he was afraid he might be out of practice. When the transformation was complete, he stretched first one wing and then the other before using them to fly up onto the limb of a nearby tree. The owl form was the favorite of all his animal forms, and while he had no desire to become stuck in a form again, if he had to choose one to be stuck in, he would choose to be an owl. After all, the ability to fly was such a freeing experience.

It didn't take long to detect his first prey. In owl form, his sight and hearing were even better than the heightened senses he had as a human. He could easily detect the movement of a small mammal on the ground below. He waited for it to move into the clearing below the tree. He then quietly launched himself into the air with a flap of his wings made virtually silent in flight by the special design of his feathers. As he descended on his prey, he identified it as a good size hare just before he fanned out his wings and knocked the rabbit over with his talons, hitting it in the head and neck. He felt the snap of the rabbit's neck and its final death throes underneath him. He looked around to see if anyone was approaching, but his silent assault assisted by the darkness had gone unnoticed.

He dragged the carcass into the bushes not far from where he had stashed his clothes, feeling fortunate that his first hunting spree had gone so well. It also dawned on him that if he could find some matches, he could start a fire and cook his meal, which sounded much more appetizing than eating it raw. He decided to give it a shot. He found his pile of clothes, transformed back into human form and retrieved the rabbit. He then stuffed it into a plastic grocery bag he had found along the pathway leading back to the lit part of the park.

Locating a book of matches took a little longer, but he finally found some that had been left behind on one of the sidewalk cafe tables along with a pack of cigarettes. He took both, figuring he might be able to trade the cigarettes for something later. He had read enough about living out in the wild to know that he needed to dress the rabbit before cooking it. *Sure wish I still had my knife*, he thought. That and the ski jacket were his two greatest losses when it came to practicality, though he also regretted losing Mimi's book and the computer game Kendra had given him.

But practical matters were becoming increasingly important to him, and right now he needed to be able to clean the rabbit carcass so he could cook it. He solved the problem with a soda pop bottle he had found on his way back to the park. Holding the bottle by its neck, he broke it on the concrete curb and came away with a sharp piece that would do nicely for cleaning the rabbit and also as a weapon in case anyone else tried to take advantage of him. Life on the streets might be hard, but it was also a good teacher if you could survive the lessons.

That night he retired to the dumpster with a full stomach of cooked rabbit and a tool and weapon of the glass bottle. He had lined one end of the dumpster with several layers of newspapers he'd accumulated during the day and had sequestered the bags of garbage that had been tossed in it to the other end. He would use the remaining newspapers as a blanket. He might be cold, but he'd be warm enough to make it to the next day. Maybe his luck in finding a job would be better tomorrow, and one thing he also added to his plans. He needed to find a better place to live than the dumpster. After all, it wouldn't be long before it would be filled with garbage again.

Miss Precious

1

By the middle of the next day, TJ had concluded that when it came to getting a job, he was in a no-win situation. Not only was his disheveled appearance a major obstacle, but even worse, he didn't have the necessary identification papers or a note from a parent or guardian. Without such papers, no one was willing to give him the time of day, much less take a chance with him by giving him a job.

I can work. Sure I'm a young kid, but I can still do things like washing dishes, waiting on people, clearing tables, you name it. So why won't someone give me a chance? The answers were all the same. No ID papers, no work, or you're dirty, and you smell, so get out of here, but it wasn't his fault he was dirty and smelled. If he could get a job, he'd be able to get his clothes cleaned and even take a bath somewhere.

He decided he needed to take a break from job hunting. As Kendra had told him more than once, "You might not be able to stop bad things from happening to you, but you are in control of your attitude about those things." Or something like that. He had to admit at the moment his attitude sucked, so he decided to change not only his attitude but also his form. Maybe seeing the city from a different perspective would help.

He returned to the park that was rapidly becoming his second home. It was the closest he could come to his old habit of taking long walks in the woods when he was having a bad day. Plus, there were places in the park where he could shift to an animal form without being seen. He thought about shifting back into the owl form but decided to save it for later when he needed to hunt for his next meal. There had been enough rabbit left over for a good sized breakfast, so he could wait until the evening to hunt. Instead, he decided to explore Asheville in his dog form. He had noticed quite a few people walking around the city with their pet dogs, so maybe he'd get better treatment as a dog than as a human. In either case, he could explore the area freely while covering a good bit of ground as well.

As he made the shift, the first thing he noticed was that he felt warmer in his canine coat than he did as a human with only a shirt and jeans to keep him warm. He also noticed a change in the people around him when he left his hiding place and started walking around the park. As a homeless person, people either ignored him completely or were antagonistic towards him. As a dog, many people continued to ignore him. Those who did notice him tended to be much friendlier and easy-going with him. A few even took the time to pat him on the head or talked to him as he walked by them.

"Where are you going, boy?"

"Lost your owner, big guy?"

"Oh, what a handsome dog you are. Dad, can we take him home with us?"

Of course, there were those who were also intimidated by his large size and would either cross the street to get away from him, or stop and wait for him to pass, but even they didn't treat him harshly.

Funny, TJ thought. *Asheville seems to be friendlier to animals than to homeless people.*

He was enjoying his afternoon romp around the city when he found himself in a new section he'd not yet explored. The houses and buildings were older here and not as well kept, and the smaller park he found appeared to be going to seed and strewn with litter. He was about to turn around and retrace his steps when his canine senses were propelled into high alert by a bark that reminded him of the rabbit squeal he'd heard on the internet. Another dog was in trouble. He trotted towards the sound, his hackles raised.

In the far corner of the park, he found an old playground with a set of swings, slides, and a merry-go-round in dire need of repair. Partially hidden under one of the slides was a small spaniel-looking dog trying to fend off the attack of three younger and larger dogs. The lead dog looked to be a cross between a pit bull and a larger, shaggier dog and was close to TJ's size. His two companions were smaller than the shaggy dog, but both the black and tan shepherd and the black short haired dog looked like they could hold their weight in any fight.

TJ could just make out the greying muzzle of the spaniel sticking out from her improvised shelter as she growled and snapped at her three tormentors. Three big bruisers against one small old girl didn't seem fair at all to TJ, but then he remembered the last time he'd tried to help out a lady in distress. His head was still sore from where she'd laid him out. He started to back away. No need to interfere. It wasn't his fight.

Just at that moment, the three dogs charged the spaniel, and the shepherd grabbed her by the nape of her neck and started pulling her out from under the slide where the other two dogs could get to her as well. Before he realized what he was doing, TJ barked his most fierce and intimidating bark, and he charged into the fracas. He snapped at the hindquarters of the shepherd and was pleased to feel his teeth sink into the muscular rump, followed a second later with a high pierced bark of pain.

The shepherd released its hold on the spaniel, who quickly retreated under the slide. As the shepherd turned to ward off his attacker, TJ took the opportunity to place him between the three assailants and the spaniel. He stood with his front legs wide apart and snarled a warning which he hoped meant something like; *You want a piece of me? Come and get it!* In dog speak. The two smaller dogs backed away, but the pit bull lunged at him, trying for his throat. Fortunately, TJ saw the attack coming and was able to sidestep as he clamped down on his attacker's right ear, ripping a large chunk of it off in his mouth. He promptly spit it out, surprised at the exhilaration he felt from the taste of blood.

The pit bull backed off, shaking his head, sending droplets of blood flying off in all directions. The three dogs stood frozen in a semi-circle facing TJ, but none of them were prepared to further the fight. They slowly backed away and finally trotted out of the park.

TJ stood watching them until he was sure they weren't going to try to counterattack, then turned back to see if the spaniel was okay, but she was no longer under the slide. She'd used his diversion to slip out the back way and was even now hightailing it out of the park in the opposite direction.

*I'll be...*TJ thought. *What an ungrateful...*but then he stopped himself. Truth be told, if he'd been in her situation, he might have done the same thing. *At least she didn't hit me with her purse.* He chuckled to himself at the thought. He'd done a good deed. That was what mattered, and he had lived to tell about it, even though he didn't have anyone to share it with at the moment.

He glanced down at the ground where the piece of ear laid in the dirt. Was the excitement he'd felt from tasting blood an indication he was becoming too much dog and in jeopardy of losing himself again? He didn't think so, but he was also not interested in finding out. Time to return to where he'd hidden his clothes so he could shift back to his human form, but he'd learned something else important today. He was warmer as a dog with his thick coat than he was as a human with just a shirt and pair of pants. If he got too cold tonight, he'd shift back to dog form at least for a little while.

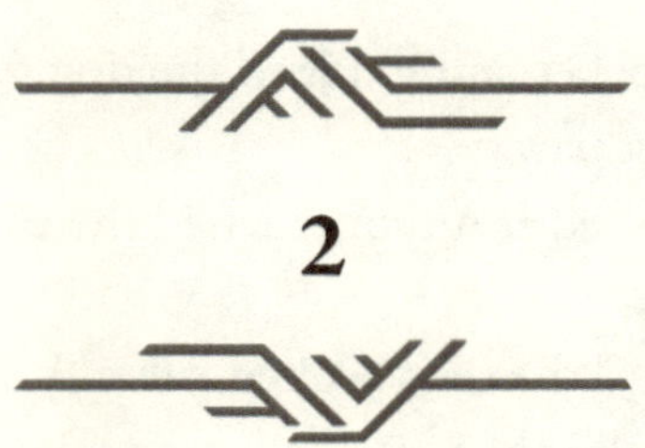

2

By the time TJ had returned to Pack Square Park, found his clothes and shifted back to his human form, the sun was dipping behind the mountains, and the temperature began to drop again. And he was growing hungry again, having finished off the last of the rabbit earlier in the day. He had noticed several others of the homeless community sitting along the streets of Asheville panhandling for change, but he wasn't quite ready to go that route, although with the temperatures dropping more each day, it wouldn't be long before he'd have to do something to come up with warmer clothes. He was still thinking about what that might be when he saw the old spaniel trotting down the sidewalk in front of him. She appeared to be favoring one of her front legs but otherwise was no worse for wear.

He decided to follow her to see where she went. She took a straight path through the park to the other side where she met up with an old man wearing khaki pants with a cardboard sign propped up beside him that read:

Homeless Vet

Support Your Troops

Beside the sign set a plastic Tupperware container with an American flag sticking out of it along with a few dollar bills. The dog leaped into the old man's lap and licked his gray-bearded face, much to the vet's satisfaction.

"Welcome home, Miss Precious," he said, laughing heartily at her antics. He placed one hand on his head to keep the camouflaged cap from falling off.

But TJ's attention focused on one particular detail that stood out over all the rest. The man was wearing his dad's blue ski jacket, complete with the rabbit foot attached to the zipper. He watched as the man took a morsel of food from his jacket pocket and fed it to the dog. While she munched on it, he gently checked her paw.

"Is she okay?" TJ asked as he approached the two of them, his eyes still focused on the jacket.

"Yeah, she'll be okay," the man replied friendly enough. "Looks like she might have gotten herself into a bit of a scrap while she was away."

"She did," TJ replied. "It was off of Hilliard Avenue in that park. Three dogs were after her." As TJ talked, the spaniel climbed down from her owner's lap and walked over to him. She sniffed at his leg for a second before jumping up on him in a friendly manner.

"She wandered that far away?" the vet asked, then noticing her antics, continued. "That's odd. She never takes to strangers, but she sure has taken to you." He studied TJ for a moment before asking, "Did you help ole Precious out?"

"Let's just say; we've met before and leave it at that."

"Okay," the man said. "Thank you kindly for whatever you might have done." He reached out his right hand. TJ hesitated for a moment before realizing he was offering to shake hands. As he took the man's hand, he noticed he was missing a couple of fingers, and the remaining ones were scarred and arthritic looking with swollen knuckles. "I'm Luke, and this here is Precious."

"I'm TJ. Good to meet the two of you."

"You new to these parts?" Luke asked as he released TJ's hand. "Don't remember seeing you around here before."

"Yeah, been here a few days," TJ answered. "Listen, I hate to bring this up, having just met and all, but well...that jacket you're wearing is mine...well, my dad's, but I borrowed it from him."

"Is it now?" Luke replied noncommittally. "You know what they say about the law around here."

"No, what do they say?"

"Possession is nine-tenths of the law," Luke replied with a chuckle. "If it's your jacket, but you and I have never met, and I'm now wearing it, how could that be?"

"I was mugged and robbed the first night I got here."

"Oh, were you now? Don't tell me you fell for the ole 'damsel in distress scam?'"

"Yeah, I guess so," TJ replied, hanging his head. "But that doesn't make it any less mine."

"No...no it don't," Luke replied, "but my possessing it sure does. Listen, let me ask you something. Where you been staying?"

"Around," TJ replied.

"You're the kid been sleeping in the dumpster off of Spruce Street, ain't you?"

"Maybe," TJ finally admitted.

"Yeah, well you sure smell like it," Luke said with a chuckle. "Listen, I'm not a big fan of slick Saul and Sally's tactics. They're the ones that welcomed you to town, but sky blue is my favorite color so when I saw him wearing this here jacket, I traded for it. So, you want it back; you'll need to trade me for it."

"I don't have anything to trade," TJ replied, upset at how much it sounded like a whine.

"How about you let me be the judge of that," Luke replied. "Now, tell me the truth. Did you help Precious out of her scrap with those three dogs?"

TJ nodded. "Yeah, but I can't tell you how."

"That don't matter," Luke replied as he took off the jacket. "That's good enough for me. There's nothing on this planet more important to me than this here ole dog, and if you saved her from being mauled by three bully dogs, I'd say that's a pretty good trade." He held the jacket out to TJ. "What do you say?"

"Yeah, I guess so," TJ finally agreed as he took the jacket from him. "But what will you wear?"

"Oh, don't worry about me. I still got my old Army coat. It's not a pretty blue like this one, but it's warm, and I think Precious likes it more on me than the blue one, but there's one more thing. You can't take that coat back to that smelly dumpster. You come with Precious and me. We'll find you somewhere to stay."

Hunting

1

Pat didn't hear back from Shack until the next evening.

"I'm betting by the time this is over, it'll be you insisting we have dinner and on your tab," Shack said as his greeting.

"Since when did you start believing in miracles?" Pat retorted. "You got something for me besides pipe dreams?"

"Yeah," Shack replied. "Word is on the street that a new kid showed up a day or two ago. Of course, a new kid on the street is hardly news, but in this case, it was. No one knows where he's from, but rumor has it he's been sleeping in a dumpster off of Market Street. He fits your boy's description."

Pat groaned at the thought of TJ sleeping in a dumpster, realizing it was her fault. "Can you follow up on it, and let me know what you find?"

"Of course, little lady," Shack replied. "Your wish is my command. I also heard of a new steak and seafood restaurant that just opened that's supposed to have a killer wine list. Want me to make reservations?"

Pat didn't bother to answer, but as she hung up the phone, she had a smile on her face.

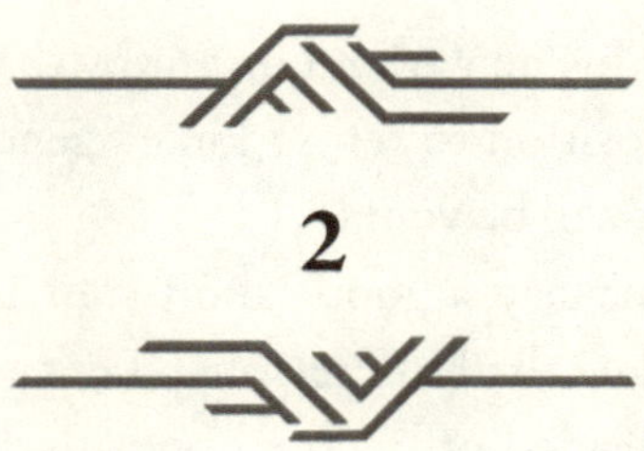

2

"Look, some of my friends and I are going to hang out tonight. It's not supposed to be all that cold. We have a place that's pretty safe, and there will be a fire and blankets for when you're ready to crash. You're welcome to come along if you don't already have other plans." Luke tried to keep from smiling as he said that last part.

"Let me check my calendar and see if I can fit something else in," TJ answered, playing along, and a second later he added, "You're in luck. I happen to have tonight free." Then he stopped himself. "Ahh, I don't have anything to contribute, but if you give me a little bit of time, I can maybe come up with a rabbit or two. If not that, how about a squirrel?"

Luke looked at him as though trying to figure out if he was serious. "How you going to get a rabbit or squirrel?" he asked.

"Oh, I've got my ways," TJ answered. "Tell me where the gathering is, and I'll be there. I'll bring what I can."

Luke gave him directions, then stood up and started packing up his belongings, which included a few dollars he'd collected during the day. He started to stick the money in his pant's pocket, then stopped.

"Here, you take this just in case the rabbits and squirrels don't cooperate."

TJ looked at the money Luke held in his gnarled hand. "I can't take your money. You worked hard for it."

"Yeah, right. Sitting on my ass all day looking pathetic is hard work, but I'm used to it," Luke replied still holding out the money. When TJ didn't move to take it, he stepped forward and stuck it into TJ's shirt pocket. "Look, man, if you're going to be on the street, you gotta learn not to let your pride get in the way. You helped out my Precious earlier today without any expectation of getting anything from it. Well, I believe in karma so consider this a little karma back to you."

TJ wasn't sure what his new friend meant by that last comment, but he realized he was in no position to refuse Luke's generosity. "Okay, but that means the fattest rabbit will be yours."

"That's fine. I haven't had a good rabbit stew in ages. Good hunting, boy. Come on, girl," Luke called to Precious. "Let's go round up the others."

The two of them headed off in the opposite direction from TJ, who strolled back into the park where he waited around for it to grow dark. He hesitated a moment before taking off his newly recovered ski jacket. He'd hate to lose it again, so he made sure it and his other clothes were well hidden before making the shift.

After shifting into the owl form, he decided to fly around a bit before settling down to hunt for his evening meal. The air was crisp and clean for being in the city, and the lights below sparkled in multiple shades of white, yellow and gold. He could see the citizens of Asheville rushing to their cars to get home to their warm homes and families. Everyone was too busy to bother looking up, so he was able to fly around without being noticed. After a few minutes, he returned to the darkened part of the park where the hunting was best.

In the space of a couple of hours, he was able to kill two rabbits and a squirrel. That should be enough to get him into the gathering. Not exactly like bringing a bottle of wine to a party, he thought, but under the circumstances, the fresh game might be preferred over booze. Besides, as he'd learned on his first day, without proper ID one's shopping choices were significantly curtailed as was one's ability to make money so you could afford to go shopping.

After making the last kill, he dragged it to where he'd stashed the others, shifting back to human form and quickly dressing. He relished putting on the ski jacket and feeling the warmth start to build inside of it. He cleaned the game, being careful not to get blood on the coat, then stuck the carcasses in a bag before hiding the makeshift bottle knife. Sure would be nice if he could somehow get his knife and other belongings back. Maybe he'd talk to Luke about that. See if he could negotiate with this Saul fellow.

Okay, time to find the party, he thought as he pulled the directions he'd scribbled down. The day had turned out alright after all.

3

Less than twenty-four hours later, Pat was back on the phone with Shack.

"I've got some more news, and it's not good...not good at all," Shack said straight away without even a hint of flirting first, which immediately set off Pat's alarm bells.

"What is it, Shack?"

"I've tracked down the knife; at least where it was as of yesterday evening."

"Okay, that's a good start," Pat replied. "Where was it?"

"Apparently cutting a couple of homeless people's throats," Shack replied.

"What? Impossible! TJ would never do such a thing." *At least I don't think he would,* Pat thought.

"Here's what happened as best as I can make out. I have a cop who owes me a couple of favors, so the story's source is strong. The police were called out to an alley behind one of the homeless shelters around 9 pm. It seems there had been an altercation. One of the shelter employees heard a ruckus outside and called them. When they arrived, they found a homeless man dead and his female companion bleeding out. They'd both had their throats cut. They managed to stop her bleeding in time to save her, but it appears her vocal chords may have been damaged. That part isn't clear. She may have been mute before the incident. Anyway, the two were identified as Saul Young and Sally Morrow. I know both of them, or at least their street rep. They're both bad apples. Whoever took them out probably did the city a big favor."

"How do they know my knife was involved?" Pat asked.

"Sally isn't able to talk, but she was able to draw. It turns out she's not a bad artist. She drew two pictures; one of a knife and one of a teenage boy then drew a line between the two. My cop friend took a picture with his cellphone and sent it to me. Sorry to say, the pictures fit your knife and boy to a T. I'll forward it on to you when I get off."

Pat sat down on the kitchen chair, the tea she was in the process of fixing forgotten. What in the hell was she going to do now? Surely it was just a matter of time before the cops tracked TJ down and then the shit was going to hit the fan. Now, it was more important than ever for her to find him, but then what? Her brain was swirling but without any solution coming to mind, a little like a computer searching for a file that simply wasn't on the hard drive. She suddenly realized Shack had asked her a question.

"What was that again?"

"I said, what do you want me to do now?"

"Find TJ before the cops do," Pat replied, an idea starting to form. "And one more thing, Shack. Do you still have that connection with the guy who prepares fake IDs?"

"Yeeaaahh..." Shack replied slowly. "I might be able to help you out there. Why?"

Gathering

As TJ followed Luke's directions to the gathering, he wondered if the old man had sent him on a wild goose chase. He found himself walking through a well-manicured residential neighborhood that seemed to TJ to be an unlikely setting for a gathering of homeless people. He felt self-conscious strolling along the streets with his plastic bag of recently killed game. He could imagine people inside their homes staring at him before rushing to their phones to call the cops. Still, he didn't have anything else to do with his time, and Luke had appeared genuine with his invitation, so he'd keep walking at least until the patrol cars arrived.

Luckily none did, and as he continued to walk the houses grew sparser, and within a few blocks, he found himself in a wooded area not yet taken over by the urban sprawl. As he followed the roadway around an outcropping of trees, he heard the sound of music in the distance and detected a scent that started his mouth to water with anticipation. Walking a little further, he saw a clearing up ahead with lights fluttering through the trees in the distance. These turned out to be from fires burning inside some large metal drums. Around each fire people stood and sat, many of them swaying to the music that came from a boombox TJ figured was probably close to twenty years old.

He suddenly felt awkward walking into such a gathering, but then relaxed as he saw Precious bounding towards him, her tongue flapping to one side like a welcome flag. Her limp appeared much better, and she seemed no worse for her adventure earlier in the day. As she reached him, she reared up on her hind legs and pawed the air with her front, obviously pleased to see him. Luke followed close behind, much more calmly but with a smile on his face as well.

"Welcome to our gathering, TJ. Come, let me introduce you to some of my family."

"You have family here?" TJ asked as he once again accepted Luke's outstretched gnarled hand in greeting.

"Yep, the best kind of family — people I've chosen to be part of my life," Luke replied. "And don't worry about remembering the names. You'll get to learn them if you stay around long enough. Hell, some of us have trouble remembering our own names these days."

TJ appreciated the warning, for within minutes he had more names and faces swirling around than he had any hope of making sense. Peggy Sue (was she the one with the red and pink hair?), Elmer Fudd (could that have really been his name?), Alley Cat (pretty sure she was the young, cute one but with the much bigger boy holding her hand), and the names and faces went on. Everyone appeared to welcome him with open arms and graciously accepted his donation to the stew that was in process.

"Let me help by cutting these into chunks," Luke said as he reached into the faded green coat with the multiple pockets and brought out a large hunting knife in a leather sheath — the knife that Pat had given TJ for his birthday.

TJ stood there staring at the knife as Luke took it out of its sheath and started to reach for the bag of game, a crooked smile beginning to play on his face.

"That's my knife." TJ finally managed to get the words out. "Where did you...?"

"Is it now?" Luke replied. "You know what they say..."

"Yeah," TJ replied with a dejected tone in his voice. "Possession is nine-tenths of the law."

"You're learning quickly, my boy," Luke replied, "Except in this case it's not true." He flipped the knife in the air, deftly grabbing the sharp end and offering the handle end to TJ.

"Several of us have pretty much had it with Saul and Sally's antics recently. Giving our little town here a bad name, so we had an 'intervention.' Under the circumstances, I'd say they were quite understanding. They both wanted to be sure you got what they 'borrowed' from you the other day."

As TJ took the knife from him, Luke reached into another of his many pockets and pulled out the CD case of TJ's video game and Mimi's book. "I believe these are yours as well. Unfortunately, they'd already hocked the backpack and clothes, but if you're not too particular about your fashion tastes, we can hunt you up some more clothes in the next day or two, but not until we get you washed up."

"How will you do that?" TJ asked. "I thought about washing off in the fountain at the park, but the idea of jumping into that frigid water was a little too much."

"Not to mention that some Big Blue would likely arrest you for indecent exposure," Luke added with a chuckle.

"Big Blue?"

"Yeah, that's what we call the cops around here. For the most part, they leave us alone as long as we don't do anything stupid," Luke replied.

"Like trying to wash in the fountain?" TJ asked.

"Exactly," Luke answered. "No, most of us use the shelter over on Patton Avenue. The shower stalls are clean, they seldom run out of hot water, and the staff there don't try to save your soul...least not too often. Of course, there's no point in cleaning yourself up just to put you back in those nasty clothes or to send you back to sleep in a dumpster."

"Yeah, that's been my dilemma," TJ admitted. "I wasn't figuring on getting mugged my first night. I'm afraid I didn't have a plan B when that happened, but I'm learning."

Luke threw his head back and laughed heartily. "I bet you are. The street is a good teacher if it doesn't kill you in the process. Most of us will spend the night here. There's plenty of wood to keep the fires stoked, and I don't expect Big Blue will be visiting us. If so, hightail it to those woods over there, and we'll meet up tomorrow in the same area we met today."

"What is this area, anyway?" TJ asked. It was fully dark by now and impossible to see more than a few yards beyond the light of the fires.

"It's a construction site," Luke replied as he took a pocket knife from his coat pocket and began cutting up one of the rabbits with it. "In a couple of weeks they'll finish paving the roads, and a few months after that, there will be rows of new houses. Jacob over there has been doing some work for the contractor and promised to clean up a lot of trash left over from the initial clearing, which is where the fires come in. We're staying warm and cleaning up all at the same time."

"Wow, that's cool," TJ said.

"Yeah, I just wished more people were willing to give us a chance. Of course, then you run into folks like Saul and Sally who end up giving the rest of us a bad rep. It can become a downward spiral if you let it."

TJ thought about what Luke said. He had sure gotten himself stuck in such a spiral. "You seem to have a pretty good outlook on life," he finally said. "How do you manage it?"

Luke looked up from his work and stared into the fire for a moment before finally answering. "I spent quite a bit of time in Vietnam when I was in the service. That's where this came from." He held up the hand without the two fingers. "I learned a little about karma from one of the Buddhist priests I met there. It took me years to get the hang of it...probably still fail more often than not, but it seems to work for me."

"Karma?" TJ asked as he pulled the other rabbit from the bag. "You mentioned that before, but I haven't a clue what you're talking about."

"I'm probably not the best one to teach it to you," Luke replied, "but this is my take on it in its simplest terms — what goes around, comes around. I had it tattooed on my arm so I wouldn't forget it." He pushed up the sleeve of his left arm to reveal the words inscribed in a circle on his arm.

"Wow, couldn't you just have written it on a piece of paper and kept it in your pocket?" TJ asked.

Luke threw his head back and laughed for a second time. "Maybe, but it wouldn't have meant the same thing."

"But what does it mean—what goes around comes around?"

"Here's how I think of it," Luke replied as he cut off a chunk of meat from the hind quarter of the rabbit and popped it in his mouth. "The results of things that one has done will someday affect the person who started the events. Take Saul and Sally, for example. They've been doing some pretty bad stuff to people. You're not the first one to fall for their scheme. They've been sowing some pretty bad 'karmic seeds,' and earlier today they reaped the results."

"What did you do to them?" TJ asked, suddenly worried.

"Let's just say my friends, and I helped keep the karmic wheel turning." Luke rotated one finger around, outlining the circle of words on his arm. "Now, finish cutting up your rabbit and let's get it in the pot. People are getting hungry."

As the two of them walked over to the large pot of simmering stew, TJ said, "You realize you ate some of that rabbit raw?"

"Did I now?" Luke said as he tossed a small chunk of it to Precious before popping another piece in his mouth. "Guess I learned that from ole Precious here. You learn to appreciate all the bounty this Earth has to offer in whatever form it comes to you."

Soul Searching

1

It took a couple of sleepless nights and more soul searching than Pat could remember ever doing before, but she felt like she finally had a plan that she could live with if she could pull it off. She had come to the conclusion she somehow needed to get TJ out of Allan and her lives if they were to have any chance of making it as a couple. At the same time, she had grown too fond of TJ to simply ruin his life by turning him over to Oliver and his crew at B.I.U.F.O. She had to give the boy the opportunity to find his place in the world—as long as that place didn't involve Allan or her.

So far, she'd managed to be vague with Allan whenever he asked how the search for TJ was coming along; a question he asked her several times a day. But she wasn't sure how much longer she could keep him in the dark before he decided to take some action on his own. As it turned out, she was assisted by a busier than usual time at the clinic.

While she waited to hear back from Shack, Pat resorted to numerous long walks through the woods. It was during one such walk that she received the call from the Asheville P.I.

"What you got for me?" she asked.

"Good news!" Shack replied. "At least some of it is good. The documents you requested are ready, but the price tag is pretty high. Rushed jobs always cost more..."

"Not a problem," Pat interrupted him. "I figured as much. What's the quality like?"

"Good," Shack replied. "They should work just fine."

"And the other news? Good or bad?" Pat asked.

"I'd say a little of both. The cops are continuing to look for the boy, but so far the case is still low on their priority list. After all, a homeless kid knocking off a couple of other homeless people isn't that big a deal to them, and they're trying to keep a low profile on it. It's not the kind of story any of the powers-that-be want to hit the newsstand, especially as we start the holiday shopping season."

"Any word on the Sally woman's condition?"

"She's out of I.C.U. and is expected to recover, but she's still not able to talk."

"Okay, thanks for keeping me up to date," Pat said. "How do I go about getting those documents?"

"Glad you asked," Shack replied with a lighter tone in his voice. "Remember that steak and seafood restaurant I mentioned the other day?"

Pat groaned but with a smile trying to break the surface of her face, something that hadn't shown up there in several days. "Yeah, I remember."

"We have reservations for 7 p.m. tonight...in your name. I'll have the papers with me. Bring the cash — five G's in small bills. And oh, do you still have that black, sequin gown you wore to that Gala a few years ago? I'd love to see you in that again."

2

"Guess what?" Mimi shouted to Kendra as she ran up to her outside their school, drawing the attention of several other kids who were also leaving the school grounds late.

Kendra hadn't seen her friend so excited or animated in quite some time, not since receiving the decree from her father that she could no longer help TJ with his homeschooling.

"I don't know, but I bet you're going to tell me, right?"

"You bet I am," Mimi said as she hugged Kendra, spinning the two of them around until Kendra felt like they'd end up falling to the ground.

"Whoa there. Not so enthusiastic," but she couldn't help but laugh. It was good to see Mimi happy again. "So what's got you so excited?"

"I just came from the D.M.V., and I passed my driver's license test! I got my license!" Mimi said as she finally let go of her friend.

"Wow! That is good news," Kendra replied. "I thought your dad wouldn't let you get one."

"Yeah, he wouldn't for the longest time, but Uncle Bo and I finally persuaded him to let me try for it. I think dear old Dad figured his dumb daughter would never pass the test, but I did!"

"Congratulations," Kendra said. "That's quite an accomplishment."

"Yeah, I guess so," Mimi replied, "but don't you realize what this means?"

"That you're not nearly as dumb as your dad thinks?" Kendra guessed.

"Well, yeah, that too, but what it means is that we can now go find TJ." And with that Mimi started her happy dance again.

"What? You're kidding. Pat said he'd run away to Asheville. That's over thirty miles away."

"Yeah, thirty-two miles to be exact," Mimi replied. "I looked it up yesterday during my study break. So, we don't have to walk now. We can drive."

"Huh, just one little detail. To take such a trip requires more than just a driver's license. We'd also need a car."

"I know that silly," Mimi replied undaunted by Kendra's lack of enthusiasm. "Uncle Bo won't lend me his truck. Hell, he won't even let his brother drive it, but he's had an old clunker of a car in the barn for ages. He got it running the other day and said I could use it."

"To go all the way to Asheville?"

"I'm not going to tell him where we're going," Mimi admitted. "You know the old saying, 'Sometimes it better to ask for forgiveness than for permission.' This is one of those times."

"Okay," Kendra replied, starting to warm to the idea. "I guess we're going on our first road trip to Asheville. When do we leave?"

"Early tomorrow morning. Uncle Bo gets up at the crack of dawn to go hunting on Saturdays this time of the year, so we can get an early start as well. I'll pick you up around 7."

"In the morning?" Kendra asked, suddenly less excited by the idea. She'd planned to sleep in since her sitting and homeschool job was temporarily on hold.

"Of course in the morning," Mimi said. "That way we'll have all day to find TJ and bring him home where he belongs."

"Okay, I guess," Kendra said. She knew it was pointless to try to talk her friend out of one of her ideas once it took hold. "Maybe we can get some early Christmas shopping in while we're there."

"There's only one thing I want for Christmas," Mimi replied. "And that's TJ."

Kendra studied her friend's face, looking for clues about what that last comment meant, but Mimi just smiled innocently back as she added, "That is, I want him back home where he belongs. For Allan and Pat's sake."

Menial Job

It had been a week since TJ had been serendipitously introduced to Luke through his dog, Precious, but much had happened during that time. For starters, Luke had taken TJ to the Salvation Army for a set of hand-me-down clothes and then on to the homeless shelter. There TJ enjoyed a thorough cleaning followed by a hot meal.

Things are beginning to look up, TJ thought, as he glanced around the dining hall that was about eighty percent filled with other homeless people and others down on their luck. As Luke had been quick to point out, "We live in a pretty great country that provides such accommodations and resources for less fortunate people."

The comment surprised TJ coming from an old Army vet who seemed to have been given the short end of the stick by his country.

"No, not at all," Luke disagreed. "This country has been good to me. Oh, I know it has its faults, don't get me wrong. I'd like to see veterans treated with more respect, and for sure the VA department needs a major overhauling. It's like my old lieutenant used to say, 'We're not perfect, just better than any of the alternatives.'"

Next, TJ learned from Luke that there were some jobs available that didn't require ID papers or written permission from a parent. They were menial jobs like unloading trucks, or at other times of the year, picking apples, and the like. Most of them paid below minimum wage for hard, back-breaking work, but you got paid at the end of the day in cash. Such work was spotty at best, but TJ had been lucky that morning and obtained his first such job. Now, although he was bone tired, it felt good to have a few bucks in his pocket. He planned to pay Luke back the money he'd given him, but that still left some money over for food. He figured he'd surprise Luke and the others with sandwiches from Subway, his treat in thanks for all they'd done for him.

Of course, he'd had to show the young lady behind the sandwich counter that he had enough money to pay for the sandwiches before she'd make them for him, but it would take more than that to dampen his spirit this evening. He grabbed the bag of sandwiches and headed to his new family's latest location.

They'd stayed at the construction site for three nights before they had to move on. He'd learned that it was safer to not stay at any one location for more than two or three days. Their latest location was at a small park known as the Bountiful Cities Edible Gardens, though in November there wasn't anything edible on the grounds as far as TJ could tell. Still, it wasn't far from Pack Square Park, where he liked to hang out during the day, and Luke had told him that it was a pretty safe place to bed down for a couple of nights.

"We should be fine as long as we keep the fire small and the boom box on low," Luke had said.

By the time TJ arrived, Luke and Precious were already there along with Alley Cat and her boyfriend, Oscar, as well as Elmer and a new family member Luke introduced as Marlin. "He loves fish and smells like one that's been kept out in the sun for about three days most of the time," Luke said by way of introduction, then noticing the bag asked, "Whatcha brung us?"

"Sandwiches from Subway," TJ said, holding the bag up for everyone to see.

"So you got the job, huh?"

"Yeah, and they paid me at the end just like you said they would."

"Good," Luke replied as he pulled one of the sandwiches from the bag. "You didn't need to spend all your money trying to feed us though."'

"I know, but I wanted to," TJ replied as he tossed a couple of the other sandwiches to Alley Cat and Oscar. "Besides, I still have a few bucks left over."

Everyone sat around the fire that Luke had built, munching quietly on the food. Finally, Luke looked over at TJ with a serious look on his face.

"How old are you, boy?"

Not knowing how to answer the question TJ answered, "Old enough."

"Do you have your high school diploma?"

"What's that?" TJ asked, taking the last bite from his sandwich, then tossing the paper into the fire.

"It's what you get when you graduate from high school," Luke replied. "Everyone knows that."

"I was homeschooled," TJ replied a little defensively. "Why all the questions?"

"Oh, I was just wondering what your plans were?" Luke replied after a moment.

"Plans?" TJ studied his new friend with a puzzled look on his face. "I don't know. I guess I plan to sleep here tonight and maybe go looking for another day job tomorrow."

"And after that?" Luke persisted.

"Hell, I don't know," TJ replied, suddenly irritated, mostly at himself because he'd been avoiding asking himself such questions.

The two of them sat quietly. Luke rubbed Precious's ear as she lay sleeping beside him, snoring quietly. Now and then he'd toss a twig into the fire. Finally, he said, "I noticed that game you have was called *Mercenaries*. You any good at it?"

"Not bad," TJ replied, though he knew he was one of the best players around, at least from what he'd read on the internet from other gamers.

"Well, playing a game ain't the same thing as being in a real war," Luke said, "but I was wondering if you ever thought about joining the Army. Sure beats working those day jobs for next to nothing."

"You trying to get rid of me?" TJ asked, only partly joking.

"Nah, that ain't it. I'm just saying a body could do a lot worse, especially someone who didn't have anything better planned. Think about it." And with that he lay back, pulling his faded green Army jacket around him and went to sleep.

Piece of Work

1

Two days after meeting Shack in Asheville to pick up TJ's fake ID papers, Pat received another call from the P.I.

"Wow! I can't believe you're calling me on a Saturday morning and before noon," Pat joked with him.

"I can't believe it either," Shack replied in a less than spritely voice, "but I just received word from one of my street connections. I think we may have found your boy."

"Really! That's good to hear," Pat replied. "Where is he?"

"My connection says that he's seen a boy that fits the description hanging around the Pack Square Park area. Seems like he's hooked up with an old Army vet named Luke Glover. If so, that's probably a good thing. I know Luke. He's not a bad guy."

"Okay, that's good to hear," Pat repeated.

"That's the good news," Shack continued. "The not so good news is that I've also heard that a local reporter has gotten wind of the throat slashing incident and is investigating it. He's been snooping around as well and could break the story at any time."

"Damn," Pat said.

"He's not the most ethical guy. You may be able to pay for his silence."

Pat groaned. Her savings account had already taken a significant hit with the purchase of the I.D. papers, but she could hardly be concerned with the cost at this point.

"Okay, see what you can do to keep him quiet for at least the next few days. I'm coming over. I can be there within the hour."

"I thought that might be the case," Shack replied less than enthusiastically. "Bring coffee, plenty of coffee. Here's the address of the park where we can meet."

After getting the address, Pat hung up the phone, pulled a thermos out of the kitchen cabinet and poured the remaining pot of coffee in it. She double checked her bag that looked like a cross between a briefcase and a purse to be sure the I.D. papers were inside, then quickly scribbled a note to Allan that she'd gone shopping. He would receive it later in the day when he returned from his half day at the clinic. She then grabbed her car keys and flew out the door.

She found Shack slouching on one of the park benches dressed in a trench coat and with a black felt hat covering his face. As she approached, Pat could hear him snoring softly.

"I brought the coffee," she said as she sat down beside him and took the thermos out of her satchel.

"Can you just shoot it into me intravenously?" Shack asked from under his hat.

"Sorry, but I left my I.V. set at home," Pat replied. "But here's a cup." She poured the coffee into the top of the thermos and placed it into Shack's hand. "Careful, it's still pretty hot."

Shack pushed the hat from his face and onto his head as he sat up. "Bless you, my child," he said, looking at Pat for the first time. "And while I'm at it, I want to thank you for a lovely evening the other night. One I will never forget. You're really quite amazing, as I knew you would be."

"You do recall that I didn't go home with you despite your many invitations?"

"Oh sure, I know," Shack replied. "I knew you never would. That really wasn't the point, anyway."

"And what, pray tell, was the point?"

"For us to be seen in public," Shack replied.

"Yes, well you certainly accomplished that. I don't recall a time when my dinner was interrupted more often."

"Yes, exactly," Shack said as he took a sip of the coffee and, finding it not so hot, he took a long slurp. "Why, I already have three other dates from three different women—women that previously wouldn't have given me the time of day."

Pat chuckled despite herself. "You know, Shack, you are one piece of work."

"Thanks," Shack replied.

"That wasn't intended as a compliment."

"I know, but that's how I'm choosing to take it. Now onto the business at hand."

"Yes, please. I can tell you've been scoping out the area before I arrived," Pat said sarcastically.

"Actually, yes, I did, just before taking a nap so I'd be fully alert for your arrival." He pointed across the park. "He's over there."

2

"I feel like we're two country bumpkins come to the big city," Kendra said, sweeping her arms out to take in the crowded sidewalk and streets before her.

"I know what you mean," Mimi agreed. "It's been well over a year since I've visited Asheville. I didn't realize it had grown so much."

"We'll never find TJ," Kendra lamented. "It's like trying to find a needle in a haystack. We've been walking around for close to three hours now, and I haven't seen anyone who even remotely looks like him."

"True," Mimi said, "but we have seen a few dreamy guys."

Kendra stopped in the middle of the sidewalk and stared at her friend. "Are you in heat?"

"No," Mimi snapped back defensively. "Least, I don't think so."

"Let's take a break and get a bite to eat on me," Kendra said. "How's that place look?"

"Looks fine to me."

They had beaten the lunch crowd, so it was easy to find a table. As they sat down, Mimi placed the picture of TJ on the table. They'd been showing it around to folks on the off chance someone may have seen him. So far, no one had.

A young woman with her blonde hair tied back in a ponytail came out from the kitchen with a tray of food. After delivering it to two couples sitting at a nearby table, she walked over to them.

"Have you had a chance to look at the menu yet? I can also go over our lunch specials if you like."

"Those sandwiches you just delivered look delicious," Kendra said. "What are they?"

"Those are one of our restaurant's specialties. They're Rubens but with a special sauce that most people say make the sandwich extra special."

Kendra looked at her friend. "What say we split one of those?"

"Sounds good to me. And I just want water to drink...lots of water."

The waitress started to turn away but then stopped when she noticed the picture lying on the table.

"You know him?" she asked, pointing down at the picture.

"Why, yes," Mimi replied. "He's a friend of ours. We've been looking for him all morning but so far, no luck. Why? Do you recognize him?"

The waitress picked up the picture to take a closer look before replying. "Yeah, that's him. He's a lot cleaner in this picture, but he's definitely the one who came in here several days ago looking for a job."

"Really? Did you give him one?" Kendra asked.

"Nah, couldn't do it. He didn't have any ID proving his age, not to mention the fact that he smelled like the town dump."

"Darn!" Mimi said, clearly disappointed. "We're back to square one."

The waitress started back to the kitchen, then stopped and returned to the table. "You might try Pack Square Park. It's just a few blocks from here. It's a pretty popular place for...for folks down on their luck. I'll draw you a map before you leave."

"Thanks. That would be great," Mimi said, a note of hope returning to her voice.

After the waitress left, she turned to Kendra. "This is a sign. Our luck is about to change. I feel certain of it."

"I sure hope so," Kendra replied. "I'm not sure how much more walking my poor feet can take."

Cheerios

"Catch!" The word shook TJ out of a warm, sun-induced stupor. Like a cat who's unexpectedly awakened from a catnap, TJ jerked his head up just in time to see a bag of Cheerios flying towards his head. Without a thought or a moment of hesitation, he snatched it out of the air with one hand, then looked around to find its source.

Pat Vogt stood about ten feet away, a smile on her face.

"You've always had amazing reflexes," she said as she stepped forward. She was wearing a stylish navy blue overcoat with a matching handbag hung over one shoulder. For just a moment, TJ had a warm glow of recognition come over him. It was good to see a familiar face. He felt a smile start on his face but then froze in place as he remembered the late night conversation from a couple of weeks ago.

"How about coming with me to get some milk to go with those?" she asked, pointing to the bag in his hand.

"I'd rather have coffee," he replied, trying to keep his voice low so it would sound as adult as possible. After all, adulthood wasn't far off. Just the other day he'd felt along his chin and was surprised to feel the first evidence of whiskers on his otherwise youthful face.

"Okay, coffee it is," Pat replied.

As TJ started to stand, he heard Precious' low growl of warning. He glanced over to where she stood next to Luke, both of them watching him closely.

"It's okay," TJ said, holding up a hand towards Precious. "She's a..." *Friend? Not really. My mom? No.* "She's someone I know. I'll be back in a little while."

Luke nodded as he reached out and patted Precious to assure her as well.

"We'll be right here if you need anything. Best coffee in town is at Double D's over on Biltmore. Just look for the double-decker bus," Luke said.

The two of them walked along in the direction Luke had indicated, neither of them saying a word. They found Double-D's without any difficulty. Sure enough, it was located in a red vintage double-decker bus that looked like it belonged on the streets of London more than in a Southern town. Despite the chilly temperatures of December, they decided to sit outside where there were fewer people and at least the illusion of privacy.

After the wait person took their order for two large coffees, TJ thought about asking Pat how she'd managed to find him, but then realized he really didn't want to know, and he wasn't in the mood for small talk anyway.

Evidently, neither was Pat who, after a couple of minutes of awkward silence, opened her handbag and took out a large business sized envelope and pushed it towards him.

"What's that?" TJ asked without picking it up.

"It's your pass to a new life," Pat replied, then went on to explain. "It's a set of ID papers—driver's license, birth certificate and a social security card all in your name or a name that you can adopt."

"Really?" TJ asked, suddenly interested despite himself. He picked up the envelope and opened it. He pulled out the largest piece of paper, which turned out to be a birth certificate.

"Todd John Jacobs," Todd read the name on the certificate. Jacobs? Where had she gotten that name and why did it sound familiar. Then he remembered. It was the last name of his favorite character in *Mercenaries*. He looked at Pat now for the first time since they'd arrived at the coffee shop, a quizzical look on his face.

"I did my research," Pat said.

TJ nodded and then looked into the envelope. It had felt heavier than he'd expected it to when he picked it up, and now he realized why. Along with two laminated cards was a one-inch stack of money held together by a thick rubber band. He could just make out that the top bill was a fifty. It was more money than he'd ever seen. He placed the certificate back in the envelope and dropped it on the table.

"What is this all about?" he finally asked. "Are you trying to bribe me to come home?"

"No," Pat replied, shaking her head. "As I said, this is your passport to a new life, one that doesn't involve Allan or me."

TJ nodded as he continued to study the envelope. "And what if I decline your generous and manipulative invitation?"

"You don't understand. This isn't an invitation. It's a demand. Take it or else."

"Or else what?" TJ shot back, feeling his hackles rise along the back of his neck.

"Remember my phone conversation the night you left?" Pat asked.

"Yes," TJ said.

"That was to my friend, Oliver. He works for B.I.U.F.O. - The Bureau of Investigation for Unidentified Flying Objects."

"So?" TJ asked. "Why would he care anything about me?"

Pat stared at him before finally answering. "Don't you know what you are? What Homlin was?"

"No," TJ replied, a puzzled look growing on his face. He had to admit he'd wondered about that—a lot lately, as he realized how different he was from everyone else.

Pat continued to study his face, finally deciding she believed he was telling the truth. He really didn't know...but how to break it to him? Was that really her job, her role in this game? She'd always believed that the direct approach was best. She'd learned it from her father while still a young girl.

"Homlin was not of this Earth," Pat said, looking straight at TJ to monitor his reaction. "While it's not yet been determined where he came from, it's very clear that he was an alien, and you are a product of what he brought with him."

TJ blinked several times as he processed her comments, finally replying, "So, you're saying that I'm an alien as well. Is that right?"

Pat nodded. "Yes, that's correct." There, it was out in the open now. Suddenly she felt a great weight lifted off her chest.

TJ continued to sit there with a blank look on his face. Then slowly he smiled. "You know, that explains a lot—a whole lot." The smile grew into a wide grin.

Pat watched him, surprised by his reaction to the news.

"Homlin is no longer a threat to this world. He's been neutralized, and his plan for world domination stopped," Pat continued. "I can't go into any more detail than that without breaking a sacred pledge, but I will say this. I don't believe you are a threat to this world; at least not at the level that Homlin was. While you are the product of his devious plan, I do not believe you are devious. Allan raised you as his son and as a human being, and I respect that. I've grown too fond of you, TJ, to simply turn you over to Oliver. I want to give you this chance, but if you refuse, then I'll have no other option but to turn you in."

TJ sat there staring at the envelope, considering what Pat had said. Finally, he picked the envelope back up and removed the birth certificate. He read the date of birth, then looked at Pat.

"This would make me eighteen...today. Today is my birthday?"

"Yeah, that's right, and this is your birthday present from Allan and me." She reached out and grasped his hand. He started to pull it away but then stopped. "At eighteen, you can get a job without permission from a parent or guardian. You can do a lot at eighteen, so I figured..."

"No, no, that's fine," TJ interrupted. "That's great. Now I can get a job." But it wasn't a job he was thinking about, at least not a job in Asheville. He'd been thinking about what Luke had said a few days ago about joining the Army. Now he had the paperwork he needed and even the last name of his favorite mercenary. Maybe Pat was right. This was the start of a whole new life.

He had walked by the Army Recruiting Station over on Oak Street a number of times, but so far hadn't had the nerve to walk in, but now he could. He could go in with his head held high with a new name and proof of his age. TJ reached out with his other hand and placed it over Pat's. He patted it gently.

"Thanks," he said with as much sincerity as he could muster. "I hope I never see you again," he added with the same sincerity. He rose from the table and picked up the envelope. He stuck it in his coat as he walked away, leaving Pat alone at the table.

Papers

1

As TJ walked back to Pack Square Park with the envelope secured away in his jacket, he felt an emotional storm brewing within. On the one hand, he was excited about the new life that lay before him as Todd John Jacobs, future mercenary extraordinaire. On the other hand, he felt a blanket of sadness trying to descend upon him at the thought of never seeing Allan again. Not only Allan, TJ realized, but also Kendra and Mimi would now be out of his life as well. Had he made the best bargain he could? He really hadn't been in a position to bargain or negotiate. He had known Pat long enough to know that she rarely if ever bluffed. If she said she'd report him to her friend at B.I.U.F.O., he knew she meant business.

And while he was cutting the cord from his past, he might as well go all out and say goodbye to Luke and Precious. He'd checked the schedule posted on the front door of the recruiting station, and he knew it was open on Saturdays. He found the two of them where he'd left them basking in the midday sunshine of the park. TJ noticed Luke's box with the flag sticking out of it had more money than usual. Evidently, the sunny skies had brought more people out to the park. As TJ approached, Luke looked up at him from where he sat crossed legged on a cushion he carried around for that purpose.

"Everything okay?" Luke asked.

"Yeah, it's cool," TJ replied as he sat down beside him and reached out to scratch behind Precious' ear. "She's a...a friend of the family. She brought me some papers from home."

"Papers?" Luke asked. "What kind of papers?"

"ID papers."

"What you need with those?"

"I've been thinking about what you said the other day when you asked me about what my plans were. I realized I didn't have any plans beyond getting away from home and getting settled here in Asheville."

Luke nodded. "And now?"

"And now I have a plan," TJ continued. "I'm going to join the Army as you suggested."

Luke nodded again, this time with a slight smile appearing on his face behind his beard and mustache. "You could do worse," he said. "You could really screw up and join the Navy or, God forbid, the Air Force. So that's what you needed with the ID papers."

"Yeah, that's right."

"And now you've come to say goodbye. Is that it?"

"Yeah, that's about the size of it." Suddenly, TJ felt a tightness in his chest. In the short time he'd been in Asheville, he'd grown fond of the old man and dog. "I mean, I can wait a day or two if you'd rather..."

"No," Luke said abruptly, then repeated in a softer tone. "No, it's good timing. If I were you, I wouldn't wait."

TJ sat there considering what Luke had said. "What do you mean, it's good timing?"

Luke reached into his coat pocket and brought out a crumpled piece of paper and handed it to him.

TJ unfolded it and studied it for a moment before looking up. "This looks like a drawing of me, and if I'm not mistaken, that must be my knife. Where did you get it?"

"Big Blue has been passing them around among the homeless," Luke replied. "They're looking for you, but want to keep it quiet and out of the public's eye if possible."

"What? Why?" TJ asked feeling a different type of tightness building. He noticed Luke looking down, avoiding him. "What is this about? Is this about Saul and Sally? Did they report me to the police or something?"

"No," Luke replied, still not able to look at TJ. "Not exactly...though it does involve Saul and Sally." He pulled the box of money towards him and pretended to count his take for the day, but TJ could tell he wasn't really counting it. Finally Luke looked up at him.

"Me and some of the other guys went to talk to Saul and Sally to try to persuade them to give back your stuff and stop scamming people, but things went bad. Saul had been drinking and, boy is he a mean drunk. He started yelling and screaming. Then he took out your knife and came for me with Sally right behind him. I guess I must have gone into counter-attack mode. I'm not too clear what happened after that. Next thing I knew, a couple of the guys were washing my hands and face, and the cloth kept coming away all bloody."

"What did you do? Why are they looking for me? I haven't done anything."

"I know, I know. The guys told me that I freaked out when Saul and Sally came at me—went all commando on them. They told me that I killed both of them, but they were wrong. I killed Saul, but Sally survived. She isn't able to talk, so she drew this picture. No one knows why for sure. Sally has always been a bit touched in the head. Big Blue put two and two together..."

"And came up with five," TJ finished. "They came to the wrong conclusion."

"It's not the first time," Luke said. After a long pause, he continued. "If you want, I'll turn myself in. I'll explain what happened and maybe..." The last words hung in the air unfinished.

"You can't do that," TJ replied. "They'll put you away for the rest of your life. I couldn't live with myself. Hell, you were just trying to help me get my stuff back." He looked down at the paper again. "But you're right. I need to get the hell out of here—fast."

Luke nodded, then reached inside his shirt and removed a set of dog tags. He held them out to TJ. "Give these to the recruiter over on Oak Street. It'll either be Starr or Lee. Every once in awhile I'll send them someone I feel would make a good soldier. I have a pretty good track record. They'll treat you right. Tell them I'm asking them to expedite your process."

TJ took the tags from him and dropped them in the envelope, then pulled a few of the bills from the stack of money and handed them to Luke who just stared at it.

"Take it," TJ said. "Someone told me once not to let my pride get in the way when someone offers to help out. You need to get yourself out of town for awhile. This will help."

After another moment of hesitation, Luke took the money and dropped it into the box. He studied TJ for a moment.

"Let me do something to earn this. It's important you make a good first impression so we'll start by getting you cleaned up and with some decent looking clothes."

He stood up and clipped the leather leash onto Precious' collar. "First stop, the Salvation Army, then to the shelter for a much-needed bath. Might need to borrow a pair of scissors to trim your hair as well. Why don't you go ahead over to the Salvation Army, and I'll meet you there. There's something I need to take care of, but it shouldn't take long."

TJ agreed, then strolled off in the direction of the store leaving Pack Square Park for the last time.

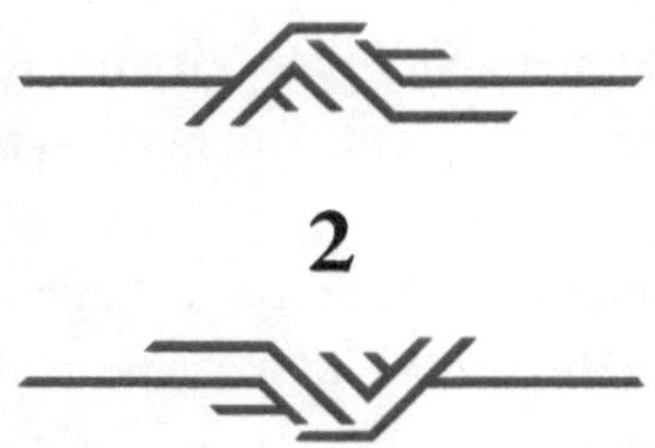

2

As Mimi and Kendra arrived at Pack Square Park, they realized their search was far from over. The park was larger than expected and filled with people enjoying the sunny weekend day. Mimi decided to show TJ's photo to a young girl with red and pink hair who looked like she might be a permanent resident of the park.

The girl glanced at the photo for a few seconds, then back to Mimi. "Yeah? What about it?" she asked with a suspicious look on her face.

"We're looking for him," Mimi replied simply.

"So?"

"So, can you help us? It's really important. I'm his sister, and our mom is very sick," Mimi lied. "He'd want to know."

"Oh," the girl replied, her look changing to one of concern. "Sorry to hear that. Yeah, I know him. He's over there with Luke and..." She stopped in mid-sentence. "They were over there near the fountain a few minutes ago. I guess they must have left."

Mimi groaned. "Where would they have gone?"

"Oh, probably back to their condo over on Reed Street," the girl replied.

"Really?" Mimi said with renewed hope.

"Of course not," the girl laughed. "What about the word 'homeless' don't you understand?"

Mimi's face turned red, a mixture of embarrassment and anger. She started to take a step towards the homeless girl, but Kendra stepped in front of her and placed a hand on her arm. "Don't," she said. "It's not worth it. We're getting closer. We just need to keep looking."

After a couple of seconds Mimi relaxed and nodded. "Yeah, you're right."

As they turned to leave, the girl spoke up again. "You might try on the other side of the park. Luke likes to change his location about this time of the day. Says it's better for business. I hope you find your friend," she added in a consoling tone. "Look for an old man with an even older looking cocker spaniel."

Mimi and Kendra headed in the direction the girl had pointed. As they approached the other side of the park, Kendra urged them on. "We're getting closer. I just know we are. I can feel it."

"I hope you're right," Mimi replied and a moment later, "There...over there. Isn't that a cocker spaniel?"

Kendra followed where Mimi pointed. "Yeah, looks like one to me, and she seems to belong to that old man sitting under that tree, but where's TJ?"

"There!" Mimi pointed off to the right where a teenage boy with shaggy black hair was waiting to cross the street.

As the two girls started running towards him, Mimi noticed a young woman rising from the park bench where she'd been sitting. She stepped in front of the two girls to block their path.

"Don't." She spoke the one-word command with such authority that it stopped both of them in their tracks. "You need to let him go," the woman added as she reached out and grasped Mimi's arm for emphasis.

"Pat!" Kendra exclaimed. "What are you doing here? We've got to..."

"You need to let him go," Pat repeated more softly this time. "We all need to let him go." She corrected herself.

"Why?" Mimi asked.

"Because TJ needs to find his place in the world. We've all done what we can to prepare him for this next leg of his journey, but we can't take it with him."

"I don't understand," Mimi replied.

"In time you will," Pat said. "For now you'll just have to trust me."

The three of them stood in silence as the light changed, and TJ crossed the street, disappearing into the crowd of other pedestrians.

Rangers

1

Luke watched until TJ was out of sight before turning around and walking in the other direction with Precious following close behind on the leash. They strolled along one of the paths of the park until they were close to the center before leaving the path to enter a thick clump of trees. When he was sure they were out of sight of any prying eyes, Luke sat down cross-legged on the ground, placing the end of the leash under one leg. He glanced around one final time before reaching into the inside pocket of his coat for his pocket knife enclosed in a worn leather case. He pulled the knife out of its case and stared at the scrimshaw picture of two ducks about to land on a lake etched on its surface. Opening the single blade of the knife he carefully held it up to his ear and spoke a series of numbers into it.

Several seconds passed before he heard a muted voice on the other end of the line.

"Yes?"

I have another one for you," Luke said. "Think this one might be special. You'll want to keep a close eye on him. His name is Todd John Jacobs. He'll be coming in through the regular channels."

"Okay," came the simple reply.

Luke nodded. His job was done...for now. He closed the knife and returned it to its case. He looked over at Precious, who lay dozing in front of him. "Let's go get something to eat, Pretty Girl." He slowly unwrapped his legs and stood up. It had been a good day's work.

2

The next couple of days were a blur for TJ. On Luke's recommendation, he made sure he took a bath at the shelter and dressed in his nicest clothes.

"If you wear a t-shirt make sure it doesn't say anything obscene or anti-American," Luke had warned. "And give them this address as your current residence." He handed TJ a slip of paper. "Starr or Lee will know it's not real, but they won't say anything since so far I've not given them any rejects. Make sure you're not the first."

After meeting briefly with Sergeant Starr and filling out some preliminary paperwork and presenting his own identifying papers, everything moved into high gear with the next days filled with aptitude tests, a thorough physical exam, and an interview with another officer who went over the various career options currently available to TJ.

"You've scored in the upper ten percentile on your aptitude test, and you're as physically fit as anyone I've seen in the past year, so you've got quite a few options available to you," the career counselor said.

"I saw a poster of someone jumping out of a plane at the recruiting station," TJ said. "What do I have to do to be able to do that?"

He'd remembered in several of the *Mercenaries* game scenarios that his namesake had often started off his clandestine mission by jumping in behind enemy lines. Besides, he already knew he enjoyed flying, though as a bird rather than in a plane.

"So you think you could be a paratrooper?" the sergeant asked.

"Maybe," TJ replied, then added, "Sure, why not? Someone has to do it."

The sergeant smiled and made a couple of notes on the paper in front of him. "Okay, duly noted. If you want to jump out of planes, maybe you should consider becoming a Ranger."

"What's a Ranger?" TJ asked.

"They're elite fighters who go in fast, hit hard, and get out."

That sounded right up Todd Jacob's alley.

Everything became very real when TJ was asked to take the Oath of Enlistment.

"I, Todd John Jacobs, do solemnly swear that I will support and defend the Constitution of the United States against all enemies, foreign and domestic; that I will bear true faith and allegiance to the same; and that I will obey the orders of the President of the United States and the orders of the officers appointed over me, according to regulations and the Uniform Code of Military Justice. So help me God."

It was the last step before he was whisked off to Basic Training.

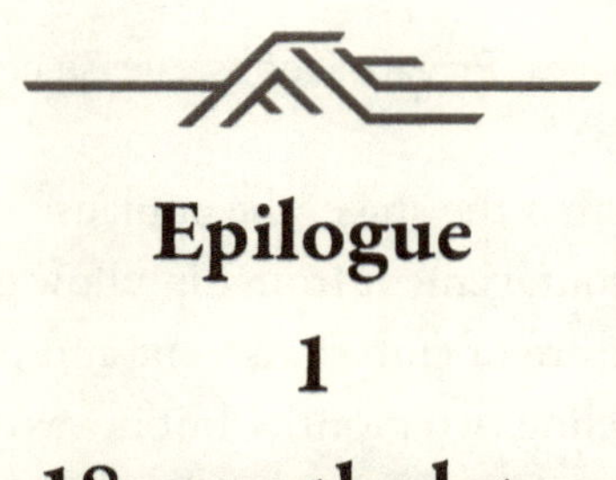

Epilogue

1

18 months later

Private First Class Todd John Jacobs paused a moment at the top of the stairs, waiting for his name to be called by his commander. He gazed out at the crowd who enjoyed the early spring-like temperatures of mid-March in Fort Benning, Georgia. It seemed like his fellow soon-to-be Rangers had invited all their family members and friends to join the graduation from Ranger School. As far as he could tell, he was the only one without anyone from his past in attendance.

He'd toyed with the idea of calling Allan and inviting him and Kendra to come down, but then quickly rejected the idea. He'd agreed with Pat, and he wasn't about to use this occasion to renege on the deal.

"Our next soldier has the distinct honor of winning two of our most esteemed awards; something that has never been done since the founding of this school over fifty years ago. Private First Class Todd Jacobs has received the Darby Award, which is bestowed on the Ranger that has shown the best tactical and administrative leadership, has the most positive spot reports, and quite frankly has demonstrated being a cut above the rest."

The crowd clapped but stopped when the commander raised his hand.

"And he also receives the Michael Kelso Enlisted Leadership Award. This award, which is selected by the Ranger's peers, is given to the Ranger who has demonstrated outstanding leadership, initiative, and motivation."

After the applause had subsided, the commander looked up from his notes and smiled. "I also have it on good authority that no one goes hungry while part of Private Jacob's team; something many of us are still trying to figure out how he manages. Private Jacobs, please come forward to receive your awards and diploma."

As Todd walked across the stage, the applause resumed, accompanied by several shouts of encouragement from his fellow graduates. Todd felt his face redden with a mixture of embarrassment and pride as he strolled forward. It had been a grueling two months, but it was now over, and he could get on with the business of being a soldier, but not just any soldier. He was now part of one of the most elite groups of fighters on the planet.

After shaking hands with his commander and receiving his diploma and awards, he exited at the other end of the stage. As he walked down the stairs, he noticed an older man in a dark gray business suit standing at the bottom, gazing up at him. He didn't recognize the man, but from the straightness of the man's stance, Todd suspected he had a military background.

"Congratulations, Private Todd," the man said as he held out his hand. As Todd shook it, he took in the graying hair around the temples and crow's nests around the eyes.

"Thank you, sir," Todd replied as he stifled a wince of pain from the firm handshake. "I'm sorry, do I know you?"

"No, least not yet," the man replied with a chuckle as he released Todd's hand. "But an old friend of yours suggested we meet. My name is Phillip Ackerson, but most of my friends just call me Jersey. I wonder if you've given much thought to what's next for you."

"No, can't say that I have," Todd replied. "Just waiting for my next assignment, I guess."

Jersey nodded. "Good. That's what I'm here to talk to you about." He placed a hand on Todd's back and started guiding him away from the stage. "Your Commander-in-chief has a very special assignment for you."

"My Commander-in-chief?" Todd asked, confused by the title.

"Yes, you know, the President of the United States."

"Oh, yeah, right," Todd replied, his face flushing once more with embarrassment. "But what on earth would he want from me? I'm just a good ole boy from the North Carolina mountains."

"That's what we need to talk about," the man answered as he pointed towards a black SUV parked illegally along the curb, its windows tinted black. It looked like it had been pulled from some Hollywood spy movie. "Right this way, if you please," but it was apparent from the man's tone that it wasn't a request, but an order.

Todd glanced over his shoulder to see if he could draw any of his friends' attention.

"Don't worry," the man said, his hand continuing to guide Todd towards the vehicle. "You're in good hands."

The last thing Todd remembered seeing before he was escorted into the SUV was his commander standing on the stage staring at him, a worried look on his face.

2

It took James almost two years to find a way to bring some semblance of control to his life as a mercenary. Becoming more selective about the missions had helped, as had insisting on knowing more about the other team members, but he knew these were just temporary steps until a better answer came along. It finally came in the form of a complaint.

Over the past year, Jersey had complained to him a couple of times about how stressful his position had become and how he really wanted to get out of the black ops business and into something quieter. When James prodded further, Jersey confessed he longed to retire to some quiet getaway and open his own restaurant.

"Besides, James, a restaurant in the right location can be a pretty good front so I could keep my hands in a bit without them getting cut off. Why do you ask?"

When James suggested he might be interested in assuming Jersey's role, his old friend had responded positively and then added. "This isn't something I'm comfortable talking about on the phone. How about meeting me in person?"

"Sure, where?"

"There's a cozy little restaurant in Bermuda called the Black Horse Tavern that I've been looking at. You can give me your opinion on whether it would be a good investment; kill two birds with one stone as it were."

As James hung up the phone, he thought, *this could be the start of a whole new phase for both of us.*

3

It started as a mild buzzing in the ears. When it persisted, Val went online to learn that such buzzing was fairly common among humans; a condition called tinnitus. Unfortunately, the buzzing grew in frequency and intensity making it next to impossible to ignore. When it started interrupting his sleep, he considered going to a doctor, but then thought better of it. Even though his "Aeo engineered" body had worked fine for the past two years, he wasn't sure if a doctor might be able to detect a difference.

It was after a week of mostly sleepless nights that he realized the second anniversary of when he'd left the cave and entered human society had been the previous week...just about the time the buzzing had begun. During those two years, he had continued to grow rapidly but decided to ignore Aeo's advice to move from family to family. Maude had turned out to be surprisingly easy to manipulate, in part because she was starving for love and attention. Over the many years they'd been married, Harold had grown increasingly reclusive, spending most of his waking hours in his workshop out back, leaving Maude and Val to themselves. It didn't take long for Val's cute and cuddly act to win her over completely.

When Val heard Maude and Harold arguing one night with Harold insisting they turn him over to social services, Val decided to take matters into his own hands. Harold would have to go. The opportunity arose the next day while Harold was working on the second floor of the barn. Val followed him upstairs, knocked the old man unconscious then broke his neck before tossing him out the window to cover it up.

Maude was devastated, but there was no more talk about social services. About a week after Harold's untimely passing, as she tucked Val in bed she said a short prayer thanking God for sending the young boy to help her through this most trying of times.

The next big challenge was when Maude began noticing Val's incredible appetite and growth. At first, she chalked it up as a growth spurt that many children experience, but when it persisted week in and week out, she became concerned. When she called to book an appointment with the local pediatrician, Val threw such a temper tantrum that she finally hung up the phone without making an appointment.

When he finally calmed down, he explained that he was deathly afraid of doctors because he'd been so poorly treated by those his previous family had taken him to. He made her promise not to repeat their mistakes.

"I know you think I'm a freak just like they did, but please don't let those mean doctors hurt me again," he pleaded as he climbed into Maude's lap and hugged her.

"Don't be silly. I don't think you're a freak at all," Maude replied returning his hug. "You're the most adorable little boy I've ever met."

"Even though I'm growing too fast?" He asked. "I'll stop eating...I'll do whatever you ask. Just don't send me away."

"Now you really are being a silly boy," Maude replied. "Who's to say what normal is, anyway. You eat as much as you like as often as you like. In fact, I think it's time for a dish of ice cream. What do you say?"

Val nodded as he wiped away the tears. "Chocolate?"

"Sure, chocolate, vanilla, or strawberry. I have all three." There was no more mention after that of his rapid growth.

4

The dust covered ellipsoid shaped object lay in the corner of the cave looking much like the other rocks around it. Shortly after Aeo had sent Val away to meet his new family, the artificial intelligence had cleaned up the cave, hiding the cocoon and FreeForm container in its deepest recesses, then tucked itself among a heap of rocks in standby mode to conserve energy. It would awaken instantly if any threats appeared in the area, but otherwise, it would hibernate much like the cave's former occupant.

It lay there just barely conscious...until two years to the day that Val had left, it started pulsating with a bluish purple glow. It was time to return to work. It switched on the beacon to call the now grown Val back to the cave.

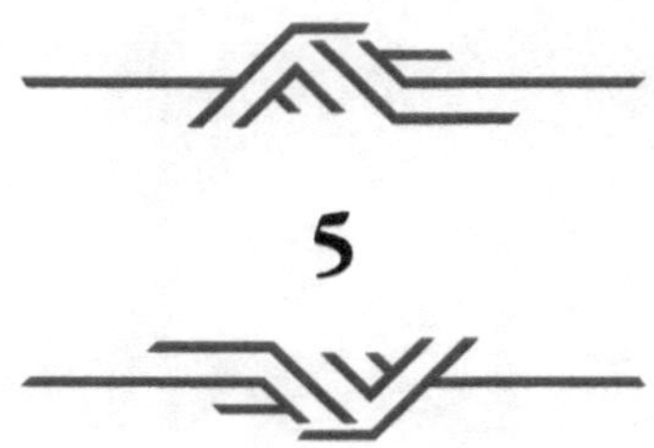

5

Val stood at the crest of the hill gazing down at the mouth of the cave that had been his birthplace. The buzzing in his ears that had continued to grow in intensity over the past two weeks was now just barely perceptible, but he knew if he turned around and tried to leave the buzzing would return.

It had taken a few days to tie up loose ends at Maude's, eliminating all signs of his presence. It hadn't been difficult. He started by suffocating her with a pillow in the middle of the night right after the weekly grocery delivery. That gave him seven days to clean up and get out of town before the young delivery boy would return to notice the front door cracked open, discover her body, and assume she'd died quietly in her sleep.

He adjusted the empty backpack that was a replica of the one he'd dreamt about for the past week, carefully made his way down the rocky slope and into the cave where he found Aeo sitting next to the cocoon and container of FreeForm pupae.

It was finally time to resume the Primary Directive. In the nearby meadow, a sudden breeze blew hundreds of dandelion seeds into the air.

Pick Up the Rest of the FreeForm Series Today

The Adventure has Just Begun

mybook.to/freeformseries[1]

1. http://mybook.to/freeformseries

Enjoy this sample chapter

Freeform: Resumed

Outside Fallujah

THE VIBRATION AND ROCKING of the helicopter combined with the moonless night sky to lull Sergeant Todd John Jacobs into a semi-trance. So much had happened in the past six months since graduating from Ranger school, most of which he still didn't fully understand. The mysterious man who'd met him as he left the graduation stage turned out to be Lieutenant Phillip Ackerson, or Jersey as he preferred to be called. Jersey, an Army officer assigned to special duty with the CIA, had all but hogtied him. He claimed he was there to offer Todd his next assignment per their commander in chief, the President of the United States. That assignment had turned out to be six more months of rigorous training and intel briefings that had eventually led to tonight's mission somewhere in the vicinity of Fallujah, Iraq.

He shook himself awake as he heard the order on his headset, "Five minutes till drop off. Get ready." As Todd looked around, he could just make out James, the pilot, and his co-pilot whose name Todd couldn't remember in front with the crew chief and a door gunner seated behind them. Farther to his right, he saw the outline of Jersey. He knew the other two men assigned to the mission were seated behind the Lieutenant on the opposite side of the helicopter. Jasper Mullins was a good ol' boy from the south so Todd found they had a natural affinity for each other. He found the shorter man, Dewey Stalins more abrasive and eager to start a fight so he'd made it a point to stay out of Dewey's way.

Todd rubbed the smooth metal of his M4 weapon sitting in his lap. He found it comforting and hoped the silencer would allow them an easy in and out if he ended up needing to use it. The weight of the backpack on his shoulders meant it was time for action—the part of military life he loved. Jersey reached over and gave a thumbs up. Todd returned the gesture. The second the aircraft hit the ground they would be running.

Todd felt the aircraft flare, settle and the doors opened. He jumped out into the pitch blackness of a moonless night, ran about fifty feet and dropped to the ground. The helicopter departed without ever coming to a full stop. Todd stood up, adjusting his night vision goggles even though he didn't really need them and looked around. It was important to play the role that he was just like the other soldiers. Three other figures also stood up. The one nearest to him pointed in a direction to the south and started off in a fast jog. The other two moved to his sides and matched stride, with Todd taking up the rear. They ran like this for what Todd calculated to be three-quarters of a mile, putting them a quarter mile from the village that was just over the rise in front of them.

Jersey, in the lead, signaled to stop and kneeled. Todd, Jasper, and Dewey caught up and kneeled beside him. "Damn, this is getting harder every mission," Jersey whispered even though he didn't appear to be at all winded. "I need to get out of this business. All right guys, you know the drill. Refresh if needed and check your weapons and gear. Let's get in there as planned, snatch the package, and get out without anyone knowing what hit them. Any questions?"

Todd looked around. No one had any. Jersey nodded and moved off in the direction of the village. Everyone else moved up to a line position and spread out. As they got closer, Todd could see the wall around the small village and the doorway of the building they were to go through. According to their intel, the door would be unlocked for them, and someone would lead them to the location of the package.

As the team approached the building, Todd noticed some lights in the distance to the west of their position but decided they were probably just goat herders. As he drew nearer to their target, he started having tremors of an odd, yet vaguely familiar feeling which grew stronger the closer he got to the building. What the hell was going on? He'd never felt anything like this on his previous training missions. Maybe those lights weren't goat herders after all.

The creaking of the door cut through the silence of the night as Jersey pushed it open, but before he could enter through it, a man dressed in traditional Arab garb stepped out from the darkness and started firing, hitting Jersey and Dewey. Todd jumped forward and struck the man in the head with the butt of his gun. He yelled for Jasper to secure the area and bolted through the door. Sensing two men on the other side of the door, he cut them both down before they had a chance to react.

Todd paused a moment leaning against one wall, allowing his heightened senses to scan the area. Detecting no one else close by, he signaled for Jasper to bring in their fallen team members. Glancing at Dewey's bloody pulp of a head, Todd knew he couldn't be helped. He started to to turn his attention to Jersey who'd been hit in the side, but Jasper was already apply pressure to the wound. Todd grabbed the unconscious Arab and slapped his face several times to revive him. The man's eyes shot open. Apparently he'd only been pretending to be unconscious.

Todd forced the barrel of the M4 into the man's mouth. "What the hell happened? Why did you shoot at us?" he screamed. The man glared back, defiantly refusing to talk. "So, that's the way you want to play this?" Todd said between clenched teeth. He yanked the gun barrel from the man's mouth and shot off the big toe of his left foot. The man screamed, his eyes growing wide with pain and fear.

"Let's try that again," Todd said. "Why are you shooting at us? You were supposed to help." The man shook his head and spit at him. Todd shrugged, pointed his weapon at the other foot and shot off the other big toe. The man screamed even louder this time. "Okay, one last chance," Todd said as he pointed the gun at the man's crotch. That did the trick.

"Please, no more. I'll talk...please," the man pleaded with a thick accent. After another moment, he continued. "We got word you were coming. We were ordered to set a trap. Please, I was only following orders."

"That's what they always say," Todd replied. He thought about smacking his captive in the head again, but paused to assess the situation first. "Damn, now what do we do?"

"Todd, we have to get out of here," Jersey answered him from where he was lying on the floor, a pool of blood beginning to form despite Jasper's pressure.

"The hell with that. We haven't completed our mission yet. We're not leaving until we've recovered the package, dead or alive."

"We've obviously been made," Jersey said, wincing in pain. "It's time to scrub the mission."

Todd leaned over him and tore the fabric away from the shoulder of his shirt where the bullet had entered. "It's just a flesh wound. Trust me. I can handle this. It's what I've been made for," Todd said. He turned to Jasper. "Take care of him. Keep pressure on the wound and stay alert. There may be others around. Contact me on the headset if things change."

"Will do," Jasper replied, not questioning Todd's self proclaimed authority.

"This asshole and I are going to take a walk..." He looked down at the man's bloody feet. "Well, I'll walk. He'll crawl."

Todd kicked his captive out the door and to the middle of the compound. "Where is he?" he growled to the man who pointed to a doorway two buildings down the street. "Are you sure?"

The man nodded vigorously.

"Good enough," Todd replied as he brought the butt of the gun down on the man's head. The answer had matched his own assessment. As he slowly approached the building, he felt the strange feeling wash over him again. This time he remembered when he'd felt it before. It had been years ago when, as a young kid, he'd run away from home the first time. It felt almost like déjà vu.

Todd crept up to the door and stopped. His senses detected someone on the other side of the door and several others nearby. He could feel the tenseness in them and could hear their elevated heart rates, all except for the person on the other side of the door who remained, calm but why? No time like the present to find out.

Todd lowered his shoulder and smashed through the door. As he burst into the room, the man sitting by a small fireplace put his hands out to his sides and stood up. "Hello, TJ. Man, how you've grown. I thought I felt you out there, but couldn't believe it at first."

Todd stared at the strange man who somehow felt familiar, but unrecognizable at the same time. The man stood over six feet tall, dressed in a long flowing robe. Todd estimated his age to be in his mid to late forties.

"Ahhh, you don't remember me, do you?"

Todd slowly shook his head.

"Well, we met only briefly at the hunting reserve before the Americans tried to wipe us out." Todd continued to stare at the man, racking his brain in an effort to remember his face. "I have often wondered when another of my brothers would show up," the man continued.

"Your brothers?" Todd asked, a confused look on his face. What in hell was he talking about, and why hadn't anyone bothered to tell him during those hours of briefings that the package might know him?

"Yes." the stranger replied. "Most have been killed or captured, but I've eluded capture. Hopefully others have as well. What are you doing here, anyway?"

"I'm here to bring you in," Todd replied, but even as he said it, his brain was busy sorting out what he'd just heard. The man had just said they'd met at a hunting reserve, and he'd called him TJ. It had been quite a while since anyone had called him by that name, and the only hunting reserve he'd ever been at...Homlin's! Holy shit. This guy must have been one of Homlin's flunkies. The pieces were finally falling into place.

"Nah, how can that be?" the man said. "You're one of us."

"One of us?" Todd repeated, trying out the term in his mouth. He remembered hoping that might be the case years ago, but he'd found out soon enough he hadn't belonged at the hunting reserve. Homlin had been up to no good. Todd still had nightmares from watching Homlin almost kill Pat Vogt, his *father's* girlfriend and his sorta stepmother, before she finally turned around and killed Homlin instead.

"I'm not your brother," Todd finally said. "I don't know what I am, but I do know I'm not one of you. I'm here to do a job, so put your hands behind your head." As the man started to comply, he suddenly moved with incredible speed, reaching inside his robes for something. Todd moved just a quickly, firing a short burst from his M4 into the man's chest. As the man slumped to the floor, a pistol fell from his hand onto the dirt floor.

"You're making a mistake," the man whispered before dying. Todd stood silently in the room still trying to make sense of it all. His senses alerted him to the presence of several people approaching from outside.

Todd silently moved to the wall nearest to the door and waited. A second or two later, a dark skinned man poked his head in through the broken door. "Lenny, are you all right?" he said just before Todd shoved his dagger up through the man's throat and into his brain. He used the dagger handle to hold the man up as he pulled his body into the room. He then stepped into the doorway and shot the two other men waiting there. Todd walked over to the man who'd called him a brother. He grabbed him by his robe and started dragging him back to where he'd left Jersey and Jasper.

As he reached the building where they'd been ambushed, everything went to hell. Guns started firing and men yelled in Arabic outside the wall. "Shit," Todd cursed as he yanked the dead man's body through the door and into the room. "What the hell is going on?" he shouted.

"There are a bunch of crazy Arabs outside in the field firing at us. We can't get out," Jasper yelled as he fired off several rounds from the doorway. *Now I'm getting pissed,* Todd thought. He was growing tired of so many people trying to kill him and his friends. "Hold them off for a few minutes, Todd said. "I have a plan."

"What the hell are you going to do?" Jasper asked.

Todd looked down at Jersey who looked pale and only semi-conscious. "We need to get him to a hospital," he replied. "Call James and get that helicopter back here."

"And if it gets shot down, what do we do then?" Jasper asked as he switched his headset on to contact the helicopter.

"Leave that to me," Todd replied, as he slipped out the back door. Todd looked around and ran to another building against the wall and vaulted to the roof. *I thought I was pissed before. Now I'm really POed,* Todd thought. As he started removing his clothes, his body started changing, looking like a much bulkier and darker version of himself except this one had a nasty set of claws and long teeth. *Let's see how they handle my alter ego,* Todd thought as he leaped to the ground and began running full speed at the flashes of light of the firestorm. Todd ran full speed at the first man, taking his head off with a single vicious swipe, then turned on the second man who looked on in horror.

A short time later, Todd returned to where Jasper and Jersey were held up. "I hear the the helicopter," he said to Jasper. "Get him up and let's get out of here."

"What happened out there? Where are the men that were firing at us?" Jasper asked, as he picked Jersey up.

"Let's just say they won't be giving us any more trouble," Todd replied, as he paused to dig a last remnant of dried blood from his fingernails.

<<<< >>>>

A Message from Orrin Jason Bradford (a.k.a. W. Bradford Swift)

As an Indie Author I know just how important readers are. Without people who enjoy reading, authors are pretty useless. Oh, I know I enjoy the thrill of writing the *next great American novel,* but that's really not enough. I need readers like you who enjoy reading my stories. So, thank you. I sincerely appreciate your taking the time to read *FreeForm: Reborn*.

Perhaps you would enjoy some of my other books and stories. If you'd like to stay up to date on new book releases, special discounts, and my occasional giveaways, you can also join my **OJB's Amazingly Awesome Readers Group**. Just go to my author's website and blog:

www.wbradfordswift.com

There's one last thing you could do if you would be so kind. Go to your favorite online bookstore and leave an honest review of *FreeForm: Reborn.* Honest reviews are really important to help other readers like you know which books to try next. And thanks for being an amazingly awesome reader.

Orrin Jason Bradford (aka W. Bradford Swift)

Acknowledgments

Writing a book is a labor of love for me as well as being a wonderful way to express my life purpose. It's also something that I could not do alone, so I want to thank some of the people who have contributed to this project. Thanks go to my #1 beta reader, James Stepp. (Yes, there's a real James Stepp as well as the fictional helicopter pilot.) James has become much more than a beta reader, but so far neither of us have come up with a better title for him. Thanks for all the time, effort and great ideas you've contributed. I also want to thank the Orrin Jason Bradford Launch Team members. Currently at 260 members, this team of awesome readers helps keep me inspired to write as well as I am able. Thanks for being part of the team. Last of all I want to thank team – Kat and Tracy Cartwright (my book editors) and Maxwell, aka dogpillow, (my book blurber) who all did an amazing job.

Porpoise Publishing

Flat Rock, NC 28731
www.wbradfordswift.com
Library of Congress Cataloging-in-Publication Data
ISBN: 9781930328884
FreeForm Combo: Beginnings & Reborn/ W. Bradford Swift.
1. Science Fiction 2. Speculative Fiction 3. Technology

Cover design by Victor Habbick ~ www.victorhabbickvisions.co.uk/
Typeset in Book Palatino
Printed in USA
First Edition

Orrin Jason Bradford's style has been compared to the "early works of Dean Koontz and the late great Michael Crichton." ***Freeform: Crash*** is the prequel everyone has been waiting for in the action-packed, sci-fi Freeform series.

Read more at www.wbradfordswift.com.

Also by Orrin Jason Bradford

Fantastic Fables Series
Fantastic Fables of Foster Flat

FreeForm
Crash
FreeForm Combo: Beginnings & Reborn

The Cosmic Conspiracy Series
Babble

Standalone
Elliot Savant
Ellenore Finds Her Muse
Stars Beckon Call: A Far Future Dystopian Sci-Fi Thriller

Watch for more at www.wbradfordswift.com.

About the Publisher

Porpoise Publishing is the imprint of indie author W. Bradford Swift who also writes under the pen name of Orrin Jason Bradford. It is best known for publishing visionary fiction--stories that entertain while also inspiring readers to imagine greater possibilities for their lives.